D0368041

THE
WEIGHT
OF
LIES

OTHER TITLES BY EMILY CARPENTER

Burying the Honeysuckle Girls

THE
WEIGHT
OF
LIES

A NOVEL

EMILY
CARPENTER

LAKE UNION
PUBLISHING

This is a work of fiction. Names, characters, organizations, places, events, and incidents are either products of the author's imagination or are used fictitiously.

Text copyright 2017 by Emily Carpenter
All rights reserved.

No part of this book may be reproduced, or stored in a retrieval system, or transmitted in any form or by any means, electronic, mechanical, photocopying, recording, or otherwise, without express written permission of the publisher.

Published by Lake Union Publishing, Seattle
www.apub.com

Amazon, the Amazon logo, and Lake Union Publishing are trademarks of Amazon.com, Inc., or its affiliates.

ISBN-13: 9781477818435
ISBN-10: 147781843X

Cover design by Rex Bonomelli

Printed in the United States of America

For Katy

KITTEN

—FROM CHAPTER 1

"Kitten"—that was what everyone called her. No proper Christian name, just Kitten.

"Kitten, dear," her mother would say at breakfast in her musical Southern drawl, and the girl would skip from the hotel's elegant dining room, reappearing with a fresh pitcher of orange juice for the guests gathered around the great mahogany table.

"Kitten, my sweet," her father would say after cognac had been poured and cigarettes lit. And the girl would turn the great iron key that dangled in the lock of the front door, curtsy, and bid everyone a good night.

Fay felt lucky to be entrusted with the care of such a poised and advanced child and in such a beautiful setting. She wasn't without worries about her small charge, though. The child had some oddities—a few secretive tendencies and strange habits.

On more than one occasion, after Kitten had locked the front door of the hotel for her father, Fay was sure she saw the girl take the key out of the old brass lock and slip it into her pocket.

Ashley, Frances. *Kitten*. New York: Drake, Richards and Weems, 1976. Print.

Chapter One

The envelope lay on the hotel's poolside chaise—a creamy ivory rectangle of heavy, premium-quality paper. Propped against the neck roll I'd been resting on less than five minutes ago, it was lit by the burning midday Vegas sun like it had been stamped with heavenly approval.

I dropped the bottles of water I'd just fetched on the nearby table and gulped air. I could picture, without even looking, the intricately swirled monogram engraved on the back flap. The tangerine tissue liner. The tasteful card inscribed with gilt words. I knew exactly what this envelope was.

A bomb. The kind that explodes without making a sound. The kind that destroys.

The needles had kicked in already. Pinpricks engulfing my fingers and toes, growing and intensifying until it felt like I was clouded all around by a swarm of stinging wasps. It had started about eight months ago, on a trip to Colorado. I'd sprained my ankle skiing and headed back early to LA. The flight had been a nightmare—along with the aching of my ankle, my other extremities had gone completely numb.

The Internet told me it was called peripheral neuropathy. I'd done the requisite online diagnosing of the tingling and discovered that causes ran the gamut from diabetes to autoimmune issues to tumors. None of which I was willing to entertain the possibility of having. I was young—just twenty-four—and perfectly healthy otherwise.

I didn't need to waste half a day so a doctor could tell me I'd twisted my ankle. Or that the tingling would probably go away when I healed. Doctors were my mother's favored territory, not mine.

The needles had hung around longer than expected. But at worst, they were an annoyance, which, I assumed, would eventually resolve itself. I had it under control, for the most part. They mostly flared up in moments of stress. Like right now, for instance.

I sat on the chaise. Inhaled. Curled my hands into fists.

What the hell had I been thinking? Frances might live in New York, but the woman had spies everywhere. Of course word would have gotten back to her—about us easing Aurora through her divorce with a Vegas party. I should've known she'd gather her intel and track me down. The CIA had nothing on Frances Ashley.

I shouldn't have used my real name to register. I sure as hell shouldn't have stuck around for three days. But I couldn't leave Aurora alone with the Glitter Girls, her party posse. They were nice enough. But divorce is a black hole of heart-hardening sorrow. (I should know. I was the child of three of them.) And the Girls weren't known for being deep wells of empathy. Their cure for heartache was a week of gambling, drinking, and indiscriminate hooking up. Even though Aurora was acting okay and kept calling it her "starter marriage," I could not allow my best friend to go it alone in this sad, smoke-filled town.

So for three days, I'd been trotting behind the squealing, amorphous, vodka-soaked blob as they migrated from casino to club to restaurant to spa. All the while keeping one eye on my phone, in case Omnia, the nonprofit I'd interviewed with the previous week, called with news. But they hadn't, not yet.

And now there was this.

My mother had found me. And delivered her elegant explosive.

I eyed the envelope again. It was from her personal bespoke stash: Smythson of Bond Street—Jackie O.'s stationers, if you were the sort of person who cared about that. My first name was written on it in a flourishy script with gold ink. *Megan*—not Meg, what everybody else in the world called me. There was no return address or stamp.

It ought to have been mailed last month—*no later than six weeks before the party, Megan, and, for God's sakes, never one of those email invites.* This one was late, just one day before her birthday. And dropped off by a messenger. Obviously, Frances had told them to wait until I stepped away, so there wouldn't be the chance of me refusing the delivery.

The tingling had now moved from my palms to the soles of my feet. I rubbed my hands together so briskly sparks should've shot out from them.

I glanced at the guy on the next chaise. His messy hair glinted reddish-brown in the sunlight, and freckles blotched his shoulders. My type. I racked my brain for his name. All I could summon was a brief but flirty conversation between us on the walk back to the hotel last night. Earlier this morning, not long after I'd gotten settled by the pool, he'd materialized and plopped down beside me. He was cute, but a faint odor of last night's drinks still hung around him, and I wasn't in the mood for company. I'd managed to slip out of the room without waking anyone—dodging Glitter Girls sprawled across beds, sofas, and overstuffed ottomans—and thought I'd found a quiet spot to wait for my phone call.

Which hadn't come yet.

I checked yet again, then replaced the phone on the teak table. I'd been volunteering with Omnia's after-school program for over a year. It had been the most fulfilling thing I'd done, maybe ever, and I'd been excited when the coordinator job opened up. It was a full-time gig, offered decent pay and benefits and, for the first time in my life, a shot at something I'd never experienced before. *Independence.* The word felt like a treasure stored in a private corner of my heart.

I'd thought I had a pretty good shot at the job when I'd initially interviewed, but now my confidence was flagging. It was past twelve thirty, three thirty in New York. How long were they going to draw this out? I cleared my constricted throat.

"You didn't happen to see who left this letter, did you?" I asked Mr. Freckled Shoulders.

He didn't stir, not even slightly. I considered the possibility that he'd passed out.

"Excuse me," I said with a sharper edge than I intended. The guy flopped his head over, and I jutted my chin at the envelope. "This. Did you see who left it?"

"No. Why don't you open it?"

I looked away. Rubbed my hands some more. He didn't understand. But, honestly, how could I expect him to? How could a stranger fathom the singular psychological torture of receiving a letter from Frances Ashley? A guy like this couldn't understand that if I picked up the damn thing—if I opened it—I couldn't keep up the lie I'd been telling myself for three years: that I didn't have a mother. That Frances Ashley didn't exist.

The guy yawned. "Looks like an invitation. Wedding, maybe."

"It's not," I snapped.

He lowered his sunglasses, and his eyes flicked from my face down to my hands. I felt myself go warm. I abruptly drew up my knees and locked my numb, tingling fingers around them. Focused on a lone kid splashing in the deep end of the pool. He was wearing green plastic frog goggles, and, in spite of a couple of giant water wings, he was still struggling to get to the edge. No mom in sight. She was probably huddled in a cabana somewhere, nursing a hangover, utterly unaware that her child was wretchedly out of place in Sin City. *Hang in there, kid. Been there, done that. You got this.*

My relationship with Frances had always been rocky. But it imploded for good three years ago. It was over a piece in the *New Yorker*—part of a series they were doing, Novelist as Mother. (I assumed they'd decided against Novelist as Block of Ice / Megalomaniac / Animal Who Eats Her Young.)

Unsurprisingly, Frances's ("reflective, raw, powerful") essay was unadulterated bullshit. For the most part she recounted fantasies, moments between us that had never happened. That is, with the exception of a charming passage about the day I got my period on a gondola in Venice. There, for some perverse reason, she chose to tell the truth.

The day the magazine came out, we squared off. It was after dinner at her Fifth Avenue apartment. While her housekeeper clattered in the kitchen, I informed Frances that she was a pandering, self-aggrandizing liar. She told me I was indifferent to her needs, an entitled, self-important princess who'd rather live on a trust fund than risk getting a real job. At which point I hurled a copy of the offending magazine at her head but missed and broke a glass bowl. She stared at me stonily for a few long moments, then glided out of the room and locked herself in her office.

Just past midnight, she found me, swaddled in an old robe, morosely watching a *Full House* marathon with a pint of mint chocolate chip. The shards of the glass bowl still littered the floor. She icily informed me that, per the editor of the *New Yorker*, I was invited to write a rebuttal to the essay. I had exactly one week to turn in some copy.

"Oh, gosh. Where to begin?" I said. "Christmas 2003? Otherwise known as 'The Year Santa Got Drunk and Forgot'?"

She sighed. "Sure, Megan. Start with that."

"Or . . . maybe I should lead with 'The Time My Mother Bribed the Headmaster with a Signed First Edition of Her Book So I Could Skip Tenth Grade.'"

"You were too smart for that school. Finishing out the year would've been a waste of your time."

"You mean a waste of *your* time. It was the only thing I had to do—be with my friends. Learn. Be normal. You just didn't want to be tied down to one place."

She sighed. Picked at the piping along the sofa arm. But I wasn't done. It wasn't enough to know I'd annoyed her; I wanted blood.

"How about this one?" I said softly, and her eyes locked onto mine. "'Lolita, the Sequel: How My Mother Looked the Other Way When Her Underage Daughter Had an Affair with a Married Man.'"

In one moment—a nanosecond—everything froze around us. It was just the two of us, mother and daughter, locked in a primal battle for survival. In that moment, I saw her inability to give me what I wanted and the pain I caused her. I saw my own meanness and desperation for her to erase the past. As we stood there, eyes blazing, pulses racing, the inevitability of it all became clear. When the two of us came in contact, we were always going to do this—react like incompatible chemicals in a lab experiment. Sizzle. Spark. Then explode.

We needed each other—possibly even loved each other in some strange, flawed way—but it didn't matter. We were doomed to destroy each other.

I spent the next three Christmases and New Years at random friends' island villas or apartments in Paris, dodging questions about why I wasn't with my mother. I eluded three birthday-dinner invitations, missed three birthday parties. Radio silence reigned supreme—no emails, phone calls, or texts passed between the two of us. For the first time in my life, I felt free. It had been three years since our fight. Three years since I'd spoken to my mother.

Three wonderful, Frances-free years. Well, *wonderful* might be stretching it, considering my stalled career and dry spell when it came to men. But it was a start. And I wasn't going back to the way things used to be.

Now, sweating in the scorching Vegas sun, with my ominously silent phone and that vile envelope, I felt lost all over again. Angry and unfocused. I was me, three years ago.

I scrubbed my face with a towel and glanced at the water bottle, wishing it was a Bloody Mary. Then abruptly turned to see the freckled guy sitting up and flipping the envelope between his fingers, a magician rolling a quarter. He grinned at me.

"I could be your plus-one." He leaned close to me and ran one finger down my leg, all the way to my ankle. He stopped at the bumpy white constellation on my skin—a birthmark—and circled there. I jerked my leg away.

"Trust me, you do not want to come to this party," I said and reached for the letter, but he snatched it back.

"Trust me, there is no party I don't want to go to." He tore into the envelope. Held up the gilt-edged, engraved card to block the sun's glare and squinted. Then guffawed in disbelief. "Oh, dude. Do you know what this is? This is from Frances Ashley." He thrust the card at me. "You just got a fucking *engraved* invitation to Frances Ashley's birthday party. Tomorrow night!"

"Hm," I said.

Another thrust of the card. "That's amazing!"

I said nothing.

"She's a legend. How old is she, like forty?"

"Sixty."

"No way." His lip curled in faint disgust. "Dude. She's hot."

I suppressed an eye roll. "Just goes to show you what bathing in the tears of purebred puppies can do."

"Frances Ashley . . ." His brow furrowed. "That bitch probably throws like the sickest birthday bash ever, man. She has got to throw the fuck down, you know what I'm saying? With, like, absinthe and clowns juggling flaming chainsaws."

I considered telling him that my mother threw down by forcing her guests to listen to tiresome stories about how she'd learned to sword fight from a reformed jihadist or how she mastered Vedic yoga in one week in Tibet with Michael Douglas's manager's ex-wife.

I wanted to laugh. Then cry. Then poke this guy's stupid eyes out.

"How do you know her?" he asked. But he'd flipped the card over and wasn't even listening. "Oh, wait," he crowed. "There's a note on the back. 'Darling, I miss you and love you. Please do come. Edgar isn't well.'" His smile faded a fraction. "Huh," he said.

I felt like someone had slapped me. Like I couldn't get a breath.

"Give it to me," I whispered hoarsely.

He handed the invitation over.

I thought I heard the kid shriek from the pool, but I wasn't sure because my heart was pounding so hard. I read the note once, twice, barely seeing the words.

"Who's Edgar?" he asked.

I ignored him, stuffed the invitation and the envelope in my bag, and grabbed my phone, knocking one of the bottles of water off the table. Its contents glugged out onto the hot deck, but I left it there. I needed to do something—call someone, make plans—but I couldn't think what that would be. I wondered if I was going to be able to make it back to the room.

"I have to go," I said. My voice sounded shaky. Like it was coming from somebody else's body.

"How do you know Frances Ashley?" he said.

"I don't," I yelled over my shoulder and fled.

KITTEN

—from Chapter 1

There had been three nannies who'd come before Fay—and they'd all left on good terms, Mrs. Murphy assured her over the phone. The previous girls simply hadn't been able to adjust to life on Bonny.

Fay thought if she could adjust to the diner, she could adjust to practically anything, especially a four-star hotel on a private island. To her, Ambletern sounded like heaven, and the child like an angel. Fay could write the previous nannies, if she wanted, but there really wasn't time. The Murphys needed the position filled right away.

The bus ticket from Norwalk to St. Marys cost her $24.50, which was almost exactly what she had left in her bank account.

Ashley, Frances. *Kitten*. New York: Drake, Richards and Weems, 1976. Print.

Chapter Two

Back in the dark suite, I tiptoed between the sleeping bodies to the bathroom. After bolting the door, I stood, trembling all over, and read and reread Frances's note. There were no specifics about Edgar. Nothing that gave any clues as to his condition. I flipped the invitation and propped it against the mirror.

PLEASE JOIN US FOR
FRANCES ASHLEY'S
BIRTHDAY CELEBRATION
SATURDAY, APRIL 7, 2016
EIGHT O' CLOCK
43 CENTRAL PARK EAST
RSVP ASA@RANKINLEWISLITERARY.COM

The party was tomorrow night, the day of my mother's birthday. Same as always. But this time she hadn't mailed it the requisite six weeks ago to the house I was renting in LA.

I thought of the last time I'd seen Frances. The way she'd looked when I'd said that last awful thing about Graeme and me. Her face had dissolved somehow, become a puddle of melted wax. All at once, I didn't recognize her. Fear had risen in my throat. Maybe regret too. I wasn't sure.

"Mom—" I'd said, then stopped. There was no going back, not even if I apologized. Somehow I knew. She'd started down the hall to her bedroom. I considered calling her back, but didn't. I'd meant what I said, and she knew it. We both knew it.

If I'd found her birthday invitation in my mailbox six weeks ago, I would have tossed it in the trash without opening it. So she'd had it hand delivered. Whether it was smart on her part or just plain stalker-ish, one thing was clear: Edgar was sick, and Frances wanted me home.

My lungs felt constricted. I retrieved my phone from my bag and looked up flights to New York. There were a few first-class seats leaving first thing in the morning and arriving in New York that evening. I booked a seat, then ordered two bouquets at Frances's favorite florist on the Upper East Side—one of hydrangea, the other, pink peonies. I showered, then sat on the toilet, yanking a comb through my hair and ordering myself not to cry.

I had to send all my positive energy—what was left of it—to Edgar.

I pictured his twinkly eyes, headful of swoopy silver hair, still handsome in his eighties. He'd been my mother's agent since the beginning. The only constant in my chaotic life. The story went that he had found the manuscript for *Kitten* buried in the slush pile of his ancient, fusty literary agency, which was teetering on the edge of bankruptcy. He'd plucked my mother from obscurity and, in a blink, turned everyone's fortunes around.

Edgar called me Pip and brought me rose macarons. He met my Omnia girls once. When I was just a kid, I overheard him confront Frances and tell her she was wrong to ship me off to boarding school and camp and the overseas leadership programs. He said she would regret her decisions one day, when she was alone. She didn't listen, but

I loved him for trying. In fact, I just loved him in general. He was the only family I had.

My phone echoed in the marble bathroom. The call from Omnia. God bless, finally. I adjusted my towel, cracked my knuckles, then jabbed at the screen.

"Hi," I said.

"Meg. Hello. Good time to talk?"

"Absolutely. Great time."

I closed my eyes. I'd seen Frances charm reporters countless times when she needed to, when the questions got a little too uncomfortable. The easy laugh, the knowing twinkle. *I'm a professional liar, darling. Whatever story I tell you, you're going to believe.* (And then she would go on about the psychology of story, narrative transportation, or some such literary gobbledygook, and everyone would fall into a worshipful trance.)

The director was already knee-deep into her spiel, talking about how the Pearce School girls up in Harlem had really taken to my French and Italian classes and commending me on the most highly attended sessions in the program. If only she'd known how woefully unprepared I'd been when I started. That my grab bag of go-to phrases for the teens to translate had mostly consisted of *double shot, kickass deejay,* and *my friend needs to vomit, please.*

I made the appropriate noises, and she segued into a description of Omnia's new direction. An expansion of the after-school program necessitated a new push in fundraising. I tried to focus, but her words were battering me like waves—*restructuring, refocusing, reassessing community partners*—making a spot throb directly behind my right eye. At last, she paused for a breath, and my brain started to catch up.

"You gave the job to someone else," I said, pressing the area around my eye socket.

"Yesterday."

I was quiet.

"Look, you've been really great with the girls," she said. "But everyone agrees that instead of coordinator, you'd be better suited to fundraising. With your . . . extensive contacts."

"My contacts."

"In the publishing world. We'd like to offer you the head of fundraising, Meg."

"I don't have contacts in the publishing world," I said numbly.

Just Edgar.

"I feel like I've just blundered," she said carefully. "Did I overstep?"

"No. It's just . . . I'm not that close to my mother," I said. "Not lately. Not for years."

She went quiet.

Six months into my Frances sabbatical, I'd confessed to Aurora that not speaking to Mom really wasn't so bad. She gave me a sympathetic, if slightly confused, look. Her mom was one of those people who organized family pictures at the beach where everybody wore the same color outfits and stood together in the dunes, loose limbed and breezy. My dear, kindhearted best friend couldn't fathom any other kind of mom, much less mine. And that was the worst feeling of all. To know I was alone.

Frances would always be my unique burden to bear.

I cleared my throat. "It's not the first time someone's made that mistake."

"Meg—"

"I appreciate your offer, but I'm not interested."

I hung up and headed back into the dark room to pack.

KITTEN

—from Chapter 2

Fay had never seen anything quite so grand as Ambletern Hotel. Situated on the southern end of Bonny Island, the huge old house was constructed of tabby—the local concrete made of crushed shells and sand. It stretched out its wings, turrets, and segmented porches in all directions, like a giant white spider. The roots of a couple of oaks had grown up through the foundation, and Fay thought immediately of a fortress. The house would certainly never fall, not even if you rammed a bulldozer right through it.

Ashley, Frances. *Kitten*. New York: Drake, Richards and Weems, 1976. Print.

Chapter Three

The New York air was starting to crisp and purple to darkness. I had just come out of my favorite macaron shop in Chelsea (one dozen pistachio-and-lavender for Frances, another dozen of coffee for Edgar) and had stepped off the curb to hail a cab, when Frances flashed into my line of sight.

Her face was huge, her pale skin and red hair filtered with some kind of grotesque, photoshopped shadow effect. I couldn't help it—my head swiveled to track her. An automatic response, I guess. Like people who light up a cigarette even when they've been told they have lung cancer.

The giant, airbrushed likeness of her plastered to the side of a city bus smiled enigmatically next to the new edition of *Kitten*. The book jacket showed the titular main character, a small blonde girl, standing in the open door of a Gothic mansion. She was dressed in a ragged green gingham dress and a turban with a drooping white ostrich feather. Garish red copy slashed down the length of the bus: **FRANCES ASHLEY AND KITTEN: STILL KILLING IT AFTER FORTY YEARS.**

The bus streaked past, grinding and squealing its way down Ninth, but in that brief glance, the lizard part of my brain managed to register every detail of the picture: my mother's pirate eyes, her auburn sweep of hair, the face collagened and Botoxed and lasered to a hard sheen. Her scarlet lips cat-curled across her pale face as she smirked out at us all. And I couldn't look away. You know what they say about the *Mona Lisa*? It was the opposite with my mother's picture—no matter where I stood, her eyes seemed to look everywhere but at me.

Screw the cab. Walking would clear my head, keep the pins and needles at bay. I turned north, using the Chrysler Building as my compass. It was unusually cold, even for April in New York, and I'd only brought my flimsy Vegas wardrobe, so I shivered in the paper-thin dress and heels. I wished for a trench coat. I had a really nice one somewhere, I couldn't quite remember where. It had been a Christmas present from one of Mom's exes. The hedge-fund guy she'd ditched in Thailand, if memory served.

Eventually, I smelled the change in the air. As Chelsea turned into Midtown, then the Upper East Side, piss and old garbage and Indian food gave way to perfumed boutique air and Town Car exhaust. It was dark now. I turned down Central Park South, breathing heavily and bathed in a fine sheen of sweat, and zigzagged up to Sixty-Third, where I ducked into the florist's shop.

After I gave her my name, the smock-clad girl behind the counter handed over two gargantuan bouquets wrapped in brown paper and cellophane. They smelled heavenly. Noticing the macarons, she offered a giant burlap shopping bag to carry everything.

"No card for the peonies?" she asked after tucking everything neatly in the bag and handing it over. She had an impossibly smooth ebony bob and two perfectly even sweeps of purple eyeliner.

I shook my head.

"How about a blank one you can fill in yourself?"

"No," I said firmly and handed over my credit card.

When she saw the name on the Amex, she lifted her brows. "Oh my God. You're *that* Megan Ashley."

"That's right." I smiled tightly. I could see the lightning assessment in her eyes, the one I always got even though I'd been photographed with my mom a million times: *Light-brown skin, vague ethnicity. Definitely not a chip off the porcelain-perfect Frances Ashley block. Which one was your father, again . . . ?*

"Would you like to put these on your mother's account?" she asked.

"No. No, thank you. The flowers are for her. I probably shouldn't make her pay."

I laughed. She laughed. Even though it was, in fact, not funny at all and something I'd become increasingly uncomfortable with: my mother paid for everything I did or consumed—indirectly, automatically, from a trust account on the fifteenth of every month. And now that the nonprofit job had evaporated, it looked like I'd be on the payroll until I could figure out what the hell I was going to do with my life.

The girl's eyes took on a disconcerting sparkle. "I just have to say. I loved *Kitten*. I mean, really loved it. I guess everybody says that, but so many people say it for the kitsch factor, you know? I don't. I actually saw the movie eleven times when they played it at the Angelika last year. I mean, *You tell me a story, you weave me a tale . . .*" She smiled expectantly, like she was waiting for me to chime in. When I didn't, she barreled on. "It just gives me goose bumps every time. Can I ask you . . . what inspired her? I mean, how did she even write something like that when she was just nineteen?

"I mean, I'm a writer, you know? Not that I could ever be Frances Ashley or anything, I'm just saying I understand the whole writing thing because I'm in the trenches. I'm working on a thing right now, a trilogy? Not that's it's published or anything. But one day, maybe." She colored slightly and touched her perfect bob. "I'm just saying, everybody always talks about the greats. But, I mean, what about the ones who aren't necessarily great? But who make a ton of money? Screw the greats, right? I think your mother is better than all those guys. I mean, not a better writer. Just a smarter one." She let out a squeak. "How did you even deal with having a mother who has managed to outsell the greatest writers of our day?"

"Well . . . ," I said.

She caught her breath, waiting for the golden nugget of wisdom I was about to drop.

"I stay fucked up one hundred percent of the time, so that I am able to drown out the shame and self-loathing."

Her face caved in on itself. "Oh. I didn't mean it in a bad way at all—"

"That was a joke." I took my card back. "A really stupid one. Sorry about that. I'll just . . ." I lifted up the bag. "Thanks for the flowers. They're beautiful. Have a nice night."

She nodded once, mutely, and I pushed through the door out into the chilly night. My face burned, even though I told myself it didn't matter. But God, did I always have to be such an asshole? What was it about being in the same city as Frances that turned me into a whiny, spiteful bitch?

And what did it say about me that I kind of enjoyed it when someone reminded me that my mother was considered a hack? Did it make me feel superior?

Ten minutes later, I arrived at my mother's building. I took a moment to gather myself on the sidewalk and looked up. The place had been designed to impress—white limestone blocks stacked like sugar cubes, brass window grilles and doors flashing in the lights of passing taxis. All the windows glowed except the ones on the top floor, which was oddly dark in the cold, blue dusk.

Strange.

When I walked in, the doorman—not Paolo, a new guy—raised his index finger at me.

"Hold up," he said. "Can I help you?"

I smiled at him, trying not to look as nervous as I felt. He smiled back, but it was more of a *Hey, chica, what's up* kind of smile, like I was here to deliver some takeout. I got that a lot. The Mexican guys always assumed I was Mexican. The Persian guys assumed I was Persian. The Colombians, Puerto Ricans, Indians—all the same. They would make me whoever they wanted me to be, their all-purpose woman of color.

I didn't mind it, honestly. I kind of considered it my own personal superpower, the ability to blend in wherever and with whomever. It allowed me to slip under the radar when I needed to. In reality, my genetic makeup was a fairly simple combination: I took after my long-deceased father, a blend of his Creole and Brazilian roots.

I straightened, shifted the bag to the other hand. "Delivery for Ashley. Penthouse."

The new doorman puffed his chest—"Just a moment"—and picked up the phone. He covered the receiver. "Who?"

I hesitated a second, then glanced down at the burlap bag. "Bramble and Bloom."

He waited, eyes flicking from me to the elevator. Finally he put down the phone. "Sorry. No one's home."

"They're home. The flowers are for a party. Try again."

He squared his shoulders. "You can leave them at the desk, and I'll see that Ms. Ashley gets them when she returns."

I sighed and chewed at my lip. "Actually, I'll just go up. I'm . . . expected."

Something flickered in his expression. "Oh, wait a second." He pointed at me. "Oh, I'm sorry. You're . . . ? You're her daughter, aren't you? Paolo told me about you . . ."

He came around the side of the desk. No more *hey-chica* eyes, that was for sure. But something else had replaced them. A spark. The look.

God, it must be a full moon.

I executed a side maneuver and darted past him, around the leather chairs and a huge arrangement of tulips spilling over the inlaid table, into the cool, perfumed air of the elevator. I hit ten. His jaunty cap appeared around the corner, hopeful eyes wide beneath the patent-leather brim.

The closing doors silenced whatever he was about to say, and next thing I knew I was rocketing up into the building. I backed into the upholstered corner and exhaled. My feet throbbed from the long walk, and I sniffed at one armpit. It smelled like a nauseating combination of airplane, taxicab, and flower shop, but I'd have to forgo a shower. It was almost eight thirty. Frances had probably already wrapped up cocktail hour and started on the first course.

I rang the buzzer on the white enameled door with the brass number *10*. Once, twice, then another long blast. No one appeared. I juggled my packages, fished my key ring out from my purse, and let myself in.

KITTEN

—from Chapter 2

Ambletern was quiet, too. Surveying it from the drive, Fay imagined it was not the kind of place to which families brought their noisy children on holiday.

Rather, lovers rendezvoused there. Scientists came to study the wildlife, and authors to write their spooky mysteries. Ambletern was a different sort of place, a house brimming with history and secrets and promise. A house where things *happened*.

With a flutter of excitement in her belly, Fay set her suitcase down on the sandy drive and lifted her long, red hair off her neck and into a clasp. She was already bathed in sweat.

Ashley, Frances. *Kitten*. New York: Drake, Richards and Weems, 1976. Print.

Chapter Four

The foyer and the rooms beyond in my mother's apartment were dark, everything strangely silent. I paused, set the flowers and macarons on a glossy table, and walked into the living room.

Nothing much had changed since I'd last been here three years ago—it still looked like a magazine spread. The room was swathed in shades of pale pink and cream and furnished with the perfect combination of antiques and elegant, custom-made furniture. A Gustavian clock ticktocked on the carved marble mantelpiece. Above that, my mother, in a green silk ball gown rendered in flattering oil brushstrokes, smiled down at me. I averted my eyes.

As usual, there was not a speck of dust anywhere. Nor were there any party guests. The place was empty.

I slipped off my shoes and padded across the thick Persian rug, turning on lights as I went. I pushed open a window, breathed in the cool, exhaust-laden air, and went into the kitchen. The marble counters were spotless, appliances tucked away in the pantry. No sign of a catering staff having been here.

I flung open the doors of the massive Sub-Zero fridge. One lone, unopened bottle of champagne sat on the shelf.

"Hello, darling," I said.

I filled a coffee mug to the brim, then continued my cursory check of the apartment. The dining room, library, and salon. Down the hall to the bedrooms. Halfway to the master, I pulled up short. The door to Frances's study was closed, but there was a sliver of light glowing under it.

I knocked softly. "Frances?"

There was a rustling sound, then a sharp thump. On instinct, I stepped back.

"Frances?" I said again.

I heard more rustling on the other side, then silence.

I'd encountered my mother's crazed fans before, and they were the real deal. Fucking one hundred percent, off-the-charts insane. The person in there could be anyone—a college student who'd recently discovered *Kitten* in his Contemporary American Horror class and wormed his way past the new doorman; some rando teenage stalker who'd dug up Frances's address and wanted to ask her to his prom. Or maybe it was one of the really crazy ones, the kooks who called themselves the Kitty Cult. Those were the ones who clotted up the Internet with their fanfic, creepy art, and nutso conspiracy theories about her book.

I wished desperately for pepper spray or a rape whistle. Or a gun.

I squared up to the door, my pulse hammering. "Whoever's in there, you better show your face right now."

Nothing.

"If you don't open this door right now, I swear to God, I'm calling the cops, and believe me, you do not want—"

The door to my mother's study swung open, revealing not a hulking monster but a thin, hunched young man. He looked like he was in his midtwenties, even though he was gray-faced, like an old man, with a feathering of colorless hair. His neck was swaddled in a gauzy, forest-green scarf. Above the scarf, two bright spots of rosacea glowed angrily on his cheeks. I took another step back.

"Megan," he said. Like a blanket of ants, a wave of pinpricks covered my body, the shock of it nearly knocking the breath out of me.

"Who are you?" I said.

"I'm Asa Bloch." He held out a slender hand. "I'm Frances's new assistant. I'm terribly, terribly sorry if I scared you. I was just doing some work, returning some correspondence for your mother."

I looked down at his hand. It was gray like the rest of him, a gray uncooked chicken cutlet. He looked nothing like my mother's past assistants—aggressive, strong-jawed kids from Westchester County, graduates of Ivy League schools who'd been plotting their takeovers of the publishing industry since they were in diapers. This guy looked so . . . anemic.

"Where is everybody?" I asked.

He withdrew his hand. "Beg pardon?"

I said it louder. "Where is everybody?"

A flicker of understanding and his mouth dropped open. "Oh, no." He gulped. "I mean, of course. You're here for the party."

"Yes. I'm here for the party. Which is today, on my mother's birthday, like it is every year."

He flushed. "I'm an absolute idiot. I should have . . . I didn't even think to . . . Your mother just assumed you weren't coming. So I guess . . . well, it seems she didn't tell you."

He offered a weak smile, but I didn't return it. I looked behind him instead, to my mother's massive glass desk, reflecting the glow of her silver computer. Everything was in its place—the ivory leather desk set and the jagged, crystal-white rock she used as a paperweight. Which, incidentally, had never fulfilled its purpose, as Frances had always immediately filed any and every loose piece of paper.

The ivory leather chair, which cost somewhere in the five figures, was pushed back at an angle. He'd been sitting there, right at her desk. I'd never known my mother to let her assistants into her study. Or on her computer. My mother was a control freak about that computer. About her files. About everything in her life.

25

I looked at him. "The invitation wasn't mailed ahead of time, like it should've been. It was hand delivered to me. Yesterday. By a pool in Vegas."

He nodded, like this was new information he was mulling over. I could feel fury rising inside me.

"Why don't you tell me what the hell is going on?"

He drew in a deep breath. "There was no invitation mailed to you because Frances decided not to include you this year." He was looking out the window, at the black smudges of trees in the park, and I was glad. My eyes had suddenly, unexpectedly filled. "She thought it was for the best," he went on. "But then, three days ago, Edgar had the stroke and they put him in the hospital. She told me she had changed her mind. She said she wanted to see you and that I should find you. It was too late to mail it, so I had the invitation messengered to you."

My mouth went dry. "Wait, Edgar had a stroke? He's in the hospital? All the note said was that he wasn't well."

"Yes, it was a stroke. Three days ago. Your mother's been very upset about it. The stroke was serious, and he's old. But, if I may, it seemed like she was really more upset about you." His eyes locked onto mine like a tractor beam. "The whole situation between you two. Which is why she decided to invite you."

The skin on my palms began to needle again. He was making all of this—Edgar and the ruined party—sound vaguely like it was my fault.

"She was distraught," he went on. "She said she didn't know if she could bear to host the party with Edgar in the hospital. And . . . she seemed convinced that even if you got the invitation, you wouldn't come. She told me she was tired of being alone and . . ." He shifted uncomfortably.

"So she ran," I prompted.

He nodded. "She canceled the party this morning. And flew to Palm Springs."

"Of course she did. So then, as my mother's humble assistant, you obviously called everybody and told them not to come. Except me. You didn't call me. Why?"

"Frances said she would."

"A tip. Don't ever assume Frances will do what she says. You'll just be disappointed."

"And also . . ." He cleared his throat. "I thought you would want to see Edgar."

My breath hitched. "Well. You were right about that."

"There's one more thing," he said, and I tensed. "And I really shouldn't be telling you this because I could lose my job, but . . ." His voice faded.

"What?" I demanded.

"It's about Palm Springs."

"Palm Springs," I repeated dully.

"And Benoît Jaffe," Asa said.

Benoît. A French artist Frances and I met at a show in Palm Springs about five or six years ago. I could see him, clear as day. Mop of black hair, thin nose, olive skin. Sexy in a disheveled, helpless kind of way. He'd been married at the time—to an American actress—and was far too young for my mother, but I had a suspicion she hadn't let that stop her.

"Frances and Benoît Jaffe went to Palm Springs. To get married," he added, and I swear, I nearly toppled over, right onto the carpet of my mother's hallway.

It was a new level of bad. Frances had gotten married without telling me.

KITTEN

—from Chapter 2

Kitten Murphy stood halfway up the wide staircase in the lobby of Ambletern, her hands twined around the carved oak banister, watching the guests from the ferry register at the big oak desk below. Her blonde hair hung in two even braids just past her thin shoulders.

From inside the door of the hotel, Fay watched her. The girl's face didn't move the way most girls' did, all untamed flashes and fits. It appeared nearly immobile, almost preternaturally composed for a girl so young. Even her braids seemed carved in stone. She watched the incoming guests with wide, green, unblinking eyes, her lips curved in what some people might've called contempt, if she'd been of age. As she was only eight years old, Fay decided it was bashfulness.

Before she could introduce herself to the girl, Fay was swept into the crowd of guests. She met a lovely young couple, the Cormleys; a boy named Henrick and his gregarious mother; and an older lady, with an imperious air, called Miss Bolan. They were all so glamorous, Fay thought, far more than she. She considered herself lucky to meet such people.

Ashley, Frances. *Kitten*. New York: Drake, Richards and Weems, 1976. Print.

Chapter Five

The next morning, I took a cab over to Presbyterian to visit Edgar. After the strokes, the doctors had hooked him up to a ventilator and dropped him into a coma in an effort to reduce the swelling in his brain. Since I wasn't immediate family, I wasn't allowed to see him.

Never mind all he had was an estranged son who lived in London; never mind I was the only one who'd shown up for the dying man. I must've looked miserable, because when I dropped the flowers on the Formica desk, one of the duty nurses took pity on me.

"Ten minutes," she whispered. "If anybody asks, you're his granddaughter."

It was dark in the room, and Edgar's bed was cranked to the highest level, so that his pale face was almost even with mine. I brushed back a lock of his hair. Leaned close and kissed his forehead.

"Edgar, it's Pip." I felt tears push behind my eyes but sniffed them back. "You don't look so hot, mister. I'm sorry I haven't called in a while." I straightened. Drew in a shaky breath. "So, Frances got married. Again. Yesterday, as a matter of fact. To Benoît Jaffe. She didn't tell me, she just went off and did it. She went to California with him, and I just . . . I don't know. I don't like him. I think he's a parasite."

I caught my breath, not sure I could go on.

"You have to be okay, Edgar, because Frances can't function without you. And this guy, Benoît? If he ditched his ex-wife for Mom, he's got to be penniless. Completely dependent on Frances. You have to get better and help me figure out what to do. Also, there's this guy, Asa. Frances's assistant . . ."

I felt the tears again, hot and threatening.

"Did you hire him? He was in her office last night. On her computer. What is going on? Has she gone completely around the bend?"

The *shush-shush-click* of the ventilator filled the room. I smoothed his hair again.

"I threw him out. Told him not to come back as long as I was in the apartment. But he's trouble, I can tell you that right now."

The tears dripped down my cheeks and my nose. I sniffed mightily.

"I know. I should call her. But Edgar . . . it's been too long, and there's so much between us. I'm just so fucking out-of-my-mind angry . . ." My voice broke.

I might say something I regret forever.

I might cut all ties. For good.

"We need you to get well, Edgar," I whispered, suddenly prickling with shame that I'd popped into the ICU and dumped my problems on a comatose man. Everybody knew you were supposed to be positive and upbeat in these situations. God, I was turning into Frances.

I kissed him, then brushed away the wetness left behind on his wrinkled face. "Don't worry about Mom, okay, Edgar? I'll take care of that. Right now, I need you to get well so I can hear you complain about how shitty the young bartenders are at Bemelmans. You hear me? I need . . . I need to hear you laugh, one more time . . ." I turned, fled the room, then stumbled down the fluorescent-lit corridors until I found a bank of elevators.

Back in the lobby, I sank onto one of the plastic benches near the automatic glass doors of the entrance. I dropped my head in my hands.

My gut was still twisting, the pinpricks stabbing me all over, but I barely even noticed. All I could think of was Edgar.

He was the person who'd sat me down on my thirteenth birthday and told me he knew how hard it was to be Frances Ashley's daughter. He told me I could come to him, no matter what, for anything. He was the one who convinced me that, even though I wasn't a great student, I should go to college and major in global and urban education, a decision that ended up being the smartest thing I'd ever done. NYU was where I got my first subway card, ventured into my first laundromat, and met my best friend.

Edgar was the one who reminded me of Frances's good points when I wanted to kill her. He was the one who kept me sane. My foundation. But now . . . now he was lying unresponsive in a hospital bed, and I didn't know what I was going to do.

It was the fortieth anniversary of *Kitten*, I remembered, scrubbing at my swollen eyes. The pressure of planning such a monumental event had worn him down. He wasn't a young man anymore. He wasn't strong. He couldn't handle things—stress or Frances—like he used to.

My eyes unfocused, and my mind rewound. I visualized life—my life, Edgar's life, Frances's—as it might've been, without *Kitten*. A carefree, rose-tinged existence where I was just a regular girl with a regular mom and a kindly uncle-figure like Edgar. No rabid fans. No strange trips featuring a revolving door of strangers. Just a family who loved each other.

And then the flecks in the blue tile at my feet swam into view, and the fantasy dissolved. Wishing was a child's game. I couldn't change the past. Frances had written her book and, for better or worse, changed all our lives.

It had taken her a mere two months in the summer of 1975, after her sophomore year in college. She was working as a housekeeper at a bed-and-breakfast on one of Georgia's sea islands to earn some extra cash. She was from Macon, Georgia. Her parents weren't rich, and Frances had held jobs since she was a kid. She was used to the hustle.

Kitten was just a little something she dashed off in her spare time between toilet cleanings. A little something that the eminent Drake, Richards and Weems published the following year to rave reviews. It wasn't her only book—she was no Emily Brontë or Margaret Mitchell—but it was the most famous.

I'd never read it. I also managed to make it all the way through high school without seeing either movie, automatically clicking past them whenever they showed up on basic cable. Mom made it easy enough for me to pretend *Kitten* didn't exist—not to mention her other work. She wrote nonstop, but she never talked about her books with me. That part of her life was work, and she was adamant that work stay separate from family. I wasn't Frances's fan, I was her daughter.

My freshman year at NYU, a rare wave of curiosity crashed over me, and I spent one Sunday afternoon researching my mother's famous book online. I found a scathing write-up at *Kirkus* in their vintage reviews. More reviews, from *Publishers Weekly, Booklist, Library Journal,* popped up. They all read pretty much the same—250-word paragraphs blasting the book's utilitarian writing with a sledgehammer plot.

Apparently, *Kitten* fans didn't give a rip what reviews said. I found dozens of elaborate websites where readers wrote their own lengthy odes to the book. As well as speculated endlessly about all the sequels, prequels, and related materials.

That night I sent Edgar a drunken, rambling, self-pitying email about the injustice of it all. Why did everyone insist on bowing down to Frances? Couldn't they see what a mediocre writer she was—not to mention a pathetic excuse for a mother? In reply, he invited me to lunch.

He ordered a bottle of Bordeaux and a tray of oysters and told me the whole story. Apparently, the public's response to *Kitten* was a cultural phenomenon. Absolutely unprecedented. Rarely had regular folks loved a book so much that its critical reception turned into white noise.

"It was her timing that . . ." He exploded his hands like fireworks. "The country was deep in a recession, and unemployment was through the roof. People were antsy. Angry." He sat back. "*The Bad Seed* came out in 1954, lighting the creepy-kid-genre fuse." He ticked off on his fingers. "Then *Rosemary's Baby* in '67, *The Exorcist* in '71, and *Carrie* in '74 whet readers' appetites for more, but for one with something meaningful to say. Concerning, say, the new wave of child-rearing and marginalized groups like the Native Americans. Not that we used those words back then."

I rolled my eyes. Hard to imagine my mother as anyone's ally.

"It wasn't Pulitzer Prize quality—we all agree; she just accidentally gave the people what they didn't know they wanted."

When a book or movie or song hits it big, he went on to say, one of two things happens: either the object of adulation sees the praise for what it is and keeps their feet on the ground, or they believe their press and demand ass-kissing in perpetuity. The latter was clearly the path my mother had chosen. Edgar didn't blame Frances entirely. He said no sane person could have kept both feet on the ground, not with that level of fame.

He didn't have to tell me the rest. I'd lived it. Frances dated billionaires, actors, and politicians. Wed four of them—conceiving me with #2, who died six months after the wedding in a motorcycle accident—and divorced the rest shortly after the unions. Then the Internet came, intensifying the *Kitten* craziness one-hundredfold. A whole new generation of the Kitty Cult took over and spun things into overdrive.

There were reams of books in *Kitten's* wake, one every six months—mostly horror, speculative, or science fiction. A highly rated anthology series for TV, *Frances Ashley Presents*, which pretty much managed to rip off both Hitchcock's show and *The Twilight Zone*. A reboot of the original film, this one featuring an ensemble of hot young actors and a darker, edgier script.

"There's one thing I've never understood." I took a long, slow slurp of Bordeaux, trying not to appear like this was the central question, the main reason I was sitting there with Edgar. "Why did Frances decide to have a child? She never told you she wanted one, did she?"

He just looked at me.

"She was single, wildly successful, and didn't have any responsibility beyond her career. I mean, I know I was a surprise, but there are ways to deal with those."

He beckoned the waiter.

"Sir?" The waiter clasped his hands. Bowed.

"Another bottle of the same, please."

The waiter swirled away.

Edgar was quiet for a minute, then refolded his napkin. "Your father wasn't right for her, Pip. And she knew it, even before he died, God rest his soul. You were a different story. And after you came, she couldn't imagine her life without you. You changed everything." He tilted his head and smiled. "Darling, precious, magnificent you."

Ah, yes. Magnificent, precious me.

Behind closed doors, Frances may not have taken to motherhood, but in public, she was Supermom. She loved to talk about me in interviews. When I was a little bit older, she took me as her escort to events and movie premieres, showed me off at celebrity-studded parties and book conventions. By thirteen, I'd become nearly as famous as her. Had learned how to deflect intrusive questions, duck fans, and pose on the red carpet like a pro.

In private, I was a mess. A moody, twitchy, difficult kid. I had trouble talking to strangers and using public bathrooms. I suffered from chronic night terrors, wet the bed, and flinched when fans mobbed my mother.

At our lunch, Edgar tried to explain her contradictions. "I know she doesn't show it in the conventional way, Pip, but Frances does love you. Very much. Look past your anger, if you can. Let her prove herself to you."

I sighed. This was just Edgar doing his job—mediating, working the deal, utilizing all the skills in his agent wheelhouse. It was in his best interests, after all, keeping my mother and me on speaking terms. For his livelihood, he needed the Frances Ashley machine to run smoothly. I could pretend for him. And I did for a while.

But now . . .

Now that he was sick, everything was different.

He couldn't keep Frances and me together from a hospital bed. If this illness was as serious as it seemed to be, if he left me, I didn't know how long the tenuous bond between us would hold.

I looked up, exhausted from my thoughts, and caught the reflection of my face in the hospital lobby's glass doors. It was raw and red from crying.

So this was what it was like to lose someone you loved. It felt like someone tearing your heart free of its veins and arteries with their bare hands. It was agony, but, in a strange way, the sadness felt cleaner and truer than anything I'd felt before.

I wiped my eyes with the back of my hand, snagged a tissue from my purse, and blew my nose. Time to get out of this place.

KITTEN

—from Chapter 3

After Fay had gotten settled in her room upstairs, she joined Delia Murphy in the library. The girl's mother launched immediately into her instructions.

"Kitten is to be allowed to play any game that amuses her, with no restriction whatsoever. Mr. Murphy and I believe children should be encouraged to pretend." She was straightening the desk as she spoke, moving piles of paper from one spot to another. Fay noticed one pile was moved to the same place three times. "Giving free rein to imagination stimulates the intellect. Kitten is allowed to pretend she is a wild pony, a pirate, or a fairy princess, and we do not interfere."

"Yes, ma'am," Fay said meekly. This was certainly not the way she'd been raised, but it sounded healthy to her. Adventurous and free.

Ashley, Frances. *Kitten*. New York: Drake, Richards and Weems, 1976. Print.

Chapter Six

Frances's apartment smelled of the housekeeper's organic lemon cleaner. I didn't know what there was to clean in this mausoleum, but she still showed up every morning from ten to noon, regardless. Asa must've told her I was here. She had stocked the fridge with two neatly arranged rows of sparkling water and diet soda, bagels from Inman's, and a stack of boxed meals from Moto, a nearby sushi restaurant.

I tossed my empty Starbucks cup in the trash, splashed water on my face, and poured a slug of the leftover champagne into my recently washed mug. I headed down the dimly lit hall, stopping at the open door of my mother's study.

It was immaculate, like the rest of the house, done entirely in ivory. She'd lined up every book she'd ever loved on shelves that wrapped around the room. Rare first editions, books her famous friends had written, even paperbacks she'd dropped in the bathtub. One entire wall, the one facing the windows that looked out over Fifth Avenue, was reserved for her own work and awards. Along the uppermost shelf were crystal polygons, silver platters, gold plaques. A dented sterling mint-julep cup (some Southern book award, maybe?) and a carved ivory spoon thing

(I couldn't begin to guess). Each engraved, each proclaiming Frances Ashley a genius.

I made a lap around the room, swirling my champagne in the mug and trailing my fingers over the spines of my mother's book collection. The skin along my own spine went to gooseflesh. I couldn't help it—the room always made me feel edgy. A little spooked.

At the end of my circuit, I reached the pièce de résistance—the *Kitten* wall. Copies of the original hardbacks, first editions and other limited editions, lined one entire shelf. Below that, every incarnation of trade and mass-market paperback in every language imaginable stood like a row of obedient children. Frances had cleared out the shelf below the awards for the new fortieth-anniversary edition, the one I'd seen on the side of the bus.

I took a step back, the way you might look at a painting that is too big to take in at close range.

All those copies of *Kitten*—they were like an army, their sheer numbers and precision making me feel slightly off balance. Christ. When you looked at it all together like that, it really was impressive. The wall loomed, there was no other way to put it. I shivered, hating the books and feeling oddly grateful for them all at the same time. My mother's books had made me what I was: a spoiled socialite, a useless dilettante. A failure. I was the girl *Kitten* built.

I touched one of the hardbacks. My finger traveled up. Hooked over the edge. A triangle of the familiar cover emerged—the black-and-pink image of a demonic little girl in a pinafore dress and that lurid '70s typeface. In my head, the bus roared past me, and I saw my mother's face, those curled scarlet lips like she had a secret.

Maybe she did. Maybe there was something of my mother buried somewhere in the pages of this book that, if I had ever bothered to read it, would've given me a key to understanding her. Something that would've made my life bearable.

I pushed the book back in line with the rest of its comrades and went to sit behind Frances's desk. I drained the rest of my champagne. Spun in her spectacularly expensive, ergonomically designed chair. There were no framed pictures on the sleek glass surface of the desk, no plants or kitschy keepsakes. Just an ivory leather cup holding a bouquet of ivory pens and the jagged stone paperweight. She'd told me, since I was a little girl, never to touch her awards. Never to touch her desk or the paperweight.

But I wasn't a little girl anymore, was I?

I plucked one of the pens out of the leather cup. Stared at it as I balanced it on the tips of my fingers. I took hold of either end and pulled the cap loose. Then unscrewed the body of the pen and drew out the cartridge. It was full of black ink. The ink she used to write her first drafts, on creamy white legal pads in an even, looping hand.

I bent the cartridge a few times and it finally split, dripping a few drops of ink onto the pad of my finger. I studied the black blob as it quivered on the surface of my skin, slowly settling into the whorls of my fingerprint, then I lowered and pressed my finger onto the paperweight. The ink left a perfect print.

I stood and walked to the *Kitten* shelf. Ran my inky finger along the row of pristine paperbacks, leaving a series of black smudgy dots and dashes along the spines. Fifth Avenue Morse code.

Help me. Help me.

I stopped at the end of the row, at the last paperback. Its spine was broken, creased so deeply the title was almost completely illegible. I pulled it out.

It was a 2007 edition, surprisingly beat up for such a relatively new book. Inside the cover, there was a name written in pencil. *Susan Evelyn Doucette, age 12. From Aunt Jo.* Ah, yes. I'd almost forgotten. Frances's most rabid fans liked to gift her back their treasured books every time new editions were released. At some point, back in the early 2000s, I think, she'd mentioned in an interview that she loved seeing readers' annotations, and ever since she'd been deluged with old copies of the book. It was a religious rite, almost, for a Kitty Cultist, to return a copy of *Kitten* to the mother ship.

Which I'd thought my mother had always promptly handed over to her assistant to dump in the garbage, unless it came from somebody like Bill Clinton or George Clooney or Ruth Bader Ginsburg. Susan Doucette wasn't a name I recognized. Maybe a Make-A-Wish kid or something. Someone special enough for her to actually hang on to it. This book definitely had the too-loved look of somebody's Velveteen Rabbit.

I lifted the book to my nose and inhaled. It smelled the way old books do, a combination of printing-press chemicals and rot. Some people liked the smell. Not me.

"Planning on doing some reading?"

I spun. It was Asa Bloch, standing in the open door. He wore a rumpled blazer with the sleeves rolled up and was swathed in a pale-blue scarf, which wasn't doing him any favors. In the light from the window, he looked even more ashen than he had last night.

"What are you doing here?" I snapped and dropped the book on the desk. "Did Frances give you a key?"

He held it up.

"I told you not to come here. When my mother is away, this place is mine."

"Okay, fair enough. But before I go, I wondered if we might talk."

"Now's not a good time."

He scanned the room, probably taking note of the inky smudges on the paperweight and across the row of books. His face didn't change.

"Did you like the food I left you?" he asked me.

"I thought that was the housekeeper."

"You thought the housekeeper bought your favorite cinnamon bagels, tuna rolls, and lemon-flavored Pellegrino?"

"Jesus. Stalk much?"

"I was trying to put my best foot forward."

"Right." I looked into my empty champagne mug. "What the little people do."

He laughed. "You're really hard to impress. I like that about you."

"Then you must love my mother. But really, you shouldn't have gone to so much trouble. Probably nobody told you this, but you don't have to impress me. I don't give a shit. Not about you or anything you have to say."

"Okay. Whatever. I just got you that stuff because I feel for you . . . with Edgar and everything. I know it's hard."

I swallowed. My body felt achy and ragged from lack of sleep. And I was fast becoming annoyed. The pinpricks would be coming next. I considered a diplomatic strategy for throwing him out of the apartment. Technically, the Rankin Lewis Literary Agency employed my mother's assistants, but in the past they had rarely showed their faces inside our home. They were harried, sleep-deprived, and bitter, running errands, delivering manuscripts, occasionally even shuttling me to appointments when the nanny couldn't. They certainly didn't give a shit about engaging me in personal conversation. This was new.

"Does that surprise you?" he said. "That somebody would take the time to find out what you like?"

Annoyance was now heading to exasperation. I folded my arms. "Don't analyze me. Just because you know where I get my bagels and sushi doesn't mean you know who I am."

"I know," he said. "But I have kept up with you. Read the articles about you and Frances. Read between the lines, I should say."

"Weird. But okay, if that's what gets you off."

I was talking tough. Using my New York socialite smart-ass act to shut him up. But I knew it wasn't going to work. He was smiling.

He spoke again. Softly. Confidently. "I know what it's been like for you, Meg, being the daughter of Frances Ashley. I know what you've lived through, and I want to help you. You were just interviewing for a job with Omnia, the nonprofit up in Harlem, weren't you?"

I froze. How did he know about that? Who had he been talking to? My mind raced, thinking of all the possibilities.

"They wanted your Rolodex, didn't they?" he said. "So they could use you to fleece your mother's friends." He shook his head. "It must be fucking awful—to go through life always being someone's daughter."

The words felt like a slap.

"Who are you?" I said. "What do you want?"

"A guy who wants to see you get a little justice."

"Speak English."

He didn't blink. "I want you to write a book about your mother."

KITTEN

—from Chapter 3

"Her best friend on the island is an American Indian girl named Cappie Strongbow. She lives with her mother, who does some work for us . . . when she's able." Delia wiped her hands on her skirt, finished with the paper moving. "Naturally, with the scope of her imagination, Kitten often pretends she's Indian as well. You aren't prejudiced, are you?"

Fay shook her head. "No . . . no, ma'am."

Delia narrowed her eyes. "If she says she's an Indian, she's not to be contradicted."

"Yes, ma'am."

"We've taught Kitten that all people are the same, no matter the color of their skin."

Ashley, Frances. *Kitten*. New York: Drake, Richards and Weems, 1976. Print.

Chapter Seven

I burst into laughter, and Asa Bloch flinched. Which, I had to admit, filled me with perverse joy.

"A book?" I said, after watching him struggle for a second or two. "What are you talking about?"

He went to the desk and pulled out the chair. Scooted up to the keyboard and tapped something out.

"You know my mother's password?" I asked.

"Mm," he said and continued typing.

"Hold up a minute. I need you to stop. Just stop, okay?"

He peered around the monitor.

"Exactly how long have you been working for my mother?"

"Seven months and ten days."

"And you came from . . . where, exactly?"

He sighed. "My résumé. Right." He inhaled. "I was one of those kid geniuses that you hear about. Created a start-up when I was twelve that matched online tutors with kids who had learning disabilities. I probably could've sold it for a nice sum if my dad hadn't been such an asshole and run the guys off with a list of crazy demands. Anyway. Undergrad at Duke. MBA from Georgetown. But ever since, I've been floundering. Searching for the right thing. I'm twenty-four, a Virgo, one hundred percent bisexual, and this is my third job."

"First was the tutoring thing. What was the second?"

He looked me in the eye. "You know those young-adult novels about the Icelandic video-gamer kids?"

I nodded.

"I found that guy. The writer. I was interning at a top agency, which shall remain nameless, when he and I were both college sophomores. I told my boss that he would sign with them if I could be his agent, so she agreed. Made me a junior agent on the spot."

"Pretty smart."

"I thought so, until he turned on me. Right after I got him a book deal, he ditched me for the woman who ran the agency. Who promptly told me 'things weren't working out,' and that was it. I was out of luck."

"You didn't make him sign a contract?"

"The agency did. Not me."

He looked kind of pathetic, standing there with his frowsy hair and red cheeks.

"Go ahead and Google me," he said. "I can wait."

"No, it's fine." I waved my hand at him. "Go back to whatever you were doing."

He leaned over the keyboard again.

"I pitched it to all the key people." He was staring intently at the screen. "All of the major houses, the top editors in New York. They all want it."

It?

"The book," he said.

"Oh. Right." I folded my arms. Shot him a withering look. "So, let's back up here: you're a former intern who got dumped by his agency, but somehow you've gotten in to all the top editors in New York to pitch a book? How exactly does that work?"

He shrugged. "A lot of them had heard of me."

"Because of the Icelandic video-gaming guy."

"Because of what he and that agent did to me. Publishing's a small world. Everyone knows everyone. But you probably already know that. A lot of people heard about what went down. A lot of them think I got screwed."

"So they had pity and took meetings with you?"

"No," he said evenly. "They took meetings with me because they know I find stuff that sells."

"Is that right?"

His eye had a gleam now. "Yeah. The first Iceland mystery book sold over ten thousand copies its first week. Your book could do that. Your memoir."

My mouth had suddenly gone dry. "I don't have a memoir."

"You should. You can, if you want." He laughed, then gestured to a chair opposite the desk. I didn't move toward the chair. His eyes were shining like a deranged person's. "Pelham Sound Books is interested."

In spite of myself, my eyes widened.

"Melissa Greenwald, who is amazing, by the way." He rattled off a list of titles I recognized. Bestsellers. "I'm thinking it'll bring at least mid six figures, maybe more. Not that that means anything to you. But to some of us, that's a lot, even fifteen percent of that. I mean, provided you agree to work with me."

"Work with you?" I echoed.

"If you agree," he repeated. "You'll give these people, the publishers, the fans, what they're dying for: a tell-all book about Frances Ashley."

"You want me to write a tell-all?"

"I want you to tell the world how Frances Ashley, everybody's favorite author, made your childhood a living hell. How she ignored you, emotionally abused you, and sent you off to the four corners of the globe so she didn't have to be a mother."

I didn't know why—maybe it was the combination of little sleep, the shock of dealing with Edgar, and now Asa's words—but I realized I wasn't going to be able to keep standing much longer. I dropped into the chair.

"No," I said. "Absolutely not."

"Just give me a minute."

"No." I looked at him. He was staring at me like he knew things—secrets. I felt a tingling along my right thumb.

"You're wondering how I know. Everybody knows, Meg. I mean, everybody who's been around you and Frances."

I held up my hand. "Trust me, nobody cares. Frances as a villain is not a narrative her adoring public is interested in."

"I think you're wrong."

"I think you're suicidal," I said.

Because if Frances Ashley could hear you right now, she would bury you.

"You're afraid," he said. "I get that."

I stared at him. This guy had no idea what he was up against. She would ruin his career. But me? It would end things for good. She would never speak to me again. I felt something twinge inside me—fear spiked with anticipation. The way you feel right before you climb onto a terrifying roller coaster. Or bungee jump off a bridge.

Asa pushed back in his chair. Turned toward the window.

"You're probably wise to be hesitant." His voice had taken on a reflective timbre. "Writing this book would effectively end your relationship. And in a very public way. You'd have to be prepared for that. Figure out what it means to be you without her."

"I know who I am," I said.

But it was a lie. He was right. I never saw myself without a ghostly image of Frances superimposed over me.

"Okay," he said mildly. "I just meant perhaps it wouldn't be such a bad thing. A clean break. Rip off the Band-Aid. So you can move on to real things."

He was talking about Omnia again, I guessed. The job I'd been offered and turned down. But Omnia wasn't the only nonprofit. There were hundreds of other charities and other opportunities in cities all over the world. Other girls I might be able to teach. I'd never considered it, going someplace new and starting over. Not with my mother looming over my life like an unexorcised demon.

"Mid six figures," he said again and then sucked in a long breath. Stroked what would've been a beard if he had a teaspoon of testosterone. "Which, I realize, means nothing to you. Although, if she cut you off, it wouldn't hurt to have a little cushion. But this is about more than the money. This book is way bigger than just your story."

"You said it was my memoir." The scared-excited roller-coaster feeling was surging through me. It was making me feel seriously nauseated.

"Right. It is. It's totally your story. But it's also someone else's." His eyes glittered. He was loving this, the rush of the pitch.

"When Frances was just a nineteen-year-old kid, working at a little rat-trap hotel on an island off the coast of Georgia, she met a little girl. She met her and she stole that little girl's life—and the life of the girl's father too. Frances made up lies about innocent people so she could become rich and famous."

I deflated. "Oh. Okay. You're talking about Kitten."

He looked positively manic now. "You're goddamn right I'm talking about Kitten. And how your mother blamed that little girl—a real, flesh-and-blood little girl named Dorothy Kitchens—for another child's murder."

He was covering old ground—the murder of Kim Baker, the little girl who'd been found dead in the marsh the summer my mother lived on Bonny Island. Old ground, old news.

"Listen to me," I said, slowly, deliberately. "Kitten isn't actually a real person. She's a composite. And Kim Baker's murder was completely unrelated to my mother, Dorothy Kitchens, or anything else in her book. *Kitten* is entirely a work of fiction." The words spilled out by rote, practiced and glib, the way they had spilled from Frances's mouth every single time any reporter or friend or fan had broached the subject. But Asa wasn't buying it.

"Kitten is definitely a real person. As real as you or me. You said her name—Dorothy Kitchens—and she still lives on Bonny Island, off the coast of Georgia."

"Stop." I held up my hand.

"Her father owned the hotel—"

"Asa—"

"—and she took it over in—"

"Stop!"

He stopped, and I fixed him with a condescending smirk.

"I know all this, Asa. Everybody who's been alive in the last decade knows about Dorothy Kitchens, as well as Kim Baker, the unfortunate child whose *mother*"—I stressed the word—"killed her. It's all been reported on, speculated over, done to death." I stood. "It's not a story, not to reasonable-minded adults. It's a conspiracy theory for pathetic, purposeless souls who have no meaning in their lives."

Eerie, how much I was sounding like Frances. So dismissive and haughty. Only she loved the Kitty Cultists and would've never dared insult them. They kept her in business.

Asa stood and came around the desk. "I'm not a Kitty Cultist, if that's what you think, not even close. But Kitten is absolutely a real person, and what happened on that island was real too, at least part of it. I'm not saying that Dorothy Kitchens killed Kim Baker. I'm just saying that Frances took some very real facts, a very real tragedy, and twisted it."

"And from what I hear, Dorothy Kitchens has been cashing in on it ever since."

"You know there was an incident." His eyes fastened onto me. "In the early '90s, fourteen years after the book was published. One of the Cultists, a guest at the hotel, attacked Dorothy. Dorothy's father,

William Kitchens, filed a lawsuit against your mother, saying it was her fault."

I blinked. "Attacked her? Like, how?"

He shrugged. "No one really knows, except William Kitchens and Dorothy. And your mother."

My head had started to feel too heavy for my neck. And it was pounding. I really needed to go to bed. Just sleep for twelve hours. He kept talking, though, his voice like an electric drill in my brain.

"Then, all of sudden, like less than a year later, out of the blue, Kitchens dropped it. Supposedly. There's nothing official on the Internet. No news stories. Nothing."

"Well, my mother's had her share of legal troubles, and she has a crackerjack team of lawyers."

He smiled. "Doesn't it strike you as odd that Kitchens dropped the lawsuit but nobody knows what really happened? Not the Cultists, not a tabloid reporter? There's got to be a reason for that, don't you agree?"

"No." I sounded like an obstinate two-year-old, but I didn't know what else to say. There was too much new information spilling around me. It felt like a dam had broken somewhere, and the water was rising. Fast. All I could do was keep pushing back.

"There's been other stuff too, Meg. Reports from guests on the island. Weird occurrences. People getting hurt or sick. They blame Dorothy. They're persecuting her because Frances has made them believe that she's Kitten. A handful have even filed charges. I can show you the stories."

I held up a weary hand. "Please, no."

"I'm proposing you split the advance with Dorothy Kitchens, the real Kitten, maybe even the royalties. She deserves as much. If you go down there and talk to her, you'll see."

"Go down there?" I burst out. "Are you out of your mind?"

"Stay at Ambletern, the old hotel, for a couple of weeks. Interview Dorothy Kitchens. Hear her story."

"You should pick up the phone and call one of the Kitty Cultists. Any one of those loons could write your book for you."

"They can't write it like you could. Not an expertly woven firsthand account of what Frances Ashley did to the both of you. No one else can write this, Megan. No one."

"Well, that's unfortunate for you. Because I'm not doing it."

"Dorothy Kitchens has never given an interview. Not to anyone. Never. Not in all the years since your mother wrote her book. Are you hearing what I'm saying? Megan, listen to me. You're the first person Dorothy has ever agreed to talk to."

And he swung the computer around to face me.

KITTEN

—from Chapter 3

The child was a wonder, the guests always said, an absolute doll.

She had the most endearing habit of catching hold of the hand of anyone standing beside her. She would clasp it and study it intently, like she was memorizing the form. Sometimes she'd press the person's hand to her own downy cheek and give it a little kiss. She was the dearest thing, everyone said. Too sweet for words.

That first night, when Kitten's father arrived upstairs to tuck her in, Fay slipped out, closing the bedroom door softly behind her. But then she moved back, as if drawn by an unseen force. She rested her fingertips against the door and listened to the low murmurs of father and daughter. She couldn't quite make out the words.

It sounded like a poem.

She thought of her own father. He'd never read to her, not once.

Ashley, Frances. *Kitten*. New York: Drake, Richards and Weems, 1976. Print.

Chapter Eight

I read the email on my mother's computer screen.

To: Asa Bloch

From: Dorothy Kitchens

Re: Book

March 30, 2016

Dear Asa,

After much thought, soul searching, and prayer, I have decided that my answer is yes. I will consult with Frances Ashley's daughter on the book.

I know my father never gave his consent to the book Ms. Ashley wrote all those years ago. He would have never agreed to allow anyone to fabricate so many lies about our hotel, our island, and me. But she did, and, while I don't believe in harboring grudges, the burden of being Kitten has become too great for me to handle in the past few years.

As a result of harassment from paying guests, I have had to close the hotel I inherited from my father, drying up my main source of income and creating no small amount of stress. I have no family now—and forming lasting relationships has been impossible with the specter of Kitten hanging over every move I make. This island is all I've ever cared about—the only thing that matters to me. Seeing that it's cared for and preserved in a manner that honors its roots and fulfills its destiny is the only thing that keeps me going. Can you understand such a thing?

I have turned down other offers because I never wanted revenge on Ms. Ashley. I never wanted recompense, but I no longer feel I have any choice. I cannot go on this way—destitute and desperate. So I will work with Megan Ashley on her book. May it bring healing to all involved, even Frances.

Please let Megan know that she is welcome on Bonny Island and that I will tell her everything I remember, exactly how it happened, about the summer of '75, the summer I spent with her mother. Ambletern's doors are wide open to her.

Warmly,

Doro Kitchens

I backed away, all the way to the door, grateful for something solid to lean against.

I still felt the nervous, buzzy fear inside me, but now, along with it, an incredible lightness too. Like I'd just shed ten pounds. Like if I didn't grab onto some anchor, I might float up and out of the apartment.

Here was a way to finally uncover the truth about my mother. To understand the past—who she'd been before, how she'd written her book, why she'd become the person she was. I could finally unpack the hows and whys of my life too. Those never-ending, exhausting questions that revolved around my mother's strange lack of love for me. Her distance. My unhappiness.

And maybe, if I could find the truth, I wouldn't feel so trapped anymore. Maybe I could finally move on with my life. The prospect was terrifying and captivating, all at the same time. I glanced down and realized I'd curled both hands into tight fists.

Asa popped backward in the desk chair. "Well?"

"You already told Dorothy Kitchens I was writing the book?" I asked. It was all I could come up with.

"I may have intimated the idea."

"You know, you're wasting your talents in the publishing industry," I said. "You should go into something like espionage. Or prisoner-of-war interrogation."

He shrugged. "Christina Crawford wrote a tell-all. And Jane Fonda. The Styron girl and Joseph Heller's daughter. And, believe me, nobody gives a shit about any of those people's parents the way they care about Frances Ashley."

"You do understand that if you actually sell this book, Rankin Lewis will immediately fire you."

I was talking tough again. Doing that thing where I played the role of Megan Ashley, Jaded Daughter of Celebrity Author. But I couldn't tell him what I was really feeling. I didn't know that I was capable of explaining it to anyone. It felt too new. Too raw.

"Then I'll start my own agency. With you as my sole client." He leaned against the desk. "Let me tell you a story. I saw the original *Kitten* when I was ten, on late-night cable. I didn't even know it was based on a book. But the next week, I found it at the library. I devoured it in a matter of hours, up in my sad little bedroom, and decided right then—somehow, someway, I was going to be a part of this . . . *magic*. Telling stories. Making books."

I nodded wearily. I'd been hearing variations on this story all my life: *I discovered* Kitten *when I was six/twelve/eighteen years old and decided then and there that I had to be a writer/agent/editor/psychotic serial killer.* But this guy took it to a whole new level. I wondered how many insults I could throw at him before he gave up. How hard I could push him until he slunk away.

I wondered if I really wanted him to.

"I can't write worth a damn," he continued. "What I can do, however, is sell the hell out of just about anything. Literary masterpieces are nice, but what I really prefer are blockbusters."

"Like video-gamer kids who solve mysteries in Iceland."

He nodded enthusiastically. "Those books weren't art, but they moved people. And that's what I'm looking for. An international best-selling phenomenon that everybody in the world is dying to read."

My mouth went dry, but I tried to look blasé. "You really think people will want to read it?"

"Of course. It's dirt. The dirtiest dirt there is. On one of the most treasured celebrities around." He smiled. "People are shitty, Megan. They're shitty, but they like to think they're smart. They want to solve a mystery. They want things set right, for justice to prevail. For the evildoers to get what they deserve. Do you see what I'm saying here? Do you see what we've got? A beloved celebrity, a neglected—dare I say abused?—daughter. A crime perpetrated on an innocent kid, way down in Asscrack, Georgia, who's now all grown up and ready to spill her guts. And to top it off . . ." He beamed. "To top that motherfucker off . . ." He spread his arms like a manic preacher behind the pulpit, his eyes aflame, his fluffy hair gone haywire. "A cover-up!"

A cover-up. My mother had participated in a cover-up.

I felt something else now—a frisson of fear shaking loose the tender vines of hope inside me. My mother was a powerful woman. I'd seen her shut people down. Put them in their place. Hurt them deeply. I didn't know how she would do it, exactly, what means she would implement, but if she was backed into a corner, she would strike. She would hit hard and hurt me, without a second's hesitation.

There were things Frances knew about me. People I had loved. Secrets I kept. If she wanted to, she could use them to hurt me . . . and others. To destroy lives.

"It's a grand slam, Megan," he said. "Yours for the taking."

I scanned the shelves, the rows and rows of books that formed her fortress walls. Maybe Asa was right. Maybe victory was mine for the taking. Maybe freedom from my mother's lies and the hold they had on me was within my reach. But that didn't mean I had to take it. Or that this was the right time.

I stepped away from the door. "You should probably go."

He stood. "It doesn't have to be about the money or the revenge. Forget those things. Think about this: there are so many victims in the world. People starving, imprisoned, dying of disease, and there's not a goddamn thing you or I can do about it. But Doro . . . Doro's different. You can actually change this woman's life, Megan. By telling the truth about your mother, you become her hero."

"I just said I wanted you to go. Do you want me to call the police to prove it?"

He stood. "Will you think about it?"

I could feel his eyes on me. They'd lost their crazy fire and were now opaque again, that murky gray color, like the rest of him.

"Probably not," I said.

He nodded once, but didn't move. He was staring at me again, this time in the most disconcerting way.

"What?"

"I know about Graeme Barnish," he said.

I felt myself redden. "What do you know?"

"That you were seen with him occasionally. Around town. Martha's Vineyard."

I swallowed. "You don't have any right . . ."

"I know that your mother knew what was going on."

I had the feeling of being slapped, and the breath whooshed out of my lungs. I cleared my throat. "Get out."

"A mom who lets her sixteen-year-old daughter party with a thirty-year-old man? A married one, at that? What a cool mom."

I held my breath. My whole body felt engulfed in flames.

"Or a neglectful one, depending on who you're talking to." He cocked his head sympathetically.

"Go." I moved toward him, but before I could push him out the door, he raised both hands.

"All I'm saying is that a good mother, a loving mother, doesn't allow that kind of thing."

I turned my face away, so he couldn't see the effect his words were having on me. The way my face was burning.

"She was trying to sabotage you, Meg. Trying to hurt you, don't you see that? Because she was jealous or insecure or something." His voice had softened.

"Get out."

"Something's wrong with her. On the inside. You know that, don't you?"

Images of Graeme were flooding my head. The feel of his scrubby beard rough against my face. The spicy smell of him. My head hitting the wall. Blood in my mouth.

If Asa didn't leave now, I was going to burst into tears. Or worse, physically assault him. I'd learned to scratch like a champion, even throw a solid punch, at a few of the boarding schools I'd attended. The offspring of the megawealthy can be an especially brutal crew. And now the guy was regarding me with something that looked a hell of a lot like pity. It was too much to bear.

"Okay, I'm leaving," he said.

He strode down the hall, then crossed the living room. I trailed him into the foyer, where he turned to me.

"I . . . ah. I actually came here today . . ." His voice seemed to constrict and sink into his chest. "I came here to . . . ," he tried again.

I wrapped my arms around my torso. "What?"

"I'm so sorry to tell you that Edgar passed earlier this morning."

My breath hitched, and everything muffled around me. It seemed like I'd been dunked underwater, sounds and lights gone wavy and distorted. I blinked a few times. Tried to fill my lungs with air. I was only vaguely aware of the needling sensation in my hands and feet.

"Megan? Are you okay?"

"I'm—" I waved him off, even though he hadn't offered his assistance.

"The hospital called me. I'm so sorry. I mean, you know. My condolences." The word sounded false coming out of his mouth.

I couldn't speak.

"I know you were really close to him."

And then, suddenly, I could speak. "Fuck you," I growled. "Fuck you for coming here and talking about some stupid *book* before you told me about Edgar!"

"Well, I . . ." He must've registered my murderous look, because he gulped down the argument. "No. You're right. Absolutely right. I'm so sorry."

I staggered back and sank down on a spindly-looking gold-leaf bamboo chair. He didn't move toward me.

"I've contacted Frances," he said. "In California. She's arranging the memorial service, but she won't be coming back for it. She said she doesn't—"

"Do funerals. I know." My voice sounded like an animal's cry.

The realization washed over me. Edgar really was gone. And my mother wasn't even coming home to say good-bye to him. The man who'd done everything for her. Who'd made her who she was.

I'd always thought she had loved him, but I'd been wrong. It was clear she'd never felt anything other than a business obligation to him. Maybe she really was an icy-hearted bitch—the *Mommie Dearest* Asa said she was. I would be Edgar's only family at his funeral. His Pip. I bit my lip to keep from screaming. Balled my fists over my eyes.

"Megan?"

All I could do was shake my head, I was so heavy with the pain and grief.

What did it matter if Frances tried to hurt me? Did I really care now? Surely she couldn't do anything worse than this—let Edgar go without so much as a good-bye.

Let her try to destroy me. I'd come back, harder and faster than she ever dreamed.

I was going to write the book. I would bring her down. Frances Ashley, brilliant creator of monsters, was the biggest monster of them all. And I had to be free of her.

KITTEN

—from Chapter 4

When Kitten had gone in for her bath, Fay opened her nightstand drawer. Inside, she found a jumble, a motley collection of treasures. One pearl-drop clip earring, a stamped leather bracelet, a man's blue silk pocket square, and a nearly empty bottle of Cacharel perfume. Under these items, she found a book. It was called *The Verselet* and had a periwinkle cover with a silhouette line drawing of a girl flying a kite.

She sat on the bed and let the pages flutter under her fingers until they fell open to a dog-eared page and a poem, only two short stanzas. She read the first lines—*You tell me a story, you weave me a tale*—then heard something.

The slap of wet feet on the wood floor.

Ashley, Frances. *Kitten*. New York: Drake, Richards and Weems, 1976. Print.

Chapter Nine

I stood at the rail of the battered blue-and-white ferry, facing the Atlantic sound. My hair whipped insistently into the corners of my mouth and the creases of my watering eyes. Finally, I scraped my curls back into an elastic and breathed in the salty air, the pungent tang expanding my lungs.

Edgar's memorial service had only been a couple of days ago, but it already seemed like ages. As did packing my bags while, in my mother's office, Asa haggled over the phone with the editor at Pelham Sound over the book deal. Strangely, ever since I'd landed in Georgia, a calmness had settled over me. There were no pinpricks. Just humidity permeating my skin and bones and muscles, making me feel like I was thawing.

Part of the reason I was breathing easier was that Asa's story had checked out.

According to everything I'd found online, what he'd told me was true—Internet start-up prodigy, Iceland guy's jilted agent, currently employed by Rankin Lewis Literary Agency. Not only that, but we'd also had a conference call with Melissa Greenwald, the editor, where she'd expressed enthusiasm and confidence in me and the project.

Further digging turned up three incidents on Bonny Island, two of them connected—charges filed by guests of Ambletern with the Camden County Sheriff's Department, claiming that Dorothy Kitchens had harassed them with threats and acts of vandalism. In response, she claimed she was acting in self-defense, that she'd felt threatened by their aggressive and violent actions. Court cases were pending. The whole situation sounded pretty minor to me.

As a bonus, while rooting around the Internet, I was smacked in the face no less than a dozen times with items on Frances's nuptials to Benoît Jaffe in Palm Springs. None of them was accompanied by pictures, thank God. Still. Every time I read about my mother and her new husband, I was engulfed in a wave of fresh fury.

But I was in Georgia now—and for the first time, incidentally. Frances had never brought me down because by the time I was born, all her family was gone. And I'd never had any reason to come here myself. It wasn't exactly Four Seasons territory—at least, not in this corner of the state. I'd been on plenty of yachts and sailboats, never a ferry.

It was actually kind of nice. A different planet altogether from New York. On the drive down from the airport in Brunswick, I think I saw every shade of green, from chartreuse to emerald to forest. There was a smattering of commercial development, but mostly flat fields dotted with cows, stretches of palmetto bushes, scrubby oaks, and towering pine trees that were mostly all trunk. The lack of buildings and people and hot-garbage smell created a pleasant negative space in my head.

Filling the space was a constant buzzing sound—grasshoppers, maybe?—and the sense that my body had almost instantaneously downshifted. I marveled how people managed to work surrounded by all this expansive light and heat and humidity. It felt like I'd stepped into a Southern gothic novel, and all I wanted to do was sit my ass on a rocking chair and drink something cool.

Adding to the relief I was feeling was the knowledge that the final deal memo between Asa, Pelham Sound Books, and me that promised a check for $300,000 was nestled securely in the bottom of my suitcase. Split with Dorothy, that money would come in handy when Frances yanked my trust.

Which she was going to do, when she found out what I was doing.

On second thought, maybe it wasn't so strange that I was feeling good. Maybe it was the idea that I was about to be free of Frances Ashley—cut off for good—that was responsible for these amazing endorphins.

Or maybe it was the book. The other book, *Kitten*, that was making me feel so . . . buoyant.

I'd slunk into Frances's office, grabbed the tattered paperback, Susan Evelyn Doucette Age Twelve's dog-eared copy, which had still been sitting on the corner of the desk. Finally, I would read the famous book. I had to now. It was research. I tucked it into my bag between the jeans and T-shirts I'd scavenged from Frances's massive closet.

On the plane, I flipped through a couple of glossy magazines, downed three Bloody Marys and lobster quiche, then halfheartedly Googled Susan Evelyn Doucette. There were next to no results. Just a handful of social-media links, none of them giving any sort of indication who she might've been to Frances. And it didn't matter anyway; I knew I was just delaying the inevitable. Finally, reluctantly, I pulled the dreaded paperback out and was surprised when, an hour later, the pilot announced our initial approach into Brunswick, Georgia. I put the book away in a fog of distraction and something resembling disappointment. I actually liked my mother's book.

I really liked the fucking thing.

After a slow, mannered opening, the book had gotten going in chapter seven with the discovery of a body—a young Native American girl, Kitten's playmate on the island. The girl, Cappie Strongbow, had been found—head caved in, drowned and half-eaten by crabs—in the salt marsh. June Strongbow, the mother and an employee of the Murphys who lived back in the shadowy tangle of the island, seemed a likely suspect. Police questioned her and, perhaps biased by the color of her skin, locked her up in the local jail to await charges.

Fay, Kitten's lovely, red-haired nanny, was obviously Frances.

The story was pure seventies horror, and—also classic seventies, I thought ruefully—bordered on racist. Nothing like kicking things off with the murder of a brown female to get your story really rolling. The character of Cappie Strongbow was your basic stereotypical Native American—no tribe mentioned or specifics about her family. Even her name sounded like it might be a white person's invention.

But the era-specific, tone-deaf elements aside, I was intrigued by the character of Kitten. The way she manipulated her less-privileged friend. And blithely appropriated her Native American culture. It was surprisingly astute.

I had to hand it to Frances. If I was reading this right, she'd attempted something incredibly daring. She'd zeroed in on the era's obsession and fetishizing of the Native American figure and was obviously condemning it. I'd never considered my mother especially sensitive to other people and cultures, but maybe I'd missed something.

Susan Doucette had meticulously underlined a bunch of random passages throughout the first chapter, fewer in the following ones, but I couldn't find any connection between the marked-up passages. Mostly they were just sentences referencing Cappie's murder and her bodily injuries—nothing that made any sense to me. I wondered what had motivated Susan. I couldn't imagine annotating a novel at twelve just for the heck of it.

But that was the Kitty Cult for you. Bunch of unbalanced creepers.

For decades, these people had mobbed Bonny Island, taking the forty-five-minute ferry ride from tiny St. Marys, Georgia, to the twelve-mile-long, three-mile-wide stretch of sand, marsh, and forest privately owned and operated by the Kitchens family. Guests stayed at Ambletern, the creepy Gothic-mansion-turned-hotel that presided over the southern half of the island. From what I could tell, it was the only operational building on the island, and I noted that Frances hadn't even bothered to change its name in the book.

Under the care of their hosts, *Kitten* enthusiasts would troop around to the iconic sites of the novel—the moss-draped ruins of the Catholic mission, the tumbledown slave cabins dating from the time when the island was a family-owned plantation—taking pictures and whatever other kooky fan activities they did.

But I could see the appeal of the isolated, windswept setting.

At any rate, I didn't have time to fangirl. I had a book to churn out . . . in sixty-one days. According to Asa's plan, I was to send the chapters as soon as I wrote them. It didn't have to be art, Asa assured me. Nothing literary or groundbreaking or even all that good. Just get it on the paper, he said, and the publisher's vast team of editors would clean it up on their end.

We had to work fast, but he assured me Pelham Sound would rush the book through typesetting and design and whatever else to publication. *Kitten*'s fortieth anniversary was six months away, October 15, right before Halloween. If all this worked, my book would be jammed right up next to Frances's on bookstore shelves that very same day. Sales would be astronomical.

At least that was the hope.

Before I left New York, I withdrew as much money from my trust as I could, cashed in a handful of random investment accounts, and moved the entire sum to a different bank. I went through Frances's apartment and collected the few things that were mine, rented a safe-deposit box at the new bank, and dumped everything inside.

I packed up my old life to make room for the new. Whatever that new life turned out to be, it had to be better than what I'd experienced thus far. On the way back, I called Aurora to tell her what I was doing, but ended up leaving a vague message on her voice mail. I hoped she would understand when I finally got the chance to explain my reasons.

But even if she didn't, I knew I was going through with my plan no matter what.

The ferry captain coughed behind me, and I nearly jumped out of my skin.

"You know anything about Bonny?" Captain Mike was rotund and grizzled, a fisherman's cap jammed down over his head and a pair of sportsman sunglasses on the tip of his nose. Santa Claus: the sea-captain version. A speck of food, roast beef it looked like, fluttered with the wind in the corner of his beard.

"A little," I lied. "Just from what I could Google."

"Sixteen major barrier islands string down Georgia's coast. Pearls in a necklace." He jerked his thumb to the right and grinned. The roast beef dislodged and went flying. "That's Florida, right over there."

I nodded.

"They were plantations, cotton mostly, then became playgrounds for the rich and famous. Every family had their own. The Carnegies had Cumberland, Rockefellers had Jekyll, and R. J. Reynolds, Sapelo."

"Who owned Bonny?"

He lifted his cap and scratched his head. "Well, now, there's some debate over that. But the Kitchens have it now." He eyed me. "Your family know where you're going?"

I pulled a rogue strand of hair out of my eye. "Excuse me?"

"Cell service on the island is spotty," he said. "Same with Internet. Landline's mostly reliable, on and off."

On and off. Which meant, by definition, unreliable.

"Good to know."

"I'm not running every day no more, now that Doro shut down the hotel. Just bring the mail and take the cook into town for supplies once a week. Sometimes you can reach me for a quick-over, if the phones are working." He grinned again.

"There aren't any shops on the island?" I asked.

He laughed. "There ain't nothing on Bonny but the old home place and a few broken-down buildings. That's it. If you want to see a movie or grab a pizza, you've got to give me a call. Or paddle yourself over."

"Got it."

"You're staying a spell, right?" he asked.

"A month or so."

"Reporter?"

"No." I shook my head. "I'm working on a book."

"Somebody already wrote a book about this place." I couldn't see his eyes for the bush of eyebrows that covered them. But they seemed to be looking toward the island, a long bony blot on the horizon.

I faced back into the wind. "You're talking about *Kitten*," I said.

"Wasn't my thing. But some people were just wild for it. Used to come from all over to see the real place. They had these murder-mystery parties. Dress up like the characters in the book. Got up to all kinds of mischief, drinking and carrying on out at the middens and the mission. A couple of times they set fires. One fella came out here and tried to kill himself by jumping off the roof of the hotel."

I made a face. "Jeez."

"People couldn't accept it was a made-up story. They wanted to figure out how much of it was real life."

"One of the murders was real. Right?"

He nodded. "An Indian girl was murdered, yes, ma'am. Back in '74."

I wondered if I was just dealing with a politically incorrect old-timer or a full-blown bigot. I couldn't seem to get my bearings down here. I was out of my element. Far, far out.

"She was murdered," he continued, "but it didn't happen like in the book. Some of the facts were right. But a list of facts isn't the same thing as the truth."

Exactly. Just what I'd told Asa. Maybe Captain Mike was one of the good guys, after all.

"So what is the truth?" I asked.

He gave me a hard look. "Don't know that it's ours to ask. It's Doro's life. And I can't say I'd want people digging up my past. I think folks should just let some things be. That woman has put up with a lot because of that book, all because her daddy couldn't say no to those kooks."

"Did you hear about the charges filed against her? For harassing guests?"

He spit over the rail. "I believe they probably harassed her, tried to get some money out of that deal. You gotta understand. That's the kind of thing those folks pull. They're a weird bunch. If I was her, I'da shut this place down right when that book came out. And sued the hell out of the lady that wrote it."

KITTEN

—from Chapter 4

Kitten, dripping from the bath and clutching a towel, walked to Fay. She caught her hand, and Fay stiffened.

But then Kitten bestowed a tiny, tender kiss atop one of her knuckles. Fay felt a rush of surprised pleasure and delight. The child was so simple, so free in her expressions of affection. It was really quite extraordinary.

Then Kitten spoke.

"Dear Fay," she said, eyes narrowed to slits. "That's my treasure drawer. I'd like it if you stayed out of it."

Ashley, Frances. *Kitten*. New York: Drake, Richards and Weems, 1976. Print.

Chapter Ten

Fifteen minutes later, I caught sight of a wide dock, banked with sea grass and scrubby pines. It seemed to be at the very southern end of the island. Behind the dock, I could see what looked like miles and miles of forest. To the north, I caught a glimpse of plains stretched out along the curve of the island. The marsh. The intricate ecosystem of interconnected creeks and sea life that rose and fell with the tides. Where Cappie, the character based on Kim Baker, had died.

There was a young man standing at the end of the dock, hand shading his eyes against the setting sun. As we neared I got a better look. He was a stunner, in his late twenties, brown-skinned, with hair that skimmed his shoulders. When we bumped the dock, he helped tie us up, loping down the dock, expertly looping ropes over huge metal cleats. He looked up at the wheelhouse behind me. His T-shirt stretched over a set of well-defined abs, and, to my shame, I actually shivered.

"Got anything for me?" he called out to the captain.

"Just her," the captain yelled back.

I crossed the deck and took the young man's offered hand (*warm, rough*), leaping from the boat to the dock in an ungainly arc. The captain shouted behind me—"Heads up!"—and a knotted plastic bag sailed over my head. "See you in a few! Tell Laila I'll have her some peach wine soon!" The guy gave him the high sign and hefted the plastic bag over his shoulder.

He had a jaw like a scythe and eyes that I couldn't look away from. It might've been a contradiction, but they were both dark and bright at the same time.

"I'm Meg," I said and awkwardly pumped his hand, the one I was already holding.

"Koa." He grabbed my Louis Vuitton duffel, which suddenly seemed wildly out of place and vulgar, and started toward a dirty, green, stripped-down Jeep that was idling at the head of the dock. I trotted after him, nearly smacking into his backside when he stopped and shifted the bags into his other hand. He whipped out his phone, listened for a moment.

"Got it," he said. "I'm on my way." He shoved the phone in his pocket and tossed both bags in the back of the Jeep, on top of a messy collection of tarps and pickaxes and rope. He secured everything with an abundance of bungee cords. Before I could ask questions, he'd slid into his seat and fastened his seatbelt.

"Sorry," he said. "But we've got a stop to make before we go to the house."

"No problem." I was still trying to strap myself in when we started to jounce over the sandy trail that rounded the southern tip of the island, presumably to the hotel. Instead of following it, he wheeled left—inland, away from the shoreline—and we headed down a wide, smooth track sheltered by gnarled oak trees. After we'd driven for a while, I cleared my throat and yelled above the wind.

"So how long have you worked on Bonny?"

"Coming up on a year," he yelled back. "From Texas, by way of Louisiana."

"And you're Native American?"

"Caddo Nation. Natchitoches."

I had no idea what that meant.

"Does your name, does Koa mean something in that . . . your language?"

"In Caddo?" He gave me a sidelong look. "No."

"Ah." I glanced away, into the tangle of trees to the right of the track. *Great.* Not ten minutes on the island, and I was showing my ignorance. I had no experience with Native culture, I couldn't remember ever having met any indigenous person, not from any tribe. But I did think I remembered hearing that they placed great significance on names and their meanings. At least, I thought I'd heard that. It was entirely possible that I had just said something completely offensive. Or, at best, fantastically dumb.

To possibly the most attractive man I'd met in a long time.

Fantastic work, Meg.

Koa gunned the engine, and the Jeep leapt forward, nearly snapping my neck. I grabbed onto the roll bar. The road narrowed to parallel sandy tracks, but this didn't seem to slow Koa at all; he stomped on the gas pedal, and we rocketed through the thicket of trees. Branches scraped at my arms, and I found myself subconsciously leaning toward my chauffeur, until he reached down to shift gears and tapped my leg.

"Hang on to whatever you can."

I clamped onto the roll bar with one hand, clutched the back of Koa's seat with the other, and set my teeth so they wouldn't rattle. We drove deeper into the forest—bounced over holes, skidded across ruts, and, after what seemed like forever, hit another stretch of the main road. It was a wide, washboard surface—sand and gravel and flattened grass. Koa spun the wheel and accelerated.

I readjusted my death grip. Was this how every guest arrived on the island? And where were we going? We were definitely heading north, away from the main house.

But then, suddenly, we cut through a thick screen of sea oats, and we were on the beach. The breathtaking expanse of flat white stretched for miles under the massive blue dome of sky. I caught my breath as the Jeep made a sharp quarter turn, spraying sand. We shot down the shore, the line of trees and scrub on our right, foamy green ocean on our left. There wasn't a beach umbrella or cooler anywhere in sight. Just the blue and the green and the white.

A blob of brown undulated just ahead of us. I squinted, not believing what I was seeing. It was a herd of horses—manes and tails streaming—galloping straight toward us. Koa slammed on the brakes.

"Unbuckle," he shouted, and I did, without a thought of protest. He shoved me, hard, out of the Jeep and onto the sand. I yelped and looked back at him. "Go to the wall," he yelled, "the wall!" and pointed behind us.

I turned to see the wall Koa was yelling about. It was a long, white, bumpy-looking structure, about nine or ten feet tall, that curved along a random portion of the shoreline. It looked like a fortress somebody had built against invaders from the sea, and it shone so bright in the glaring sun, I had to squint to even look at it. I scrambled to my feet and started toward it, just as Koa and the Jeep leapt forward, straight into the path of the stampeding horses.

I scrambled up the narrow slope of the white wall, about two-thirds of the way to the top. It was a good three feet wide, but not exactly a level surface. The whole thing appeared to be made of razor-sharp shells that tore at my hands as I climbed. When I stopped for a breath, I was standing maybe eight or nine feet above the sand. If I slipped and hit the wall on my way down, I'd be in serious trouble.

On the beach below, Koa's Jeep was speeding toward the herd, playing some kind of game of chicken with them. I could see the lead horse—a stallion, I guessed, the alpha that the others followed. He formed the tip of the spear. He was black and streaked with foam, from either the waves he was kicking up or sweat. His hooves sent out arcs of sand as he ran, and I stood there, transfixed by the imminent clash of horseflesh, fiberglass, and steel.

I covered my mouth with my hand.

When there was only a couple of yards between them, the Jeep spun out, sheeting sand. The horses didn't waver or slow. They bore down on the Jeep and smoothly parted, galloping past in a blur of brown and black and gray. As soon as the last horse galloped past, Koa jerked the wheel and gunned it, following them. And then another Jeep—identical to his—appeared, speeding up behind him.

The stallion was angling toward the wall now, toward me. He'd changed gears, adjusting his stride so that he would be able to cut just inside the wall. If the herd followed him, I guessed the wall would guide them along the deserted stretch of beach and to the marsh behind me. For some reason, Koa and the other Jeep drivers didn't seem to want that to happen.

From my perch on top of the wall, I threw up both arms. "Hey!" I yelled at the horses. Then, for some boneheaded reason, maybe because I was trying to impress the hot guy in the Jeep and thought I could help slow the herd, I scurried down the sloped wall and ran toward the oncoming herd.

"Stop! Stop!" I yelled at them. They were less than fifteen yards away, but I just kept waving my arms and yelling, like they could understand me.

When the stallion was about a dozen or so yards from me, he tossed his head. His foam-flecked legs seemed to stutter and tangle beneath him. The next instant, legs clattering and buckling, his head dipped, and he stumbled to a halt. He was so close, I could've taken just a few more steps forward and touched him.

I let out a whoosh of breath. I was shaking, like I'd just taken a swan dive off a cliff.

The herd had stopped with him. They massed around him, circling and stamping and nodding their heads. A few moved toward the dunes and started cropping the grass along the edge of the trees.

The two Jeeps roared up behind the herd. Koa stood in his seat and stared at me, and, from the other vehicle, a blonde woman swung down out of the driver's seat. She wore a faded denim shirt and tan overalls that were rolled up over heavy leather work boots. She approached me, cutting her way through the center of the herd. She pushed her wind-blown hair out of her eyes.

"Are you okay?" she said.

Doro.

I opened my mouth, but nothing came out. I knew she had to be in her late forties, maybe early fifties, but she looked far younger. Her hair was twisted into a knot on the top of her head and she had crystal-blue eyes. No makeup covered the freckles that sprayed her nose and cheeks, and her lips looked chapped from the sea air. A fine fretwork of wrinkles traced her face: webbing out across her forehead, from the corners of her eyes, around her mouth. I thought of Frances's lineless, perfect face. The contrast was almost laughable.

"Nice work," the woman said with a grin. "Impressive herding skills."

"Ah, thanks," I said.

"Almost got herself trampled," Koa said. He was still staring at me. I couldn't tell if he was annoyed or impressed.

"Looks like she handled it just fine." She stuck out her hand. "Doro Kitchens."

I took it. "Megan Ashley."

Her hand was slim and warm and strong, and as she held on to mine, she gave me a thorough examination. "I don't know why I expected red hair," she said finally and laughed. I smiled back at her. I didn't know what I'd expected, exactly, either, but Doro Kitchens was pretty and clear-eyed. I immediately liked her.

She jutted her chin toward the horses. "We try to manage the herd so they won't completely destroy the environment. The marsh, mainly. And also so the parks service won't come down here and cull them or ship them out for adoption inland. We herd them every couple of weeks to different quadrants of the island. But because we don't pen them, sometimes they break out and run for the marsh."

"They were heading to the marsh?"

"Until you stopped them. Now they've slowed down and found the grass, they'll forget about the marsh. They have really short memories." She nodded at the horses, who were busy tearing away at the scrub.

"I don't know anything about horses," I said. "I used to cry at summer camp when they made us go on trail rides."

Koa had circled behind Doro. I took in the outline of his chest under his shirt and the way his jeans dipped slightly between his hip bones. I felt my whole body heat up and looked away. Not what I was here for. Not even close.

"I don't know," Doro said. "Next time these guys decide to go on a rampage, I'm bringing you along. They must sense something in you. Something they respect. A horsewoman in the making." She held my gaze, and I felt myself flushing. "I hope you'll find your room satisfactory. We're a little on the rustic end of the spectrum here at Ambletern." She slapped one of the horses on the rump, and it scooted out of her way.

"I'll be fine." She probably had an idea about what I was like. Probably expected the requisite entitled-rich-girl behavior. But I was determined she wouldn't get it. Even if she stuck me in a broom closet.

"Okay, then," she called over her shoulder as she sauntered away. "Meet you guys back at the house. Laila's pot roast at seven."

She swung back into her Jeep, her shirt cuffs revealing ropey forearms. The woman looked like she dug ditches or chopped down trees on a regular basis.

I turned. Koa was watching me watch Doro.

"Ready?" I said.

"Whenever you are," he answered.

∾

We drove between two slightly crumbling columns made of the pinkish-gray tabby concrete and down the sandy drive, which was lined with palmetto trees. Frances had described the tabby in *Kitten*. In fact, she'd described everything about the place, down to the most minute detail. Asa had been right. From the looks of it, Frances had just written what she'd seen.

At least, the version she experienced forty years ago. Now Ambletern appeared to be long past its glory days.

The estate encompassed four acres (I'd read that), the whole expanse of smooth lawn ringed by pines, magnolias, and live oaks festooned with Spanish moss that waved in the light breeze. The mansion loomed at the center in the settling dusk. It was made of that same mottled tabby and arranged in a haphazard hodgepodge of wings and porches, towers and chimneys, each ascending higher than the part next to it. The windows were all grouped in sets of three—arched and Gothic— and there was a turret-looking thing that rose up in the center. I'd never seen anything like it. The place resembled a complicated, multitiered wedding cake. I wondered if anyone had ever gotten lost in it.

The tabby blocks had an even rosier tinge to them in the light of the dying sun. Lush ivy had grown over a better part of the walls, almost up to the trio of turrets crowning the house. It looked like it might be home to all manner of creepy, crawly creatures.

The perfect setting for a horror novel.

"The original plantation house, built in the seventeen hundreds, burned," Koa said. "This one was built in the eighteen-eighties. Doro says her ancestors grew Sea Island cotton and oranges, too, I think."

"What was that wall I climbed up at the beach?"

"The middens. Built out of clamshells by the Guale. They probably started off as a dump spot, maybe doubling as a fortification later."

I nodded and stood for a minute, allowing myself to settle. Everything expanded in this viscous air—my hair, the pores of my skin, my fingers and toes. I felt swollen here, without boundaries. Like my body had spread and overrun its personal space.

He started up the wide tabby front steps, which were flanked with iron lanterns, all of them flickering with gaslight. The windows, at least the ones on the first floor, glowed warmly. I hobbled behind him; my feet were once again tingling with the familiar, infuriating neuropathy.

"I'll take this up to your room." He hitched my bag. "Then you can . . . do whatever you need to do for dinner."

I wondered how ragged I looked. Judging by the expression on his face, extremely.

"Do we dress?" I asked.

He looked at me blankly. "Uh, yeah. Yes. We dress."

"I mean, like . . . up. Dress up. For dinner."

"Oh." One corner of his mouth lifted, and for a split second, I thought he was going to laugh, but he didn't. "Ah, no, not really," he said.

I felt a pang. He probably had a really nice laugh.

He led me inside, and I took in the vast front hall—flagstone floors, plaster and wood-paneled walls. Gleaming timbers arching overhead. Oil paintings, deer heads, all manner of strange antique swords and shields covered the walls. To my left, I caught a glimpse of a cavernous room crammed with massive carved Victorian furniture. Silk chaises, dusty bookshelves, and rococo screens.

To my right was a long, gleaming, dark wood desk sitting between two arched openings. The closest one led into the dining room. The other, Koa said, led back to the library and Doro's quarters.

In the front hall, I stopped in front of a curio cabinet containing mounds of arrowheads, potsherds, antlers, and beaded necklaces. Portraits of Native warriors and chiefs, turbaned and befeathered, were propped along the shelves. In one etching, the man wore a green tunic and a red turban that held a drooping feather. At the bottom, in a fine cursive, was written *Osceola*.

Koa cleared his throat from halfway up the wide staircase, which was carpeted in threadbare red wool.

"Sorry," I said and caught up to him. We twisted and turned, to landings and down hallways until, finally, he stopped. We were standing in front of a door at the deserted end of a short corridor. On the third floor, if I'd been paying attention.

"Your room," he said and pushed the door open.

The room was a suite, actually, made up of three interconnected spaces—a vast bedroom with a canopied bed, a spacious sitting room, and an attached bathroom. Each space was cluttered with mismatched antiques, everything else upholstered in a dingy pale-blue fabric. The walls were hung with paintings, and there were elaborate, fringed silk draperies over the windows and double doors that led onto a balcony.

It was definitely nowhere near as nice as places I was used to—*forlorn* was the word that came to mind as I took in the moth holes in the curtains, worn carpet, and chipped paint. But it would do. My princess days were behind me. Koa dropped my bag at the foot of the bed and looked at me.

"Okay?" he said.

"It's lovely." I dropped my tote on a doll-size blue chair, hoping my face did not betray my thoughts. "I just hope I can find my way back through that maze of halls in time for dinner."

This would've been where a guy smiled and said something flirty, but Koa just stared at me, like he felt uncomfortable standing in the room with me. I suddenly felt immensely tired.

"Okay, then," I said. "Thanks for the help."

After he was gone, I staggered to the bed and fell face-first onto the spread. A vivid loop of the day—the plane ride, the ferry, and especially the horse stampede—played through my exhausted brain. I was on Bonny Island. In Ambletern. With Kitten. I rolled over and gazed up at the ceiling. *I should probably call Asa to let him know I'd arrived safely.* Or let Aurora know what I was up to.

I fell asleep instead and didn't wake until sometime in the deep of the night, at which point I shed my dusty clothes, crawled under the covers, and drifted back into unconsciousness.

KITTEN

—from Chapter 5

One overcast morning, Fay lost track of Kitten. Most of the guests had been taken to tour the mission ruins on the north side of the island, so she was able to search the house unnoticed. Coming upon Dr. and Mrs. Cormley's room, she heard voices. She shrank back into an alcove that held a bamboo chair and potted fern.

"It's so pretty." It was Kitten's voice, wheedling and insistent.

"I hardly think a child has any use for a silk scarf," came a man's voice in answer. Carl Cormley.

"Your wife said I could have it. Beverly did."

He chortled. "Oh, she did, did she? *Beverly* said that?"

"Yes."

Cormley's voice was a growl. "You're a right little liar. And a nasty girl, too. Lurking around, nosing into people's business."

"What about this?" came Kitten's voice from inside the Cormleys' room. "Is this yours?"

There was a heavy silence. The air seemed shot through with electricity, even out in the hallway. Fay held her breath.

Ashley, Frances. *Kitten*. New York: Drake, Richards and Weems, 1976. Print.

Chapter Eleven

I didn't remember waking.

That is, I didn't remember waking up in my bed. The first thing I was conscious of was a panoramic view of Ambletern's lush backyard, covered in mist. An ornate tabby-and-blue-tile fountain that appeared to be dried up was at the center of it. I realized then that I was standing on a balcony that jutted off the sitting-room section of my suite, wrapped in my bedsheet.

I was naked underneath it, which set me on edge. I'd never been a sleepwalker, but there was a first time for everything. I'd had half a Xanax and a couple of drinks on the plane. It was hard to remember. The ferry ride, the horse stampede, the conversation with Koa. It all seemed like a dream. I looked down at the balcony railing. There was a series of letters scratched into it, dirt and grime highlighting them. I started to run my fingers over them, then reconsidered.

Welcome, Cappie, the letters spelled out. Over and over, in a repeating string, all the way down the length of the railing. I felt a draft coming from the open balcony door. A whiff of something deep and smoky, like it came from the forest. I turned. The door was still closed.

I heard a noise and looked out over the yard, to the far edge, near the woods. It was one of the wild horses, the stallion, standing in the curling mist. He was alone, near a clump of pines. Head up, ears pricked forward, he seemed to be looking right at the balcony where I stood.

A faint knock sounded behind me. I hurried back inside the room, rummaged through my suitcase, and threw on a T-shirt and sweats.

"Come in," I yelled.

Doro stuck her head in the cracked door. "Morning," she said.

"Hi," I said. "Come in."

She was wearing jeans and a stretched-out, faded brown tank with a yellow sports bra underneath. Her hair hung in one white-blonde braid over her shoulder. It was hard to believe a woman her age still had that shade of hair. "Didn't want you to miss breakfast too," she said. "Food goes fast around here."

I pulled at the hem of the T-shirt. "Sorry about that. About last night. I must've been more tired than I thought."

She flicked her wrist, dismissing my words. "Don't worry about it. Meals aren't command performances."

"All right," I said.

"So—what else? It's just the four of us left—me, Koa, the housekeeper and cook. The only staff I absolutely needed to keep this place from caving in around me. The only ones I could still afford with no more paying guests." She sighed. "Everybody's pretty independent. Koa and Laila and Esther get their work done, but their off-time is theirs, to enjoy however they choose. We've got two Jeeps, keys under the seats; feel free to use them."

"Got it."

"How do you like the room?"

"Oh"—I looked around and nodded enthusiastically—"it's great." I hoped I sounded convincing. Truthfully, the bed had been sinfully soft.

"I've got a lot of empty bedrooms, eighteen to be exact, and, if you can believe it, this one's not even the biggest. Laila and Esther live on the first floor, in a double, and Koa lives in a cabin, near the marsh. I thought you might like this one, though, because it was your mother's room. The summer she lived here."

I looked around the room. At the desk. The bookshelves. The mussed bed. A chill fingered up my spine.

"Pretty nice digs for a member of the staff," I said. Her brows lifted. "I mean, for somebody who vacuumed rooms and changed sheets."

Doro shook her head. "Frances didn't work at Ambletern. She was a guest."

"What?"

"She didn't . . . ?" Doro looked stricken.

I flashed the smile I used to remind people I was just regular-gal Megan Ashley, that I wasn't famous, like my mother, and they could talk to me normally. I hoped it worked. Doro had suddenly gotten a nervous look on her face.

"I know this feels strange," I said quickly, "talking about the past like this, right off the bat. But I don't have a lot of time to write this book, and I need to get to the heart of things. You can tell me anything about Frances. Or anything else. In fact, I need you to."

She shut the door quietly. Faced me again. "Frances told you she was a member of the staff?"

"She told everybody that. It's in all the interviews. She's always said she worked here that summer—cleaning toilets and stuff—while she was writing the book."

"I know, I just . . . I thought she would've told you the truth." Doro's expression softened. "Her parents were looking for a place where she could rest. She'd had a tough year at college. She'd . . ." She faltered again.

I was going to have to push, I saw that now. I had to make Doro feel comfortable confiding in me, and quickly, even though I felt massively uncomfortable.

"Doro," I said. "What?"

"Gosh. I feel like I'm really talking out of turn here."

"Doro, please. If I'm going to write a book about my mother, I need to know the truth, no matter how bad it makes her look."

I would need to know the truth about other things as well—like the Kitty Cultist who'd attacked Doro, and why her father dropped the lawsuit against Frances—but that could wait until I'd established some sort of trust between us. Later.

She inhaled. "The way I understand it, toward the end of the semester at school, your mother got pregnant. From what I was told, the relationship wasn't . . . well, it had no future, so she terminated the pregnancy."

"Oh," I said. "Wow."

Frances had definitely left that part out, although I couldn't blame her. It was nobody's business.

Doro continued. "Her parents were looking for someplace far enough from Macon but close enough to get to her if she needed them. A place with some privacy where she could recuperate psychologically from the whole ordeal. She wasn't here as an employee. She was hiding."

I sat on the tufted chaise. I wasn't here twenty-four hours and already Frances's story was crumbling. For her fans, she was all supercilious cat smiles, but, in the end, they didn't know the first thing about her. Nor, apparently, did I.

"Maybe some things you shouldn't include," Doro said.

I gave her a wry smile. "You're protecting her now?"

Doro hesitated. "I know it sounds crazy, but when she was here, she was really great to me. She was the cool college girl and I was eight years old. She played with me in the backyard, at the beach. Took me on long walks all over the island. She used to tell me wonderful stories. I thought she was a movie star, you know, with the red hair and the big sunglasses and the halter tops. I was a lonely little girl, and she was my friend."

"Some friend."

She looked down at the floor.

"Sorry. I'm just . . ." I shook my head. "If I'm going to do this, I can't start feeling sorry for her and tiptoeing around the details. She ruined your life. Your father's life. She ruined my life too."

The words hung in the air, jagged and raw, but full of an odd pulsing power. It was the first time I'd said something like that so directly. I enjoyed the feeling. In fact, I relished it.

Doro raised her head, and our eyes met. Something that felt like the striking of a match against a rough surface sparked between us. We were two people whose hurt had come from the same source, and we were ready to do something about it. But we had to be smart. And we had to do it together.

"I hope I haven't upset you," Doro said.

"I'm not upset," I said. "Not in the least."

KITTEN

—FROM CHAPTER 5

"Give that to me," Carl growled—and then, "or I'll tell them where they can find Miss Bolan's necklace."

Fay heard a thump and clatter. Then another, louder thump. A blur of blonde pigtails and overalls streaked past Fay, out into the hallway. In its wake, a flat, pale-blue plastic compact clattered to the floor, splitting into two pieces.

Fay's heart thumped. She'd seen her friends with compacts like that, containing foil packets of tiny pills. She'd seen her friends furtively tuck the compacts into purses and between mattresses. She hadn't a reason to get pills like that, not yet anyway, but she knew what they were for.

Carl Cormley stumbled out of the room, and Fay melted back into the shadowy alcove. He knelt, retrieved the pieces of plastic, and pocketed them. After looking down the hall each way, he withdrew into his room and slammed the door.

Ashley, Frances. *Kitten*. New York: Drake, Richards and Weems, 1976. Print.

Chapter Twelve

At the end of a long hall that led (and led, and led) from just beyond the main staircase to the back of the house was the enormous, old-fashioned kitchen. Doro introduced me to Laila, a rangy Cherokee woman in her fifties whose ears were loaded with rows of sparkly studs, who'd cooked a breakfast of waffles and wild-boar sausage and kiwi.

Doro told me Laila had run her own fleet of food trucks back in Florida, and it showed. The woman worked with lightning speed. After we sat at the long, scarred wooden worktable, she leaned against the counter, drinking coffee and shooting us furtive looks.

"Laila, sit," Doro said. "Fix a plate."

"I already ate."

Koa, hunched over his food, shook his head. "Woman never eats. I don't know how she stays upright."

"Pure meanness," Esther, Laila's shorter, rounder mother, said from across the table, and Laila swatted her with a dish towel.

"Cooking for such a small group makes me nervous," Laila said. "I'm used to crowds."

Doro's eyes flicked to me. "Those days are over. We're going to have to get used to having this island to ourselves."

Esther dabbed at her mouth with a cloth napkin. "I, for one, have no problem with that. None whatsoever."

"It's going to be yours soon. All of you will be part owners of Bonny with me, and then you can do whatever you want to here. Retire or start a restaurant or . . . whatever."

Doro lifted her orange-juice glass and they all followed suit. I lifted mine too.

"Praise you, Maker of Breath," Doro said and drank. "And Megan, for writing this book. Making a future for all of us possible."

I snuck a glance around the table and found everyone staring at me.

The deal memo wasn't an actual, official contract. There were a lot of variables at work here—the imprint, the editor, Asa—and they all made me seriously skittish. But Asa had promised to help me get this book written. He'd sure as hell better. These people were counting on me.

As we ate, Doro recounted a brief history of the hotel. Turning the island over to his Native employees had been her father's original plan, she said. But it wasn't long until he realized that managing an island was more expensive than he'd expected. The employees would need guests in order to pay for keeping up the place. And guests would only come if William Kitchens and his daughter were there, putting on the real-life *Kitten* show. So he stayed, toiling away at the Sisyphean task of running Ambletern.

Doro didn't mention any attacks or her father's lawsuit against Frances.

When we'd cleaned up the breakfast dishes (and Koa kissed Laila on the cheek for the meal, which she clearly enjoyed), I went back upstairs. I made a couple of wrong turns, but eventually found my room and settled on a wrought-iron chair on the balcony to call Asa. My phone only showed one bar, but I gave it a try anyway, propping my feet up and studying my chipped bright-red pedicure. After a couple of rings, I heard Asa's nasal voice.

"Give me some good news." He sounded like he was deep underground.

"Asa?" I yelled. "Are you there? Connection's shit."

"I can hear you. Fire away."

"Okay, well, I'm here. On the island. And Doro's talking to me."

"Excellent."

"The hotel's enormous. Kind of run down, though. Definitely in need of a major spruce-up. Money's tight for Doro now, but before that, it sounds like she made a killing."

"Oh, good. Puns. Please tell me you're writing all this down."

"I will be, soon."

I looked back into the room. *I should probably make the bed and put away my clothes.* I didn't want Doro or any of the staff thinking I believed room-cleaning fairies always trailed after me. Even though, technically, they had.

"Looks like Doro's email to you was spot-on. It seems like, until a couple of months ago, Ambletern was a money machine. Booked solid, year-round. Mostly die-hard Kitty Cult members, coming here to do their freaky murder-mystery, cosplay stuff. The weirdos were her bread and butter. So, the book—my book—is her lifeline."

Asa grunted. "No pressure there."

"I'm trying not to dwell on it. She's only got three people left on staff. A cook, a housekeeper, and a grounds guy. All Native American, and she's worked out some deal with them, to sign over ownership of the island at some point. She's all about preserving the heritage of the place."

"An American hero. I love it. Play that up, for sure."

I looked out over the banister and the string of carved *Welcome, Cappie*s. I repressed a shiver of revulsion. Below me, Koa, on a rust-laced riding mower, was circling the fountain in ever-widening spirals. He wasn't wearing a shirt. I ducked a little to get a better view through the balusters.

"It's actually quite beautiful here," I said, taking in Koa's torso.

"Nice," he said. "Look, Meg, I don't mean to cut you short, but you should be writing, not talking to me. Remember, I'm going to need the first ten chapters next week."

"I know."

"Do your childhood stuff first. Purge the shit, then you can move on to the Kitten/Doro section. It's going to be great, Meg. Don't think, just write. I have someone who's going to go over everything you send in and put it in order."

My fingertips did their little tingle thing. "Who?"

"Nobody you know. An editor. A friend of mine. A trusted friend."

"A ghostwriter?"

"Meg." Asa's voice lowered. I pictured his pale eyes narrowing. "You know as well as I do, it's going to take a team to get this project to print in the amount of time we have. All this guy's going to do is take your stuff and polish it. Make it shine. He's not going to change anything. Just bump it up to the next level. His name is Ethan Saito; you can check him out. He worked on the Iceland books in the final stages. Melissa loves him."

"I can't have my mother finding out what we're doing."

"She won't. He's very discreet."

"And no announcement in the trades."

"Yes, but Meg, be realistic. She's going to find out about this book sooner or later. You might want to think about how you want it to go down. Sometimes firing the first shot gives you the upper hand."

Koa's mower roared under my window, drowning out Asa's voice.

"Anyway," Asa said. "For now, you're still under the—"

The call dropped. Even though I tried repeatedly, I couldn't connect again.

KITTEN

—from Chapter 6

"The deer eat them. Indians ate them," Kitten was saying.

She and Cappie were settled at the far end of the porch because the day had gotten too hot to play outside. Even the near-constant breeze seemed to have given up and died. Fay herself felt wrung out and listless. It was all she could do to drape herself on the wicker chaise and listen to the low hum of their chatter.

They'd been playing house contentedly on a large grass mat—arranging a collection of rocks and tree bark and dried locust shells into some order only they understood—when their conversation grew louder.

"No, they didn't," Cappie replied. "They ate corn and fish and other things. Things they grew."

"And acorns too," Kitten declared. "I read it."

"Let's play horse," Cappie suggested.

"No," Kitten said. There was that tone in her voice again, Fay thought with alarm—that certain whispery pitch that she had come to associate with bad things.

Ashley, Frances. *Kitten*. New York: Drake, Richards and Weems, 1976. Print.

Chapter Thirteen

I sat for hours in front of a blank white sheet of virtual paper on my laptop and managed to not type one single word. Not one damn word.

The Wi-Fi seemed to be humming along with no hitch, so I checked my email and all my social-media pages. Aurora had dashed off a quick message on one of them, telling me about her foray back into the dating world and asking where the hell I was. I typed a brief reply, giving her a cryptic explanation: I've finally decided to piss Frances off for good, Rors. I can't talk about it yet, but it's going to be big and bad. I'm going to need a friend.

A message pinged right back. You got it, doll. XOXO. Don't stay gone too long.

In the kitchen, I found the makings of a sandwich and plucked an apple from a bowl of fruit on the table. I took the food back in my room and ate slowly, then lay down. I fell into a deep sleep, lulled by the sea breezes ruffling the curtains from the open balcony doors, then woke up feeling disoriented and inexplicably gloomy.

Outside, the sky swirled with storm clouds. I shut the doors and gulped a glass of water. I was wondering just how quickly I could book a flight from Brunswick or Jacksonville to San Francisco, to hang with Aurora, when there was a knock on my door.

"How's it going?" Doro said. Her eyes wandered around the room, and I remembered my earlier plan to tidy up.

"Great," I said.

"You need to get out of this room. Breathe some fresh air."

"Oh, I was just—"

"Get dressed," she said. So I threw on a clean tank top and a pair of baggy men's chinos I'd found in Frances's closet.

I followed Doro through the maze of corridors, landings, and twist-backs that deposited us at a side door. Esther was just bustling past with a duster and an armload of rags.

"Field trip," Doro called to her. "You can do her room while we're gone."

"Oh, no," I said. "I'll handle that."

"Absolutely not," Doro said.

"You're our guest," Esther chimed in and vanished down the hallway.

The door opened to a porte cochere where one of the Jeeps was waiting. We took off, Doro taking a shortcut to the main road, then turning onto a smaller trail and plunging us into the woods. It was even darker than usual, storm clouds gathering overhead. Cooler too.

"Might get a little bumpy," Doro shouted over the wind. "So hang on. I want to show you something."

I grabbed the roll bar and closed my eyes. Asa was going to kill me if I didn't deliver some chapters in the next couple of days. Or maybe he would just bypass me altogether and give the project to the ghostwriter. The two of them could bang out an unauthorized biography; people did it all the time.

In a sickening instant, I realized something: I needed Asa more than he needed me. This book was the only weapon I had in my arsenal. A chance, at last, to own my story. To tell what had happened to me, the way I wanted to tell it. How was I going to do it?

"Stop thinking about the book," Doro said.

I looked at her in surprise. A couple of hanks of hair had come loose from her braid and were whipping in the air. She was smiling.

"You some kind of mind reader?" I said.

"No. Your face is just really . . . expressive, I guess. That's what I'd be thinking about, if I was you." She maneuvered around a hole in the road.

"I haven't written much." Actually, not a single thing.

"Oh, you've got a touch of writer's block. Happens all the time, right? At least, that's what I've heard." She looked at her watch. "We've got about a half hour until sunset. But you have to promise me something."

"Okay."

"Don't think about writing or your mother or the book until after the sun goes down."

I growled in frustration. But I was smiling now too. A certain lightness had stolen over me. I was having fun. It should be unsettling, probably, how easy it was to be with Doro. How talking to her felt like talking to an old friend. Or maybe this was what it should feel like to talk to your mother. I smiled to myself. This place was sucking me in already.

"Close your eyes." She stomped on the gas, and I felt us shoot up a slight rise, then level out. The Jeep ground to a halt. "Now open," she said.

We were on a low ridge that overlooked a large, flat expanse. Soft mounds rippling, a pale-green-and-golden ocean. There were no trees, just tall waving grass and the pink-and-lavender sky above it.

And the smell . . .

The only way to describe it was that it smelled like the beginning of life—like you'd been hanging around that warm pond of Darwin's when the light and heat and salt and whatever else sparked and formed the first living organism. The air was redolent with warm mud and brine—the birth and decay of a million different living creatures.

"Look at it, Meg. The land. It's everything. Do you see? If you let the land talk to you, show you itself, you will understand."

She went on to tell me the saltwater marsh contained the most diverse ecosystem on the planet. In other words, there was more going on in these few acres than on entire continents. She ticked off the organisms that made the marsh their home: fish, shellfish, birds, and all manner of plant life. How the ebb and flow of the tides brought in food and oxygen and flushed the debris and silt from the rivers. The whole cycle was mind boggling. I zoned out a little as she spoke, mesmerized by the way the sun was sinking into undulating grass.

"Look," she said, pointing.

All the time she'd been talking, the intricate fretwork of water that bisected the clumps of grass, mere muddy ribbons when we'd first gotten there, was rising before my eyes, widening and joining in less than thirty minutes. We were now looking at a pond. Suddenly, there was the sound of gentle splashes and I saw a fin cruising in lazy circuits. The land become sea.

"At high tide, porpoises come in here to feed," Doro said. "Then they head back out for the night."

We watched the porpoise circle and loop and crest the water. He arced and dove, like he was performing just for us. And then there were three of them, a trio of fins tracing languid figure eights.

Doro's hair lifted in the breeze. Her eyes had gone unfocused.

"This is where they found Kim Baker, my friend. When the tide went out, she was out there, in the middle of the marsh. She had drowned when the tide came in."

She was still, her face turned away from me now. Her hand rested on the gearshift, her thumb twisted the turquoise-and-silver band on her middle finger.

"Kim's mother, Vera Baker, had worked at Ambletern for years. Lived in one of the old slave cabins my dad fixed up. She was a housekeeper at first, then worked in the garden. My dad used her wherever he needed someone. Anyway. The sheriff came over from the mainland and investigated. He said Mrs. Baker had been depressed or something. Disturbed. Wandered out of the house one night. Kim went to find her. Her mother . . ." She shook her head, unable to speak for a moment. "Vera hit Kimmy on the head. Fractured her skull, knocked her out, of course. And when the water rose, she drowned.

"After they found the body, the staff went out to look for Vera. They found her in less than an hour. On the beach up on the north end of the island, at the middens. She was all bloody. She'd cut herself, up and down her arms. Been at it all night with an oyster shell."

"Jesus. Because she killed her daughter?"

"Some people said she didn't know what had happened to Kim and had gone up to the middens to kill herself. But we all were pretty sure she was the one who did it."

Doro nodded. "They took her to the jail over at St. Marys. She died there, before she even went to trial. She had a brain tumor. Which might've been why she lost her mind and attacked her own daughter."

"It's so sad."

"Kim was my only real friend on this island. Other than Frances."

I thought it was a good time to seize a new subject. "So you really considered Frances a friend?"

"I was a little girl. And even though she cast me as the villain in her book, there are moments in it where you can see how she must have felt about me. It's not just me, right?"

I must've looked blank because her mouth dropped.

"Wait a second," she said. "Are you telling me you haven't read the book?"

I lowered my eyes.

"Megan!"

"I'm on chapter five."

Laughter bubbled out of Doro. "Your own mother wrote arguably one of the most famous books in recent history, and you haven't gotten around to reading it? A psychologist would have a field day with that."

I sighed.

She chuckled again. "Well. They'd have a field day with the lot of us, I expect. My dad was a good-hearted man. But naive. Terribly naive. When *Kitten* first came out, he could've sued her to stop the publication. But when it hit the bestseller list, it was like our fortunes turned around overnight. The hotel became famous. It was hard to say no to all those bookings. All that money."

"All the weirdos."

She hugged her torso. Watched the threatening clouds. "I feel like I haven't earned the right to complain. Not when I think about Kim and all she lost. Most of the time, I think of it as something that happened to someone else. But if I want to remember, really remember, all I have to do is come out here. Watch the sun set and the tide come in." She touched my shoulder. "Do me a favor, Meg? Will you write about her in your book? The real Kim? My friend?"

I nodded, biting my lip. I could make all the promises I liked, but I had to get to work. I had to put words on the page.

"Forget the book. Let's talk about you," Doro said. "You live in New York?"

"Sometimes. LA too."

Her eyebrows lifted. "How many homes do you have?"

"My mother has"—I ticked off on my fingers—"a beach house in Uruguay. Castle in Scotland. Condo in Switzerland. Not that I spent all that much time in any of those places. When I was a kid, I was away at school most of the time."

"What do you do now?"

I focused on the dark tidal pool, the waving grasses beyond it. I thought of my girls at Omnia, their bright eyes and loud chatter as they crowded into our room at the community center, tossed their book bags against the wall. Composing wildly vulgar questions in Italian or French to see who could make me laugh first.

"Not really much of anything," I said.

"You have yet to find your calling."

I looked at her. She was watching me closely.

"I like your spin on it," I said.

She caught my hand, and, reflexively, I flinched. I wasn't used to anyone touching me, not like that. "It's hard to think about, isn't it?" she said. "The past?"

I looked away to hide the fact that my eyes had started to water. "Yeah."

"I think you can do it, Meg," she said. "I believe in you."

I felt something rise in my throat.

"Close your eyes," Doro said.

I did. She was quiet for a moment, but she was still holding my hand, and I tried to ignore how strange it felt to be touched that way. Her hands were rough but soft at the same time. Strong.

"Remember the times you were home, wherever that happened to be, with your mom. Remember the sounds and the smells. See it all, just as it was."

I filled my lungs with the marsh air. Imagined I was moving with the porpoises under and over the dark water.

"Just remember it, that's all. Don't judge."

A strange thing happened, then. When she spoke, I saw everything. My mother, her husbands, each one of them. The swarm of staff, the flurry of appointments and meetings. It was ironic, I thought, the way I always found myself alone in rooms. Empty bedrooms, deserted pool decks, dining rooms with tables set for one.

I might be alone, but I could always count on a certain sound—my mother shrieking about something that was not done correctly or quickly enough or the precise way she had specified. I could always count on hearing one of her tantrums just beyond whatever empty room I was in.

It was all there.

All right there, tucked away in the back of my mind.

My eyes snapped open. "Can you take me back?" I asked, and she let go of my hand.

When she dropped me at Ambletern, I found my way through the maze back to my room. I jammed in a pair of earbuds, turned up the music, and wrote until the sky had gone from stormy black to gray to orange-streaked pink.

KITTEN

—FROM CHAPTER 6

Cappie said something back to Kitten, but Fay couldn't hear what it was. The girl's voice was too soft and the buzzing of the cicadas too loud. She wondered if there was lemonade in the kitchen. The girls might like some. She would like a glass.

"See, I'll do it, then you can," Kitten said.

Fay bolted upright. "Kitten! What are you doing?"

But Kitten was already swallowing whatever it was she'd cupped in her hand. Cappie's face had gone ashen. Fay scrambled up and ran to the girls. The joints of her knees felt liquid.

"Kitten, what did you eat? Spit it out right now!"

Ashley, Frances. *Kitten*. New York: Drake, Richards and Weems, 1976. Print.

Chapter Fourteen

Writing the bad stuff was surprisingly easy. Giver that she was, Frances had provided tons of raw material to draw from.

All through my childhood, I had been the recipient of her rages, ravings, and preening. Bouts of helicoptering alternated with long stretches of forgetting I existed. My tantrums were dismissed as silly. Hers were treated like global crises. If Frances was the sun . . . I was that dinky planet at the end of the line with a number for a name.

Then there was her endless line of suitors. Men who either barely noticed me or gave me lingering, full-frontal hugs. Men who didn't stick around long enough for me to care when they eventually, inevitably, slunk away.

Then there was the time I brought my college boyfriend home for Thanksgiving dinner. He was a lacrosse-playing English-literature major with soulful eyes and legs of Roman marble. I was smitten. At three in the morning, I found him with my mother in the living room, stretched out on the sofa in a horrifying, half-naked cuddle. She claimed she'd been on the verge of sending him away, so I went ahead and sent him myself. I followed him out, my own bags packed, less than ten minutes later.

I wrote all of it. Or almost all of it. The worst thing my mother ever did, her gravest sin, wasn't something I intended to share with anyone. Asa might've acted like he'd known about it. He might've thrown out the name *Graeme Barnish* and said we'd been seen together, but he didn't know anything. He couldn't. I'd never said a word to anybody. Nor had Graeme.

I was sixteen, in my junior year in high school, miserable and deathly lonely at a girls' school in Connecticut. It was the fourth school I'd attended in three years, thanks to my inability to fit in. The experimental hippie/art institute in the backcountry area of Greenwich had been recommended by Frances's film pals. I had no friends there, not that I'd made any effort. Mostly, I drew Sharpie tattoos on my arms and took full advantage of the freedom granted upperclassmen by taking a train to the city whenever possible. I went to see the man I was obsessed with.

He was one of Edgar's other clients, a married author known mostly for a science-fiction series he was avoiding finishing. We'd met at one of Frances's literary events the previous summer, when he cornered me in the coat check and told me I was beautiful, in a sexy Scottish accent. I took him back to our empty apartment, let him undress me and do a lot of things to me that I'd only seen on the Internet.

I was scared out of my mind the whole time and, at the same time, exhilarated. I was a woman. A beautiful, desirable woman who now had a delicious secret. Afterward, he told me I had ruined him for anybody else, and he was completely and utterly in love. Then asked me to loan him two hundred dollars for a Town Car back to Jersey.

In the following months, our rendezvous took on a perfunctory quality. We no longer ordered room service, watched movies, and talked, in the hotels where we met. It was sex and sex only, and then he always had an appointment he had to get to afterward.

Afraid he was losing interest, I was desperate to return to New York for good. Back at school, I jumped off a low bridge into a river, breaking my ankle and dislocating my jaw. Frances brought me home. I don't recall anyone uttering the word *suicide*, at least not in my presence, but I sensed the change of atmosphere. I wouldn't be returning to Connecticut.

I saw a child psychologist and told the woman a bunch of bullshit stories about the kids who bullied me at the school—and even one true story about one of my stepfathers who used to "accidentally" walk in on me while I was in the shower. I kept the truth about Graeme to myself.

The move back to New York seemed to have renewed his interest.

I thought of him incessantly. Felt panicked when we weren't together, euphoric when we were. We met at least once or twice a week in town at hotels, restaurants, clubs, and every time, even though we were in public and could have easily been spotted, he could barely contain himself. He pulled my chair close to him at our tables, nuzzled the crook of my neck. His hands roamed my body. He whispered that since I'd been back, he was flooded with inspiration—brilliant ideas for new books—but he couldn't work. He couldn't focus on anything but me.

"This is crazy, love. I'm crazy. What are you doing to me?"

I finally had a purpose: being the center of Graeme Barnish's universe.

It never occurred to me, though I'd been raised by a master manipulator, that he was one too. It should have. I knew enough about the publishing world to understand that anyone five years over deadline would have to be spouting some pretty persuasive bullshit to still be everybody's darling. But I ignored my inner warning bells. I ignored everything but him.

One June morning, the summer between my junior and senior years in high school, Frances caught him leaving the apartment. Not walking out the street entrance leaving the building; she literally bumped into him on our floor, waiting at the private, key-only elevator.

Later, over our ordered-in sushi dinner, she broached the subject.

"So Graeme Barnish, is it?" she asked. She was tapping away on her laptop, peering over her reading glasses at a new manuscript. Her sushi lay untouched.

I looked at her, the blood draining from my face. "What do you mean?"

"Was he here for a rousing game of bridge? To tutor you for the SATs?"

I kept my eyes on my box of rice. "He's too old for me. And he's married."

"Right on both points."

I expected a tirade forbidding me to see him again, an explosive ordeal that involved yelling and threatening—but she just went back to her computer. There was nothing further. She had a deadline to meet.

Graeme got busy on the final book of his series, and I didn't hear from him much. I took it hard, imagining the worst until he'd call or email, assuring me he still loved me and no other. But meet-ups were fewer and much farther between. By my seventeenth birthday, I'd lost twenty pounds, bit my fingernails down to ragged stubs, and stopped menstruating from the stress.

And then the day came when I happened to catch him on a network morning show talking about the new baby he and his wife were expecting. He said the baby was a girl. They were going to name her Athena, after the main character in his books. The host congratulated him on his nomination for a prestigious award. It was the nudge I needed.

The night of the ceremony, at a swanky hotel, we met in an abandoned stairwell, and I broke up with him.

He didn't take it well. Turned out he wanted me even when he didn't want me. Which he demonstrated by grabbing my throat, banging my head against the wall, and biting my lip until it bled. He hugged me afterward. Cried. Told me he'd call me—and we'd go away somewhere, but right now he had to go—then he took a cab back to Westchester County with his pregnant wife. I never heard from him again.

Later that night, when I was sobbing on my bed, my mother asked me what was wrong. I said I had gotten in a fight with one of my friends. She told me to get up and wash my face, that I was being melodramatic. Then she went to her office to write.

That was the worst thing my mother ever did. She believed my lie.

∾

"This is some seriously sad shit," Asa crowed. "Your mother is the devil. And you deserve the Presidential Medal of Awesomeness. I kid you not."

His speech was slurred, and, even though our connection was buzzy, I was pretty sure I could hear the clink of ice in a glass in the background. I felt a pang of envy. As far as I could tell, Doro kept nothing but sweet tea and lemonade at Ambletern. At that point, I would've killed for a glass of red wine.

"She really made the lawyer be your nanny?" he asked.

"Temporary nanny. Just for one summer." Good old Burt, the tax attorney. "He played a mean game of poker."

"Put that in. And did you really have to go home with one of your teachers over winter break because your mother was traveling?"

"Frances was on her third honeymoon. And, yes," I went on. "When I was eight she did, in fact, take my security blanket while I was sleeping and burned it." Jeez. Was he trying to make me sadder than I already was?

He took another noisy sip. "I'm dumbfounded, I really am. She was a spectacularly terrible mother. She's lucky you didn't murder her in her sleep. You're truly an amazing person. And, you know, you're a better writer than she is," he added.

What a flatterer.

"I guess I'm passionate about my subject," I said.

"Frances isn't passionate?" he asked.

I sighed. I wished I didn't have to talk to this guy. It was bad enough writing about all this stuff, but getting his commentary on every detail of my life was starting to really grate on me.

"She's passionate about being famous," I said. "Getting the right table at the right restaurant. About money and handbags and jewelry and shoes. But about her books? No, I don't think so. Not anymore."

"Put that in," he said. "Put it in the last chapter, where you have the stuff about the birthday party and you showing up with the flowers and her favorite macarons, but she's left to marry Benoît."

I pinched the bridge of my nose.

"Okay, moving on," he said, brisk. "How much more of the child-hood stuff you got?"

"I don't know."

"Like two or three chapters? Or ten? I mean, you could go deeper into college. But, frankly, I don't know that we need more of the same. It's all feeling kind of . . ."

"Kind of what?"

"I don't know . . ." He was quiet for a long moment, then cleared his phlegmy throat. "A bit poor-little-rich-girl, I guess. It's sad stuff, it's just not shocking. We need more blood and guts, you know what I'm saying?"

I sat up. *Ah, yes. Here we go.*

"We don't want people reading this and just feeling sorry for you," he said. "We want them to feel outrage. If they don't feel that, we lose them." He cleared his throat again, delicately. "Can I ask you something?"

The alarm inside me clanged deafeningly. "What?"

"Is there any sex stuff? Like with the stepfathers? Did any of them ever, you know, step over the line?"

"Asa, God." I held the phone away from my ear. "No!"

His voice came through the phone, thin and defensive. "Calm down, don't be such a pussy. You know people are going to wonder about that kind of stuff. You know that's what they're going to expect."

"I don't give a shit what they expect. This is my story. My actual life story."

"It is your story. But, look, I'm just saying what everybody else is going to say when they read it. If you don't put in the sex stuff, they're going to know you're holding back."

"There is no sex stuff."

"Bullshit. Come on."

I clenched my jaw.

"Meg?" he said slowly, his voice syrupy with supportiveness. "What about Graeme?"

"What about him?"

"What happened?"

"I already wrote what I'm going to write. And that's all I'm going to say, except that you're a dick."

"That may be the case, but I'm a dick who happens to know you're not telling the whole truth."

This conversation was giving me a headache. My back hurt from sitting, and I felt like I stank with narcissism and self-pity. I was dying to get out of that room. I'd been cooped up for three days straight, only breaking for meals and sleep. Doro had left me alone, and, in a flash, I realized I was starved for human contact.

And not the kind Asa offered.

I could've used a slug of alcohol, some fresh air, and the sight of Koa's chest in a T-shirt.

"Do me a favor and think about it," Asa said. "In the meantime, send me the last two childhood chapters, and I'll have Ethan go through it all. Then you can get started on the *Kitten* portion. That'll be the second half of the book. You and Doro hitting it off okay?"

I could feel my jaw aching from all the teeth grinding. "I think so."

"Does she trust you? Is she going to talk? I mean, really talk?"

"I don't know, Asa. I've been locked up in my room with my nose in my computer. I haven't spent that much time with her."

"Well, two more chapters and then leave your room. And be friendly. We have to know everything."

I sighed again and promised he'd have the remaining chapters in forty-eight hours. After we hung up, I stared balefully at my laptop, the pinpricks, an army of ants, crawling over every square inch of my skin. I couldn't sit there—my brain running a loop of Graeme. It wasn't healthy.

I changed into running shorts and twisted my hair into a knot. Esther had left a can of bug spray in my bathroom, and I sprayed and sprayed until my skin glistened. I grabbed the earbuds and my phone and started out. I stopped when I noticed my copy of *Kitten* lying face-down on my nightstand.

I knew I really should read some more—I'd left off at the part where they'd found poor little Cappie, the Native American girl, dead. Maybe I could get a few more chapters in before I ran. Get my mind off Graeme.

I picked up the book, and noticed it had been opened to a new chapter. A later section, midway through the book. I skimmed the passage. It was about a carved-rock ashtray that Fay had found hidden in the hotel library. Susan Doucette, Age Twelve, had made a notation in pencil out in the margin.

William/Frances.

KITTEN

—from Chapter 6

Kitten wiped her mouth. "Indians do eat them. Real Indians."

She sent Cappie a sideways glance as Fay examined her all over. The girl seemed perfectly fine, and, after glasses of lemonade, Cappie went home. Fay decided not to tell Delia about the acorn-eating episode since Kitten seemed unharmed, and later, when tucking Kitten into bed for her afternoon rest, she gave her an extra kiss.

"Did the acorns give you a headache? I read they can make you quite sick if they're not cooked first."

Kitten rolled away from her. "I don't want to play with Cappie anymore. She never wants to do what I want to do."

"You'll feel better tomorrow," Fay said and gave her a little pat.

She went downstairs and out to the porch to straighten up the children's mess. While she was cleaning, she found a pile of smashed acorns under a corner of the grass mat. She felt a momentary pang of confusion, then a cold, seeping realization.

Kitten hadn't eaten the acorns at all. She'd only wanted Cappie to think she had.

Ashley, Frances. *Kitten*. New York: Drake, Richards and Weems, 1976. Print.

Chapter Fifteen

After tearing through several chapters, I tucked my paperback copy of *Kitten* under a bench at the edge of the lawn, then found a path that led into the woods for my run. It was a rut, really, layered with pine straw and twigs and the occasional fallen tree. Running was slow going—I had to hold my arms out like a tightrope walker to keep from twisting my ankle and toppling into the trees that flanked me. Also my lungs had to extract enough oxygen from the humidity that threatened to suffocate me.

After twenty minutes, I stopped, scratched all over and bathed in sweat.

Instantly, a blanket of mosquitoes descended on me. They were enormous, long-legged, prehistoric creatures, bigger than any I'd ever witnessed. I tried to slap them, but within seconds, my skin lumped with their weird island voodoo poison, and I was covered in wheals. The bug spray had been completely ineffective; I was being eaten alive.

I hightailed it back in the direction of the house, hoping my movement would discourage the little fuckers or at least disorient them long enough for me to make it back to cover. It seemed to work for a while, then, suddenly, I became aware that the rutted trail had taken an unfamiliar turn, and I was now in a cooler, deeper part of the forest.

I slowed and ripped my earbuds out. A choir of bugs—the mosquitoes, maybe—chirruped around me. Above the canopy of trees, a gull cawed. I couldn't stand there trying to decide which way to go, or the bugs would suck every last drop of blood out of my body. Or the sun would go down and I'd be eaten by . . . something else in this godforsaken tangle. I reinserted the earbuds and pushed ahead.

After another twenty-five or thirty minutes, my pulse was thundering in my ears, and my legs ached. I was spent with exertion and fear. Too tired to keep going, too scared to stop. The undergrowth in this part of the woods was thick, palm fronds and ferns crowding the path, tripping me up. Which must have been why I didn't see the horse—the mare that was lying on her side—until I stumbled, pitching against the high, hard curve of her belly.

"Jesus," I squeaked and scrambled back into the matted greenery. The grass around her, a circle roughly the size of a kiddie pool, had been flattened. At her hindquarters lay a foal, small and slick. Newly born, from the looks of it. I clapped both hands over my mouth. "Jesus," I said again, softer, more reverential. Like a prayer.

The foal was all the way out but still partly encased in the birth sac, which looked like a plastic shopping bag around the lower half of its body. I leaned closer. The slimy creature was breathing but just barely, its head resting on its knobby front knees. The mother arched her neck and nosed back at the foal, nipping her rubbery lips to remove the sac. The task accomplished, she dropped her head back down on the ground with a loud shudder.

She'd already bitten the umbilical cord—I could see the frayed end snaked through the grass, and the two of them were just resting there. Which was probably normal, I thought. I hoped. I didn't know anything about horses giving birth, but I couldn't imagine getting a gangly, knobby, hoofy thing like that out of your body was easy.

I squatted, staring, my fingers woven over my mouth. I was entranced. I'd stumbled upon this rare, private moment, here in this wild place. Life was happening here, without the help of doctors—vets—or shots or pills or any other kind of man-made props. Life was pushing its way forward, no matter what, everywhere.

Suddenly, the mare groaned, and the afterbirth slipped out. I gasped.

She whinnied and thrust out her front legs—two stiff, trembly lengths of tendon and matted hair—then heaved herself up and twisted back, searching for her baby. That's when I saw something rustle behind her. A snake.

It curved and coiled between them, the mare and the foal. The mare thrashed, and the snake drew back and raised its diamond head. I watched in horror as one of the foal's ears flipped forward in curiosity and then the foal nosed at it.

I cried out just as the snake struck the foal dead between the nostrils. The baby snapped back. I stood and screamed again. To my horror, the snake slithered toward me. I pedaled back, ramming into something solid. It caught my arms, and I screamed for a third time, then felt my earbuds ripped out.

"Be still," a low voice said. Koa.

Hefting a shovel with one hand, he maneuvered me out of the way with the other. I scuttled behind him just as he brought the shovel's blade down on the rattler. The body split free from the head and spiraled through the grass, flipping belly up. I could hear the dry rattle, still going.

"Oh God, oh God, oh God," I chanted. That sound was definitely going to give me nightmares.

Koa shouldered the shovel. "Come on," he said. "I'll get you back to the house."

I searched for the mare and her foal. The mare was up now, dancing in a tight circle, favoring one of her hind legs. The foal lay flat, its neck stretched out, forelegs splayed. Its mouth gaped open, bony flank rising and falling rapidly.

"She's hurt," I said. "And the foal. It bit the foal, too."

Koa stood there for a moment, his head bowed.

"You're not going to leave them, are you?" I asked.

He brushed past me and tossed the shovel in the back of the Jeep. "We have to."

I didn't move. "What do you mean?"

"Herd management. Natural selection has to take its course." He swung into the driver's seat, but I couldn't see his face. Couldn't see if he hated the thought of leaving the foal like I did.

"So we're just supposed to let them die?"

"It was a rattlesnake, so the foal, for sure. The mare, hopefully not."

"The snake looked small. Maybe it was a baby."

"Young ones are just as venomous, sometimes more. When they bite, they dump all their venom at once. They don't know any better." His eyes flicked to mine, held the gaze, then slid away.

I looked back at the pair. The mare was a few feet away, pawing the sand, twisting around in an effort to find her wounded leg. She seemed to have completely forgotten about her newborn.

Koa started up the Jeep but I found myself propelled forward. I knelt beside the foal and began stroking its neck—his neck?—with uncertain fingers. The poor thing was gasping for breath.

"His nose is swelling," I called over my shoulder. "He can't breathe."

Without so much as a thought as to what I was doing and how I intended to do it, I scooped the foal into my arms and stood. My legs trembled, and I staggered, ragged bits of the birth sac dangling from my arms. Koa stared at me in disbelief.

"I'm taking him back to the house," I gasped. "I don't give a damn about Doro's herd-management policy."

I took a few ungainly steps—lurches, really, that only zigzagged in place. The foal felt like a slippery, warm anvil in my arms; its bony legs dangled, kicking me periodically. I managed a few steps down the path and stopped, winded.

"Fucking hell," Koa said and heaved himself out of the Jeep. He strode to me and grabbed the foal, depositing him with ease into the bed of the Jeep, on top of a pile of tarps. In a couple of brief swipes, he pulled the birth debris off the newborn foal, then turned and scowled at me. But his eyes had gone soft. So unexpectedly soft that I nearly melted into a puddle of combined lust and gratitude.

"Get in," he said.

The next thing I knew, we were flying through the forest, whipping around trees and chunking over puddles. After a few minutes, he wheeled up to one of those tiny tumbledown shacks we'd passed on my first day here—one of the former slave cabins. Except this one appeared to be in fairly livable shape, with a set of crumbled brick steps and a wobbly-looking stone chimney. The front yard was scattered with oyster shells, and a neat row of boots and shoes lined the steps.

Koa booted open the door and carried the foal inside. I followed and looked around cautiously. It was a simple structure—one main room with a huge fireplace, a kitchenette, a ratty-looking floral sofa. A door that probably led to a bedroom. All along the fireplace mantel were shards of pottery, red and white and brown. A few had intricate markings on them. I stood awkwardly in the doorway as Koa lowered the foal onto a rag rug in the center of the room.

"Don't you have a bed?" I asked as he threw open the door on a huge, rickety linen press.

He snorted. "I'm not putting a horse on my bed."

He began pulling supplies from the top shelf. Bags and vials and bandages. He dumped it all beside the foal, slapping a pair of heavy-duty shears in my hand.

"Side of the house, find the hose. Cut about a foot."

I stared at the scissors for a moment. He put a hand on my arm.

"Meg?" he said gently. "Go."

116

When I returned, he'd rigged up an IV over a metal lawn chair for the foal. He snipped the length of hose I handed him in half and threaded one into each nostril, taping them down with duct tape.

"The main thing you have to worry about is keeping their breathing unobstructed. The hose will keep her nostrils from swelling shut completely. Keep the airways clear."

"You can't give her antivenom?" I asked.

"We could. But we try to save it for humans. Believe me, if you need it, you'll thank me for not giving it to her." He sat back on his heels and brushed away the lock of hair that had fallen across his eyes.

"Looks like you've done this before," I said.

He started cleaning up, tossing ripped packages and empty bottles into the trash. He went to wash his hands at the sink, then turned. His eyes were soft again. And so brown, it was almost unbearable to look at him.

"You can't talk about this," he said. "You can't tell anyone she's here."

"She?"

"It's a girl. A filly."

I smiled. "Oh. Okay."

"Not to anyone."

"Okay," I said, slightly irritated that I'd let him distract me. "I won't."

"We have to let nature take the weakest ones, or the herd will grow too large. They'll eat everything, destroy the environment. That's when the guys in the suits swoop in and start culling the herd themselves."

"I get it."

I looked down at the foal. She was breathing easier now, and didn't seem to be bothered at all by the needle bandaged to her neck. Her ears flipped forward and back like two antennae, and she kept nosing at the rug.

"She's got to be hungry," I said. "Are we going to try to find her mother?"

I felt Koa move behind me. I could smell him, actually. He seemed to carry the scent of the island around with him: sun and salt and some other smell under all that. Something sweet. Maybe it was jasmine, the blooming vine I'd seen climbing most of the buildings and even some trees. I'd never met a man who smelled like flowers. It was not a bad thing. On the contrary, it was good. And somewhat disconcerting.

He crouched beside me, pried the foal's lips open, and stuck a huge bottle into her mouth. She immediately started sucking with gusto.

I gave him a reproachful look. "So you've never done this before?"

"I didn't say that. These wild mares are notoriously bad mothers. They abandon their foals all the time."

I studied him. A smear of blood bisected his cheek, right along the cheekbone. "Aw. You do have a heart."

"The old fuckers can gallop off into the sea, go Virginia Woolf, for all I care. They're mean as hell and don't do anything but eat everything in sight and shit all over the beach."

"And you're telling me you just happened to be passing through that spot in the woods at the exact moment when that mare was giving birth? It was pure luck?"

He didn't answer.

"Well, either you were following the mare or . . ."

He was following me.

"Guilty," he said, but when he looked at me, the hint of a smile was playing around his lips. I felt myself redden, and my arms and legs began to tingle, little bursts of energy zinging up and down the muscles. The side effect every time I felt the slightest bit tired or self-conscious. Vulnerable. The neuropathy would never let me forget just how far from normal I really was. I stood and rubbed my arms.

"Want a ride back?" Koa said.

I brushed off my shorts, suddenly conscious that they'd become a mess of horse blood, saliva, and mucus. "I'll walk," I said. "You should stay with her."

He didn't argue.

"I'm just not looking forward to the Old Testament swarms of mosquitoes that are going to attack me."

"Can I make a suggestion?" he said.

He motioned to me, and I followed him down the steps, to a faucet on the side of the cabin. The ground beneath it was muddy, and he scooped out a dollop.

"Do you mind?" he asked.

He took my wrist and rotated my arm, exposing the tender skin. Then, in one deft stroke, he smeared the mud from my wrist to elbow, all the way up to my shoulder. He talked as he worked.

"So the Caddo lived in what became Oklahoma, east Texas, and Louisiana. They were farmers, generally. They also constructed mounds and made bows to sell to other tribes. They were peaceable, with only one real enemy."

His fingers traveled around the curve of my arms, slowing ever so slightly, covering the entire surface of my arm with mud. I watched, entranced.

"This enemy was a formidable foe. A tireless one who attacked with unmatched stealth and persistence."

My shellacked arm now resembled a tree branch more than a human limb. I looked up at him. His eyes were liquid in the porch light.

"Mosquito," he whispered. The word felt positively sensual coming out of his mouth. I concentrated on keeping my knees from buckling.

He dropped my arm. "I would've tried to show off and say it in Caddo, but I grew up in the suburbs of Baton Rouge, never lived on the rez. And I was a dumb-ass kid who thought he was too cool to pay attention at summer culture camp." He smiled. "Anyway, there you go. Native American bug repellent."

"Where is the Caddo reservation?"

"Western Oklahoma."

"Do you think you'll ever live there?"

"I don't know. I'm not sure that's where my life is, you know?"

"Yeah."

"I feel like I'm still looking for that."

I nodded. I knew what he meant.

He went to work on my face then. A quick swipe across my forehead, temples, and cheeks. My chin and nose and around my lips. He caught my fingers and scraped a lump of mud onto them.

"I'll let you handle the rest," he said.

He nodded in the general direction of my exposed chest, and I hastily smeared the area. When I was thoroughly coated, I presented myself for inspection.

"How do I look?"

"Like Swamp Thing. But you won't get bit."

"Please tell me this is a real thing people do and not just some elaborate practical joke," I said. I could already feel the crackle of drying mud on my face. And imagine Laila, Esther, and Doro's laughter when they saw me.

"Don't trust me?" He smiled, and my belly flipped.

"I do," I said. "I think that's the problem."

His eyes flashed in the light from the cabin window, but he didn't answer. I couldn't read this guy. Couldn't tell whether he was interested or just being nice. I couldn't seem to read anyone on Bonny Island. This place had knocked me off balance in some way.

So I smiled back at him, said, "Thanks," and trotted off in the direction of Ambletern.

"Watch out for snakes," he called behind me. I thought I heard him laughing.

KITTEN

—FROM CHAPTER 7

Fay woke from a dream of Kitten and Cappie arguing over something, she couldn't remember what. Even after she'd showered, had her breakfast, and taken Kitten down to the beach, the dream stayed with her.

It expanded inside her mind, filling her with dread. It was like that horror movie she'd seen when she was a child, the one she'd accidentally come across on late-night TV. She had no memory now what the film was about, but she'd never been able to shake one particular image—a dismembered arm crawling on its own across the floor.

When Herb returned with the guests from the marsh tour, and Fay heard the news that Cappie had been found there, drowned, she suddenly remembered the dream. And one detail specifically: Kitten, repeatedly screaming a strange word, over and over.

Mico.

Ashley, Frances. Kitten. New York: Drake, Richards and Weems, 1976. Print.

Chapter Sixteen

No one was around when I got back to the hotel. Thank God.

Upstairs in my room, I climbed into the shower and scrubbed myself raw with a washcloth. As I toweled off in the steam-filled bathroom, something caught my eye—an aloe plant in a tiny pink ceramic pot and a vial of tea-tree oil, sitting on the edge of the tub. There was a note tented beside them. *Dab me*, it said. I smiled—Doro—then dashed a couple of drops of the oil onto the welts on my arms and legs and neck. It was pitch black outside now, so I climbed into bed and opened *Kitten*.

Ambletern's guests had started coming down with a mysterious stomach ailment—except Kitten, Fay, the Murphys. A local doctor appeared on Bonny to investigate. He seemed to suspect young Kitten, which made me wonder if he would be the next to go.

The storyline was spooky, if a bit on the predictable side. But it was easy to see why people loved it. Grotesque characters doing weird stuff in a creepy Southern setting—who wouldn't love that? It was a mash-up of William Faulkner and Flannery O'Connor, if you dumbed down the prose and multiplied the splatter factor. And my mother had come up with that shit. Pretty impressive.

Meanwhile, Susan Doucette—superfan, micro–Kitty Cultist, and über-annotator of books—seemed determined to prove that there was a real-life mystery to be solved. The same mystery all the Kitty Cultists wanted to crack—if the real Kitten, Dorothy Kitchens, had actually murdered the real Cappie Strongbow, Kim Baker.

Susan's notes were plentiful. Every time the word *Guale* appeared, it was circled in red pen, and in the section where guests were vomiting and passing out, she'd repeatedly scrawled the word. On other pages, more words, like penciled vines of ivy, twined along the margins: *father, land grant, cassina, GTO, AIM, rock.*

I had no idea what any of them meant.

I grabbed my computer, climbed back in bed, and searched the word *cassina* first.

The little blue line shot halfway across my address bar, then stopped. The Wi-Fi must have been down.

"Great," I muttered, then eyed the bookcase, its shelves bowed with the weight of dozens of musty, linen-bound books. I set aside my computer and climbed out of bed. There was a row of books about the island—one in particular, *Barrier Islands of Georgia*, seemed appropriately thick. I took it back to the bed and skimmed the table of contents. Nothing helpful jumped out at me.

A search on the shelves in the library downstairs yielded more. I found three books on local plant life and another on Muskogee Native American history and customs. I hauled them back to my room and, after twenty minutes, found what I was looking for.

> *Ilex vomitoria*, commonly known as yaupon holly or "cassina," was sacred to the Native people of the Golden Isles. A tea made from the leaves of the plant—often called "black drink"—was purported to have spiritually cleansing properties and was used in many religious ceremonies. The cleansing

usually resulted in heavy sweats, intense vomiting, and occasionally out-of-body trance experiences. The berries are known to be deadly.

The leaves must have been what Kitten used to make everybody sick. And my little researcher extraordinaire, Susan Doucette, figured it out. Smart girl.

I grabbed my phone, switched off the wireless, and waited to see if the cell network would kick in. Right away, four beautiful dots appeared.

I typed GTO into the search bar, and a bunch of links to old cars popped up. No surprise there. I entered AIM. At the bottom of the page, under the expected AOL-related suggestions, I saw the heading American Indian Movement. I clicked on it.

The website that loaded seem to be mostly press releases and news about different regional councils and their decisions; no mention of the defunct Guale tribe or Bonny Island, Georgia, or anything about the Kitchens family. After poking around a while, I decided I'd hit a dead end, so I swiped over to my newsfeed. Immediately an ominous headline flashed up on my screen.

I sat up and clicked the link.

ASHLEY SAYS FIFTH TIME IS THE REAL DEAL, read the headline. The picture below showed Frances, pale in a black swimsuit, floppy hat, and giant sunglasses, leading poor Benoît down a beach. He resembled a translucent shrimp, squinting in the sun like he'd just been dragged up from the ocean floor. A knot formed in my stomach, and I tossed the phone away. Just as I did, it rang. I snatched it up.

"Hello?"

"Good God, you're hard to reach," Asa said.

"Spotty cell service," I said. "I told you that. Listen, I need to ask you a question. Have you ever heard of anyone named Susan Doucette in connection with the Kitty Cult? Or maybe with the TV show or one of the movies?"

"Nooo . . . can't say that I have."

"I'm wondering exactly who she is to Frances. Why she would've kept this kid's book. Frances never mentioned her?"

"No." He said it quietly, and, inexplicably, my stomach fluttered. It was nothing, just a feeling, but I was going with it. "Meg?" he said. "You there?"

"Have you talked to her lately? Frances?"

"Um." He paused. "Last week, I think."

I hesitated. Closed my eyes. "Are you really her assistant, Asa?"

He laughed. "What are you talking about?"

"It's a pretty straightforward question. Are you Frances Ashley's assistant? Or have you concocted this whole bullshit story so that I would write your book?"

"No! I mean, yes. Of course I'm her assistant. Jesus. Rankin Lewis hired me eight months ago to be her assistant."

"And she gave you the password to her email. And told you to handle her correspondence."

"Right." His voice had gone flat. "She told me that she was overwhelmed with all the fortieth-anniversary stuff and needed some help."

Take a breath, Meg. I was overthinking this. Being paranoid. It was this place.

"Look," he said. "If you don't believe me, I can send you some pay stubs."

I sighed. "No. I believe you. I'm just . . . This place is getting to me."

"Meg." His voice gentled. "If you don't mind me saying, you have work to do, and quite frankly, all this feels like a giant avoidance tactic. You're investigating some Kitty Cultist because you've got a touch of writer's block. Am I right?"

"Maybe." I rubbed my eyes. "Probably. But if I knew what really happened—"

"Look. All you have to do is open that laptop and write one sentence. Then another, then another after that. Okay? I feel for you, but we really, really don't have time for this. We have a book to sell."

"Okay."

"Now go do your thing."

I tossed the phone into the covers beside me. Glanced at the computer.

I dropped back on the pillows. Asa was right. I was avoiding the inevitable, imagining conspiracies where there weren't any. I needed to pull myself together. I told myself to relax, then conjured up Koa's face . . . followed by his well-defined, knotty shoulders . . . his sculpted chest and taut stomach. The enticing shadow just below the waistband of his jeans.

My fingers had just started to drift south when I heard a noise outside, right below my balcony. A muffled thump like something had been flung against the side of the house. I sat up, points of light pulsating at the edges of my sight.

Now a scraping sound, higher up.

Something was scaling the tabby walls outside my bedroom.

I flew to the balcony doors and cracked them open. Slipped out into the night air, being careful not to let the doors squeak. I tried to get a view of the wedding-cake walls on either side of my balcony, but the darkness was so thick, and the angle of my position so awkward, I couldn't make out a thing.

I didn't hear anything either. Not for the excruciating ten minutes I waited, motionless, sweat rolling down my back, shallow breath in my ears. Finally, I gave up and slipped back into my room. Whatever it had been was long gone. I made sure the door was locked securely behind me and crept back to bed.

I didn't think of Koa again.

KITTEN

—from Chapter 8

For two days in a row, Beverly Cormley and her husband missed breakfast. It wasn't entirely unexpected.

The paramedics had bundled up Cappie Strongbow's small, decomposing body and shuttled it away, and the police had carted June Strongbow off in handcuffs. After that, most of the guests had retired to the safety of their rooms. The Talberts, the Del Riccios, and the Walthinghams had ferried back to the mainland. There was a feeling of doom clinging to the walls of the hotel.

The fourth morning, Carl Cormley joined everyone in the large dining room. He fell into the buffet line at the sideboard, nodding to the others.

From the back of the room, Delia Murphy spoke. "Dr. Cormley, may I send a cup of tea and milk of magnesia upstairs to your wife?"

His head jerked up, looking shocked that someone was addressing him.

"Dr. Cormley?" Delia repeated.

"No, thank you," he said. "I'll take her coffee and toast. It's nothing but a bit of female trouble." He turned back to the spread.

Kitten piped up. "Maybe she's sick because she's going to have a baby. Wouldn't that be something, Mother, a baby for the Cormleys?" She turned to the doctor. "What would you like the most, a boy or a girl?"

Ashley, Frances. *Kitten*. New York: Drake, Richards and Weems, 1976. Print.

Chapter Seventeen

I worked every day, from sunup to sundown—with short breaks for eating, jogs, and the occasional shower—but it still took me another full week to write the final childhood chapters.

As always, the best parts came at dawn. It was a Monday, or Tuesday—I didn't know, I'd lost all track of time—when the last drops of nastiness poured out of me. The sun had risen above Bonny's oaks, and I marveled over the pink-and-lavender show. I'd never seen a sunrise like it.

I composed an email to Asa and sent the pages rocketing into cyberspace. I crossed my fingers that they would be either so chilling or so pathetic, he'd drop the whole sex angle. I couldn't deal with more questions about that. Or the threat of the ghostwriter conducting his own independent research.

This was my story. My story, my mother, my book. Period.

I showered and headed down to breakfast. Doro, dressed in nylon fishing shorts and a frayed denim work shirt, was on her way out. Two plastic baskets were hooked over each arm.

"Run to the kitchen, grab a croissant," she said. "And a long-sleeve shirt. Your mother ever teach you how to bake a pie?"

I snorted. "I'll give you one guess."

"Go," she said. "I'll wait."

Five minutes later, Doro and I were standing under the porte cochere off the side of the house, on the drive. I crammed one of Laila's impossibly flaky, airy croissants into my mouth and then posed—arms out, eyes screwed shut—while Doro sprayed me down with her heavy-duty industrial-size can of bug spray. My bug bites burned like miniature erupting volcanoes all over my body.

"Agh." I let out another muffled scream through the half-chewed croissant.

"Close your mouth." She sprayed again.

"Get her good, Doro," I heard. "They love the taste of her blood."

I cracked open one eye. Koa slouched against a tabby post, holding a grass-coated weed whacker. His jeans looked like he'd slept in them, and a portion of his gnarled hair was tied up on top of his head. Annoying how good he made a man-bun look.

"Or you could do it the Caddo way," he said.

Doro laughed and sprayed some more. "I don't think Meg would like the Caddo way."

My eyes met Koa's for a brief second.

"Pie Night," Doro said, still spraying away. "You got a big day?"

"List as long as my arm," he said.

I coughed in the cloud of bug spray. "There was something making weird sounds outside my balcony last night," I said.

"Sounds?" Doro asked.

"Thumps. Scrapes up along the wall." I glanced from her to Koa.

"Oh, yeah. That'd be Cappie Strongbow," he said.

"It was raccoons, probably," Doro said, shaking her head. "Nothing to worry about. As long as your door is locked. Just lock your balcony door."

"And say a protection prayer, maybe," he added. "Just in case."

"Stop it, Koa." Doro put a hand on my sticky arm. "We've got work to do. See you around."

"See you around," he said.

As we headed into the woods, I threw a casual look over my shoulder. He was already at work, waving the weed whacker along the edge of the drive, a faded red bandanna pulled up over his nose and mouth.

"You gotten to know Koa at all?" Doro asked.

"Oh, no. Not really. He's just . . ." I fell silent.

She dimpled. "You know, he's not just pretty, he's smart too. Did he tell you he was a physician's assistant? He worked on the geriatric floor of a hospital in Texas before he came here to weed whack for me."

Of course. All the medical supplies in his cabin. His way with the foal.

"Why did he leave Texas?"

"I don't know. You'll have to ask him." She elbowed me and cocked her eyebrow. "He's a man of few words. And I think I've used up his quota with me."

The slanting rays of the sun lit up the bleached white streaks in her hair. Her skin was the perfect shade of golden brown with a spray of freckles drifting across both shoulders. And there wasn't a mosquito bite anywhere on her. Maybe she'd developed an immunity, living here all her life.

We were farther down the path now, and she pressed through a thick hedge. "The Guale people ruled this place once. They'd live on the island in the winter when the shellfish were in season, and then move over to the mainland to hunt or cultivate crops the rest of the year. Then the Spanish came, the Jesuits and Franciscans. Once the Guale figured out the priests wanted them to give up their seasonal relocating and tried to make them settle around the missions, they massacred them."

"Yikes."

"They stoned them, cut them into pieces. Put their heads on pikes outside the mission. The English came, the soldiers and pirates. That's who the island is named after, you know—Anne Bonny, the most famous female Caribbean pirate. The Europeans brought weapons and disease and the tradition of scalping. Did you know that?"

"No."

"True story. Eventually the Guale scattered inland and down to Florida. Their tribe—their culture, artifacts, language—it all vanished."

Interesting. In *Kitten*, there was one family left with Guale blood: the Strongbows. And then there was Kitten, who imagined she was part of the tribe—but maybe Frances had made that part up, it was hard to tell. There was no rhyme or reason to Frances's methods.

Doro went on to explain that Bonny was given as a royal land grant to one of her ancestors—Samuel Kitchens, a general in the British army. He was the one who built the original Ambletern in 1780 and carved out the plantation. There was a fire at some point, and the house was rebuilt in the 1880s. Somewhere in the '40s, Doro's grandmother turned the property into a hotel.

When she finished, I was quiet.

"What is it?" Doro asked. "Something I said?"

I shrugged. "It's nothing."

"You thought I would say I was Guale, didn't you?" She looked back at me, her eyes lit with understanding. "You've been doing your homework, I see. Reading the book."

I swallowed. Stepped over a puddle.

"That was just one of Frances's many embellishments, Kitten imagining that she was Native. Frances made all that stuff up. I never said anything like that. I never believed I was Guale or thought I was adopted into any Native tribe." Her voice sounded calm but I couldn't see her face. I had no idea if she was angry or just explaining how things were. "Kim Baker, my friend who died, was Cherokee, I think. She and her mother came up from somewhere—Jacksonville, maybe—to work at Ambletern. But not me. I wasn't Native, and I knew it."

"Right," I said. "Got it. Sorry."

She went on, thrashing through the woods at a steady pace. I could barely keep up with her. "I don't suffer any delusions; I know exactly who I am. I'm an immigrant. One hundred percent white imperialist, through and through. And I guess some people might call me crazy because I believe in the kooky notion that this island—this whole country, in fact—still belongs to Native people."

"It does, I guess, in a way."

"If you have a shred of decency in you, you understand that truth. After Kim died, I made a promise to myself that when Ambletern was mine, I would do everything in my power to see that the island was returned, once and for all, to its rightful owners. The Guale are gone, so I went and found the next best thing."

The next best thing? It was a bizarre way of putting it. Like Native people were nothing more than one big, nonspecific ethnic group. And they would want Bonny even though it hadn't been their ancestors' original territory.

She finally stopped. Turned to face me. She was breathing hard and pouring sweat. I could see where a branch had caught her along the neck. There was a line of red, a scratch, oozing and angry, leading down to the hollow of her throat.

"I can't undo the past. But I can do my part to change the future . . . at least when it comes to Bonny."

"That's pretty amazing," I said. But I couldn't help wondering if Laila, Esther, and Koa ever got together and had a good laugh about Doro's white-savior complex. It felt a little on the self-congratulatory side. A little weird.

"You sure you're not Native?" Doro studied me.

"No. I'm Creole, Brazilian, and who knows whatever else. From my father."

She nodded.

"I didn't know him," I blurted. "He died soon after I was born."

She straightened. And smiled at me. I smiled back, even though I wasn't sure why, exactly, since I'd just said my father was dead. Sometimes, I had to admit, Doro made me uneasy.

"Ah," Doro said. "Here we are."

We were standing before a bramble of long, sharp-leafed branches, all of them loaded with dark-purple fruit. She tossed one of the buckets to me.

"Only get the ripest ones," she said. "We should have more than enough for a pie and Laila's jam."

I hesitated, feeling the woods rustle around me. Or maybe I was sensing the presence of something that didn't belong. Someone watching us. Once I read that there's a special area of your brain devoted to detecting the gaze of others. Even though you may not be looking directly at them, you sense them watching at the fringes of your awareness. Right at that moment, I felt like prey being stared down by a predator.

I reached for the first blackberry and felt a sharp sting on my hand. I snatched it back and pressed it against my mouth. "Ouch."

"Oh, yeah," Doro said from her spot. "Watch for the thorns."

KITTEN

—from Chapter 8

"Darling," Delia said to Kitten.

"May I go upstairs and see Mrs. Cormley?" Kitten asked.

Cormley steadfastly kept at work on his plate.

"Kitten, dear," Delia said. "Let's leave the Cormleys alone, all right? Fay will find something else for you to do today, so poor Mrs. Cormley can get her rest."

Kitten turned her cool gaze on Dr. Cormley. "It's just that I'm so lonesome for a friend. And Mrs. Cormley is so sweet."

Cormley didn't respond, he just carried the plate out of the room like he hadn't even heard. Kitten looked at the boy, Henrick, who was sitting across the table from her.

"Would you like to go swimming?"

Ashley, Frances. *Kitten*. New York: Drake, Richards and Weems, 1976. Print.

Chapter Eighteen

Apparently, I was expected to make the blackberry pie, the whole thing, entirely on my own. The idea struck me as a particularly merciless form of hazing. Especially since I'd never baked anything in my entire life, with the exception of chocolate-chip freezer cookies.

Doro ignored my litany of protests and propped a tattered, food-stained cookbook in front of me on the counter. It was opened to a recipe entitled "Mama Peg's Blackberry Pie." She informed me that everything I needed in order to do Mama Peg proud could be found right there, in that very kitchen.

"Exactly, and her name is Laila," I said.

Doro threw open the fridge. She pulled out a bottle of icy white wine. "Funny, Meg," she said, uncorking it.

I perked up. "Wine?"

"From my private stash," Doro said. "If your pie passes the test tonight, I'll share."

"We keep it in the cellar," Esther said. "You're welcome to it anytime."

"Traitor," Doro said.

Laila, taking pity on me—and possibly worried that I was about to do irreversible damage to her kitchen—began to stack bowls and measuring spoons and sifters around me. Then she, Esther, and Doro sat and proceeded to knock back glass after glass of wine (as well as a plate of brie and grapes) as they shouted instructions and encouragement from their perches.

After I threw out the first batch of runny dough, I begged for my own glass.

"No drinking and baking," Doro declared.

"She's all tight in the shoulders," Laila said. "She's nervous. You can't bake nervous."

"Okay. Give her some wine."

Esther poured a glass and trotted it over to me.

"But you have to stay focused, Meg," Doro said. "Portions are essential here. You can't just throw in a little of this and a little of that."

"My mother didn't teach me to bake, you know," I grumbled and guzzled half the glass. Then I upended more flour into the measuring cup. "She taught me how to tip a concierge and order enough champagne for a table of thirty."

"Maybe we should get Koa in here," Doro said. "He'd get her loose." The three women cackled and clinked their glasses.

"Jeez," I muttered.

"You think he's pretty cute, eh, Meg?" Laila asked.

I poured in the ice water and went at the new batch of dough with a wooden spoon. "You will not break my spirit. You will not."

"He's been working here an entire year, and I've never seen him so on top of the lawn maintenance," Doro said. "He's been so attentive to everything around the house. He's edged about ten times in the last week."

"Ladies." I dumped out the dough and started kneading. "Your drunk is showing."

"Don't mind us," Doro said. "You just do your job and bake the damn pie."

"What about the rest of supper?" I said. "I mean, I hope this thing turns out, but Laila's making other stuff, right?"

"Nope," Laila said.

I twisted around, my hands buried in the dough, hair curtaining my face. "What?"

"No supper on Pie Night. Just pie on Pie Night." She took a swig of wine.

"What if it doesn't turn out?" I asked.

"Koa goes back to hanging out at the mission ruins, and the lawn grows back to its original shaggy state," Esther hooted, and they clinked glasses.

"Why does Koa hang out at the mission?" I asked.

"He likes to look for artifacts out there," Esther said. "Like pottery and rocks."

I glanced at Doro.

"Not *that* rock, surely," I said. "He's not one of those nutcases." I looked at the other two women. "Is he?"

Laila waved me off. "No, no. He just likes archaeology. Indiana Jones stuff."

Doro met my gaze over the rim of her wineglass. It seemed like we were thinking the same thing. That it was a strange hobby. That he might be interested in what else could be found up at the mission.

I rolled out a better pastry this time—thin and flexible and floury. A badass pastry. A poetic pastry. A pastry for the ages. I followed, as best I could, Mama Peg's complicated instructions of creating a kind of jam concoction out of half the blackberries and folding in the rest of them whole, with an extensive list of sugars and spices. I had the distinct impression that there was an easier way to produce a decent pie than following Mama Peg's instructions, but I dutifully forged ahead.

When I pulled the finished product out of the oven, Doro, Esther, and Laila did an impromptu celebration dance. I took a couple of bows, then carefully laid it on the counter.

"Sure is pretty. Hope it tastes good," Doro said and filled my glass all the way up to the top with wine.

We lifted our glasses and something caught my eye in the settling twilight of the backyard. Koa. He was standing by the fountain, watching us, a phone pressed to his ear.

∞

Doro and Laila weren't kidding about Pie Night. My blackberry pie was appetizer, first course, entrée, and dessert, all in one. That and a couple more bottles of wine made for an interesting, if one-note, meal.

Before we dug in, Doro stood, her glass lifted.

"To Meg," she said. "A true daughter of Bonny Island." Her eyes flashed. "Charmer of horses, high priestess of pastry."

I felt my breath catch in my throat.

Then, "A Native. One of our tribe, our own special tribe. Praise to the Maker of Breath."

Koa cleared his throat and looked at his plate. I thought I caught something pass between Laila and Esther, a subtle exchange between the two. But the moment passed, and everyone lifted their glasses, chorusing, "Hear, hear." I decided I'd imagined it.

"We're so thankful you came, Meg," Doro said.

For a moment, while her words still hung in the air, I couldn't seem to breathe. It was the heat, probably. The oppressive heat and humidity, and the hours writing about my childhood and my mother. I was overcome.

Or maybe it was that Doro was looking at me in a way that made me feel like I belonged. Because I did feel that. I also felt teary and soft and maybe a little drunk too.

And happy. I felt happy.

"Pie's getting cold," Koa said. I tried to catch his eye, but he seemed thoroughly engrossed by the feast laid out before us.

We demolished the whole thing, layering the thick, crusty wedges oozing bluish-purple fruit with ice cream or whipped cream or both, in Koa's case. After everybody had dispersed, I convinced Laila to leave the kitchen cleanup to me. She finally, reluctantly, went out to the porch with the others, and I stacked the dirty dishes, bundled up the table-cloth and napkins, and lugged the whole thing back to the kitchen. I found Koa in front of the fridge, door flung open. His arms were loaded with sandwich makings. He froze.

"I was craving some protein," he said. "No offense."

I ran the water and pulled open the dishwasher. "None taken. Go for it." I thought of the way he kissed Laila after every meal. He hadn't attempted any such thing with me.

"You want a turkey sandwich?" he asked.

"No. The pie was plenty."

For a moment or two we worked side by side—me at the sink, him at the counter—in silence. Then we both spoke at the same time.

"You first," I said.

"Doro said you were going to write a book about your mother. About what she did to the Kitchenses."

"Yeah."

"She said you were going to set the record straight. Put the truth out there for all the world to see."

"I'm going to try."

"That's great. Really brave of you," he said, his expression dubious.

"Yeah, you don't approve. Clearly."

"I just . . . think you might be poking a hornet's nest, that's all." He went back to his sandwich, tore a bite out.

"What's that supposed to mean?"

He shook his head. "Just that it seems a bit naive to think you can come down here and get the truth by being friendly and charming and asking what happened." He took another wolfish bite.

"Okay." I laughed in disbelief. "Wow."

He swallowed. "I mean, have you considered you may not like what you find out?"

"Yes. Have you considered that you're being sort of a condescending dick?"

He frowned. Two deep lines appeared between his eyebrows. "I didn't . . . I just meant Doro could stand to lose a lot, if she tells her story. Her real story. I mean, depending on what that actually is." He shook his head, like he might want to say more. I was glad he didn't. I was fighting an urge to grab a handful of that luscious hair and yank it with all my strength.

"Koa," I said loftily. "Why don't you consider this? Maybe I'm being friendly and charming because I *like* being that way. Because that's the kind of person I really am." It was a load of BS. But I was on a roll, pissed off and not ready to back down.

"Maybe," I continued, "I actually like Doro and want to be her friend. And"—I jabbed a finger in his direction—"*and* maybe I am an adult, and it's none of your business how I *handle* things."

We stared at each other, locked in a breathless, churning standoff. Part of me was pissed. The other part, forlorn. He was so goddamn cute, standing there, a crestfallen look on his face. I wanted to kiss him in the biggest way.

He turned away first. "Look, forget it. I don't know what I'm talking about. You're right. I'm a dick. I'm sorry."

"Fine." I sighed.

He picked a wedge of turkey from the bread and dropped it in his mouth. Focused on some spot on the wall behind me.

"Why don't you tell me what really brought you to Bonny Island from Texas? And then I can decide how valid your reasons are."

He sighed. "I said I was sorry."

"No. I actually want to know why you came here."

He finished the sandwich in two bites, then swiped at a stray shred of lettuce at the corner of his mouth.

I groaned. "Come on, do it. Just tell me your stupid story so we can move on and be friends already."

He swallowed and grinned. "Okay, fine." He leaned against the counter and folded his arms. "I was a physician's assistant in Texas. And I had a bit of a habit. Just a recreational thing, nothing earth shattering, but it was a little too easy to keep it going in a cancer center with lots of pain pills and scrip pads lying around. Anyway, one day they brought this old guy in from an assisted-living facility. Midseventies, in shitty health. He was alone, had to admit himself, sitting there in a wheelchair, spitting up blood." He shook his head. Looked out the window into the black backyard like he'd gone into a trance. "No one in the world gave a damn about whether he lived or died. It wasn't like he was a bad guy. He was nice to the staff. Patient, even when he was having a bad day, which every day seemed to be. Lung cancer. Might be common, but it's still the worst way to go."

He opened the fridge, pulled out a gallon jug of milk, and thunked it on the counter.

"He told me once he regretted the way he'd wasted his life—running from his responsibilities, living like none of it would catch up to him. Funny thing, what he said really sank in. So I quit doing what I was doing. I left that job, that town. The whole shebang. So I could start over."

I'd calmed down and was feeling a little sheepish about our earlier spat. My prickliness. This was a good person, standing in front of me. Someone with an expansive, flesh-and-blood heart.

"Talk about brave," I said.

"For once in my life." He opened a couple of the upper cabinets, banging cupboard doors open and closed, finally pulling out a small blue box.

"How is he . . . the guy?" I asked.

"Still hanging in there, I think. I hope. We haven't spoken in a while." He peered inside the box. "Anyway, I found Doro's ad, hopped on a bus, and came to Bonny. Partly to get away from the temptations of the workplace. Partly to try and do something that mattered with my life." He grinned and held up the blue box. "Pectin. Laila uses it to make jam. We put it in the milk, so the foal can digest it more easily."

"Do you mind if I come over? To see her?" I asked.

"I don't know. We're friends now?" His eyes were soft, a strand of hair had fallen across them and I wondered what it would be like to brush it away. To touch him.

"I think so. What about you?"

He appraised me, then smiled. "Grab another milk. I'm parked out back."

∞

I followed Koa to a ramshackle shed just behind his cabin. A lantern hung on a nail beside the rotted wood door, pooling light around us.

"You put her out here?" I asked.

"She shits wherever she happens to be standing. I wasn't going to keep her in my house."

Inside the shed, Koa clicked on a single bare bulb. He'd rigged up a temporary stall for the foal with sheets of plywood and an odd door wedged between a variety of lawn equipment. The floor was layered with mounds of grass clippings. He unhooked a series of bungee cords and pulled aside one of the boards, just far enough to slip inside, but the foal barely took notice of him. She was standing at the far wall, her head buried in a bucket that hung on a nail.

"She took to the bucket right away. Doesn't even miss the bottle."

"She's a fighter, isn't she?" The foal's bony, mottled rump shone in the light as she slurped up the milk, and I pulled up some distant memory of a favorite childhood book. "She's a roan."

He shot me a surprised look.

"Thank you, *Misty of Chincoteague* and *Black Beauty*," I said. "I knew you'd come in handy one day."

Koa went to work, scooping the piles of manure out and tossing them over the barricade into the wheelbarrow. Bits of dried grass eddied into the air. I moved closer to the plywood wall.

"What about the snakebite? Is she going to be okay?"

Koa bent over his work. "I'm still giving her antibiotics, and the swelling's already started to go down. She's going to be fine."

The foal wobbled around Koa and nosed over the plywood. Her head was too big for her body, and with the two lengths of hose sticking out of each nostril, she looked like some kind of alien creature. I stuck my hand out, and she nuzzled it in greeting.

Koa tossed another forkful into the wheelbarrow. "Why don't you take out the hose while I'm dealing with this?"

"Sure."

"Just go slow on the tape so you don't pull her skin. You okay to do this?"

"Of course."

We changed places, slipping past each other through the narrow opening. I could feel the heat of his body, caught a whiff of his warm perspiration as he brushed past me. That sweet jasmine-y smell that hung around him. I tried not to smile. He went outside, and I regarded the foal.

"Hey, girl," I said.

Right then a jangling noise pierced the air. Shit. Oh, shit, my phone. I'd forgotten I even had it. I felt in my pockets, but it abruptly went silent again. Probably a bad connection. I eased closer to the foal and put out my hand.

My phone rang again. This time, the foal jerked back, clattering against the back wall and upsetting the milk pail. My hand brushed my back pocket, but before I could pull the phone out, a blur of long legs and flapping tail blew past me. I whirled to see the filly break the plywood barrier and trot out of the shed into the night.

KITTEN

—FROM CHAPTER 9

"Where do you think Cappie's gone?"

Kitten had finally tired of playing in the waves and come back to settle herself on the blanket Fay had spread on the hard-packed sand. Fay stubbed out the cigarette she'd been smoking, while Kitten helped herself to chicken salad.

"To heaven, of course," said Fay.

"Christian heaven or Guale heaven?" asked Kitten.

"God takes all children to his heaven, the only heaven, no matter what the color of their skin. So that's where Cappie's gone."

"Cappie can't be a ghost, can she?" Kitten persisted.

For no apparent reason, Fay's insides quivered. She didn't believe in ghosts, never had, but somehow the thought of Cappie's spirit, floating anywhere nearby, filled her with disgust. "Of course not. Why would you say such a thing?"

"The Guale believe the dead become ghosts if they're murdered."

Ashley, Frances. *Kitten*. New York: Drake, Richards and Weems, 1976. Print.

Chapter Nineteen

An image of Ursula from *The Little Mermaid* flashed on the screen of my phone.

Frances. *Shit.*

I sent the call to voice mail, then bear-crawled over the collapsed boards, tripping over the scattered tools and bags of organic soil. When I finally stumbled out of the shed, I found the foal in the yard, prancing in figure eights like a drunken, knock-kneed baby.

Koa pushed the empty wheelbarrow around the corner. It clanked, once out of his hands, then over on its side. "What the hell?" he said. He didn't wait for an answer, just sprang at the foal. She skittered away from him, her hooves tangling and then untangling. Then she melted into the darkness.

He whirled toward me with a questioning look.

"My phone rang. She freaked out."

We crashed through the woods—Koa holding the lantern aloft and gliding through the scrub, and me pulling up the rear, catching branches in my face and chanting a frenzied curse/prayer against the snakes.

Moonlight spilled between the swaying moss, but even in the splashes of pale light, the horse was nowhere to be seen. We pushed farther into the woods, until my skin burned with bites and scratches. Koa thrust out an arm and lifted the lantern. We were standing at the edge of a large clearing, at least an acre in size—a gentle rise of sandy grass laced with an intricate fretwork of low stone walls that bisected each other in random patterns. Behind the lines of stone rose a building whose walls were almost completely intact. There was no roof on it, and the walls pointed jaggedly toward the sky; scattered along the side facing us, I saw a few high windows and one crumbling arched doorway. The mission ruins.

Somebody had built a campfire in the middle of this outside courtyard area, and the blacked remains were ringed with logs. So strange, I thought, that people would want to roast hot dogs and marshmallows in front of a spooky old Catholic mission. Where actual human beings had been murdered.

"She went in there." Koa pointed toward the rising jagged walls. I tried to see something, anything, in the darkness.

My arms and legs prickled as I swept my gaze over the rubble. It couldn't be safe in there, back in that dark warren of rooms. The foal could knock stones loose, topple one of the precarious stone walls. We needed to get her out. I stamped the ground absently, trying to lessen the needling sensation.

"What are you doing?" Koa whispered. "Stop it."

I shook my hands, trying to get the tingling to stop. "It's this thing I've got. Makes my hands and feet tingle sometimes. And go numb."

"What is it?"

"Nothing. Just something from stress."

"A doctor said that?" He was fully focused on me now. Great.

"I'm okay. Let's just find her."

We made our way through the strange maze of stones—which resembled a life-size, arcane board game laid out by a giant—until we came to the main structure and a high arched doorway. I gazed up.

"She's probably in there," he whispered, handing me the lantern. "But we should flank her. You go left. Sneak in from the side, if you can. I'll go in the doorway, and we'll meet at the back. Take it slow so you don't spook her."

We separated, and I crept around the edge of the crumbled wall. It was almost entirely intact, and I doubted I'd find any way in. Just then, I saw a small opening, only about three feet high, like a miniature doorway. I crawled under, then grabbed the lantern.

I was in a cramped room, a cell, really, with hard-packed dirt floors and a single window at least three feet above my head. The roof was gone, and when I looked up, the blanket of stars dizzied me. I brushed my fingers along the wall—plaster over stone, I thought.

I imagined the priests who'd come here, compelled by a divine cause. What priest had lived here in this tiny cubicle? Had he known his mission was doomed? That he'd be hacked to pieces, his blood pooling in this house of worship, his head decorating a pike?

I raised the lantern and moved to the adjacent room. It was a duplicate of the last one, and there was no sign of the foal, so I kept going. Creeping around stone corners, switching back through crooked passageways and narrow rooms, ducking in and out of gaps in the walls. I'd just stepped into what looked like a wider, more open corridor, when I heard something—the rustle of an animal or a person, maybe—and froze.

I thought of the scraping sounds outside my balcony. The way it had seemed something was making its way up the wall to the roof. It could've been anything up there, looking down on me. Watching.

Raccoons. Or ghosts.

No one had mentioned a third option—some unwelcome trespasser, sneaking around the island, spying on me.

The spell was broken by a gentle whicker and velvet nose at my back, and the next instant, Koa appeared. Maybe it had been nothing at all.

Back at the shed, Koa and I secured the temporary stall with stacks of more junk and bungee cords. Koa refilled her milk pail, and when the foal dunked her face in, we headed outside.

The pinpricks were still going like gangbusters. I realized I was feeling them all over now, even along my chest and down my torso. And I had a pounding headache to top it off. I stretched, and something cracked ominously in my back.

"Feels late," I said.

Koa looked at his watch. "Nine thirty. You okay?"

"Totally." I stopped rubbing my hands.

"The neuropathy's still bothering you?"

A physician's assistant. I'd forgotten. Of course he knew the real word for it. But tonight had been great—fun, actually. What I really, desperately didn't want was for it to turn into a doctor's visit.

"I'm good," I said cheerily.

"You writing tomorrow?"

I nodded. "I'm really behind schedule."

"Sounds good." He adjusted his stance. Looked at the ground.

"Sorry for bringing complete and utter chaos upon your home," I said. "And also for calling you a dick."

He smiled. My nerves were jangling now, but it wasn't the neuropathy. On impulse, I grabbed hold of his hand. It was big and warm, and his fingers automatically curled around mine.

"Thank you," I said. "For what you did."

"What was that?" he said.

"The foal," I said.

"Oh."

I leaned toward him. I could've sworn he'd begun to move too, to lean toward me, then he stopped.

"We shouldn't," he whispered.

"Why not?" I whispered back. "You worried what Doro would think?"

He was inches from my face and looking at me intently. I felt dizzy, and I wondered if it was what I was seeing in his eyes or just my exhaustion. And in spite of his words, he wasn't moving away. He was so close I could feel his breath caress my skin, see the new growth of whiskers as it ran along his jaw and up his cheek.

"Something about me you should know," he said in a measured voice. "I don't care what anyone thinks."

I raised my eyebrows. "I've never met anybody like that. Any other secrets?"

He didn't answer. His eyes dropped down to my lips.

My phone jangled against my rear end, and we both jumped.

"You should get that," he said and spun away.

It rang again. "Go ahead," he said, waving.

I pulled the phone out. "Hello?"

"Very nice, Megan. VERY. FUCKING. NICE!" my mother screamed from the other end. I bobbled the phone, accidentally triggering the speaker, and it fell to the ground. The name *Frances* flashed, superimposed over the picture of Ursula. Koa's eyebrows shot up.

"You are the . . . sort of human . . . !" she shrieked amid the static. "I hope you know that! The kind who . . . LIE and FABRICATE and . . . ON HER FAMILY NAME for a paltry, pathetic fifteen . . . a TRAITOR . . ."

I snuck a look at Koa. His eyes had widened considerably, his mouth agape. I scooped up the phone, clicked off the speaker.

"Hi, Frances," I said. "I don't think our connection is very—"

"No," she snapped, and, maddeningly, the line went perfectly clear. "No excuses out of you. You'll be interested to hear, I found your little friend, Asa. The little sycophant Edgar hired, who *betrayed* the both of us. While Edgar was on his deathbed, I remind you, this mongrel was going behind his back and pitching this abomination of a book. While the man was *dying*."

"He said he was your assistant."

"He was," she snapped. "Until he decided to start a war and become a *nothing*. Because that is what he is going to be when I get through with him. *A nothing*."

I was quiet.

"This is my fault," she sighed. "For giving you everything you ever wanted . . . For not teaching you the value of an honest day's work. Sweating over something. Staying with it until you've got it just right. This is my fault."

Koa spoke beside me. "Meg."

I shook my head.

"You want me to stay?"

I stepped back, waved him away. He retreated into the shadows.

"Were you not *aware*"—she was back to screaming now—"that I know every executive editor who works at Pelham Sound? Every assistant editor? Every marketing manager? Are you not aware that I've been invited to their homes, Megan? Attended their weddings and their children's bar mitzvahs? Those people are not only my colleagues, they are my friends."

"Pretty lame set of friends, who'd agree to publish a tell-all book about you."

I could feel Koa's gaze burning into me. I angled myself away from him.

"Can we talk about this later?" I said quietly into the phone.

"I want you to stop what you're doing, Megan. I want you to stop writing this book this instant, and come home to New York."

"I'm not coming to New York."

"Where shall we meet, then? Tell me. Paris? San Francisco?"

"No, Frances, you're not getting it."

"Then explain it to me, Megan. Enlighten me."

"I'm saying"—my voice had risen a couple of notches—"I'm writing this book, no matter what you say. No matter what you do. I'm writing it. Period. End of discussion."

But of course, with Frances, there was no period. Just one neverending, gargantuan run-on sentence.

"The fortieth anniversary is in less than six months," she said. "You'll ruin everything. But that's just what you intended, isn't it?" she asked.

I let out a long, tremulous breath. My calm was slipping, I could tell. Soon I'd be screaming back at her. Fighting tears. Overwhelmed with the old feelings of loneliness and desperation.

"Frances," I said in a measured tone. "I'm not changing my mind. I'm writing the book, they're publishing it. That's all." My eyes flicked up. Koa had hung the lantern beside his cabin door and was standing there, shoulders squared, hands clasped in front like a nightclub bouncer.

"I'm sure they've hired a ghostwriter for you," Frances said. "That's not even a question. But did you sign a contract? Did you have a lawyer review it?"

"I'm not going to discuss this with you."

"Megan, you have no idea how to read a contract. No idea how they can slip in clauses and exhibits that will trap you. These people are sharks, darling, you can't even imagine. You could have been swindled by this Asa person or God-knows-who at Pelham Sound—"

"It doesn't concern you."

"You're my daughter. Everything you do concerns me."

My breath hitched. Why did she have to say things like this? Clichés she tossed out that felt like a knife ripping through me.

"Come to California, then," she continued. "Come to Carmel. Benoît has a ranch. A very secluded, beautiful, peaceful ranch. We can talk there. Talk about why you feel like you have to do this. I want you to just take a moment here, Megan. Think about how this book is going to change everything."

"I wish to God it would."

"What does that mean? I don't know what that means, Meg."

"Why don't you? You're the one who ran off and got married without even telling your only daughter. You got married, Frances, and Asa, your assistant—"

"That anemic little turd—"

"He was the one who broke the news to me, okay, Frances? Your traitorous, turdy assistant. I got your birthday invitation. And I showed up for the party, and Asa told me you and Benoît had gotten married."

"I didn't know you were coming. You never called."

"We don't call each other, Frances." My voice broke, and I stopped. Took a breath. "We communicate through other people. You never called me about Edgar."

Here was the moment, I was offering it up to her—the opportunity to say, *I'm sorry, Megan. I'll do better.*

I love you.

But nothing came. No soft words. No apologies. Just a crystalline silence. To my profound dismay, I felt my eyes fill. I ground my fist into my forehead.

"I hear that you're angry, Megan. I understand."

I glanced at Koa. He was still standing by the cabin door, arms folded, eyes on the ground. Probably wondering how a grown woman could have such a difficult time talking to her own mother. I wished he would leave. The humiliation of this was unbearable.

"I'm not angry, Frances. Not anymore," I said.

I saw Koa pull his phone out of his pocket and frown at it.

The electrical zings were zooming up and down my arms and legs, and my head was pounding. I closed my eyes, felt the woods and the night around me, the warmth of the island. I breathed in and out. In and out. The breeze lifted strands of my hair, cooling where sweat filmed my skin.

"What, Megan?" Frances demanded.

I could hear her short, sharp breaths on the line, waiting for me. For the next blow. The killing one. But something was wrong. I couldn't seem to speak. All I could think was her name. *Frances. Frances . . .*

"Mom," I gasped.

Just as Koa put his phone to his ear and said in a low voice, "I can't talk right now."

"What, Megan? What is it?" Frances said.

And then I felt the ground rush up to meet me. Tasted sand and straw and grass and watched as everything, like in the final scene of a movie, faded to black.

KITTEN

—FROM CHAPTER 9

"Did your daddy tell you that?" Fay asked. She was hoping her voice didn't betray her fear.

"No, Cappie's mama did. She told Cappie and me about the ghosts and the Jesuits and all the ceremonies. She made me a member of the tribe."

"That was awfully nice of her. But you know you're not really Guale."

"I am. Mrs. Strongbow did the ceremony one day when I was playing with Cappie. It was real. I'm really Guale. And I'm the *mico* now, too."

Mico.

That word again, that Fay had dreamed about. She swallowed. Carefully, so she wouldn't choke.

"What's the *mico*?" she asked quietly.

"The chief. The head of the tribe. Cappie's mama said that we were the last of the Guale, and now that she and Cappie are gone, it's just me." She drew herself up. "I'm the only one left on the island. So I'm the *mico*."

Ashley, Frances. *Kitten*. New York: Drake, Richards and Weems, 1976. Print.

Chapter Twenty

The next morning at breakfast, Doro announced she was escorting me over to the mainland to see her doctor. After my fainting episode, Koa had told her about my neuropathy, and they both thought I could use a medical opinion.

Captain Mike met Doro and me and Laila, who had some shopping to do, at the dock. After a breezy forty-five-minute trip over the calm sound, we were in St. Marys. The medical complex was a cluster of one-story pink stucco buildings an easy half-mile walk from the marina.

Dr. Lodi, a sharp-eyed woman with a sparkling diamond chip in her nose, shooed the nurse out of the examination room and proceeded to take all my vitals and prick my finger herself. I rattled off my history as she jotted on a chart. She left, returning after twenty long minutes.

"Your hemoglobin and hematocrit are low," she announced. "Which would indicate anemia. This is not that uncommon for young women. Usually you can be treated with iron supplements. I'll need to do some follow-up tests to check your iron and ferritin levels. While the dizziness and fainting can be associated with anemia, the tingling and numbness in your extremities—the neuropathy—is not usually connected. Have you ever fainted before?"

"Not that I can remember. Although stress does make the tingling worse."

"Were you under particular stress last night?"

I hesitated. "My mother called."

"Ah. Any other symptoms besides fainting, after the call? Any general symptoms you've noticed lately?"

"I feel tired, I guess. I don't sleep great, but I never have. And I have headaches sometimes. A lot."

She looked down at her notes. "You said you first noticed the tingling when you hurt your ankle skiing? But you never went to see a doctor?"

"No. I wrapped up my ankle and figured it would work itself out."

"All right. Lie back, please."

She did the routine full-body poking and prodding, then patted my arm and picked up my file. "Hang here with me for a little longer?"

I nodded, and she stepped out. When she returned, she had a strange look on her face.

"So your blood smear is showing something that concerns me. Some cell abnormalities. Have you noticed any changes in your nails lately?"

"Not really. What is it?"

"Something that's been on my radar recently. Let me look at them."

I held out my hands.

"Okay," she said. "Can you open your mouth for me?"

She pulled down my lower lip, then, after a moment, stepped back and spoke.

"Truthfully, Meg, I think the anemia is a symptom of a larger problem. You have white spots, sometimes called *Mees' lines*, on your nails and a bluish discoloration in a line along your gum. These findings, along with the tingling, the fainting, and general fatigue, lead me to believe that you may have lead poisoning. Of course, this would have to be confirmed with further blood tests."

I was dumbfounded. "I can't believe this."

"Lead can absolutely affect your body on a cellular and molecular level, months, even years, after exposure. In the brain, for instance, it can block certain channels, interfere with neurotransmitters and synapses as well as protein kinases, which would cause fatigue. The peripheral neuropathy, or the tingling and numbness you feel in your extremities, is caused by this effect on your peripheral nerves. We'll need to do a heavy-metal screen to confirm it, of course."

I felt short of breath.

"I'd like to talk about any exposure you've had to lead in the past few years. I'm wondering, in particular, if you were exposed to lead-based paint or dust on that ski trip. Were you staying in an older resort, one built before 1978?"

"I think so, yes. And they were remodeling. Not our floor but some of the others."

She put my file aside. "I would like to admit you into the hospital for the night. I know it may sound extreme, but given your symptoms, I'm suspicious that your blood-lead level will not only be elevated, but will be in the acute range, which requires urgent treatment. Also, in the hospital, I can get results from your heavy-metal levels quickly and simultaneously begin chelation therapy."

"What's that?"

"It's an IV infusion of EDTA with dimercaprol. These agents have a clawlike effect on lead, grabbing and binding it so that it can be excreted through the kidneys. Initially you will probably receive several infusions in a week, then we can retest your levels and be able to adjust the schedule. Once we determine that you have no problems with sensitivity to the medication, these infusions could be given at home with a visiting infusion service."

The medical jargon was whizzing right past me. But it sounded good, and Doro had sworn by Dr. Lodi's skill, so I nodded like I understood it all.

"Koa is actually qualified to handle the treatments. We'll check your other levels too, tonight, but I'll probably recommend dietary changes as well, to ensure you're getting plenty of calories, as well as iron, zinc, calcium, vitamins C and E."

I must've looked like death, because she patted my knee comfortingly.

"The most important thing is you're no longer being exposed to the source. The effects of lead poisoning can sometimes be ameliorated, but in light of the movement of lead in the body, whether it's gotten into the bone, it could take up to a year."

I sighed, feeling the weariness from the past couple of days wash over me. And I had thought Frances was the biggest poison in my life. What irony.

"Megan?"

I snapped to attention. Dr. Lodi was studying me.

"Okay," I said. "Hospital. Let's do it."

⁓

The St. Marys hospital was less than a five-minute taxi drive away—a quaint little brick building nestled in a grove of palmettos on the far side of town. It reminded me of an old-fashioned schoolhouse.

"You don't have to stay," I said to Doro, on my way to the bathroom to change into the flimsy gown the nurse had given me.

"I want to. Any special requests?" she asked. "I'm going on a snack run."

Something about the way she said it, the motherly way she assumed she would take care of me, and I would let her, touched me. I didn't move, letting the unfamiliar prickle of pleasure wash over me.

"No, I'm fine."

"Nothing?"

I shook my head, and she gave me a little pat.

"See you soon."

A nurse and tech came to draw blood and to insert the IV for the chelation, and when Doro got back I was channel-surfing from my bed. She had an armful of plastic bags, and, after asking if the coast was clear and closing the door, she emptied them on my bed. I surveyed the stash with wide eyes. There was a stack of magazines; a rainbow of candy bars, chips, and nuts; and enough mini-bottles of bourbon to get the entire hospital staff hammered. It looked like a ten-year-old had robbed a combo five-and-dime/liquor store.

"Wow," I said.

"For me, not you. Oh, also, I picked up these." She fished out two shot glasses emblazoned with a picture of Ambletern. "Official collectors' shot glasses of Bonny Island. They sell these gems all over St. Marys."

She poured a shot for her and filled mine with water.

"To answers," she said.

"Answers." I clinked my glass against hers and threw back the lukewarm water. I fell back on the sad excuse for a pillow and heaved a sigh.

Doro settled into a chair and popped her feet up on the ottoman while I sorted through the pile of treasures on the bed. One of the magazines had a cover story about *Kitten*'s upcoming fortieth anniversary. **Frances Ashley Talks Horror, Happiness and Honeymoon.** I pushed it away.

"Whoops." Doro picked up the magazine, and her eyes swept the copy. "Sorry about that." She dropped the rag in the trashcan. I could smell Doro's perfume, the faintest trace of something familiar. I couldn't quite place it. But the doctor had said my neurons weren't firing normally. Maybe it was a scent Frances used to wear and it was messing with my head.

Doro leaned over and touched my hair—picked something and drew it down a strand. She held the thing up—a tiny, prickly pod.

"Cocklebur," she said. Her eyes strayed back to the top of my head. "Your hair is full of them." She pulled another out. "What were you and Koa up to, out there in the woods last night?" I could feel her smile as she worked, combing the bristly husks down the strands of hair and depositing them into a little pile on the nightstand.

"We were just walking, scout's honor."

I was tired now, the long day finally catching up to me. The way Doro was pulling the burs out of my hair was sending waves of goose-flesh all over my body. I was so tired, and it felt good. I dropped my head back, let my eyes flutter closed.

"Do you have a boyfriend?" I asked.

"No. Never been married either. Not really on my to-do list. I had my dad to look after. I've always had my freedom. And done whatever I wanted, whenever I wanted. I haven't missed anything."

"You've never been in love."

"I didn't say that." She pulled a couple more burs in silence. Stroked my tangled hair.

"Tell me," I said. "I won't write about it, I swear."

Her voice was unusually soft. "I don't think he relished a life with the girl who was Kitten." She shrugged in resignation. "It was for the best, I think. I wasn't going to leave the island or my father; I was the hotel's ringer. As long as the real Kitten was at Ambletern, my dad was making money."

"But your dad was using you, Doro. Just like my mother did."

She sighed. "I'm not angry. He did the best he could. We made the best of a bad situation, but I'm not proud of how I handled everything." She sat up, inhaled deeply.

My mind flitted to the handful of harassment charges.

"Did you really threaten some guests?" I asked.

A beat of silence passed, then she spoke.

"The past couple of years . . . I just couldn't play the game anymore. When they spray-painted Ambletern and boarded up some of the windows, broke into my bedroom and took personal items—I admit, I lost my temper. I shoved one of them, pretty hard, once. Threw another's suitcase in the sound."

I laughed. "You're kidding. I kind of love that."

"You should rest." She swept up the contraband candy and liquor and stuffed it under the vinyl foldout chair, then found a pillow and extra blanket in the closet. "I'll be right here if you need me," she said, settling onto the narrow chair. It looked no bigger than a cot.

She stared up at the ceiling for a few long moments, then spoke again. "I was born four weeks premature. My father is the one who started calling me Kitten. He said I was as small as a newborn kitten. Then my mom picked it up, then everyone else. Nobody ever called me Dorothy."

"So Frances stole your nickname for her book," I said.

"I guess she did." She stretched and yawned. "Did you ever have a nickname?"

"Pip," I said, and a weird pain tore at my throat. "But Frances always called me Megan. Megan Frances, if I got into big trouble."

Doro settled on her side. "Your middle name is Frances?"

"Mm-hm."

"She makes everything hers, doesn't she?"

I didn't answer.

"You need a nickname," she said. Her voice sounded strange.

I felt something strange flutter in my chest in response, equal parts pain and pleasure. It was like a shot of whiskey. Or looking at Koa's face, which could go from tender to flinty in a nanosecond when he looked at me. None of the good in life was purely so. None was untainted. It was all a mix. Dark and light.

"Just not Chubby. Or Stinky," I said, and Doro laughed. "And I want some of that whiskey when I get out of here."

"Noted."

I pressed my face against the bleach-scented pillow, reveling in the pleasant floating sensation I was feeling. Just then, Doro picked up my hand and lifted it to her face. She pressed it against her cheek and then brushed a kiss across the knuckles.

KITTEN

—from Chapter 9

"Now, Kitten," Fay began in a reasonable tone. "The Guale were a primitive people. They didn't know about the Bible or have Sunday school, so they had to make things up. Cappie's mama was pretending with you."

Now that she thought about it, Fay realized Kitten probably had never been to Sunday school either, way out here on Bonny Island. There was no church or proper school. Why, she thought with a pang of pity, the Murphys were no better than pagans.

"Anyway," Fay continued, patting her arm just to show the girl she didn't hold her faithlessness against her. "You mustn't think about such things. There are no ghosts, Cappie's gone to heaven with God, and that is that."

She was saying it for her own benefit as much as Kitten's, and she did feel better having said it out loud.

Ashley, Frances. *Kitten*. New York: Drake, Richards and Weems, 1976. Print.

Chapter Twenty-One

"I was right about the lead," Dr. Lodi said. "Your BLL was seventy-two."

She was standing in my sun-splashed hospital room, her glasses pushed up on her head. Doro stood at the mirror, winding her hair into a knot at the top of her head.

I glanced at Doro. The side of her face looked pale, and her lips were set in a thin line.

"Looks like you tolerated the chelation well," Dr. Lodi said. "The nurse says you ate. Are you feeling okay?"

I nodded. "I am."

"Good. So we'll get you discharged. But first, I do want to confirm that there's no chance of exposure to lead-based paint at Ambletern."

Doro spoke up. "Everything's up to date there. Nothing toxic at all."

"Okay, then." Dr. Lodi gave us both a brilliant smile. "Meg, if you're comfortable with it, Koa can handle your future treatments. I'll mix up a couple of bags for you to take back and you can give him a call. Sound good?"

"Yes," I said.

"Let's keep in touch, Meg," Dr. Lodi said. "I want to hear how you're feeling as the treatments progress. And I'd like to see you in my office next week, okay?"

I nodded and sought Doro's eyes again, but she was already busy folding the sheets and blanket she'd slept under last night. She looked agitated. Nervous, almost.

∞

Koa hooked the plastic bag to the IV stand and pulled it closer to the ancient brocade sofa. It bumped over the carpet and clattered against the table. He tightened the tourniquet around my arm, swabbed the crook of my elbow, then inserted the catheter—neatly, quickly—into a vein. I barely felt a thing. He attached a piece of clear tubing to the catheter and taped the whole thing down.

"We'll alternate arms, okay?" He attached the line from the bag into the cath. "Try not to turn you into a pincushion."

"I appreciate that." I felt the cold stream of chemical cocktails sluice into my arm and relaxed into the cushions.

It was two days later, and we were in the salon, the vast forest-green living room at Ambletern, which boasted an impressive collection of Victorian furniture and, at the far end, a cavernous brown-marble fireplace. The walls were crammed with oil paintings, animal heads, and the occasional framed sepia snapshot. Velvet curtains blocked the scorching rays of the sun. I was ensconced on the lumpy sofa while Doro reclined on a threadbare tufted chaise.

Behind me, along the wall, was a gleaming mahogany bar, above which hung mirrored shelves stacked with every imaginable form of wineglass, cut-crystal tumbler, silver julep cup, and shot glass, all monogrammed with the ubiquitous Ambletern *A*. The only thing missing was liquor. I wondered if Doro had stashed it in the basement with the wine when she'd shut down the hotel. It probably wasn't a great idea to drink my way through a treatment, but my mouth still watered at the thought of an extra-dirty martini.

After I'd been released from the hospital, Doro and I had ferried back to Bonny and I'd slept for nine straight hours. When I woke, I'd found eleven voice mails on my phone. Six were from Frances, most of which I deleted. The last one I listened to.

"Megan, darling, listen. About the call—I was just in shock, that's all, really, and I overreacted. I didn't realize you had any interest in the time I spent at Ambletern. I can assure you, you're not going to get the full story from Dorothy—"

I erased it.

The remaining voice mails were from Asa. He recounted, in a series of patchy, broken-up messages, the latest. Frances had contacted the rest of the agents at Rankin Lewis, and he'd been kicked out of the building. No matter—he was now happily fielding calls from every cable and Internet news outlet in existence. We were officially in business.

"This thing has exploded," he said in his final, breathless call. "It's huge. And, by the way, crucial point: Pelham Sound is one thousand percent still on board with us. They *love* the pages. They're upping the publicity budget; you're going to be everywhere, at every show, on every site."

A knot formed in my stomach.

Asa went on. "People are dying for this book. They're *salivating*."

I clenched my tingling hands into fists. What if I didn't want hype or publicity or talk shows? What if the only thing I wanted was to get this . . . this crushing weight that went along with being the daughter of Frances Ashley off my shoulders? I decided not to call Asa back. Not until I was sure I could put my feelings into words. Let him have his day in the sun.

I'd worked on the book until dinner, then slept until five o'clock the next morning, and, spurred on by Asa's news, I'd been writing ever since.

Koa bent over me and examined the cath taped to my arm. The scent of jasmine clung to him.

"Where does the doc think you were exposed to the lead?" he asked.

"Ski resort. They were removing lead paint, I think."

"Let's talk about something else," Doro said. "I know. Let's Google me."

I laughed. A touch uncomfortably, since I'd already done that. Extensively.

"You don't have to sacrifice yourself to make me feel better," I said.

"It'll be fun," she said. "And research for your book. We can have a shitty-childhood contest."

"I don't know," I said. It seemed unnecessarily cruel to delve into the freaky world of the Kitty Cultists in Doro's presence.

"We're doing this."

She popped out and returned a few minutes later, depositing my computer in my lap. I powered up the computer, and she settled herself back on the chaise—feet propped, arms crossed behind her head. "Do regale us with what the Kitty Cult says about Ms. Dorothy Kitchens, a.k.a. Kitten," she said.

Koa sighed. "This is too painful. I need coffee."

"Me too. Cream, no sugar," Doro said.

"Sure." He disappeared into the hallway.

It didn't take me long to find the top Kitty Cult fan sites: www.kittylitter.fan, www.kittenskills.fan, www.kittenandkafka.fan. They were forums, pretty well-trafficked ones too, essentially just the ramblings of kooks with either too little to do or psychological conditions that made them obsess over a book written forty years ago.

"Listen to this." I read to Doro. "'Kitten exemplifies the human struggle with God, with the government, with our need to constantly be transforming, metamorphosing into the latest, purest life form. Kitten is the existential end game, the apotheosis of our desires, the antithesis of our strivings. What Jesus meant when he said, *Anyone who wants to see the kingdom of heaven must become like a little child.*'"

Doro shook her head.

"Do you realize these people have the right to vote?" I said.

"I think it means kids can get away with shit because they're kids. They act out of the id, a pure place. And even if they kill, it's only because that's what's needed." She looked at me. "They're what we all want to be."

"I guess."

"It's kind of a beautiful thought."

"Not sure I'm with you there. You want to hear the rest?"

"Sure."

"Okay." I swallowed. "They say you killed your friend, Kimmy. They say you hurt Frances when she was living here, maybe even tried to kill her, and she wrote the book to get revenge. This one says you somehow got into the jail cell where they were holding Vera Baker, Kimmy's mother, and killed her as well."

She laughed, a short harsh sound. "Impressive."

I went on, clicking on more links. "This one says you're responsible for two coeds who went missing back in 1993 from a college in Savannah—"

"Right. I drove to Savannah, kidnapped them, brought them back here, and stuffed them in the cellar."

Koa walked back in with two mugs. He gave one to Doro, then to me, then checked the bag hanging over my head.

"Almost a third of the way. You feeling okay?"

"Never better."

"Meg was just telling me about all the murders I've committed."

He sat on a huge carved-mahogany chair and slurped his coffee. "Oh, well. By all means, carry on."

I gaped at the computer screen. "Says here you killed your father." I glanced at Doro and noticed she'd gone very still.

"Oh, God, Doro, I'm so sorry," I said. "I shouldn't have read that one. I'm such an idiot."

She gave me a rueful smile. "No, it's okay. Hearing that again . . . that people actually think I could kill my own father . . . it's hard. I guess I wasn't ready, after all. It's good to remember why I closed the hotel." She put down her mug. "This place was my dad's heart. It took a lot of energy and money to keep it going, and he did what he had to do. He let them come and play their games. Live out their fantasies."

She toyed with a velvet tassel on a cushion.

"He used to take on this persona when guests were around . . . this meek, cowed man, like Herb Murphy in the book. He would skulk around the grounds, doing little needless repairs. Generally spooking people, which they loved, of course." She sighed. "He used to hammer the hurricane boards into the windows. Totally freaked the guests out."

"What about you?" I asked. "Did you ever play Kitten?"

"Not intentionally. But the truth was, it didn't matter what I did. If I was quiet, they thought I was creepy. If I was friendly, they'd say I was manipulative. It was a game I couldn't win. I didn't really understand what was going on, not until I was eleven or twelve and I actually read the book."

"Were you angry then?"

She looked thoughtful. "In a weird way, I felt honored. I know it's messed up. But I didn't have a mother, and I was a lonely kid. Being Kitten rescued me, in a way. It gave me an identity. Made me feel special. I had some fun with it too." She laughed. "There was this one family, the Darnells. They had a son about my age. Pete. They came every summer, and Pete and I were friends. Or so I thought.

"The summer we were sixteen, he seemed different. Whenever we were around other kids, he made a big deal out of talking to me. And bringing up the book. It was like, in some twisted way, he was suddenly this big shot because we were friends."

"Oh, Doro."

"I thought he was different, but he was just like everybody else, and it made things strange between us. Not that it's a federal crime, reading *Kitten*. Or even drawing certain conclusions about me." She sighed. "But then he started in with the questions . . . about Kimmy, the Native American stuff. I was crushed.

"One day, I said I'd show him where Kimmy's ghost walked around in the marsh. I told him he'd have to be there, waiting for me, at midnight. He had to be naked, though, because Kimmy could sense he wasn't Native, like I was, from his white-man clothes."

She sent me a rueful grin. I glanced at Koa, still sitting in the shadows of the room. He hadn't moved.

"At that time of year, at midnight, the tide rises in the marsh like a freight train. Around one or two, Pete came dragging back to the hotel, half-drowned, covered in mosquito bites and mud. I know because I saw him from my window. He wouldn't tell his parents where he'd been, he was so ashamed. But he was quite pleasant to me at breakfast the next morning. Didn't ask me another thing about Kim."

I nestled back onto the cushiony arm of the sofa. So Doro had learned the hard way to take care of herself. I guess I shouldn't have been surprised.

"Did the two of you stay in touch?" I asked.

She gazed past me. "No."

"What happened to him?"

"He married, I think. Moved." She twirled a strand of hair absently. "I spoke to him once after that. We actually . . ." She stopped.

I tried to keep my voice light. "You what?"

She fluttered her hand, as if to wave off the line of questioning. "Nothing. It was a bad idea, having any contact with him."

"I'm sorry," I said.

"Anyway. That's what really killed my father. The tricks. The harassment. Everyone coming to Bonny, expecting us to be characters in a book. To playact for them."

She was staring at the floor, gone someplace else in her mind. "Sometimes, in our lives, we do what other people want us to. Simply because we can't muster the strength to go another, braver way." She dabbed at the corner of one eye. "My father wanted to return this island to what it had been, before the white man came. Before the missionaries, before the government. He wanted Bonny Island to be a refuge and a home for indigenous people. But he didn't think he would be successful without the Cultists and their money. So he let them use him. And it killed him."

I was quiet.

"It was heart trouble, that's what the doctors said. And they were right. His heart was broken."

"Was that when he brought the lawsuit against Frances? All those years after the book was published?"

Her head jerked up. "How do you know about that?"

"Asa told me."

She bit her lip. "All those records were closed. Or they were supposed to be. There was a gag order."

The air in the room had grown still and heavy. The sharp smell of must and mildew tickled my nose. The IV bag had flattened out, but Koa hadn't noticed. He was hunched over his phone, engrossed in something.

"I respect that, Doro." I looked down at my laptop. "But it's part of what Frances did to your family," I went on carefully. "It's part of your story. I wish you would tell me."

"Are you telling every part of your story in that book?"

I opened my mouth, then closed it.

"Exactly." She leveled a look at me. "They don't get everything from us, do they?"

I swallowed.

"So," she said. "Tell me who else I supposedly killed."

I looked down at my screen. She wasn't going to budge. If I wanted to know more about the lawsuit, I was going to have to get it from another source. I might not put it in the book—in fact, I wouldn't if it violated her privacy—but, chalk it up to morbid curiosity, I was itching to know what had happened.

"Meg?" Doro said.

I scrolled randomly across the site, my vision a blur. "Um. You killed a National Parks employee."

"Not yet. But tomorrow's another day."

"Okay. Here we go. There also appears to be speculation that you killed Kimmy's father, Neal Dwayne Baker."

I was dimly aware, across the room, of Koa moving.

Doro snorted. "He abandoned his family when Kimmy was a baby. I don't know where he moved, I don't even think Kimmy knew where he ended up. My father said he was a bum."

"So he's still alive?" I tapped out a search.

"As far as I know, yes. I certainly didn't kill him."

"Okay. Here we go. Kimmy's father . . ." My voice trailed off as the list of search results for Neal Dwayne Baker loaded on the screen. Out of the entire list there was only one headline that looked promising—a news feature written for a local paper on a new cancer facility in Corpus Christi, Texas.

Across the room, I sensed movement. I glanced over. Koa was staring at me with the most peculiar expression. A look of such intensity that my heart thudded. I dropped my eyes back down to my laptop screen. Silently scanned the article that had loaded:

Resident Neal D. Baker, 84, a retired chiropractor
undergoing treatment for lung cancer, sings the
praises of the staff at the recently opened Pine

Grove Cancer Center. "I've met some of the most caring people in this place. I consider one or two of them family. Closer than family."

My eyes slid back to Koa. He was still staring at me, his mouth set in a grim line. I stared back, my mind racing. Neal Baker, Kimmy's father, was the man Koa had told me about that night in the kitchen. The patient at his facility, who'd inspired Koa to come to Bonny and turn his life around.

Koa knew Kimmy Baker's father.

"Ah," I said. As thoughts whirled through my brain, I glanced at Doro. Her head was tilted back, eyes closed.

Did she have any idea that Koa was here because of Kimmy's father? Surely she would've mentioned that back when we discussed him before. And if she didn't know about their connection, was I obligated to tell her? She'd suffered so much because of people's whims and ulterior motives. But dammit, I had no interest in ratting out Koa or causing any trouble between him and Doro. And what would I say, anyway?

Just want to let you know Koa is tight with the father of the little girl everybody thinks you murdered.

That could not go over well. Not in any scenario.

I decided to sidestep the issue, for the time being. I'd get Koa to tell me what the hell he was doing here and then figure out what to do.

"No luck," I said. "I can't seem to find anything about Kim's father."

Koa leapt up and crossed the room. He checked the bag, rattled the IV stand beside me. "How are you feeling?" he asked briskly.

"Good," I said. Snapped the laptop shut. "Good."

"Ready to get this cath out?"

"Is it done?"

He didn't meet my eyes, just dropped beside me and motioned for my arm. I offered it to him, and, unceremoniously, he ripped off the tape.

"Ow," I said.

Doro stood, was stretching and going to collect Koa's mug. "Take it easy on her, Koa."

"I'm fine," I said.

Koa removed the needle. A drop of blood oozed from the hole in my arm and dripped down to my wrist. He grabbed my arm, pulled it straight, and smacked a bandage over the spot. I tried to pull away, but he didn't release me. His fingers dug into my arms until I lifted my eyes to meet his. In them, I saw a glint that was clearly a warning.

KITTEN

—FROM CHAPTER 10

Herb Murphy announced at breakfast that he felt the early signs of a hurricane. The remaining guests—most of them still pale and dyspeptic from the ravages of the stomach virus—trudged to their rooms to pack their belongings.

A grim-faced Delia pulled Herb into the library, and Fay heard the woman's high, sharp voice. She hustled Kitten away, down to the dock to see everyone off.

"She's angry," Herb told Fay when he joined them later. He waved at the departing guests. No one waved back.

For a minute Fay couldn't formulate a reply. Then she managed, "I suppose it's because some of them will expect a refund. It's hard to believe—the sky is as blue as can be."

Herb looked at her for a moment, like he didn't comprehend her words. Then he glanced over at Kitten. She had climbed one of the slick piers and was balancing perfectly on its top, on her toes, arms out like a trapeze artist.

"Storm's still a ways off."

Ashley, Frances. *Kitten*. New York: Drake, Richards and Weems, 1976. Print.

Chapter Twenty-Two

It had been two days since I figured out Koa knew Neal Dwayne Baker, but even then, I didn't have any actual proof of their connection. Well, none other than the look on Koa's face when he realized I'd stumbled upon Baker's blurb on the Internet.

After ripping out my IV, he had practically run out of the house, and I hadn't seen a trace of him since. Which was probably all the answer I needed—Koa was linked to Neal Baker, maybe even in a father-son sort of way, and he had, in all probability, come to Bonny at the behest of the man.

The motivation was murkier. But only two options seemed viable: he was on a mission either to gather information on Doro or to execute some sort of revenge for Kimmy's death.

He was supposed to give me my final treatment for the week either today or tomorrow. Which was definitely going to be awkward. Would he talk to me or ignore the Neal Baker situation completely? Maybe I should take the lead and address it head-on, I thought. I'd either clear the air or blow the whole damn thing up.

I needed answers. Well, scratch that—I wanted answers. What I *needed* to do was get this book finished. When I spotted an email in my inbox from Asa, relief flooded me.

> Stellar stuff, Meg. You're a magician. Keep going. Don't stop, don't let up. I want a detailed blow-by-blow on how Frances screwed the whole Kitchens family over. And look, I'm not going to bother you anymore. No more needy voice mails, scout's honor. I'll handle the Frances fallout. You just work. Cheers, Asa.

The poor guy sounded desperate. Frances had probably set her team of lawyers on him, deluged him with threatening emails and letters. I was willing to bet she'd called him as well, treated him to one of her famous terrifying tirades.

I closed my computer and sat back in the desk chair. Chewed on my thumbnail. I thought I should get in a few more *Kitten* chapters before breakfast. I could afford to take a break. I'd already worked on my book for the past hour and a half, and was close to finishing the full draft in the next day or so.

I reached for *Kitten*, found the last dog-eared page, and settled down to read. After a couple of paragraphs, however, something began to nag at me. I stared at the words. The page was pristine. No annotation marred the spaces. Susan Doucette hadn't underlined a single sentence or scribbled any notes in the margins. Not on this page or in the previous chapter.

I pushed myself against the bank of pillows and flipped through the next chapters. All the annotations were gone. The margins were blank, no words circled or underlined. I paged to the end of the book. Nothing. It was as if Susan Doucette had given up.

A coil of tension tightened inside me. I held my place and flipped to the cover page. It was blank.

No Susan Doucette, Age Twelve.

No Aunt Jo.

I thumbed through the first half of the book, frantically searching for any trace of Susan. There were no notes or underlined passages. It was all gone.

I scrambled up and ran out of the room. Clattered down the steps and out the front door. Esther was on the front porch, pushing a mop over the red tiles, having an animated conversation with what appeared to be an invisible person. I positioned myself in her path, fists planted on my hips.

"I'll call you back." Esther touched the Bluetooth in her ear. "Everything all right, Miss Meg?"

I held up the paperback. "Where's my book?"

"Miss Meg—"

"What have you done with it?"

Her face darkened. "I'm sorry. Really sorry, Miss Meg."

"It's fine, just . . . just tell me what happened and, for God's sake, stop . . . Just call me Meg, okay?"

She dunked the mop in the pail. "I was cleaning your room. Your bathroom, and I saw the book by the tub. I'd never read it, so I picked it up and sort of . . . went through it."

"Okay."

"But I . . . I dropped it in the toilet, Miss—Meg. I truly apologize. It was messed up bad. Completely soaked. I told Doro about it, and she said she'd get another copy from the basement. She used to sell them, you know, to the tourists and whatnot and even autograph them. That one's from her leftover supply."

I paused, flummoxed. It was a plausible enough story. So why didn't I believe her?

She put one gnarled hand over her heart. "Was that a special book? I didn't know."

I shook my head. "It's okay, it really is. I'll talk to Doro. But . . ." I cocked my head. "You wouldn't happen to have the book, would you? I had made some notes in it. Some important notes, and I'd like to see if I could retrieve them."

She looked stricken. "I'm sorry. I . . ."

"What?"

"Koa was burning the garbage earlier, when I was cleaning, and I threw it in the fire along with the rest of the trash."

I lifted my eyebrows.

"So sorry."

I stared at her for an uncomfortable minute. She didn't flinch.

As I turned to go, I could feel her eyes on me. I turned back. She was watching me—only her hand had dropped from her chest, and her face looked suddenly and inexplicably placid. I hurried to the library and was about to rap on the door when I heard voices coming from inside. Doro's, then Koa's. My hand froze in midair.

"I don't think that's a wise move," I heard him say.

There was a pause, then Doro said something I couldn't hear.

"Doro," he cut in. "I really don't think you want to do that." His voice had a deliberate, ominous tone to it. Maybe even threatening—I couldn't tell for sure.

I waited, hoping for more. What was he saying that Doro shouldn't do? Call Neal Baker? Or something to do with me? The possibilities seemed hopelessly unclear. I had no idea what anyone around here was up to.

It dawned on me, then, that no one was saying anything, that their conversation was over, and Koa might be headed for the door. Panicked, I knocked quickly on the door. It swung open.

"Hi," Koa said.

"Sorry. Uh . . ." I peered around him. "Is Doro there? I mean, available?"

"Come in, Meg," I heard her trill.

Koa stepped aside, let me pass.

The dusty, wood-paneled room was lined, ceiling to floor, with ancient-looking books. The tall, narrow windows were shuttered and the floors bare wood except for a yellowed zebra hide. Toward the rear of the room, near the far wall of books, was an old oak desk.

A large leather checkbook lay open in the middle of the desk, flanked by precarious towers of paper. It appeared Esther hadn't been in here to clean, in maybe . . . forever. Behind the desk, Doro nodded a greeting. A pair of green-rimmed reading glasses perched at the end of her nose. Her hair looked windblown, even though she was sitting inside.

"Morning," she said. "How are you feeling?"

"Better, thanks. I was wondering if I could speak to you about something."

"Of course. You can talk to me about anything. Anytime."

"Okay," I said. "I just talked to Esther."

Her eyes traveled to the paperback tucked underneath my arm. "Oh, dear."

"She told me what happened."

She removed her glasses and tapped them on the desk. "You know, I used to order them in bulk from the publisher. Nothing better than a souvenir copy of *Kitten* signed by the little devil-girl herself, right? I happen to have boxes of them left over from back then. So when you came back from the hospital, I rummaged around and found one just like it."

I laid the book on the desk. "Not exactly."

"What do you mean?" Her eyes went wide.

I cleared my throat. "It's just . . . that book, the one that got ruined, it was my mother's. So, it felt a little sentimental, I guess."

Her brows knit together. "Really? You're sentimental about one of Frances's books?"

She studied me. I shrugged. Offered a hangdog smile.

"Okay, well." She put her hands on the desk. "I had no idea. I thought I could take care of it without bothering you." Her face was neutral, but her blue eyes lasered into mine.

I swallowed. "It's just . . . You should've said something. There's no reason to keep secrets from me."

She pushed her hair back from her face. "You're absolutely right. Absolutely right. I was trying to protect Esther. She's been with me for a long time."

I wavered. I was starting to feel like I was being an asshole.

"I'm glad you felt like you could come to me with this. I want you to feel that way, that we're friends. That you can trust me. Because you can."

"Okay."

"In fact"—she stood—"I want to trust you with something too."

I raised my eyebrows.

"Ambletern's attic. It's full of boxes. Guest registers, ledgers. Odds and ends." Her eyes were bright. "I don't know if there's anything up there that relates to your research. But you're welcome to rummage around, if you think there is."

"Thank you. I will."

I headed back upstairs, tossed the replacement book on a table, and dropped on the bed. I flipped open my laptop, gnawing at the inside of my lip and thinking. I didn't believe Esther, not for one minute. Or Doro. The hitch was, there was only one thing that made that particular paperback of *Kitten* unique.

Susan's notes.

I adjusted the screen on my laptop, went to Facebook, and typed her name.

Assuming Aunt Jo had given her darling niece a brand-spanking-new book, Susan had been twelve in 2007, which made her roughly twenty-one now.

Eight Susan Doucettes popped up, none with the middle name Evelyn. Six of the pages were public, only two were the right age. One, a redhead with yellow cat glasses and a houseful of actual cats. The other looked like she could hang with Aurora's Glitter Girls.

This Susan Doucette wasn't age twelve anymore, that was for damn sure. Her profile was full of pictures of her partying—taking bong rips, throwing back shots, guzzling from kegs. She had smudged eyeliner, cropped tops that showed too much under-boob, side-boob, plain old boob. She was all sticky coral lips and sweaty hair, perpetually surrounded by her blurred-out girl squad. I went through the pictures in a haze of nostalgia. I used to take pictures like this, but it seemed like a lifetime ago.

This Susan Doucette had over a thousand friends and was in her junior year at Georgia Southern, double majoring in English lit and women's studies. Cat Lady Susan only had a handful of posts—cats, cats, and more cats—and thirty-one friends. Both Susans' contact information was sparse—no emails for either one of them. I requested friend status with both, then clicked over to my page.

In my photos, I found a picture of me and Frances from about six years ago at an awards ceremony. I was wearing a strapless yellow dress and my hair was swept up in an artfully messy twist. Frances was holding a plaque—she must've won something that night, I didn't remember. Come to think of it, I didn't remember anything about the night—which hotel ballroom we'd been in, what we'd eaten or drunk. How I'd felt—if I was proud or indifferent or uncomfortable in the strapless dress. We were smiling, but that didn't mean anything. We always smiled when a camera flashed.

It didn't matter what that night had been about. What mattered was that the picture made it appear that Frances and I were close. I made it my cover photo and waited for both Susan Doucettes to accept my invitations.

KITTEN

—FROM CHAPTER 11

Herb had said it was the change in the barometric pressure that had made the guests sick. He said it with such an air of finality, Fay didn't argue.

But she knew better. It had been Kitten's tarts. She must've put something in them—acorns, maybe. Fay knew the guests suspected the girl of murdering Cappie. Kitten was the real reason the guests had left.

The days that followed felt endless. Every morning after breakfast, Herb went out to haul up the plywood storm panels stored in the cellar and lay them out on the lawn in their places below the windows. Delia scolded him for it, saying he was imagining things and scaring their daughter and that he must put a stop to this nonsense immediately. He ignored her and went about his task. Delia locked herself in the library.

Ashley, Frances. *Kitten*. New York: Drake, Richards and Weems, 1976. Print.

Chapter Twenty-Three

After forty minutes of obsessively refreshing both Susan Doucettes' Facebook pages, I had bitten all my fingernails down to ragged half-moons and neither had accepted my friend request. I took a bathroom break and then, for what seemed like the millionth time, clicked on Cat Lady Susan's page. I hit the Message button.

Hi Susan, I hope you get this message. My name is Meg Ashley. I'm the daughter of Frances Ashley, the author of Kitten. I'm writing a book about my mother, and I was wondering

My fingers froze on the keyboard. If Susan was a member of the Kitty Cult, she worshipped the ground my mother walked on. There was little chance she'd have any part of a nasty tell-all from her hero's ungrateful daughter. She might even go so far as to try to discredit what I was doing.

Or—who knows—maybe she'd go full-on *Housewives* and make up a bunch of baloney to get more attention.

I deleted the message and slammed my laptop closed. One thing I knew: I had to wait. I needed to let Susan Doucette, whichever one it turned out to be, come to me. In the meantime, I needed a break. I needed a break from my problems. I needed to see the foal.

I climbed out of bed and threw on a long-sleeve T-shirt, a pair of yoga pants, and sneakers. I might suffocate from the heat, but if I ran across another rattlesnake, that fucker wouldn't be able to find an inch of bare skin. I jammed a baseball cap on my head, threading my tangled ponytail through the hole in back, and doused every inch of my body with bug repellent.

Outside, the humidity-thickened air closed around me. It sank into the pores of my face, filled my lungs, and dampened my clothes. If I found the horses, maybe I'd find Koa. I knew he and Doro kept them on a rotation among about four grazing sites around the island. They should be in the center now, in the few patchy spots of grass that bordered the forest between Koa's cabin and the mission ruins.

I set off in that direction, keeping to the main road that bisected the island. It was the road Koa had driven me on when I first came to Bonny. After a good forty minutes, when I was thoroughly coated in sweat and dust, I caught a glimpse of a chestnut flank and swishing tail through the brush to my right. I slowed my pace. The horses were here, just as I thought, weaving their way through the trees, browsing in pools of sunlight. I crept closer, searching through the herd for the roan mare or the foal.

And then I saw her. The foal, butting against her mother's belly, trying to nurse. The mare kept walking away. I pressed myself against the rough bark of a gnarled old oak and watched the foal trot after her.

"C'mon," I muttered. "Have a heart."

I heard a scrape of metal against dirt, then saw Koa on the opposite side of the herd, his trusty snake-killing shovel arcing over his head. I sucked in my breath and pressed myself against the tree. He circled around, then stopped a couple of yards away from my hiding spot.

"Meg," he said. "Hey."

I stepped away from the tree. "Oh, hey."

We stared awkwardly at each other.

"So, you saw me right off?" I said. "I guess I suck at hiding."

"Well, you kind of"—he gestured with his free hand—"don't blend into the woodland habitat too well."

Was that a compliment? Or just Koa being blunt? Regardless, I felt myself go warmer than I already was.

"I was thinking I could find the foal." I smiled at him. "I wanted to check on her. See how she was doing."

"Yeah. I was checking on her too."

I twisted my fingers. "Looks like her mom's kind of a deadbeat."

"Give her time. Sometimes they come around." His eyes dropped briefly down to the yoga pants, then back up to my face. He adjusted the shovel.

"Also, to be truthful, I was hoping to find you," I started. "I wanted to tell you not to worry. I'm not going to tell Doro you know Kim Baker's father."

"Okay."

"I mean, I don't want to tell her . . ."

He started to say something.

". . . that Neal Baker thought of you as family. As a son."

His eyes slid away from me. He swung the shovel down to the ground. Planted it with a *whump*.

"Although," I went on, "you realize, she's a smart woman; she knows how Google works, and she's going to stumble across the same information I stumbled across, if she hasn't already. And when she does, she's going to flip out."

His eyes stayed unreadable.

"Unless she's already found out, and that's what you guys were talking about in the library earlier."

"We were just talking about the horses."

"Koa, come on. I know it's none of my business, but we're friends, right? You trusted me enough to tell me about him that night in the kitchen."

His eyes met mine. "We're friends."

"Then talk to me. Did Neal Baker send you to Bonny Island to find out who killed his daughter?"

He shifted. "I can't say. I made a promise I have to keep."

I nodded. Just when I thought I had him on the ropes, this guy went and showed just what a loyal, steadfast person he could be. Shit.

"But even if I was here for that," he said, "why would you care? It doesn't have anything to do with your book."

"Well, no. Not directly."

"And, if I may be so bold, it seems like you're doing your own Sherlock Holmes–ing around here, too."

His face might've been indecipherable, but his eyes were soft, the same way they were the other night at his cabin, after we'd rescued the foal. I fought the urge to run to him and put my hands on his face. Breathe in his jasmine scent and bare my soul—about the paperback, Esther and Doro, and the way it seemed like the island was messing with my head. But I couldn't. I shouldn't. Getting physical with this guy would just cloud things. I wrapped my arms around my torso, just in case my hands suddenly started acting independently of my brain.

I sighed. "So I guess we both have . . . extracurricular reasons for being here that we don't want to discuss. But can you promise me one thing?"

"What?"

"Don't hurt Doro. She doesn't deserve that."

He regarded me with a look I couldn't quite identify. "I assure you, I don't want to hurt Doro." He hesitated. "Or you. That's why I think we should just . . . play it smart. In terms of the way we"—he gestured between himself and me—"interact. I don't think we should—"

Doro broke through the trees, wiping her forehead with a bandanna. She stuffed it in her back pocket and looked from me to Koa. "Who needs to play it smart?"

"Oh, hey, Doro," Koa said in an unnaturally loud voice. "We were just talking."

I grimaced. What a terrible liar.

"I was just out for a run," I said. "And bumped into Koa." I glanced at him. "I was telling Koa about my best friend. She got a divorce and wants to date again."

"Ah." Doro's head swiveled from me to Koa. "Okay."

The foal chose that moment to butt her bony head up under my arm, her ears swinging forward. I sprang away, but she click-clacked her hooves, lining them up with her body, and came at me again. When her oversize nose tried to snuffle under my shirt, Doro crowed.

"Will you look at that?" She put her hand out to stroke the foal. The horse danced away from her, circling around, and came at me again. I felt Doro's eyes move from me to the foal and then back again. "She really likes you."

Our eyes met.

Then a low, mechanical rumble reverberated through the woods. Doro craned her neck and peered through the thicket of trees. The foal skittered back to the rest of the herd, just as one of Ambletern's Jeeps burst into view. Laila was at the wheel.

She fumbled with the clutch, and the Jeep skittered to a halt, then died. "Goddammit!" she chirped and hit the wheel with both hands.

We formed a half ring around the car, and she blinked out at us.

"There's a guest, Doro," she said. "Two of them. Captain Mike just dropped them at the dock."

Doro pushed a couple of blonde strands behind her bandanna. "We're closed to guests," she said.

Laila nodded. "I told them that, but she . . . the woman insisted."

Doro cut in. "I don't care what she says, Laila. It's my hotel, and I say it's closed. Go back. Radio Mike. Tell him I'll pay him for the extra fuel. And tell them I said the hotel is closed."

Laila's eyes slid to me, then back to Doro. Her voice lowered. "They came for her. For Meg. It's her mother."

KITTEN

—FROM CHAPTER 12

That night, when Fay checked on Kitten, she found the child standing in the middle of the room, every one of her windows flung open. She looked like a little marble statue, staring out into the dark.

Fay moved to the window that faced north, over the marsh. Looking down over the lawn, she saw the rectangles of plywood, the storm panels Herb had laid out on the grass, ready to be fitted to the windows. She pulled down the sash and drew the bolt and hurried Kitten to bed.

The next morning, rising before dawn, Fay saw that Herb Murphy had drilled every one of the panels to Kitten's bedroom windows sometime in the night.

Ashley, Frances. *Kitten*. New York: Drake, Richards and Weems, 1976. Print.

Chapter Twenty-Four

Esther met us on the porch, her eyes starry, her face wreathed in smiles. She was wringing her hands maniacally.

"I see you've met my mother," I said.

"I did," she crowed. "And who would have thought it—me, Esther Tafton, meeting Frances Ashley? She said she'd sign a book for me, if I wanted."

"How nice," I said.

Doro flung open the heavy front door and strode into the shadowy foyer. Koa and I followed, Laila and Esther bringing up the rear. I tried to maintain my breathing. I was safe. These people wouldn't let Frances come down here and destroy me. They were my friends.

When I saw her, I stopped. Let the familiar burning sensation rip through me. It was always the same, the first millisecond of laying my eyes on my mother felt like somebody had pressed defibrillator paddles against my chest, sent a slug of electricity through me. Pushing out my breath and wiping my brain.

I concentrated on staying vertical. The last thing I needed was another fainting spell. I had to be strong now. Fight.

On first inspection, Frances looked the same as always. Tall. On the too-thin side of svelte. Prettier and younger looking than most women her age. She wore an expensive emerald-green dress and stilettos. Crimson lipstick. Batwing sweep of eyeliner. Today, though, there was one significant difference about my mother's appearance: her red hair, which was usually smoothed back in her impeccable signature chignon, tumbled over her shoulders instead, in an avalanche of messy waves. This made her look impossibly sexy, like she'd just been making out with her boyfriend in the backseat of his car. It was wholly disconcerting.

For some reason, it infuriated me.

And then another thing struck me. Her eyes were wide and bright with unshed tears. Which was not, on any level, normal. My mother never cried.

She was drifting along the walls, surveying the room. Occasionally, she would lower her hand to a picture frame or paperweight, then withdraw it before she actually made contact. It was like the room fascinated her—pulling her in and repelling her at the same.

One finger pressed her lips. They appeared to be trembling. She turned to us, her audience.

Here we go.

"It's just like I remember," she said in a tremulous whisper. The sun, leaking through a crack in the heavy curtains, bathed her in a weak, watery light. She was either genuinely moved or putting on a show for the crowd. I was inclined toward the latter, but either way, it was a hell of a thing to witness Frances Ashley welling up.

I glanced across the room. Benoît, a skinny man in his midforties with a mop of dark curls and an overly tailored Italian suit, receded into the shadows beside a wing chair. *Good.* That's where he belonged. In the background. He raised a hand and sent me what he probably considered a stepfatherly smile. I looked away.

Beside me, Doro planted her hands on her hips, and I felt a tidal wave of confidence wash over me. Next to Frances, she looked like some kind of bedraggled vagabond. Her shirt was dirty. Her work pants were cinched up with a cracked leather belt. My mother stopped at the gleaming bar and glanced across the room at her. I wondered, wildly, for a moment if the two of them would crouch and begin circling like a couple of cage fighters.

I clenched my fists. Open and closed, open and closed. Slow and easy. The neuropathy hadn't started up yet, but it would. Any minute now.

"Doro," Frances said and, in the same instant, flew across the room to her. She took the other woman in her arms and hugged her—the real deal with both arms and full-body contact—then pulled back and went in for round two. I blinked in disbelief. Who was this person—this crier and now, apparently, hugger? I didn't recognize her.

Meanwhile, Esther made a circuit around the room, flinging open all the curtains. The late-afternoon sunlight drenched the walls and rugs. Frances squinted and turned her face into the glare.

"Oh, yes! My God, yes! I haven't felt sun like that in years." She closed her eyes. She clasped her hands in front of her. A huge diamond flashed. "It's divine. Makes you want to shuck off your skivvies and run absolutely wild." She giggled and her eyes snapped open again. "I am so happy to have met you all—Esther and Laila and Koa. And I'm horrified I'm descending on you with no warning. I'm so sorry about that," she said, and now her voice was back to its usual part-Southern, part-faux-European timbre. "My husband and I heard Megan was here, and we had to see her. Unfortunately, she wasn't able to make our wedding."

"I wasn't invited," I said. All the heads in the room swiveled to me.

"Megan. Darling." She walked to me and hugged me too, just like Doro. Her loose hair swung into my face. It smelled like expensive shampoo and her perfume. She held me by the arms. "You're looking so well. Lovely. Robust."

I raised my eyebrows. "Robust?"

She shook me and giggled playfully. "It's an adjective meaning strong and healthy. I meant you look perfect, of course."

That's when my fingers went. They began to tingle, then the whole length of my right arm. I felt wrung out and exhausted. Confused by my mother's game. I wanted to scream.

"What are you doing here?" I tried to keep my voice modulated.

"I said, we missed you at the wedding. It was . . ." She gave the room a smile. "Hard, not having you there."

I pressed my lips together. She wanted this, she wanted me to get angry and fight with her. She wanted me to lose my shit in front of all these people, but I wouldn't. I wouldn't give her the pleasure.

"I'm sorry I missed it," I said. "Congratulations to you both. Benoît?" The mop-haired man brightened in the corner. "I can't tell you how thrilled I am to have another stepfather."

Out of the corner of my eye, I saw Frances frown. But I knew she wasn't upset. I'd just given her the dig she'd been waiting for. But that was it—that was all she was getting. If she was going to play nicey-nice, so would I.

"As much as I'd love to spend more time with you and Benoît," I went on, "it's going to be impossible. Doro closed Ambletern months ago, and she can't accommodate guests any longer."

Frances looked crestfallen. "Oh, that's bad news. I'd looked forward to spending a day or two here, visiting our old haunts." She flashed a hopeful smile toward Doro. "Are you sure you can't put up with us for just a few days before we have to whisk Megan away?"

"I'm not leaving," I replied. "You are, but I'm not."

I could've sworn I heard Esther or Laila make a *tsk-tsk*ing sound behind me. I didn't care. They had no idea what—who—I was dealing with.

Doro fished out a small white business card from the desk and handed it to Benoît.

"It's a bed-and-breakfast on the main street in St. Marys," she said. "I'll call Mike and have him ferry you back. Tell the owner I sent you, and maybe she'll take off ten percent. Or maybe she'll charge you double. She's never really been thrilled about all the business your wife had a hand in bringing to this place."

"Touché," Frances said as Benoît started toward her, holding out the card like a puppy who'd just fetched a stick. She took it and gave him a brief, soulful look. I sighed audibly.

"Megan, do you think we could speak in private?" Frances was tracing the business card now and had her eyes fixed on me.

"We can talk here," I said. "These are my friends."

She said nothing, but her gaze was steady.

I inhaled deeply, evenly. "Frances, I want you to hear me."

"I'm listening."

"I am writing this book. I'm writing it, and you know why, and there's nothing you can do to stop me."

She smiled. And executed a deft, yet somehow careless, hair toss. "We don't need to go into the book right now. It's beside the point."

"It's not beside the point, Frances. It's the only point. It's why you came here."

Her voice stayed maddeningly even. "I came because you missed my wedding, and I was heartbroken over it."

"No you weren't." I was going to cry. Or throw something. I could feel it. The neuropathy was raging, and I could feel my control slipping. She was doing it again—manipulating me. Twisting things in front of people who didn't know any better. Baiting me.

"I was," she said.

"You missed Edgar's funeral," I burst out.

Her lips parted.

"Edgar died, and instead of attending his memorial, you went on your honeymoon."

Her chin went up, ever so slightly.

"If it was the first time you'd done something like that, I'd let it go. But it isn't close to the first time, is it? It's been our life, from the beginning. So don't play innocent."

"I never claimed to be innocent." Her eyes darted toward the others, but she soldiered on. "But you don't have to do this, Meg, just to get back at me."

"It won't be as bad as you think," I said in a softer voice, remembering Asa's words. "It'll hurt at first, like when you rip off a Band-Aid."

She pressed her lips into a tight line.

"Just think of all the publicity. That should lessen the sting."

My voice was trembling, but I meant what I was saying. I wouldn't be swayed or cajoled or bullied into changing my mind. I was going to sever our relationship, once and for all. And I was going to do it with a book.

Out of the corner of my eye, I saw Esther and Laila slip out of the room. Then Koa trailed behind them, hesitating under the arched opening. I caught his eye. He looked torn, like he wanted to help, and somehow that broke my heart even more.

I looked away. There was nothing he could do. My mother could never be trusted. I would always be alone.

"Anyway." I turned to Doro. "This is Doro's place, and she has the final say."

Doro laid a hand on my shoulder. It felt warm. Solid.

"Actually, Meg, I say the decision is yours. You have a lot of research to do for your book. Maybe your mother could help you. Share what she knows about Bonny Island and Ambletern and what happened all those years ago. I could make an exception and let her stay."

Frances brightened, and she turned to Benoît.

Keep your enemies close. That had to be Doro's angle.

I jutted my chin at Benoît. "But he has to go."

Frances shook her head. "Absolutely not."

"If he goes, you can stay."

"No. I won't allow it."

Benoît met my gaze. I flipped him a mental bird, and, like he was some kind of circus-freak mind reader, he grinned back at me.

"It's your choice, Frances," I said. "Go home with him. Or stay here with me."

He looked down at his new wife. "I'll only be a phone call away. But you have to do this." He looked pointedly at me.

"Benoît," Frances sniffed pitifully.

God. My eyelids fluttered closed. What a performance.

"No," he said. "You're a strong woman. You can do this." He leaned in and kissed her, then glowered at me. "Take care of her."

"She'll be fine," I said.

"I'll call the ferry," Doro said and the two of them left.

In the salon, the air conditioning clicked on and began to grind away. Somewhere, a clock ticked ponderously. It was finally just the two of us. Frances's smile had vanished, her face settled into a collection of flat, hard planes. Her cold eyes glittered at me. This was the woman I knew. If she bared her teeth right now, I wouldn't have been surprised to see they'd transformed into fangs.

She crossed the room, and I flinched, steeling myself for the onslaught. She grabbed me around the shoulders and looked at me, her eyes hard.

"I'm so happy to see you . . . looking so well," she declared. But her face didn't match her words. It was taut.

She pulled me in like before, crushing my body against hers. I felt her arms circle around me, desperately, it seemed, her hands grabbing at my shoulder blades. Then the pressure of a kiss on my temple. I held my breath and stayed very still. Something was different. Frances was different.

Crazy thoughts whirled in my head. Was it too late for us? Was it possible to think we could spend a couple of days together and actually change things between us?

Before I could take this line of thought any further, she put her mouth close to my ear.

"Megan, listen to me," she rasped in a voice so low I could barely hear it. "You're in danger here. I know you don't trust me, but you have to listen." Her voice dropped even lower. "You need to get out of here."

KITTEN

—from Chapter 13

Fay woke, her heart thundering. She raised a hand to her throat. It felt as if she'd been screaming while she slept.

It had been three days and nights since Herb had locked himself in the library with his wife. Fay hadn't left Kitten's side in all that time. She even slept on the uncomfortable chaise in the girl's bedroom, although she tossed restlessly, plagued by nightmares.

This night, Kitten's bedroom wasn't as dark as it should have been with the plywood storm panels blocking the windows. It was bathed in a silvery moonlight. The center window in the bay had been flung open and its panel pushed out. The room creaked, as the wind whipped around the eaves of the house and into the room where Kitten stood in the center. She was staring out the open window, her nightgown billowing.

"Kitten, darling," Fay croaked. "What have you done?"

The girl turned to face her. Her eyes were wide with fright. "I saw her. I saw Cappie."

Ashley, Frances. *Kitten*. New York: Drake, Richards and Weems, 1976. Print.

Chapter Twenty-Five

Up in my room, I drank one of Doro's mini whiskeys left over from the hospital and cursed my mother's name in as many creatively disgusting ways as I could think of. After about twenty minutes of that, I was still seething. I showered. Brushed my teeth and blew out my hair, then wandered back into my room. I did crunches until my abdomen knotted and then about ten woozy, drunken pushups.

My arms still smarted from where Frances had held me.

I'd lain down and fallen into a dizzying sleep when I felt my laptop buzz on my legs. My eyes flew open, and, on autopilot, I checked Facebook. I had a message. I bolted upright, shock jolting through me.

Cat Lady Susan had accepted my friend request.

And Glitter Girl Susan had sent me a message. I clicked on it with trembling fingers. It was short, just two lines, but I read them hungrily.

I know who you are. Don't contact me again.

My stomach leapt, and I tasted soured whiskey in my mouth. I pulled the computer closer, hovered my fingers over the keyboard for a couple of moments, then typed.

I have your copy of Kitten, Susan, from your Aunt Jo. I mean, I used to have it—it was stolen recently. Do you have any idea why anyone would do that?

I waited, chewing at a jagged piece of cuticle on the side of my thumb. The laptop buzzed.

I can't talk to you.

But she was talking to me. Which was something. I thought for a minute, then typed.

You're in the Kitty Cult, right?

Bag of dicks, she sent back.

Okay. A little defensive, considering her copy of *Kitten* resembled the fabled Velveteen Rabbit, well loved and worn to pieces.

But you used to be? I wrote.

I waited. There was no response, so I tried again.

Susan, please. I have to talk to you. Something's going on, and it's really weird.

I CAN'T.

No one has to know we've spoken. I know how to keep a secret, and, believe me, I have no interest in getting you in trouble. I just want to know about my mother and Dorothy and William Kitchens. The real story of Kitten. I read some of your notes, but I didn't get to them all. Can you just tell me—what exactly was your interest in them? It seemed like you were doing some kind of investigation. Can you tell me what you discovered? And how you figured it out?

The computer buzzed. Can't. Sorry.

I gazed out over the yard and the trees. A breeze stirred the hanging moss, and the early-morning light warmed the tabby walls of the house to a pinkish gray.

I'm writing my own book now.

No reply. Of course. What did Susan Doucette care about my petty, small-minded revenge book? I added to the single line.

I had never read Kitten until just recently. I happened to pick up your copy—your book from your Aunt Jo was on my mother's shelf. How did it end up in my mother's apartment in New York? Did you give it to her? I find that hard to believe you would do that. You did a lot of research, back then, maybe hit on something important. All I know is now the book's gone, and I want to know why. Don't you?

I held my breath.

They made me give it to them.

Who? I wrote.

Then came her reply. This is illegal, us talking.

I shot back, How is it illegal?

I signed an agreement I wouldn't talk.

The fuck . . .

About Kitten? How is that possible? Who made you sign that?

There was a long beat, then the answer buzzed back.

Rankin Lewis Literary.

When?

Six years ago.

My mother's literary agency made a teenage girl sign a gag order?

Nothing.

And confiscated your copy of Kitten? I asked.

Can't talk about it.

I sat back, staring at the chain of messages. I ran a hand over my mouth, then hunched forward.

We HAVE to talk, Susan, I typed. The book—your book was stolen a couple of days ago from my room in Ambletern on Bonny Island. I think Dorothy Kitchens might have done it.

Everybody blames Dorothy for everything.

You don't? I typed. And then, Just tell me who you think murdered Kim Baker/Cappie Strongbow. Just one word is all I need. One name.

Someone knocked on my door, and I scrambled up. Koa hoisted the IV stand and a fresh bag of chelation cocktail in greeting. His face was a careful blank.

"Come in," I said, annoyed.

I left the door open and while he was setting things up, I shut my computer, slid it under my pillow, and settled back.

"Writing?" he asked.

"Research." I offered my arm and our eyes met.

He went about his work, and then, after he checked to see the solution was dripping down the tubing, he put his hands on his hips.

"See you in two hours?"

"I'll be here." I held up my pierced, taped-up arm.

After he left, I pulled out my computer and pried it open, my whole body pulsing like one giant nerve ending. The screen blinked and flashed a notification:

Susan Doucette is offline.

KITTEN

—FROM CHAPTER 13

Fay could barely think. "You pushed out the panel."

"I didn't," Kitten said. "I woke up and it was gone." She leaned out the open window.

"Kitten, come away from there!"

"Come, look. There's something here."

Fay moved closer and leaned over. And then she saw scratches cut into the wood sill. She ran her fingers over the markings, letters that spelled out the word *Cappie*, and then, *welcome*. Over and over again the words, *Cappie welcome. Cappie welcome.* She snatched her hand back like she'd touched a flame.

"You called her and she came," Kitten whispered.

"No." Fay's voice quavered.

"She spoke to me."

"No, Kitten—"

"You pushed out the panel! You carved her name on my window! And Cappie's ghost came to haunt us!"

Ashley, Frances. *Kitten*. New York: Drake, Richards and Weems, 1976. Print.

Chapter Twenty-Six

The next morning, I found Laila darting around the kitchen, frantically flinging open cupboard doors.

"She says her food has to be gluten-free," she puffed. "And all I have is canned peaches."

"Okay," I said, not really understanding.

"Gluten can really mess with a person's system."

"Laila, stop. I know this is hard to believe, but I've actually seen my mother eat an entire loaf of French bread and wash it down with a beer. Not kidding. She's not gluten sensitive. She's just regular sensitive."

The cabinets continued to fly open and shut at a dizzying rate. "I want to make her something she likes. She offered to sign a copy of *Kitten* for me. Told me all about the television show and all the famous people she's met. She's very down to earth."

My mother was the opposite of down to earth, but whatever.

"Okay, well, knock yourself out. Just know that she's fine eating the same food we all eat."

She planted her hands on her hips and regarded me. "Look. Before she passed, my grandmother used to make me rub her hammer toe. So what if your mother's a little high maintenance? You should consider yourself lucky you have family and she's here."

She directed me to a pot of oatmeal on the stove. I doctored up a bowl with brown sugar and milk, then poured myself a cup of coffee and mounted the stairs.

I settled at the desk and, between spoonfuls of oatmeal, got started on my research. Thirty minutes in, I hit on something promising. Susan Doucette was originally from Savannah, and her parents still lived there. Don Doucette worked at an HVAC company and Millie, his wife, ran a housecleaning service called Millie Mops. I dialed the number I found on the Yelp page, gulping the last of my coffee. A chirpy female voice answered.

"Millie Doucette?" I said.

"No, but I can help you schedule your cleaning, if you like."

"Actually, I need to talk to Millie. Is she there?"

"Hold on, sugar."

The line clicked over to music, and I was treated to a couple of bars of vintage nineties George Michael.

"Millie Doucette." The voice came across the line, deep and smoke-rasped.

I straightened. "Hi, Mrs. Doucette. You don't know me, but my name is Megan Ashley and my mother, Frances Ashley, wrote a book called—"

"I know you," she said in a flat voice. "And I know your mother."

I swallowed. "Oh. Good. I was hoping—"

"What do you want?"

"I'm not sure exactly how to explain all this, but yesterday I spoke to your daughter Susan—"

"That's impossible. She wouldn't talk to you."

"I reached out to her on Facebook, and she responded."

There was silence on the other end.

"Mrs. Doucette?"

"She knows not to say nothing about all that. We haven't ever gone back on our word, not once."

"I'm not saying she did anything wrong. I was badgering her, Mrs. Doucette, trying to get her to talk to me. She told me about the nondisclosure or gag order or whatever it was she signed."

"We all signed it. And we've honored it, every day since."

"Are you aware that you were asked to sign that under false pretenses? That there was a crime committed, or there was knowledge of a crime, and that's why Rankin Lewis Literary and my mother wanted to keep Susan and the rest of you quiet?"

I was spitballing now, quite frankly, but it sounded reasonable. And maybe it would convince Millie Doucette that I actually knew something. After a moment or two, she spoke.

"Susie was one of those Kitty Cultists," she began. "She used to hang out in the forums, talking to people. She had Kitten parties with her friends. She even wrote a paper for English class about the book. She read that book about a hundred times, marked up passages. She thought she was gonna solve the mystery, if Kitten really killed that girl."

"You mean Kim Baker?"

"You know they put her mama in jail, just like in the book, but all the Kitty Cult people thought maybe Kitten did it. The real Kitten, Dorothy Kitchens. Susie was really into the subject, so she started a blog with all her theories."

"A blog?" I felt a thrill run up my spine.

"Stuff she'd figured out from clues in the book. Her father and I thought it was harmless, just something to do for fun. Then we got a letter from the agency. Frances Ashley's fancy-pants literary agency in New York"—here she laughed—"saying Susan's blog was invading Ms. Ashley's privacy and, if she kept it up, we would all be sued for libel."

"Did Susan shut down the blog?"

"My husband and I made her. The very same day. We didn't want to start no fight with people like that."

So Edgar had known all about Susan Doucette and her theories. He hadn't hesitated—not from what Millie was saying—to shut her down. Naturally, he'd never mentioned the situation to me. He wouldn't have wanted me worrying over something like this. He was a protector.

"Mrs. Doucette," I said. "You should know the agency had no right to make Susan shut down her blog. There's something called free speech in this country, and as long as Susan was expressing her opinion, they can't call it libel."

That might've been a load of horseshit too, but I was on a roll. And I could tell what I was saying was having its intended effect. Millie Doucette had grown quiet.

"We don't have the kind of money to fight nothing. My husband thought Susan should concentrate on school, anyway, instead of spending all her time on that Kitten nonsense. She was smart. Had a chance at a scholarship."

"Right." I paused. "Is there any way I could access the website now?"

"She took it down."

I'd already started typing. "What about one of those archive sites? Do you think it'll be there?"

"I gotta go," Millie said.

"Wait a second—"

But she had already hung up.

Less than three minutes later, while I was searching—unsuccessfully—for the site on any web archives, Susan Doucette pinged my Facebook.

Fuck you and stay away from my mother

I waited. The laptop buzzed again.

She's terrified now thanks

Another buzz.

She is a simple woman a good woman who cleans the shit off rich peoples toilets so she can bring home a paycheck for my lazy father who sits in the garage under a sunlamp and plays video poker all day this is who you're trying to intimidate nice

I rested my chin on my hand.

Rich bitch

And then:

She doesn't know anything anyway not what I know.

I suppressed a smile. Pressed my fists to my mouth.

Just leave my mom out of this

I typed quickly. Can we meet? I can come to you. To Statesboro. Now.

It was only a two-hour drive. I'd already clocked it. I could probably call Captain Mike, rent a car in St. Marys, and be up there by lunchtime.

I'll come to you

I thought for a minute, then answered. St. Marys Public Library, I typed, tomorrow at noon. They had no right to shut you down, Susan. You deserve to be heard.

She didn't reply.

KITTEN

—from Chapter 13

"Kitten, I didn't carve those words into the windowsill. And I didn't push out the panel." Fay reached for the girl, but she shrank away.

Fay's throat constricted, because the truth was clear. She had to have done it; Kitten wasn't strong enough. Fay must have pushed the window open in her sleep. She didn't know about the carvings. Was she capable of doing such a thing without knowing it? Was she losing her grip on reality?

"I told you she would be unhappy," said Kitten. "I told you she would be angry that I'm the mico. But now you've gone and called her back." She moved across the room to the door.

"Where are you going?" Fay felt desperate. Terrified and exhausted and confused. The room seemed to have filled with a black, suffocating cloud of fear.

Kitten fixed her with a glare. "She told me it was in the library. She said to throw it in the water." She flung open the bedroom door.

"What's in the library? What are you talking about? Kitten, darling, come back."

Fay was conscious that she must sound unhinged, that she was begging a child not to leave her alone in a room. But she didn't care. She didn't want to be here with Cappie Strongbow's ghost.

"You called Cappie. You stay with her," Kitten said and vanished into the dark corridor.

Ashley, Frances. *Kitten*. New York: Drake, Richards and Weems, 1976. Print.

Chapter Twenty-Seven

After a fruitless half hour of waiting for Susan Doucette to resurface online, I gave up. I showered, dressed, and went downstairs. The foyer was deserted, but through the large bay window, I caught a glimpse of a huge, floppy straw hat. Frances. I felt a hand on my arm and turned.

Doro lifted her eyebrows. "You going out there?"

"Gotta face the lion at some point," I said.

"Bit of unsolicited advice?"

"Sure."

"Try being nice. Get her to relax, and maybe she'll drop her guard with you."

I watched Frances out the window. The floppy hat was motionless. She was gazing out across the yard, movie-star-style. It was her way, to strike poses like that. Making it easy for the paparazzi. Only there were no photographers here on Bonny Island to get her picture.

"Frances doesn't drop her guard," I said. "Not ever."

"Oh, Meg, come on. Everybody has weak moments. Everybody wants to be seen and tell someone about the awful, horrendous, incomparable shit they've endured. Why do you think I've been talking to you?" She caught my hand. "It's been a long time since I had a friend."

I swallowed, let this sink in.

"Frances has a story too. Maybe it's about the unplanned pregnancy, who knows? Who really cares—just let her talk. If it's the truth, you can put it in your book. If it's lies, well, you can put that in too."

She gave me a wink, squeezed my hand, and sent me outside.

Frances had settled on the porch swing, her head tilted back and eyes closed. She was dressed in jeans and a white tank top and, frankly, looked better than I did, which rankled. I could hear the faint hum of music from the buds in her ears. I gave the swing a knock with my knee.

She bolted up and squinted at me. Her eyes were heavily made up, but underneath I could see the deep-purple shadows she'd tried to conceal. She looked tired in the harsh morning light. Vulnerable. She pulled out the earbuds, and a blast of static assaulted me.

She clicked off her phone with a sheepish laugh. "Riot grrrl music. Benoît's got me into it. I'm thinking of setting a book in that universe."

"You can drop the act. No one's here but me."

She hesitated. "I was just making conversation."

"You had breakfast yet?"

She shook her head.

"You want to grab a banana or something?" I asked.

"I'm not hungry," she said. "I didn't sleep well."

"Sorry to hear that."

She stood. Pulled off the hat and frisbeed it back onto the swing, then fluffed her hair. She pursed her lips and stared at the huge windows. On the other side of the wavy glass, I could see a distorted image of Esther vacuuming the massive, red-carpeted front stairs.

"Are you?" she said. "I didn't think you cared how I felt."

"Frances."

"Come home with me, Megan." She took a step toward me. Her pupils had shrunk to inky pinpoints in the bright light. "I'm begging you."

I almost laughed. "You're begging me?"

"I'm serious. Please."

"Okay. I'm listening."

Her voice was fervent. "We can't talk here. She'll hear us." Her eyes slid to the house.

"Okay." I bit my lip to keep from smiling. "I'm going to Kim Baker's cabin to look for a murder weapon. You want to come along?" Her face pinched, and she looked away. "Come on, Frances. It'll be fun. You can tell me everything you've been hiding. All your deep, dark secrets."

She produced a pair of giant sunglasses from somewhere and slid them on.

"'Atta girl." I pointed her toward the waiting Jeep and she followed me. I slipped behind the wheel and pulled the keys from under the seat.

"You have access to the vehicles, I see," she groused, hopping in.

I started the engine. "Doro's been great. She's really made me feel welcome."

"Why wouldn't she? You're going to tell her side of the story." Frances ran her hands through her mane of red hair. It had started to curl wildly in the humidity, and I couldn't quit looking at it. "What," she said.

"The hair. It just . . . it's throwing me off."

She hooted with laughter. "Good. Do you know where the cabin is?"

"No. But I figured you did."

She clucked in exasperation. "I'll try. It's been forty years."

When we were headed down the main road, however, she directed me past the turnoff to Koa's place, then deeper into the forest. Right before we hit the marsh, Frances flung out her arm, and I turned down another track. The woods were choked with spiky palmetto. Moss dripped from the overhead branches like stalactites from the roof of a cave. We jounced down the track, which narrowed and narrowed, until, suddenly, the trail ended, and we were in a clearing in front of a mossy, tumbledown cabin.

I switched off the Jeep, but Frances didn't move. Her eyes traveled from the fern-laden roof to the crumbled chimney to the half-rotted front door. There was an old sawhorse, cracked down the middle, its two jagged ends forming an M.

"They used to put blankets on those," she murmured. "Pretend they were horses. Kimmy and Kitten." She glanced at me. "Doro, I mean." She climbed out of the Jeep and walked to the sawhorse. Ran her fingers over it. "How is this still here?"

"I'm sure it's not the same one, Frances. Koa said they still use the old cabins for storage. For repairs and stuff."

Up the sagging steps, I pushed open the door, and we walked inside. I pulled the light cord, and one bare bulb buzzed yellow in the dusty space. The main room was grimy and cobwebbed and airless, piled high with gardening supplies and tools. There was a whole wall of shelves filled with mildewed cardboard boxes labeled *Taxes*. Pushed into a far corner, a motley collection of furniture formed a barricade: a vinyl-covered sofa, a ladder-back chair, a metal dinette set. A long, rolled rug balanced across the whole clutter.

Frances moved to the kitchen area. Ran her fingers along a cracked yellow counter, metal sink, and rust-eaten stove. She leaned against the counter, staring out the window.

I pushed past her, into the stub of a hallway. This cabin had two bedrooms.

"The one on the right was Mrs. Baker's. Kimmy's was on the left," Frances said behind me.

I could smell her perfume and the ripe scent of sweat. That was a first; I'd never known my mother to sweat. I pushed open the doorway on the left and heard her sharp intake of breath.

I moved to her. "What is it?"

The tips of her red-lacquered nails were tented over her mouth, and her eyes had gone huge. The circles beneath them stood out starkly, like two blue moon crescents. She was trembling. She made a soft sound, a cross between a sob and a sigh.

"I'm so sorry, Kimmy," she said. "So sorry."

Panic bubbled up in me. The next second, the pinpricks kicked in.

"Come on," I said to my mother, rubbing my hands together. "Don't say that."

I scanned the room, trying to figure out what had set her off. She must've seen something of Kim's—a framed picture, an old doll, something. She seemed to be working through some real emotion, which was a shocker. Perhaps this was the moment she was going to open up and talk to me.

"You should sit down." I tugged on her arm, but she resisted.

"Megan, no," she said softly.

I let go of her. What was wrong with me? It was like I couldn't bear to see her feel hurt, even as she wallowed in it.

She turned to me, her eyes red and watery. "I knew that Kim's mother was sick. That she had problems and missed a lot of work. She neglected Kim. I suspected she beat Kim sometimes, but I . . . I was just a girl myself. And you know, back then, people didn't bat an eye at spanking your children. But I should've told someone that the girl wasn't safe. She wasn't safe."

I deflated in relief. Frances wasn't confessing some huge secret. She was just doing her thing—gathering the drama, trying to make it revolve around her.

"I should have done something." She gave a little wail, and it was all I could do not to slap her.

"C'mon, Frances," I said. "Buck up. How many kids in the world have parents who are depressed? Or can't manage to get their shit together? Probably every other obnoxious little brat in existence. So, at least a million. A billion, more likely. There's no way you could've known what would happen to Kim."

"I had a feeling something was wrong."

I sighed.

"I had a feeling that little girl wasn't properly looked after."

"Why? Because she was Native?"

"No. Of course not." Self-righteous indignation flashed in her eyes. "Because her mother was overwhelmed. And all alone. Not every single mother has the kind of wonderful help I did."

Help. So that was what she was calling the people who raised me.

"Well, it's all in the past," I said. "There's nothing you can do now. Except maybe forgive yourself."

She ignored my sarcasm and floated toward the far wall. She brushed at the dirty windowpane but it was a futile act; the dirt was on the outside. "I came here a lot with Kitten."

I folded my arms. Waited for the story.

"Kitten—Doro—wanted to show me something she and Kimmy had made. A dollhouse they'd made from an old set of bookshelves. It was really quite clever. The shelves were floors in the house. She and Kimmy made furniture from scraps of wood and shells. And they had their Barbies . . ."

She spotted something and brightened. "There it is!" She drifted to the other side of the room, to a small, dingy bookshelf. She knelt and pointed to the top shelf. "Oh my gosh. Look at this. They made this an attic. They made little chests to store treasures in it. Just like the attic at Ambletern. Such interesting, resourceful girls." She paused, lost in her memories. "I made up a story for them. For their dolls who lived here."

I nodded, chewing the inside of my lip. I couldn't remember my mother ever making up a story for me.

"Kimmy's mother, Vera, stayed in her bedroom the whole time. She was sick, Kimmy said. Kimmy invited us to stay, though. She was making dinner. Those TV dinners people used to heat up. Poor little girl, left to take care of herself."

I ran my hands through my hair. "Why don't you think they ever found a murder weapon?"

"I don't know." Frances's gaze wandered back to the bookshelf. "Maybe there wasn't one. You can kill a child with your bare hands, you know."

"Nice."

"It's true."

"But I read that the police thought a weapon was used. A tool or a bat. A rock, possibly."

Her opaque eyes flicked to me. "Ah. The mico's bowl. You're reading the book."

I shrugged. "For research."

"Well, well. Wonders never cease."

"It's not bad. I'm actually kind of enjoying it."

She laughed. "Oh my, such effusive praise. It threatens to overwhelm me."

"The book is spectacular," I said. "There. Is that better?"

"I'm only interested in the truth, Megan."

"Ha."

She rolled her eyes.

"That's the truth. I like the book. I really do."

She shook her head, like she was physically shaking me off. "Well, at any rate, I made up the mico's bowl—the ashtray, actually—about it being the murder weapon. There was no bowl like that."

"Really? Because all the Kitty Cultists think the murder weapon was a rock."

"I know."

"Some of them have done a lot of research."

"Look, Megan. The police had no idea what the murder weapon was and neither did I. So I did what writers do. I used my imagination."

"What do you think happened to it? The murder weapon?"

"No one knows."

"But you have a theory. And don't give me that bull about being a novelist, not a true-crime writer. Don't feed me the same crap you feed everybody else."

She didn't answer. She wouldn't even look at me.

"Frances. I brought you out here because you said you wanted to talk. So talk."

KITTEN

—from Chapter 13

"Wait," Fay cried, throwing out a protective hand to block Kitten.

Herb and Delia had been holed up in the library for days, ever since the last of the guests left. She couldn't imagine why or what they were doing in there, but she felt sure it was something terrible. Something Kitten did not need to see.

Fay gently moved Kitten away from the library door and tried the knob. To her surprise, it turned easily. When the door swung open, the stench of piss, sweat, and cigarette smoke hit her, and her hand flew to her nose. She crept forward into the room, Kitten behind her, clutching at the back of her nightgown. The library was empty, except for a swath of blankets nested on the floor and a mound of books heaped up like sticks in a bonfire. When Fay moved closer, she saw they were guest registries, ledgers, and reams of files.

"Where have they gone?" Fay asked.

"I don't know," Kitten said. "You're the grown-up."

Ashley, Frances. *Kitten*. New York: Drake, Richards and Weems, 1976. Print.

Chapter Twenty-Eight

Frances still wouldn't look at me. "I wish you wouldn't call me that."

"What?"

"Frances."

"Okay. *Mom.* What do you think happened to the murder weapon?"

She wandered into the middle of the room, her eyes focused on some faraway point. "The real situation was unbearable to witness. Vera Baker was distraught when they took her into custody. Screaming for her daughter. Sobbing, tearing her hair out by the roots. It was horrific. A travesty."

She hadn't answered the question, but I didn't want to interrupt. Who knew where this would lead?

"Billy Kitchens had hired a few Native Americans to work on the island. He told the guests they were the last remaining Guale, the original inhabitants of Bonny. But there haven't been any Guale anywhere since the seventeenth century. The Bakers were Cherokee, I think? But, you know, calling them Guale upped the sizzle factor. Made Ambletern sexier."

"A Native American Epcot."

"It's vulgar, I know." She sighed. "But it was the seventies and cultural appropriation wasn't a word. People were less politically correct."

"Or more racist," I said. "Tomato, tomahto."

"Yes. It was completely unacceptable, what the Kitchenses did, setting those people up as these exotic creatures—parading them like animals in a zoo. When they arrested Vera Baker and took her down to the ferry, it was a circus. All the guests at the hotel gathering to watch the psychotic Native American woman being marched away by the white man."

"It is unfortunate," I admitted. "And kind of sickening. But, honestly, she did kill her daughter. Right?"

She didn't answer.

"You don't think Vera killed Kim?"

Frances snapped out of her reverie. "It just seemed like an unnecessary display of shaming, that's all." She moved to the door. "But, like I said, perfect veracity isn't one of my concerns. I write fiction." She leveled a look at me. "Unlike you."

I pointed at her. "Ah. Good one."

She lifted an eyebrow. "What exactly are you writing about, anyway?"

"What do you think I'm writing about?"

"I don't know—your miserable childhood? Our tragic, fractured relationship? Or are you writing about who really murdered Kim Baker?"

I shrugged. "All of it."

"Can you be more specific?"

"How about you be more specific? The lawsuit that William Kitchens supposedly filed against you in the nineties. I never heard anything about it. And there's nothing online. What was that all about?"

For a fraction of a second, I thought I saw worry in her eyes. Then she rallied.

"I don't know. My lawyers took care of it." And then she shook her head, did her new signature hair flip, and walked out of the room. I followed her.

"Why did Kitchens wait so long to sue you? The book had been out for fourteen years at least. Cultists had been coming to Bonny Island in droves for years."

"Making the Kitchens family very rich," she added.

"Rumor was Doro was attacked. They say one of the Kitty Cultists who was visiting the island did it. And her father couldn't take it anymore."

"If that's true, it's terrible. But I don't know. I don't know anything about it."

"Do you know why he dropped the suit just a couple of months later? Did you settle with him?"

"I don't know. My lawyers must have dealt with it and made it go away."

"Convenient, don't you think?"

"Yes, I do." She picked around her manicure. "That's why I have lawyers, Megan, in order to make my life more convenient. I probably shouldn't have sheltered you from this reality, but as a public figure with a substantial net worth, I'm a target. I've been sued hundreds of times, but I've always considered it part of the job. I simply don't have the time to look into each one, not when I'm writing. So . . . lawyers."

"But this was William Kitchens and Doro. This was *Kitten*. You didn't find that the least bit compelling?"

"No, Megan. I didn't, because I was busy. Do you have any other questions?"

"I do, as a matter of fact. What happened to Benoît's wife?"

She turned to face me. The fear I'd thought I'd seen was gone, and her face had settled back into its usual cool mask.

"The actress, remember?" I repeated. "That he was married to when you met him? What happened to her?"

She swept her hand, like her husband's ex-wife was nothing but a sprinkling of crumbs that needed to be wiped off a table. "They're no longer together, okay? But we don't need to talk about it, because I know you don't really want to. You just want to make me feel bad. But you can't. Benoît and I love each other."

I showed my hands. "Fair enough."

"It's a complex situation with Benoît's wife—his ex-wife—but we are managing to work it out. And he and I love each other, which is the most important thing. Of all people, you should understand."

I swallowed uneasily. What did she mean by that? Was she talking about me and Graeme? Or the two of us?

"Remember the time we saw that revival of *Oleanna* in LA?" she said suddenly. "Remember how we argued about the ending?"

I did remember. It was one of the few nights we'd done something just ourselves, out of the spotlight. We'd gotten hamburgers afterward in a dumpy diner and argued until closing time and they chased us out. I'd had fun.

"I remember," I said.

"I do too." She folded her arms. "I enjoyed that argument we had more than any pleasant conversation I've ever had with anyone."

I didn't know what to say. Just when you thought Frances had opened a door that you could walk through, you got that shit slammed in your face. I wasn't venturing into the open door. Not yet.

"Anyway," she said and turned away from me.

"You get a prenup?" I asked, angry but not wanting the conversation to end.

"Ironclad. But I trust him. He's not going to hurt me."

"Everybody hurts everybody, Frances."

She gave me a twist of a smile. "I know you believe that, and maybe it's my fault. That's what I taught you. But he's committed to this marriage, just like I am."

I snorted.

"Is that so hard for you to believe?" she asked. "That someone could actually love me?"

"Oh, Mom." I heaved a sigh. "Not what I meant."

"But that's what you think, isn't it? That no one could possibly love me?"

"No." I took a deep breath. "You've got it backward, actually."

The look she gave me was so wounded, so utterly full of despair, that my throat constricted. But I meant it. And she knew it. I couldn't apologize to cover my intentions or lessen the sting.

"I'm sorry, Megan," she said. Her voice was a ragged croak. "I'm truly sorry for whatever it is I did that turned you against me."

She moved to me. Touched her fingers to my cheek, then flattened one palm against my skin. I shivered. Her hand was cold.

"So I'll tell you what you want to know."

I waited.

"Doro killed Kim Baker all those years ago," she said simply. "I knew the truth, Megan. I mean, I suspected it. I suspected it strongly."

My thoughts rose and whirled together like a tornado. How could this be? How could she be saying this? After all these years?

"Why didn't you tell anyone that what you wrote in the book was true? Why did you keep saying it was fiction?" I said. "I don't understand."

"I . . ." Her eyes softened. "I was nineteen years old. Immature and foolish. So foolish." She faltered. "And because . . . because I saw that the story was good—*so good*. I wanted it for myself, Megan. It was a horrible, selfish thing to do, to keep quiet, but I wanted Doro's story for myself. I wanted people to think I had come up with it."

I pushed her hand from my cheek. Backed away. "Stop it."

"Megan—"

"No." I held up one finger. "The rest of the world might enjoy being led down your dark, twisted trail, but I don't."

"It's not a story, Megan. I'm telling you the truth. I lied to everyone else. I always have."

"No!" I was trembling now. "No, you can't throw that bullshit reverse-reverse psychology at me now. Doro is my friend. My friend. I'm not going to let you slander her. I'm not going to let you keep tearing her world apart so I'll stop writing this book."

"So write your book. But do it somewhere else. In Carmel or LA or New York. Just not here. Anywhere but here."

I stood taller. "No. I'm staying. You lose, Frances. Do you understand? You lose."

She stared at me for a moment, her face unreadable. Then she said, "I need some air," and turned and slipped out the front door of the cabin.

I stood in the middle of the fusty room, frozen in a fighter's stance. Panting as if I'd just gone six rounds in a boxing ring. I'd won, but I didn't know how much longer I could keep this up.

When I finally went outside, Frances was standing just off the side of the house, close to the dense thicket of trees.

"Come on," I said wearily. "Let's go back."

She didn't turn, just kept staring. "There was someone here. They were watching us."

KITTEN

—from Chapter 13

Kitten spoke again, in a quiet voice. "Fay? Cappie says it's in Father's desk. In the back." She pointed to the lower drawer, then stepped back, her eyes darting from the drawer to Fay.

Fay took a wadded handkerchief from the desk, opened the drawer, and reached behind stacks of papers and folders. A few seconds later, she felt something hard. She pulled the thing out—a jagged, reddish-brown, oblong stone with one flat side and a shallow depression on the other.

"Goodness," she said. "Did Cappie's ghost happen to mention it was an ashtray?"

Kitten glared. "It's the mico's bowl. The chieftain used it for grinding herbs." Fay held the rock up in the moonlight and studied it. It had traces of black ash in the depression.

Then something on the underside caught her eye—a dark, irregular stain along the jagged edge. A stain that resembled blood. Kitten snatched the rock from her and pressed it to her chest.

"We have to throw it in the ocean," she said. "Then Cappie will leave us alone."

Ashley, Frances. *Kitten*. New York: Drake, Richards and Weems, 1976. Print.

Chapter Twenty-Nine

Frances and I pulled into Ambletern's front drive, passing Doro along
the way. A basket was looped over her arm. She smiled and waved at
us. When I parked, Frances made a beeline for the porch. Like magic,
Laila materialized beside her with a cocktail and a plate of something
that looked suspiciously like hors d'oeuvres.

"Well, how do you like that," I muttered as Doro sauntered up.

"I guess you're used to the royal treatment." She nodded at the pair
of them. "But I'll tell you—I have a hard time thinking of Frances as
anything but that sweet, redheaded college girl who played with me the
summer I was eight."

"If you say so. I wish I'd known her then. Maybe I'd be able to look
past all the shit she armors herself with, and see who she is. She's just
so damn . . . opaque."

"Sometimes the best people have the hardest shells to crack."

I eyed Doro's basket. "More blackberries?"

"Got to get them when they're ripe."

I peered up at the porch where Frances was slumped in the swing.
Marie Antoinette, after a long day pretending to milk cows. Then I
looked back down at Doro and her basket of berries.

"Pie tonight?" I said.

"Berry tarts." She gave me a sly wink. "Just like in the book."

"Need any help?"

"No, thanks. Laila and I have got it. You keep working on your project."

We walked up the steps.

"Will you be joining us for supper, Frances?" Doro called out brightly.

"I'd love to, but I'm exhausted and on deadline. Would Laila mind terribly bringing it up to my room?" Frances stood. Sighed. Tossed her hair.

"Mom," I said.

"It's all right, Meg. We don't mind a special request now and then," Doro said.

"Thank you, Doro," Frances said. The two women seemed to size each other up for a minute, then Frances broke the silence. "Well, good night."

She disappeared inside. I followed her. Caught her arm at the foot of the stairs. She whipped around to face me.

"What do you want?" She did look tired, and for a minute I regretted what I knew I was about to do. I withdrew my hand.

"What are you writing?"

She shook her head like the question didn't warrant an answer.

"What's the deadline, Mom?"

"I can't talk about it. Nothing's official yet."

"What are you up to?" I hissed.

"What am *I* up to?" she snapped. "You should be asking Doro what she's up to. There was someone watching us, back there at Kim Baker's cabin. I saw them, running away through the woods."

"It was a deer. Or a horse. Or a raccoon or an armadillo or whatever the hell else lives on this island."

"It wasn't an animal. It was a person."

"What do you want me to do about it, Frances?"

"Come home with me. This place isn't safe."

I clenched my fists.

"You can't stop this book," I said evenly. "You won't. And I'm warning you, if you try, I'll make you sorry."

She seemed to float for a moment, to turn to one side then the other like she couldn't find a way of escape. Then her hand hit the heavy wood banister and her back went straight. She started up the stairs, her jeans sagging at the waist, and there was a sweat stain on the back of her tank. I watched her round the landing and then head up the second flight.

I gulped air and smeared the tears I hadn't realized I'd been crying off my face. I felt a hand on my arm. Doro.

"Go upstairs," she said quietly. "Take a shower. Get some rest. I'll have your supper sent up too."

I hesitated. "No. I need to work. You mentioned the other day that I could go up in the attic to look through the old guest registries. Would you mind if I did that now?"

"Of course not. Can I ask what you're looking for, exactly?"

I shook my head. "I don't know. A name I recognize? Someone my mother knew who might've come down here to tidy up for her? Or maybe she came down here again and used one of her aliases I might recognize. I don't know."

"She couldn't have come here without me or my father recognizing her. Or all the fans."

I nodded and she hugged me, hard. "It's going to be okay, Meg. You'll figure it out."

She released me, and I ran upstairs to my room, soaped off the bug spray and sweat, threw on pajama pants and a T-shirt. I twisted my wet hair into a knot on the top of my head and grabbed my notepad. I hadn't discovered anything noteworthy at the Baker house, but I hoped to have better luck with the hotel records. Best-case scenario: the attic would prove to be a treasure trove of information, and it would keep me busy—and distracted—for hours.

Ambletern's attic reminded me of a set designer's idea of Manderley's garret. The whole place was bathed in amber light from a row of port-hole windows under the eaves. Discarded furniture rose in ghostly, sheet-draped forms. Massive wardrobes, moth-eaten Victorian sofas and matching rocking chairs trimmed with braid and fringe and sitting on dark-stained, carved claw feet. Scattered Tiffany lamps, dusty taxider-mied animal heads, and china figurines that all seemed to be missing at least one crucial part.

Along the right wall, cardboard file boxes were stacked in neat rows, three high and ten across. Arranged on the left wall was a collection of trunks, those old-fashioned camp lockers with metal fittings and latches. There were rings for padlocks, but most of them appeared to be open. I sighed. Going through every one of these boxes would be a tedious process. And I had no idea what I was even looking for.

I lifted the lid off the first box. It was filled with stacks of neatly folded clothing, men's shirts and pants. I touched the one on top—it was soft, threadbare, and faded, a denim work shirt with pearl snap buttons, the kind that Doro liked to wear. There were more under it, the same style but plaid and khaki and olive green. The next trunk held hats: floppy fisherman's hats, bandannas, and straw fedoras, and three pairs of work boots.

The rest of the trunks held little girl's clothing: small capri pants and jean shorts, T-shirts, and a couple of dingy sundresses. A two-piece swimsuit, bright red with a navy-and-white plastic flower on the strap. There was also a box with a carefully folded lace wedding dress wrapped in tissue. I didn't pull it out.

The last trunk, the one farthest against the far wall, was locked. I pulled at the latch, even hit the tiny padlock a couple of times, but I didn't want to break it. I tilted the trunk back and crowed softly.

Attacked to the underside, with a starburst of yellowed tape, was a tiny key.

I pulled it loose, opened the lock, and lifted the lid.

A cloud of dirt and mildew enveloped me as I pulled out the items and laid them side by side. There was a small dark-green gingham dress, edged with ruffles. A gauzy red shawl, torn in half. A white ostrich feather and a cheap silver necklace.

My breath caught.

I flashed to the bus and the ad with Frances's picture beside the fortieth-anniversary book jacket. This was the exact outfit Kitten was wearing on the cover, down to the faux-Incan choker necklace. It must've been Doro's when she was young. How easy it would've been for Frances to change things up, to have her demonic little protagonist wear something else. What a cruelty, then, to duplicate the costume so precisely. Almost as if she wanted Doro forever, irrevocably connected to the horror of the book.

How like my mother.

I returned everything to the trunk, locked it, and tucked the key underneath the loose tape. Then I crossed to the file boxes and began riffling through the files. They were mostly invoices, receipts, tax records—nothing of interest. I made my way down the row, and found, in the third-to-the-last box, the stack of registry books, starting with the year 1942. I worked my way through the stack, searching for 1975, the year Frances came to the island. When I found it, I lifted it out and carried it to a table by one of the porthole windows.

I ran my finger down the list of names until I hit a certain one.

Frances Ashley, the signature read in a careful hand. *May 15, 1975.* Beside the date, a little flower, a daisy drawn to look like it was growing directly out of the number five. I touched it.

I scanned the rest of the page, my eyes blurring, until I came across another familiar name: *Mr. & Mrs. Milton Darnell. Dalton, Georgia.*

Pete Darnell, Doro's friend. These must have been his parents.

Doro said the Darnells were regulars at Ambletern; maybe they'd show up in later registries. I ran back over to the box and pulled out a stack of three more books. Sure enough, the Darnells appeared regularly in each one, every summer for the next eight years. They seemed to always come in May and stay for two weeks exactly. After 1983, there was no sign of Pete or his family.

I thought back to what Doro had told me about Pete, how she'd lured him to the marsh without his clothes to teach him a lesson, one that had humiliated but not actually done any damage, and that seemed to be the end of it.

I searched through the rest of the eighties and into the nineties. Pete Darnell's name didn't appear once. And there was something else. The ledger from 1990 was missing. The same year William Kitchens filed his hush-hush lawsuit against Frances that nobody—*nobody*—seemed to remember. Now that was just way too much of a fucking coincidence, if you asked me. A little too convenient.

I dialed Asa's number. It immediately rolled to voice mail.

"Asa, hi." I scanned the pile of leather guest ledgers. "So . . . I hope Frances hasn't torn you to shreds. Doro's being a little cagey." I hesitated. "Okay, a lot cagey. She lies some. Hides things." I looked at the stack of ledgers. "But I think it's just out of self-protection, and I can understand that. She's been through a lot. I've got some other sources I think I can mine for info . . ."

I trailed off. He didn't know about Susan Doucette or her notes. Or, at least, he'd never mentioned her. Maybe he had known. It had been Rankin Lewis, his employer, who had shut Susan down, after all; maybe Asa had known all about her from the start. But then why wouldn't he have said something?

There were too many unanswered questions. Too many blank spaces, and I wasn't feeling like I should show Asa all my cards. Not yet. Something told me he hadn't shown me his.

I realized the line had gone unusually quiet. I looked at the screen on my phone.

"Dammit." While I was off in la-la land, the call had dropped. It had probably cut off half my message too. I shoved the phone in the waistband of my yoga pants and hauled the registry books back over to the boxes. There was something to be learned here, something to be understood, but I couldn't get past the feeling I was looking in the wrong place.

I got back to my room and powered up my laptop. As I jotted a few notes on what I'd found in the attic, I noticed the printer icon in the dock. Weird. It didn't usually pop up unless it had just finished a job. I clicked on it and pulled up the recent print jobs. The only one it showed was the second half of my manuscript. Someone had just printed it.

KITTEN

—FROM CHAPTER 14

At sundown, the sheriff's patrol skiff drew up to the Ambletern dock. Fay told Kitten to stay in the house, and she met the deputy on the front steps. He was holding his hat in his hands, and his hair was plastered with sweat. She'd gotten so used to the heat and humidity, she barely noticed it anymore.

"Did you find the ashtray?" Fay asked him in a low whisper.

He shook his head. "It wasn't under the tree."

"The one lying on its side, on the bank by the dock? That looks like a skeleton?"

"I'm sorry, ma'am. I looked. There wasn't any ashtray there."

Fay's stomach churned. She cast a furtive glance back at the house. The windows, covered in their plywood panels, seemed like eyes squeezed shut. A house that kept its secrets locked inside.

"We weren't able to locate the Murphys either." He nodded toward the forest. "Herb and Delia have been living here on Bonny a long time. They know this island well. They're hiding out there, somewhere. Or else they've cut and run to the mainland."

"Because they murdered Cappie?"

"I'm afraid it's starting to look that way." He scratched his head. "It's been suggested . . . well, some folks are saying that the Murphy girl should be brought back to town. It's been suggested she would be safer there."

Ashley, Frances. *Kitten*. New York: Drake, Richards and Weems, 1976. Print.

Chapter Thirty

Frances stayed in her room all the next day—which didn't surprise me. She had undoubtedly snuck into my room when I wasn't around and printed my book, that snake. No wonder she couldn't face me.

Down in the kitchen, Laila told me she'd climbed the stairs multiple times with food, but the trays had all been left outside the door, barely touched.

"She doesn't eat when she's working. Blocks the flow," I said. We'd brought supper out on the porch and were eating cold fried chicken and raw, slender green beans from the garden on the edge of the lawn. I pulled a strip of golden fry off the chicken breast and popped it in my mouth. Considered my own flow.

I'd written everything I could for the second half of the book—how Frances had turned Ambletern into a carnival sideshow, how Doro had been forced to play along with it, ruining her chances at love and basically sending her father to an early grave. But it was lacking something, an element that connected the disparate parts.

Maybe that missing piece would be a new clue about the elusive murder weapon. Or a story I hadn't heard from a source I hadn't met yet. I didn't know. I didn't care. I just wanted something.

If I could find that, I thought, I would finally blow away all the lies.

Not that snooping around for whatever killed Kimmy was actually the same as getting words on paper. But if I did happen to stumble upon something, it couldn't hurt. And it would definitely make it sexier, that was for sure. Maybe then Asa would leave the Graeme stuff alone.

He still hadn't called me back. When I could manage to snag a decent signal, I'd left him a couple of messages. I'd sent him the latest pages, such as they were, but since I hadn't heard from him, I hoped it meant he was too busy setting up his new agency, or slamming back drinks with the Pelham Sound folks.

I was counting on him.

And Susan Doucette. She felt like my only chance to make any sense of the loose threads.

Tomorrow was our meeting in St. Marys. Captain Mike's ferry always appeared at the dock Friday mornings at nine o'clock to drop off the mail and any extra groceries Laila had ordered. I planned to be there waiting. My cover story? I was going inland to drop off my latest blood samples to Dr. Lodi in town. With Frances at Ambletern now, I doubted anyone would be surprised if I stayed gone the remainder of the day.

∞

On my way out of Dr. Lodi's office, the doctor caught me at the door.

"How are the treatments going?"

I smiled. "Very well, thanks."

"Good to hear." She signed the chart, unclipped the folder, and handed it to the woman behind the desk. "I've been thinking—if you have time, I'd like to do some X-rays. I know we think this is lead-paint exposure, but I want to rule out any additional factors."

"Ah . . ." I glanced at the clock in the waiting room. Eleven thirty. A half an hour before I was supposed to meet with Susan.

"My tech goes on vacation tomorrow."

"I have an appointment."

"He's quick, I promise. Any chance of you being pregnant?"

"No."

I signed a couple of papers, then she hustled me down the hall and into a room where a guy wrapped me in lead blankets and took pictures from every imaginable angle. Shortly afterward, I was jogging down the street, computer tucked under my arm, in the direction of the library.

The St. Marys library was one large octagonal room—bright, pleasantly cool, and mostly empty. The room was bordered four shelves thick, around a collection of scarred oak tables. As I shivered in the air conditioning, I scanned the tables. There were old men reading and students drumming away on laptops. No sign of Susan. I strolled to the shelves and began casually perusing the books, a row of military biographies. After about five minutes, I peeked out from behind the stacks. Still no Susan.

I ambled around the room, inspecting nearly every nook of the place, save the children's reading corner, which was jam-packed with kids and their harried moms or nannies. By one o'clock, Susan still hadn't showed, and I was in a foul mood.

I had to be at the St. Marys dock no later than five p.m. in order for Captain Mike to ferry me back to the island. He had a standing Friday-night dinner with his wife at the local pizza place, and no amount of bargaining would persuade him to miss it. If Susan was late or lost, I was screwed. And I didn't have her phone number, just her Facebook page. At exactly one fifteen, I found a deserted corner and typed a message on my phone.

Where the hell are you?

I waited five endless minutes, but an answer never came.

Susan, I wrote, I'm here at the library? Are you coming?

Nothing.

Suppressing a growl, I headed to the front desk. I smiled at the librarian, a man who looked like he should be on an NFL defensive line instead of sitting behind a desk.

"Hi," I said, smiling through gritted teeth. I was starting to feel light-headed and numb all over. "I was supposed to meet someone here. Has anybody called . . . or left a message or something? My name is Meg."

His head tilted, eyes filled with commiseration. "Stood up for the hookup. Exactly why I don't do Tinder anymore."

I darkened. "So, no message?"

"No message."

I turned, my jaw working in frustration. The library had just about cleared out, and it was nowhere near five o'clock. I might as well check the stacks one more time to see if Susan was hiding somewhere in their depths before I gave up.

I started with the kids' section, stepping over the detritus of story time, then headed over to adult fiction. I peered down each aisle but found nothing except one teenage boy, ears plugged with buds, wagging his head and reading a fat paperback. Third row, fourth, fifth. I headed down the last row, where, at the end, one book—a hardback—had been halfway pulled out. It perched precariously over the edge of the shelf, and I moved to push it back in. The title on the spine jumped out at me—*Kitten*—and my hand froze.

Feeling my pulse hammer in my neck, I gingerly pulled the book out. Opened it. Turned a page or two. As I proceeded to flip through the pages, a scrap of paper slipped out and fell to the carpet. I crouched, scooped the paper up, tucked it into my bag, and strode toward the main entrance.

I hurried down the sunny street. She'd been there; Susan Doucette had been in the library and left me a clue. But why hadn't she approached

239

me? Was she too scared somebody would see her with me? Did some stupid contract she signed with a literary agency really hold that much power over her?

It seemed almost too far-fetched to believe.

I felt the slip of paper between my fingers, then stopped, realizing I'd been walking for a good ten minutes and had no idea where I was. I leaned against a brick-walled storefront and read the words written on the scrap. Then grabbed my phone and typed in one more Facebook message to Susan Doucette.

Thank you.

KITTEN

—from Chapter 14

The deputy settled his hat on his head. "Everything's a muddle with the Strongbow girl being murdered and her mama . . ." He frowned down at his dusty boots. "Anyway, the sheriff decided the kid might be better off here, with you. So that's that for now. You'll be her temporary guardian until we can figure out a plan."

While Fay was trying to formulate her protest, she realized the deputy had taken her silence as consent and had started talking again.

"The sheriff thought that if the Murphys did come back, well, we wouldn't want them to be alarmed or anything, that their daughter wasn't here. We wouldn't want to spook them. Tip 'em off, you understand. If they killed the Strongbow girl."

Fay felt herself grow faint. She didn't relish staying one day longer on the island, even for Kitten's sake. Herb and Delia were gone. They might be fugitives from the law or just two unbalanced people who'd been cut off from civilization so long they'd lost their marbles. Regardless, if they were hiding out there in the woods, she did not feel safe.

"There's something else," the deputy said. "Bad news, I'm afraid." Fay managed to focus again on his narrow, sweating face. "Last night, June Strongbow went and killed herself. How about that? Hanged herself right in her jail cell."

Ashley, Frances. *Kitten*. New York: Drake, Richards and Weems, 1976. Print.

Chapter Thirty-One

I popped into the little indie bookstore I'd stopped in front of and got directions to the Bloody Bowl, as Susan had instructed me.

I walked for fifteen minutes or so, all the way to the other side of town, finally arriving at an old brick building with an English-pub-style sign swinging over the heavy oak door. The sign was carved with a Native American chief headdress and tomahawk and, below that, the words **THE BLOODY BOWL**.

Inside, the place was dim and deserted, except for the rotund bartender, who sported an enormous, waxed handlebar mustache and matching beetle-brow. The place looked like a Kitty Cult clubhouse: its walls papered with photos of cosplayers dressed as Herb Murphy, Fay, Cappie Strongbow, and, of course, every version of Kitten. There were blonde-wigged, pigtailed Kittens; Kittens in pinafore dresses and overalls; Native American Kittens in the iconic green dress, red turban, and ostrich feather. Also several homicidal-maniac Kittens, smeared in blood and wielding chunky rocks as weapons.

I was definitely in the right place.

A loop of the original '70s movie played on TVs suspended overhead. The scene currently playing showed Kitten rifling through the newly arrived guests' rooms, presumably looking for items for her Indian-princess getup. I turned my back to the TVs and found a stool at the bar. The bartender ambled over and leaned on the polished bar. He looked like somebody's uncool but perfectly nice dad.

"Afternoon," he said, putting down a coaster. "You want a drink?"

I nodded. "Food too, if you have it."

He cast a look over his shoulder. "Not usually this early, but the cook likes me. If I ask her real nice, she could make you a cheeseburger."

"Add a glass of your house red, and I'll love you forever."

He lifted one enormous brow. "Well, don't tell the cook. She's my wife." He headed to the back, kicked through the swinging door. "If you need the Wi-Fi, password is *BobbisSweetAss*—three *b*'s, one *i*, no *e*, no apostrophe."

"Thanks."

"Mac and cheese okay?" he asked when he returned, setting down the glass of wine. "She already made a batch."

"Sounds great."

"Anything else I can do for you?" He had one elbow on the bar and was studying me with interest. Like he maybe recognized me. It wouldn't be so out of the question, in this place.

"Um." I stared at him. "Not right now." I sipped the wine and pulled out my laptop. Pretended to peruse something interesting. Susan hadn't said what I was supposed to do once I got here, and now I wasn't sure exactly how to proceed. I was feeling wary. The whole thing felt a little Jason Bourne.

The bartender finally gave up staring and sidled down the bar, busying himself pulling glasses out of a dishwasher and wiping them down.

After a few minutes he returned, an apologetic look on his face.

"Hey, you mind solving a bet?"

I looked up. "I guess not. Sure."

"Bobbi!" he yelled. Then gave the bar a few swipes with his towel.

A painfully pretty young woman, with beauty-queen bone structure and two fat plaits of blonde hair that hung over her impossibly huge breasts, emerged from the back bearing a steaming bowl. She plunked it down in front of me—the mac and cheese aroma rose up and made my mouth water—then pressed herself against the bartender. She nuzzled his cheek.

"Don't yell for me, Shug. I don't like it."

He gently pushed her back, reached to the top shelf, and pulled out a crisp hundred-dollar bill. He pointed at me, held it out to her, and then she squealed.

"Are you sure?" she asked him.

"Ask her."

She turned, aimed the most intense stare I'd ever been the recipient of, and then flashed a blindingly white smile. "Megan Ashley?" she breathed. "Frances Ashley's daughter?"

My heart did a funny little jig in my chest. And I nodded.

She flapped the hundred-dollar bill and giggled maniacally. "I told him so! I said, 'Build it and they will come.' And you did. You did! I mean, technically, what I meant was your mom would show up, but you count. You totally count!"

She screamed. She literally screamed, then started jumping up and down, her enormous chest jouncing half a beat behind each leap. I smiled gamely.

"What are you doing here?" Shug asked.

"I'm trying to find a defunct Kitty Cult website," I said.

Bobbi stopped jumping and fixed me with a stare. "Oh my *God*, you are?" She lowered her voice. "Which one?"

"Ah . . ." I said.

Bobbi's eyes flamed in the shadows. "I know every Kitty Cult site that has ever existed."

"She speaks the truth," Shug said.

"Okay," I said. "There was this girl . . . she was young, twelve, back in 2006 or 2007—"

"Who is Susan Doucette, Kitten Kid Detective!" Bobbi screamed out.

"It's not *Jeopardy*, babe," Shug said.

I blinked in disbelief. "You've heard of Susan Doucette?"

"Sure," Bobbi said. "Kitten Kid Detective was a website, a really popular one. The hardcore Cultists were all over it. For some reason, they took it down."

"Even off the archive sites?"

She nodded and then smiled.

"What?"

"I mean, I don't like to show off—"

"Please. By all means."

"Do you mind?" She pointed at my computer.

Her fingers flew over the keyboard, then, after a couple of minutes, she swiveled the laptop back to me. It was Susan's website—or at least screenshots of it, rows and rows of them.

"I kept a folder," Bobbi said. "I always had a feeling that kid was on to something. She came here once. Had a hot dog."

"Oh my God," I breathed, drinking in the site.

It was classic early-2000s look, black with cramped pink and green text in a bubble font. I scanned a page, which was a long thread where about five different people discussed their recent visits to Ambletern.

. . . and then one night I caught Dorothy standing outside our door at three a.m. She said she was just passing by, but she was HOLDING A CROWBAR WITH GLOVES ON.

. . . my fiancé found a bloodstain on the desk in the library. He gouged out the wood and put it in a baggie. Anybody know anyone who works in a freelance CSI lab?

. . . she's soooooo weird. OMG. Dead eyes. Motherfucking dead eyes. She might wear blue contacts because I KNOW her eyes are green. Bitch carries this thermos around with her all the time, even drinks out of it at meals, like the water's poisoned or something. During dinner, she was like lurking in the corner and watching us. That woman gave me the fucking heebie-jeebies, seriously.

"Okay," I said, looking back up at Bobbi. "Are there any pictures of earlier posts? Any of the originals?"

"Sure."

Within seconds, she crowed and swiveled the laptop. My eyes widened as I took in the site.

"Oh my God. That's it. I can't believe it."

"I'll get you a berry tart, house special, okay?" Bobbi said. "And would you mind signing my first edition? I'd be so honored."

From
www.kittenkiddetective.com

Hi! My name is Susan Evelyn Doucette. I am fourteen years old, and I go to Newberry High School in Savannah, Georgia. I read Kitten for the first time when I was eleven years old. I snuck it off my aunt's bookshelf when my family was on vacation at her beach house. She found out, and secretly gave me my own copy the next Christmas. Since then, I have read the book fifteen times (at least), read online articles, police reports, court transcripts, and basically done a lot (a ton) of research, possibly more than anyone else. Let's get started. Welcome to Susan Doucette, Kitten Kid Detective!

Theory #1: Most Kitty Cultists don't know this, but Frances Ashley went to stay at Ambletern because she had an affair with one of her married professors at college (George Tinley O'Brien). She became pregnant with his child but terminated the pregnancy. GTO was young, handsome, and the head of the English department. Frances Ashley probably took at least one or more of his classes her freshman year, specifically a Shakespeare class entitled "Macbeth and the Literature of Blood." She took his creative writing class her sophomore year as well. To avoid scandal about the relationship and pregnancy, Frances had to lay low for the summer, but I think she was still in love with George Tinley O'Brien. I think she wrote the book, not to reveal the identity of some mystery killer (Dorothy Kitchens, the girl she based Kitten on) by planting a bunch of Easter eggs, but as a love/revenge ode to him and to ultimately protect herself. (See Theory #4) Here are a couple of examples that support my theory (and that I posted last year on the forums).

"Brian O'Hanlon": The name of the doctor who investigates the guests' "stomach virus" is Brian O'Hanlon, very close to "George Tinley O'Brien." Even though he's a villain supposedly, he is handsome and rather sympathetic—Kitten poisons him, but he survives. He has a "cowlick that made a lock of hair fall over his blue eyes." (page 49) I couldn't tell from the following link if GTO had blue eyes, but he definitely had a cowlick. (www.facultyarchives.asc.edu)

Miss Bolan's silver necklace (Chapter Two): A GTO reference appears again—this time when Kitten tells Miss Bolan, the reclusive spinster, that another guest, "George" (an imaginary, and ultimately disappointing, suitor who she has invented), has been asking about when she's going to join the rest of them at their nightly after-dinner drinks. (Miss Bolan falls for Kitten's story, of course, and this is when Kitten steals the necklace.)

The Stained Green Gingham Dress (Chapter Four): GTO and Frances's abortion is referred to indirectly here. When Kitten tells the young divorcée's son, Henrick, she wants him to give her the dress that's hidden in his mother's suitcase, she says he must do it or else something dire will happen. Or as she puts it, "blood will have blood" (page 51). This is actually a quote from the play Macbeth, and refers to the above-mentioned undergraduate course that GTO taught at Agnes Scott College and later at Emory University. There's no specific mention of the type of stains on the dress (e.g. semen, blood, sweat, etc.) but I believe this is a sort of homage to the way

Frances felt "stained" after the failed relationship (and possibly after the abortion). More later on that "blood will have blood" quote.

Theory #2: All the Kitty Cultists are wrong about who murdered the real Cappie Strongbow. To review, let's look at a list of their favorite suspects:

DOROTHY KITCHENS (Kitten) was not Kim Baker's killer. She was only eight at the time of Kim Baker's murder and according to the book was "undersized and anemic-looking." A petite child of eight years would have difficulty bashing a skull hard enough to fracture it. The disappearances of staff and government officials can't be confirmed via online articles and therefore must be considered mere rumors.

VERA BAKER (June Strongbow) was not Kim Baker's killer. Although Vera was arrested and put in jail, indicted, she was never brought to trial because she had a diabetic stroke before the court date and died (she did NOT commit suicide like in the book, FYI). She never confessed to the murder, only to occasionally spanking her daughter.

VICKY KITCHENS (Delia Murphy), Dorothy's mother, was not Kim Baker's killer. She died in Custer, South Dakota in 1973, while taking part in an American Indian Movement (AIM) protest. Immediately after this, William, her husband, and Dorothy responded to an ad, buying Ambletern and moving to Bonny Island. (The Kitty Cultists who say Vicky Kitchens murdered Kim prove just how dumb they are. Just a small amount of research would show that was impossible.)

WILLIAM KITCHENS (Herb Murphy), Dorothy's father, was not Kim Baker's killer, even though he is, by far, everyone's second favorite suspect, next to Dorothy Kitchens (Kitten). In the book, Herb Murphy did handyman work for June Strongbow, and he helped Vera Baker out in real life as well. William admitted this in the police reports and in The Camden County Tribune. It IS my belief that William and Vera Baker were conducting a secret relationship, as she made statements after her arrest to the sheriff alluding to the fact that he could provide an alibi for her. William WAS obsessed with Native American culture, was involved with AIM (American Indian Movement) and even took part in several protests. His wife, Vicky (who he claimed was of Native ancestry, although that is unproven), was accidentally killed in Custer, South Dakota. I DO believe this incident influenced William Kitchens's behavior (more on this later). But I don't think these beliefs or events spurred him to commit murder.

Theory #3: **The murder weapon** (WHICH SHOULD BE THE KITTY CULT'S FOCUS, NOT THE SUSPECTS) has never been found on Bonny Island, even though the police believe it to still be there (everyone who left the island after the murder was searched thoroughly). That's why I believe William Kitchens hid it. However, I don't think William would have thrown it into the water or done anything to permanently get rid of it, because I believe he thought he might need it for leverage with the police or killer later on. I do think he would have hid it in a place that would be protected somehow, for example:

The Mission Ruins: I believe William Kitchens might think hiding the murder weapon in a sacred place was a sort of poetic justice.

Vera Baker's house: As he was a frequent visitor there, William could have easily hidden a rock on her property, and, as an original slave cabin from the 1800s, it's designated as a historical place by the state of Georgia, so no one is allowed to raze or remodel it.

The Middens: The wall of shells protecting the northern shore of the island remains a site of historical value. Although the Guale probably only used it for a trash heap, since Vera Baker was found here the morning Kimmy's body was discovered, trying to slash her wrists, I believe William might have viewed the spot as secure, as well as significant. Which leads me to . . .

Theory #4: FRANCES ASHLEY KILLED KIM BAKER. Then, somehow William Kitchens found the weapon (covered in blood possibly) and hid it. He did this because he either believed Kitten had committed the murder or thought Frances did it, and hoped to blackmail her in the future. Hang with me here, but Frances may have known Kitchens suspected his own daughter. Thus, there was a sort of standoff between Frances Ashley and William Kitchens. So then, for Ashley, writing a book was a masterful act of revenge (on GTO, who was a failed novelist) and of self-preservation. She KNEW that by writing a story that pinned a murder on Dorothy Kitchens, she would a) automatically muddy the waters of public opinion on Dorothy's presumed innocence and simultaneously, b) intimidate William Kitchens, knowing his precious daughter could be inches away from being arrested for murder. Frances wrote the book to protect herself. Frances Ashley is the murderer—a violent, brilliant, homicidal psychopath. And here is what I believe is strong evidence . . .

I had the opportunity to correspond with a former student of GTO's (ANONYMOUS SOURCE). A. SOURCE described a class lecture (Emory University, 1976) where he used excerpts of papers written by former students in lectures. One such paper, notated in the upper left-hand corner as written by an F. Ashley, explored the subject of Shakespeare's use of real-life murders on which he based his plays. F. Ashley then went on to name contemporary authors who had taken this idea one step further to advance their careers—ACTUALLY WRITING NOVELS BASED ON CRIMES (murders specifically) THEY HAD COMMITTED!!!! When A. SOURCE commented to GTO that she guessed the paper might have been written by Frances Ashley, he denied it. But the passage was immediately pulled from the curriculum and not mentioned again in classroom discussion.

***UPDATE!!!!!!** **2010**: I've found William Kitchens!!!! He is alive and well, living inland, in Farrow, Georgia, a small farming town near St. Marys. Sometime in the early '90s, he turned the hotel over to Dorothy and moved to Farrow. (Deeds for the property on file in the Camden County Courthouse. Property purchased in 1991 by William Kitchens.) He doesn't work, but seems to live comfortably. (?) I met a lady who used to work at the courthouse in Camden County (name withheld) and found out that, in 1990—fourteen years after the publication of Kitten—William Kitchens filed a defamation lawsuit against Frances Ashley for libel and invasion of privacy. The lawsuit was dropped in 1991, or settled—there are no official records that I was able to dig up and none of the lawyers will return a call from a kid. Go figure.

My theory is that, after all these years, William and Frances worked out some kind of deal. Since each had something the other wanted—Frances had money and William Kitchens had the murder weapon—I believe an exchange took place.

Chapter Thirty-Two

If Susan Doucette's website was to be trusted, Doro had lied to me. Not once or twice but multiple times. Which excited and confused and pissed me off, all at the same time.

I ran down Main Street, in the direction of the St. Marys marina, my hair kinking into corkscrew curls in the humidity. Macaroni and cheese and red wine sloshed in my stomach, but my body pulsated in triumph. I finally had something.

I mentally tabulated a list of Doro's falsehoods:

Vera Baker had not died from a brain tumor that made her violent toward her daughter, but a diabetic stroke. That was the minor one, granted. But still a lie.

Next. The Kitchenses had not inherited Bonny Island and Ambletern as part of a blue-blood-type land-grant situation. They had seen an ad and bought the place in the 1970s.

And finally, Doro's father, William Kitchens, wasn't dead, but actually living just down the road. In fact, Bobbi at the Bloody Bowl had even tracked down his address for me.

This last one was the kicker—the lie that really got me wondering what else Doro might be hiding. Whatever it was, I was determined to figure it out. I made it to the marina with three minutes to spare, but when I relayed my plan, Captain Mike looked incredulous.

"Don't know why you'd want to go to Farrow," he said in his gruff voice. "It's not a town, it's a turd. A blot on the good state of Georgia."

"How long would it take me to get there?" I asked.

"You don't listen, do you?"

I smiled and shook my head.

"You don't have a car," he pointed out.

My eyes drifted to his giant, silver truck parked in the lot. "I can pay you. Like it's a rental."

His gray eyes felt like lasers on me. "What's in Farrow?"

"Research," I said. "For my book."

His eyes clouded, and he hooked his thumb in one belt loop. "It's a good forty-five, fifty minutes there. I got a full tank of gas. Look, I can walk home; it ain't far. Just have it back here at ten o'clock tonight, you hear? I'll run you back over to Bonny then."

"Thank you." I dug in my purse, but he held up his hand.

"I don't need no money. Just be back by ten." His face looked grim.

Fifteen minutes later, squinting into the sunset on westbound 40, I fumbled for my phone. Coverage was decent here, but the call still rolled over to voice mail. I almost screamed in frustration.

"Asa! Call me," I yelled into the phone. "I'm working on some new sources. Is Pelham Sound liking the chapters? When are they going to send back the edits?"

The wide highway seemed to stretch ahead of me into the unobstructed horizon like the proverbial road to hell. What had happened to Asa? Had Frances finally managed to shut him down for good?

"Anyway," I said to Asa's voice mail. "Call me, okay?"

I caught a glimpse of a shack, the entire thing—door, trim, siding— painted a startling shade of lapis blue. I slowed, taking in the strange sight. As I neared the house, I saw a giant black dog chained to a tree in the front yard. He leapt forward, his chain snapping taut, and started barking ferociously.

I stomped the gas pedal. A call buzzed in, and I answered it.

It was Koa. "Hey. Are you on your way home?"

An unexpected frisson of pleasure shot through me. *Home.*

"No," I said, checking out the weird blue house in my rearview mirror. "Not quite. Turns out I need to make one more stop."

"Okay, well, I wanted to let you know, your mom is really sick," he said.

"What?"

"She's been vomiting all day. She's lethargic, and her blood pressure's low."

"Okay."

"I thought you'd want to know."

"Oh, I do. What is it? Lupus? Lyme—"

"Um—"

"—fibromyalgia, cancer, precancer, shingles, Parkinson's, Graves', Turner's, Huntington's, Bright's—"

"What are you talking about?"

"If it's named after a man, my mother either has had or will have it. She's a blue-ribbon hypochondriac, Koa. Ignore her."

"I've been with her, Meg," he said. "She really is sick."

I chuffed impatiently. "Okay, well, I guess it's possible she could be sick. But you're there with her, and I'm sure she'll be just dandy before you know it. Tell her I'll be back later tonight, and I'll check on her then."

"Okay." He was quiet again, no doubt thinking what a shitty daughter and terrible person I was. Unfortunately, I didn't have the time or mental energy to convince him otherwise. All I could think of was finding William Kitchens. "What are you doing?" he asked.

I passed another house—a shack, just like the other one—except this one was deserted. Half-burned and caved in on one side. Beside a small pink tricycle, turned over on its side, was a crude cross made of two thin slats, driven into the ground out front. It was also charred black, like the walls and roof of the house, and it had a wreath of white silk flowers hung over it.

"Just some research," I said. "I'll be back tonight, I promise." I hung up.

It wasn't until after I hit another stretch of empty highway that I realized the cluster of sad buildings I'd just blown past was the actual town. I did a clumsy U-turn in Captain Mike's giant truck, then headed back. Once I hit the main drag, I pulled up to the curb and parked beside the buckled, weed-sprouted sidewalk. There were no meters or signs on the road. Not a soul in sight.

I glanced around. Captain Mike had been generous. Worse than being a turd town, Farrow, Georgia, appeared to be headquarters of the local KKK chapter. Other than one grimy hardware store a few doors down, most of the storefronts were boarded up with plywood. Everything baked under the relentless sun. The bricks of the buildings along the street were either a flat yellow or else painted over in charcoal. The sky was enormous above me—white, with a bank of thick, gray clouds rising up behind the buildings. Windows were smashed; half-hearted graffiti decorated the brick facades: *God and KKKountry*, they read. *Trojans 14—Rebels 0, Boo-Yah!*

Besides the hardware store, only one other establishment seemed to be open for business. Its cracked, masking-taped display windows were festooned with a couple of bedraggled, sun-washed Confederate flags. The door was blacked out and a plywood sign hung on two chains. **WAR ROOM**, it read in block letters, and under that, **KIDS KADET KLUB AT 6.**

My God.

How had William Kitchens, the man who'd gone to Custer, South Dakota, with the American Indian Movement, losing his wife in the process, ended up in this nightmare of a town? How could he stand to live here?

The sharp tang of rain hung in the air, making my mouth feel even drier. I had thought I'd grab a Coke or a cup of coffee at a local diner before heading to Kitchens's place, but there didn't appear to be anywhere to do that. No quick-mart or grocery or deli anywhere in sight. I was going to have to power through.

I pulled away from the curb, maneuvered through the sad downtown and along a series of potholed roads lined with sagging shacks. The neighborhood—if you could call it that—led to fields littered with broken stalks, the remains of a harvest I couldn't identify.

Kitchens's house stood in the middle of one of these fields, flanked on one side by a huge oak that had been shredded by lightning. A ring of wood spikes crowned the trunk, and one of the partially amputated branches, itself as big as a small tree, lay at an angle across the front yard. A small johnboat on a rusted trailer sat on the other side of the house. I parked a dozen or so yards away from the house, the nose of Mike's truck pointed out, positioned for a quick getaway.

I marched up onto the dirty porch (anchored on one end by a rusty white porch glider, on the other by a miniature fake Christmas tree) and rapped on the door. There was no answer. I moved to the window and peered through the blind. A large framed photograph hung above the sofa. The beach at Bonny Island. A fallen tree—probably yanked up by a storm and dumped on the beach, sea-washed and slick. A horse stood beside it, looking out over the roiling Atlantic. I stared, entranced. I'd just begun to think no one was home, when I heard a voice coming from the other side of the door.

"What's your business?" The voice had a distinct Midwestern twang.

I backed away from the window. "Hi, Mr. Kitchens. My name is Meg Ashley. I've come from New York. I . . . I wondered if I could talk to you about your daughter, Dorothy."

"Meg Ashley?"

"Frances Ashley's daughter."

Silence.

"Mr. Kitchens, I'm here on my own behalf, not my mother's. I want to help, if I can." I scanned the desolate yard, the dry-bark pines, the puddles of yellow water teeming with mosquitoes. "I want to fix what my mother broke."

"I don't have anything to say," came the reply.

"I'm writing a book," I said. "It's an account of what Frances . . . what my mother did to me . . . and to you and Dorothy."

"She didn't do anything to us." There was a pause. "So you can go on, back to wherever you came from."

But his voice sounded unsure. Weighed down with some long-held, unnamed burden. I shifted, put a hand on the doorknob. It was blazing hot, even in the shade of the porch, but I gripped it tightly. I wasn't going to be turned away, not having come this far.

I leaned into the door. Spoke loudly. "Mr. Kitchens, would you be willing to talk about Susan Doucette's theories? About where you think the murder weapon might be?"

The door flew open so quickly, I didn't think to let go of the knob, and I stumbled into the house. When I finally righted myself, I saw William Kitchens. He had backed against the far wall and held a gun, a black and silver pistol. It was leveled at me.

KITTEN

—from Chapter 15

Smashed crystal goblets and shards of glass tumblers littered the carpet of the grand salon. Curtains pooled on the floor under cracked rods. One velvet sofa cushion was ripped nearly in two, its wadded cotton viscera spilled out.

It was Kitten's handiwork. She'd flown into a rage when she learned that Fay intended to give the deputy the ashtray.

"You've done it now, you stupid cow!" the child had screamed, taking a carved wooden pipe from a table and pitching it at the shelf over the bar. A row of silver julep cups toppled, smashing the champagne flutes below them. "Cappie's angry and she's come back. She's taken the bowl because you called the sheriff instead of throwing it in the ocean. And now she'll never leave us alone!"

Ashley, Frances. *Kitten*. New York: Drake, Richards and Weems, 1976. Print.

Chapter Thirty-Three

"Drop the gun, asshole," I blurted on reflex, like I was a character on a cop show.

He lowered the gun, and, to my amazement, I saw he was grinning. "New York, huh?"

I glared at him.

"There's some strange folks around here. You never know." He leaned past me, then executed a Clint Eastwood coast-clearing-type maneuver to make sure my team of ninjas wasn't hiding behind the rusted porch glider or Christmas tree.

"That your truck?" he asked, looking past me.

"My boyfriend's. I dropped him back in town. He's waiting for me."

"Uh-huh." He didn't look like he believed me but motioned at me with the gun. "Come on in. We can talk about . . . what you said . . . inside."

I didn't move.

"Come on. I swear, I'll put the gun away."

He crossed the room and put the gun on top of a boxy TV. I assessed him. Somewhere in his late seventies. Rangy and blond—like Doro—or, rather, he had been blond at one time. Now his hair was a thin, sandy white. Blue eyes sparked out of a sun-leathered face. Deep grooves etched either side of his mouth. A faded plaid shirt flapped around his wiry torso. I could take him if I had to. Provided a hefty dose of adrenaline kicked in.

I crossed the threshold and glanced around the room. It was shabby but tidy and smelled of some kind of bleachy cleaner. A sofa, recliner, and coffee table—a slab of particle board and two cinder blocks—made up the decor. On the surface, a neat stack of magazines sat next to a row of three remotes, which looked like they'd been lined up with a ruler.

I could feel him studying my skin, my hair, my eyes. Cataloguing me. My scalp prickled in alarm. Was he assuming I was black? Or some other unknown but offensive-to-him combination of ethnicity? Forty years ago, he'd been a freedom fighter for the Natives. Had he come full circle in his old age and turned into a raging bigot? Was he a regular over at the KKK hangout downtown, the War Room? Or did that strange light in his eyes mean something altogether different?

He held out one freckled, chapped hand. I hesitated, then took it. "Billy Kitchens," he said.

"Meg Ashley."

He was squeezing my hand tightly, still staring.

"Sorry about the gun. Side effect of living alone too long, I guess." I withdrew my hand from his grasp.

"It's fine."

"Something to drink?" he asked.

"No, thanks." I wasn't thrilled about letting the guy out of my sight. Not yet. He'd just pointed a gun at my head. "Look, Mr. Kitchens, I know this is unexpected—me showing up at your house like this. But I really need to talk to you. Would it be possible to do that? Talk?"

"I guess we could give it a whirl." He gestured to a scarred Formica table set with matching vinyl chairs on the far side of the room, and we sat. He leaned back, laced his hands over his stomach. "We could start with your mother. How is our dear Frances Ashley?"

"Going strong. Gearing up for *Kitten*'s fortieth anniversary. The publisher's planning quite a celebration."

"Good for her."

"I imagine it might be a difficult time for you, the anniversary. I know she's been the cause of a lot of heartache in your lives."

He shrugged. "The cause of good things too. Everything balances out in the end, I think, don't you? Speaking of. Why don't you tell me a little bit about your book?"

It took me a minute to recalibrate. He was obviously reluctant to talk about *Kitten*, but maybe if I got this line of conversation going, he'd warm up. I cleared my throat.

"The book's about Frances and me. Our relationship. What it was like growing up the daughter of a world-famous bestselling author and a pop-culture icon."

"Hm," he said.

"It's also about what Frances did to Doro and you. How, even though it might appear that you've benefited from her book, she actually ruined your lives."

"I wouldn't say ruined. More like, complicated. Personally, I always liked Frances. All my employees did. The cook used to bake those Italian wedding cookies for her. You know the ones, with sugar all over them."

I nodded like I knew.

"None of us had a clue she was writing a book, not until it showed up in the stores. Next thing we know, we're famous. Phone's ringing off the hook. Hotel's booked a year or more in advance. People come from all over the country. Washington state. New Mexico. People even come from Europe. You believe that? We had Canadians, German, French, and Swiss, all of them nuts over *Kitten*."

"So you didn't consider suing her?"

He squinted at me like I had said something outlandish. "Why, no."

"What about later? Did you want to sue her later on, when the Kitty Cultists started showing up?"

He gave me a rueful smile. "Listen. I was no dummy. With all that business, I could finally afford to hire a big staff—every one of them Native. I could finally do what mattered most to me—help those folks claim what was rightly theirs. I gave everyone who worked for me ownership in the island and a share of the hotel profits. If I'd have sued her, back in the beginning, I'd have lost all of that." When he looked up, his eyes sparkled. If he was lying, he did it as well as Doro.

"But then you left Bonny," I said. "You handed it over to Doro. What happened?"

He glanced around the room. At the door, the window. The red digital clock on the cable box. My stomach twisted the slightest bit. Nerves. I took a deep breath.

"Well, she did what kids do. Grew up. I'd always coddled her a bit, maybe filled her head with some grandiose ideas, but she was an only child without a mother. I felt like she could use all the building-up she could get. But I admit it. Some of it came back to bite me."

"What do you mean?"

He smiled to himself like there was some private joke only he could understand. Shook his head.

"You can trust me, Mr. Kitchens."

He leveled a look at me. "Doro loves Bonny Island. I mean really loves it, in a kind of obsessive-type way, you might say. She believes that she has a unique connection to it. Which may be true, I don't know. Doro's always been an odd one. Anyway, by the time she was grown, she'd developed some pretty particular ideas about her role there and how things should be run."

I raised my eyebrows, but he waved his hand.

"I'm not going to go into it. Suffice it to say I got tired of fighting with her, day in and day out. So I handed the reins over to her and left."

"And came here. In 1991," I said.

Around the same time he brought a lawsuit against my mother. An interesting coincidence.

"Why here?" I asked.

"Couldn't stay in St. Marys where we'd be running into each other at the Winn-Dixie. This place is close enough so I could keep an eye on her and stay out of her way at the same time."

"Keep an eye on her?"

He cleared his throat. "I might visit the island every now and then. To check up on things."

"In the dead of night? I think that's called spying."

He shot me an apologetic grin. "At the end of the day, she's my girl. And I'm her daddy. I told you, she's an odd one. Sensitive and vulnerable. It's my job to look after her, even if she doesn't want me to. No matter how much of a pain in the ass she might be, I couldn't live with myself if I left and something happened to her. Anyway. I heard Doro had a lot of turnover with the staff. Dustups with the guests. Didn't surprise me much. She can be prickly. Hard to work with. I hear she got her a whole new crew, before she decided to shut the place down."

"What do you think about that?"

"It's hers now. She can do what she wants."

Including tell everyone that you're dead, I thought.

He drummed his fingers on the table, then eyed me. He seemed on the verge of saying more. I wondered how long it had been since he'd had a visitor. Since he'd unburdened himself to someone. I felt another ripple of discomfort.

"So why didn't you go back to wherever you were from? Why did you come here?" I asked. "To Farrow?"

"Don't get me wrong; I know the town is a shithole. And it's full of racist assholes. But it's cheap, and I keep to myself. And it's nice out here in the country. Quiet."

Then, without warning, he leapt out of his chair and crossed the length of the room to the boxy TV. He drummed his fingers on the top a few times, then ricocheted to the opposite wall, the one with the horse photograph. He stared up at it, rubbing his chin.

"Billy?"

He spun back to me, his jaw set, arms limp at his side, and spoke.

"There are direct flights from Jacksonville International to LaGuardia, all day, every day. Just pick a time."

I stared at him in disbelief. He'd started shifting his weight from foot to foot.

"Are you kidding me?" I asked. He didn't look like he was. He looked deadly serious. Afraid, even.

"I can get you a ticket," he said. "First class, if that's what you want." His voice had risen the slightest bit.

I stayed very still. "I don't understand what's going on here. Why don't you just tell me the truth, Billy?"

He seemed to hug the other wall. And now he was plucking at his shirt like he was on the verge of having a panic attack.

"Billy?"

"You don't know what you've gotten yourself into. You got no damn idea. So, like it or not, I'm taking you to Jacksonville, putting you on a plane, and sending you home."

And then he lunged toward me.

KITTEN

—FROM CHAPTER 16

Fay screamed Kitten's name through the oaks, into the nettle bushes, and across the vast, flat beach. The wind whipped her voice up and into its hot, swirling currents, carrying it away before there was an answer. The only sound that remained was the echo of the endless waves. Even the birds had stopped singing.

At the northern end of the island, she stood on the pinnacle of the middens, looking out over the crashing greenish-brown Atlantic, savoring the lash of her hair on her face. She hated herself for the thought, but she had not ruled out the chance she might catch a glimpse of Kitten's form, bobbing lifeless in the surf. When she got up her courage, she looked.

The water was clear.

She returned to the house, exhausted, sunburned, coated in sand and mosquito bites. She was starving as well, having run out of the house without the slightest thought of breakfast. She told herself not to cry. A little something to eat would make things seem brighter.

Ashley, Frances. *Kitten*. New York: Drake, Richards and Weems, 1976. Print.

Chapter Thirty-Four

I scrambled up out of my chair as Billy crossed the room. But he didn't intend to hurt me; all he did was slap a wad of crumpled bills on the table between us. He looked at me with a beseeching expression.

"Take it," he said. "It's all I got. Just take it and get the hell out of here."

"I don't want your money. I'm not leaving." I was shaking a little. Breathing hard. He'd scared the shit out of me, again. What was it with this guy? "Look, Billy, I'm going to find out what went on between you and Frances and Doro, and I'm going to put it in my book. So if you know anything, if you have anything to get off your chest, now would be the time."

His eyes met mine. The fire was gone, his whole body had deflated, and I saw where a couple of beads of sweat had tracked down his face. He let out a long sigh.

"I need a drink." He pointed at me. "You? Beer? Iced tea?"

The man was a disaster, possibly an unreliable source. But I needed to calm him down enough to open up to me.

"Sure," I said. "Whatever you're having."

He returned from the kitchen and we sipped rum and iced tea from cups with Confederate flags emblazoned across them, and the words *DIXIE OR DIE*.

"Sorry about the . . ." He glanced at my cup. "They're free at the Dollar Store in town."

"Just tell me about Doro, Billy."

He leaned back. "You don't know how it was for her all those years. You wouldn't believe it. No one could, not if they hadn't seen it for themselves."

"So make me understand."

"Weirdos and freaks." His voice was gruff and unsteady now. "Maybe even some of them perverts, I don't know. And I let them . . . I gave them complete access to the island. They used to spy on her, you know, all hours of the day. Snuck into her room at night. They said nasty, hurtful things—like how did it feel to kill her best friend? Was there blood or brains that spilled out when she did it? Where did she hide the murder weapon?"

I was silent.

"And I didn't stop them." His face sagged in regret. "About four years after the book came out, a group of kids, teenagers, told her they were kidnapping her and tied her up. Left her on the north end of the island in some cove while we searched for her for hours. Did she tell you that?"

"My God. No."

"She was twelve years old. She went back to sleeping with her baby blanket after that."

His fingers frantically drummed the table for a moment or two. Then he stood. Began pacing the tiny den, matting the grungy shag carpet in long twin tracks under his work boots. "She never made any friends. The boys she liked never liked her back. One broke her heart so bad I thought I'd lost her forever. Her mind, you know. I thought it might be gone for good."

"Pete Darnell?"

He stopped in front of the photograph. His skin was mottled, pale beneath the sun spots, and a blue vein stood out on his forehead.

He rubbed his bristled jaw. "Ah. Maybe that was him. Hard to say."

It was a lie, I was almost sure of it. The man looked antsy, like he might make a run for it, right out the front door. I wondered if it had anything to do with his defamation lawsuit against Frances. The mysterious, disappearing lawsuit.

"Doro told me some things," I said. "But I'd like to hear it from you so I can understand better. Would you be willing to talk about how you came to own Ambletern?"

"What did Doro say?"

"That Bonny Island was a land grant to your family after the Revolutionary War." I sipped the tea.

"It looked good on the brochures. And back then, there wasn't any Google to prove it wrong. The real story was my wife found an auction notice in the newspaper, and suggested we buy it with some money she had from an inheritance. We were up in South Dakota at the time—"

"At Custer," I said.

"That's right." He studied me. "She died up there, as I'm sure you already know. I decided me and Kitten would go ahead and buy the island anyway. Even though Vicky wouldn't . . ." His eyes strayed back to the other side of the room. The window. The door. The clock. Jesus, this guy. Now he was making me jumpy.

"Don't be too hard on Doro for sticking with our old story," he said. "Sometimes adults find comfort in childhood tales."

"Look, Mr. Kitchens, I'm not here to call Doro out for lying. But there are so many rumors about you guys. Frances and the murder weapon. I just want to clear some of it up."

"All those Kitty Cult rumors," he said. "I don't like talking about them."

"But say, for instance, Frances knew what happened to Kimmy or what became of the murder weapon." *Or you did,* I thought. "The world deserves to know the truth."

"The world doesn't deserve a damn thing. The cops agreed that Vera probably did it. And she's gone now. Died of a stroke in jail before she ever went to trial. So it doesn't matter."

"But there are other theories. Like Susan Doucette's."

His head jerked up. "How do you know her?"

"I'd rather not say."

He let out his breath. It made a whistling, wheezy sound.

"Susan said you sued my mother, back in the early nineties," I added casually.

"That was nothing." He waved his hand. But he glanced away. Out the window again.

"Susan thought you and my mother worked out some kind of deal. A trade."

"There was no trade. I just changed my mind, is all. And I don't want to talk about it."

I started to say something more, but before I could, my stomach twisted the slightest bit. Just enough to send me to the edge of my seat. The pinpricks started too, rising up and rolling over me.

"You okay?" he asked.

"I, uh . . ." I rubbed my stomach. Dr. Lodi had said nausea was one of the symptoms of lead poisoning. Maybe now that the lead was being pulled out of my system, this was how it was going to be.

"I'm fine. I've got lead poisoning. I have symptoms—"

He cocked his head. "Mind if I ask you a question now?"

"Okay." My stomach cramped again. Then, as quickly as it came, it passed. I inhaled deeply. Prayed I wouldn't have to ask this man to let me use the facilities.

"Where are you from?" he asked. He was still standing by the sofa, but he seemed farther away than just a minute ago. The weak sunlight in the little house had become strange all of a sudden. Greenish gray and dancing with dust.

I rubbed my temples. "Where am I from?" I repeated. My voice sounded strange and tinny in my ears.

He moved closer. "What nationality are you?"

"American," I said.

"But you don't look a thing like your mother." I could feel his eyes travel the length of me. Not in a lecherous way, exactly, but a bit off, all the same. "Your skin is . . . beautiful but different than hers. And your hair. Not a hint of red in it. Not a hint. No resemblance, that I can see. Was your father foreign?"

My heart thudded. "I don't see how that's relevant."

"So what?" His eyes flicked briefly up to mine. "I welcomed you into my house. You can tell me a thing or two in return. Out of courtesy."

"It doesn't matter." A wave of cramps hit me, and I clenched my jaw.

"It's hard to tell," he mused. "You could be African or Indian. Caribbean. Or Egyptian, maybe. A modern-day Cleopatra."

Normally, if anybody talked to me like that, I wouldn't hesitate to tell them to fuck off. But the pain from my stomach silenced me, twisting violently. And I could taste a metallic tang. My mouth felt unwieldy and numb and wouldn't form the words I was thinking in my brain.

This wasn't the lead. This was something else. Something different. Suddenly, I was afraid.

"You're pretty, either way. I mean that."

Thoughts careened through my head, spun past me so I couldn't seem to grab hold of them. Something was happening, but I couldn't figure out exactly what it was.

"I—" My throat felt tight and hot, my head like it was detached from my body. The strangest sensation. I licked my lips and managed to stand. "Bathroom?"

I wasn't thinking bathroom. I was thinking *door*. Or *window*.

Billy Kitchens smiled what looked like an apologetic smile. His eyes looked dark to me all of a sudden. Animals' eyes did that, I thought, dilated before they pounced on their prey. So they could focus on the kill. I imagined Billy's face had become a wolf's face—covered in fur, his teeth lengthening to razor-sharp fangs.

Jesus. I was losing my mind.

"Easy now," I heard from somewhere. I felt a rough hand encircle my wrist and give a gentle tug. I stumbled forward.

Toward the wolf.

"No," I said. The fear spiked now, but no adrenaline accompanied it. I couldn't run away. Or take a swing at him. I could barely move.

I pulled against Billy with what little strength I had left.

"No," I moaned. "No, no, no . . ."

"You're safe, Meggie, don't worry. I was just gonna let you lie down on the sofa for a bit and talk to you. I needed to give you a drink so you'd listen to me. So you wouldn't fight me or try to run out on me."

"Fight you . . ."

"It's okay. Come on." He pulled me, and I staggered forward, then I sank down, surprised to feel the scratchy sofa beneath me. I leaned my head back. Closed my eyes. I felt two hands guide my shoulders until I was prone.

Oh God. If only the pain would stop.

If only . . .

"I've got you, little Meggie," Billy said in a singsong voice. "Don't you worry now, I've got you."

KITTEN

—from Chapter 16

Fay hoped she would go upstairs to find Kitten in her bedroom, curled up on her window seat, reading her *Verselet* book.

She imagined the girl sucking on a butterscotch, her composed, alabaster face set in a childish pout. Perhaps, if she were up there and Fay were very calm and firm, the child would understand that Fay had been duty bound to call the sheriff instead of throwing the ashtray in the sound.

Maybe Kitten would let Fay comfort her. She was a child, after all, and children were vulnerable when they were frightened. Fay would explain in the most convincing way she could that Kitten's parents would return soon and there was nothing at all to worry about—and then afterward, maybe the two of them would go down to the kitchen and find some ice cream.

Fay climbed the front steps of the hotel and crossed the porch, but even as her hand twisted the corroded iron doorknob, she knew something was wrong. Terribly wrong. The heavy front door of Ambletern was locked.

Ashley, Frances. *Kitten*. New York: Drake, Richards and Weems, 1976. Print.

Chapter Thirty-Five

I lay on Billy Kitchens's sofa and stared up at his stained ceiling. My head spun, and sour saliva filled my mouth. I wanted to throw up, but the possibility, the relief of it, felt light-years away.

"I need to be sick," I said, struggling to sit up.

He pressed me back down, easily, with just one hand. "Lie still. Go with it. If you don't fight it, it can actually be quite an enjoyable experience. A spiritual one, in fact." I swiveled to face him. He was on his knees by the sofa, watching me.

"Forgive me." He reached for me, but I shrank back. "I didn't mean to scare you. You're stubborn, which isn't surprising. It's just that now I got to figure out what to do now."

"I've got a medical condition," I said. "Whatever you gave me—" I sat up fast, the room tilted, and he pushed me back down. Firmly this time.

"What I gave you won't kill you. I, on the other hand, could."

I froze.

He shook his head, like he regretted the statement. "Poor choice of words. You just need to lie still. Okay?"

I shut my mouth and scanned the room. The gun was still on the TV. And across the room, my purse on the table. I looked back at him. His eyes were narrow and cold, studying me. I could smell his breath. Toothpasty, with a hint of rum. He touched my arm, and I flinched.

"I'm sorry I said that."

I turned my face away.

"You have to know I would never do that. I would never hurt you, not on my life. You can trust me. I just didn't expect you to come out here. I wasn't ready." He ran his fingers down my arm, and I jerked away.

"What did Susan Doucette tell you?" he asked.

"Nothing," I answered through clenched teeth.

He grabbed my face, and I cried out.

"Nothing. She just told me how to find her blog. That's all." I squeezed my eyes shut. Envisioned running to the table, reaching my hand into my purse. Digging beneath the wallet, Kleenex pack, and compact.

He moved closer. I held my breath.

"I saw that site when she put it up," he said. "I know everything it said. She didn't tell you anything else? You swear?"

"No."

He let go of me, and I cracked open my eyes. He'd dropped back on his heels. Was rubbing the scruff on his cheek. This lunatic, hiding in this disgusting yellow town—I wanted to claw out his eyes, kick him in the balls. I rolled my head so I could see the TV, where the silver pistol still gleamed. My purse was still on the table too.

"Susan Doucette," I panted, "was nothing but a nerdy little kid. She didn't know what she was saying."

He slumped. "Oh, Jesus. Goddammit all to hell."

I struggled to keep my eyes open. To swallow down the sour liquid rising up my esophagus. "Just tell me the truth. Did Frances really do it? Did she pay you in exchange for the murder weapon?"

He looked really distracted now, plucking at his beard, scratching his chest.

"I gave everything I had to that godforsaken place." He was looking over my head, at the picture of the sea-washed tree trunk and the horse on the beach. His eyes were shiny. "Perfect Bonny. Paradise." He smiled down at me. "You know, no one even knows what the Guale called it originally because there's no record of their language. It died, along with a whole people. It was paradise, at first. But things happen. Doro and I had a falling-out, and I had to go. Paradise lost. People have to move on, for their own good. You understand that. That's why you're writing the book."

"I have to go," I said. "They're expecting me back at Ambletern."

He looked at me, his eyes full of pity. "You can't go back there, Meggie."

I lay completely, utterly still. Maybe, if I could sit up and hold on to something, I could walk. I could take him by surprise, if I could just get control of my limbs.

"You're not safe," he said. "Not at Ambletern. Not on Bonny Island."

Did he mean Doro was dangerous? Or Frances? Or just that he had concocted some horrible plan for me?

He was still talking. "You need to stay here, in this house, with me. I won't let anyone hurt you. I swear it on my wife's grave."

My eyes slid past him to my purse. I was feeling a break in the nausea, and suddenly, my thoughts arranged themselves in something resembling logic. A plan.

A handy trick I'd picked up from the girls in boarding school.

I opened my mouth and jammed my finger down my throat as far as it would go. I bucked once, heaved, and vomited up a fountain of macaroni and cheese, red wine, and rum iced tea, directly onto Billy Kitchens's soft plaid shirt. He jerked back, hitting the coffee table and knocking the board off its base. The magazines and remotes flew in every direction. I rolled off the sofa and scrambled around him, just as he grabbed at my ankle. His nails tore my skin.

I ran to the TV, reached for the gun, but felt a shove. I pitched forward, crashing headfirst into the TV and toppling it off its stand. The gun glanced off the wall. As Billy pawed through the broken tangle of cart and TV and wires, I ran to the table and tore open my purse. The contents sprayed out—wallet, phone, coins, tampons, lipstick, and my little pink canister of pepper spray. I grabbed the spray, flipped open the cap, and pivoted.

He was coming at me, fast. Hands trembling, I aimed and pressed hard, arcing the stream in the general direction of his face. As the spray hit its target, I saw his eyes bulge and mouth gape. He leapt back with a strangled cry. Flung one arm over his face.

"Shit!" he yelped. He staggered back, moving in circles. "What the hell—"

I scrabbled through the spilled contents of my purse. My keys. Where were my keys?

Pocket.

I patted my jeans pocket and, feeling the lump of keys there, went to snatch up the wallet and phone. I jammed them back in my purse and ran for the door. I flung it open so hard it banged against the wall and smacked me on the shoulder.

The yellow-clay drive was empty. Captain Mike's truck was gone. Gone.

I felt two hands grab my shirt and pull me back. I twisted around. Billy, his chest slicked in vomit, head tucked, and eyes blinking frantically to rid themselves of the pepper spray. He pushed me toward the sofa.

"You aren't safe," he gasped. "I'm telling you, you have to stay with me."

I ducked, and he tripped over me. I swung an elbow then, hard, against the side of his head. He gasped and staggered away.

"Where's my truck?" I screamed at him.

He straightened, a puzzled look on his face.

"Who stole my truck?"

He just stared at me in confusion. I clutched my purse to my chest and sprinted for the open door. The outside.

"Meg!" I heard him shout behind me.

I clattered down the porch steps and across the cracked clay yard. It was dark, and I tripped over a few branches and rocks as I ran, but I made it to the end of the rutted drive and hit the street without feeling Billy's iron grasp. I didn't look over my shoulder, didn't slow down until I'd made my way through the lonely, darkening neighborhood and back to the main street in downtown.

Mike's truck was there, I could see it three blocks away. It was parked in front of the KKK headquarters beside the blinking yellow light, a tow truck in the spot in front of it. I slowed to a jog and glanced over my shoulder. The street was deserted, same as earlier, but this time I was pretty sure I was being watched.

I walked all the way around the truck. Someone had taken a bat or crowbar or something to the headlights and back lights and the grille. The lights were a mess, but the dents were minor and the paint job was mostly intact. Captain Mike was going to kill me. Maybe if I gave him every bit of cash I had in my wallet—

I stopped at the front grille. A huge Confederate flag was draped over the hood; it had been secured with a web of black electrical tape. I felt the eyes then. I turned and saw them, pinpoints of light in the gloom of the storefront, and the beards and dirty caps and cigarettes glowing.

I grabbed a fistful of the flag, yanked it off, and climbed in the cab. Mike's veteran's cap, the navy one with the gold stitched leaves on the brim, perched on the dash. I popped it on, tucking my hair up under, and pulled it low. I started the truck—the light on the radio blinked on. *9:17.* I had just enough time.

Not that I was in any shape to drive. It would not be good if I got pulled over.

My hands had gone numb from the pinpricks, but I wiped my mouth on my sleeve, pulled down the drive shaft, and popped off the emergency brake as best I could. I'd stop to clean up when I got out of this nightmare of a town. When I was far enough away that I no longer felt the burn of eyes on me. When I got back to the marina, I'd tell Mike that rednecks from Farrow had defaced his truck and promise to cover all the damages.

When I pulled out, trembling all over, I made sure to screech the truck's tires over the crumpled flag where it lay on the hot asphalt.

KITTEN

—from Chapter 17

Ambletern remained an unassailable fortress, indifferent to Fay's attempts to enter it. She could not manage to pry off the storm panels. And after a day and a half of watching for boats in the sound and nights of sleeping on the porch swing, Fay despaired of seeing Kitten, the Murphys, or anyone else, ever again.

She despaired of escaping Bonny Island.

Ashley, Frances. *Kitten*. New York: Drake, Richards and Weems, 1976. Print.

Chapter Thirty-Six

It was pitch dark when I finally got back to Ambletern. I climbed the stairs, turned down one of the hallways that bisected the third floor, and rapped on Frances's bedroom door. Somewhere in the distance, crickets chirped a rhythmic lullaby. There must have been a window open in one of the rooms up there.

I tried her door. It was unlocked. Inside, one lone lamp glowed at the desk, but shadows layered the rest of the room. I could still see that it was done up in rose toile. Wallpaper, upholstered loveseat, curtains, all of it the same pattern. On the bed, the toile coverlet stirred.

"Frances?" I whispered.

She sat up. Her hair gleamed in the pale light, a halo of burnished copper. Her face was pale and drawn. She looked so much older in the weak light, it took my breath. I felt a pang. A yearning so intense, it surprised me. What would she do, I wondered, if I ran to her? Crawled beside her in bed?

It would be so easy to tell her I'd decided not to write the book. With just a sentence, I could turn this ship around and make all of it go away. We'd go home. And maybe, because of this experience, she'd be softer. And maybe I wouldn't be such a bitter asshole. Maybe we could actually try to love each other.

Maybe.

She squinted at me. "What happened to you?"

I moved to the bed. "Nothing. I'm fine. Just a crazy day. How are you feeling?" I handed her the glass of water from the nightstand. She gulped the whole thing down and handed it back to me.

"Less like a corpse now. What are you talking about, a crazy day? Where have you been? Where did you go? You don't look good."

So. This was the mother-act I was going to get: the firing-squad version. I steeled myself and tried to arrange my face in a nonchalant expression.

"I went to St. Marys. To do research."

She stiffened. "You shouldn't be running around by yourself. It's not a good idea."

"You're kidding, right?"

She lay back on the pillows. "Did you find what you needed?"

"Might have."

She stared at me expectantly. "Well?"

I didn't answer.

She shrugged. "All right, fine. Suit yourself."

"Can I get you anything?"

"A teleportation device," she said.

I smiled. "Are you hungry?"

"God, no. From now on, I will not be consuming anything Doro Kitchens has touched. I swear that woman put something in my soup."

"Or maybe you have a virus. Or a reaction from something you ate before you got here."

She sniffed, fumbled under the covers, and produced her phone. She began to scroll, and I sat on the edge of the bed.

"Phone blowing up?" I asked.

"Benoît is incredibly attentive."

I watched her thumb her phone. "Is there something you want to say to me, Frances? Something, possibly, about a document you printed that you shouldn't have?"

She kept scrolling. "I'm sure I don't know what you're talking about. Is there anything you would like to say to me?"

I sighed. So she wasn't going to cop to going into my computer and printing out my book. I didn't even care. "I'm sorry I wasn't here for you. I'm sorry you were sick."

"Are you?"

The sadness in her voice caught me off guard. "Mom. Why would I be happy that you were sick?"

"Let's see: your tragic childhood, my recent nuptials"—she glanced at me—"Graeme Barnish."

"I would never wish you pain or sickness."

"Just a ruined reputation."

I bit my lip. She had a point. "Look. I don't know that we're ever going to come to any kind of agreement about Graeme. Or the rest of everything. I just wish things had gone differently, that's all."

She'd let the phone fall and was gazing at the dark French doors. "No one drew the curtains."

I stood up and walked across the room.

"Why don't you want to tell me about your research?" she said. "Did you uncover anything that's going to blow the Kitten story wide open? The murder weapon? Proof that Doro did it?" There was an edge in her voice.

"I really don't want to talk about it."

"Megan"—she plumped a pillow behind her—"let me explain something. If the Kitty Cultists haven't been able to prove the deep, dark, mysterious truth, you won't either."

"Right, I forgot. You already told me. Doro killed Kim." I folded my arms. "Only you have always been and will always be full of shit, so I don't believe a word you said."

She ran her fingers through her hair, and I could see the white roots. "All right, then. If you're so smart, go figure it out for yourself."

"I'm trying to." I narrowed my eyes at her. "Only I don't think I should be asking the same questions all those imbecile Cultists ask—about the murder weapon and clues and blah, blah, blah. I think I have to go deeper. All the way down to each of the characters' innermost desires."

She let out a delighted laugh. "Excellent imitation of me, darling."

"I've heard you interviewed a million times, you forget. Haven't you always said mysteries aren't just about Mrs. Peacock doing it in the library with the candlestick? They're about *why* Mrs. Peacock had to do what she did."

She struggled up against the bank of pillows. "And who she needed to protect."

Our eyes locked for a brief moment, and I felt a blip of excitement. Time seemed to have dropped away. We were working on something together.

"Okay, then," I said softly. "What was your motivation, Mom? And who were you protecting?"

She shook her head. "I told you, Megan. I had my suspicions about Kim Baker's murder. So I fit my story to them. I didn't think about the implications, because I was just a silly girl. A child. I just wrote it down and it became . . . what it became."

"But there has to be more."

"Why? Some mysteries are never solved, that's the sad truth. There is no more. No proof, no way of finding proof. It's all over. I wish everybody would move on."

That was the first time I'd ever heard her say that. *Interesting.* I pinched the bridge of my nose. I could still feel the last vestiges of the poison in my system—the rolling of my stomach, the pounding right behind my eyes. I wondered if it was cassina that Billy had given me. I wondered if that's what had made my mother sick too.

"Billy Kitchens is alive," I said. "He lives not too far from St. Marys."

She blinked a couple of times, then let out a great sigh. "That was your research. You met with him," she said. Her voice had a toneless quality to it.

I nodded. Spoke carefully. "We talked briefly. He told me some things. Not much. He's a . . . bizarre guy. Definitely hiding something— information—and possibly the murder weapon."

Or you're hiding it.

"He told you that?" she asked. She looked the slightest bit afraid.

"Not in so many words."

"Ah." Her lips curved in a knowing smile. "You found Susan Doucette's website. Baker's house, mission ruins, or middens?"

"Or at one of your many houses," I said. "Susan believed you did it. Did you? Did you kill Kim Baker?"

She met my eyes. Hers were unreadable now. Opaque, like I'd said to Doro.

"Come home with me, Megan," she said.

"No."

She lay back. Turned her head away.

"Then go." Her voice was weary. "Do your research. Decide what the truth is and put it in your book. Write that your horrible mother killed Kim Baker, and Billy Kitchens covered for her so he could turn a profit." She turned her face to the ceiling. "Go finish your book, Megan. Tell the world your heartbreaking story."

Tears rose in my eyes, and a hollowed-out sensation in my chest I'd never felt before.

"Go," she said again.

So I did.

I pulled the door shut behind me, then headed down the dark corridor and a flight of stairs in the direction of my room. When I rounded the shadowy corner before my door, Doro appeared like an apparition in the center of the hall.

KITTEN

—from Chapter 18

Upon returning from her latest vigil at the dock, Fay noticed something sitting at the top of the porch steps. It was a lumpy object, shiny and silver. It looked like a gift left for her by an island elf. She stopped, glanced over both shoulders, then back at the silver ball.

There was no one around, no telltale sway of branches or whiff of a scent of the departed messenger.

On closer inspection, the silver turned out to be a ball of aluminum foil. She collapsed on a middle step and pried it apart with trembling fingers. Inside she found three sugar-white wedding cookies. She scanned the grounds again but saw no one. Her mouth watered furiously, even as she remembered the tarts.

What if Kitten was trying to poison her now? She really shouldn't risk eating anything the child could have touched, but she was dizzy with pain and hunger. She lifted one of the cookies to her mouth and inhaled. An invisible cloud of sugar filled her mouth.

Ashley, Frances. *Kitten*. New York: Drake, Richards and Weems, 1976. Print.

Chapter Thirty-Seven

I jumped back and clapped my hands over my chest. "Doro! You scared me."

She stood unmoving in the darkness—and I flashed to an image of her as a little pigtailed girl, creeping around the deserted halls of Ambletern. Skulking. Plotting. Eavesdropping.

"Sorry," she said. "Didn't mean to. I was just making the rounds." She touched my arm. "How is she?"

"Fine." I managed a rueful grin. "She's always fine. She's a cockroach."

"How were things in town? You were gone a long time."

"Good. Good. I just needed a break, you know? From . . . everything."

She nodded. "Are you hungry? I can fix you something."

"No," I said, then realized I hadn't seen Esther or Laila since I'd gotten back. Or Koa. In their absence, the noises of the house seemed more pronounced than usual, like the place ached with emptiness. "Where is everybody?"

"Laila and Esther went to visit their uncle down in Florida. They'll be back next week."

"How did they get to shore? Captain Mike was in St. Marys."

"Water taxi. One from town."

"But Koa's still here?" I was starting to feel strange. Sick and exhausted and disoriented from my argument with Frances.

"He's downstairs." She gave me a cursory look. Her nose wrinkled, I was sure from the reek of sick coming off me. "Have you been sick?" she said.

"Yeah. The lead. It makes me nauseated. I went to town to drop off my blood samples. Then I stopped for a drink or two. Didn't sit well with me."

"You were alone?"

Yes, alone, I thought. *Always alone.*

Doro caught my hand and squeezed it. "Megs."

The tears were so close—threatening to overwhelm me—that I didn't trust myself to speak.

"Did you have your chelation today?" she asked.

I shook my head. Pulled my hand out of hers. Her face changed in the shadows.

"I'll get Koa to come up," she said.

"No—"

"You tried with her, Meg," she went on. "But it didn't work. So now she'll go home. You'll be able to relax and write your book with—"

"No." I stepped back. "No. Just . . . stop talking, okay?"

I could feel the heat from outside emanating from her. It was like she soaked up the sand and sea and sun of the island and then radiated it back, everywhere she went. It was easy to be drawn to her. I was. But I didn't want to be.

"We can do the treatment later. I'm going to bed," I said.

I brushed past her. Turned my face so she couldn't see.

"Meg, I don't understand. Did I do something?"

I stopped. Turned back to her.

She was standing there, in the dark, waiting. Waiting to hear what I had to say. Not defending herself or hurling insults, like my mother. Not preparing herself to batter me with smart retorts and below-the-belt jabs. I couldn't just run off.

"You lied," I said.

"Okay." She lifted her chin. "Tell me what you're talking about specifically."

"I don't want to. You've lied over and over to me, and I don't feel like talking to you right now."

I stumbled past her, to my room, slamming the door behind me. I shucked my clothes in a pile on the carpet and headed to the bathroom. The shower was glorious, hot, pounding, steamy, and I wished I could stay there forever. Wash away all my fuckups with Frances and Graeme and Doro and start clean. How had I let things get so tangled? Why did I keep allowing people like this—deceivers—to bulldoze my life? I didn't have any answers, but after twenty minutes, I did feel calmer. At least until, wet hair dampening the shoulders of my fresh T-shirt, I stepped out of the bathroom.

Doro and Koa stood by the balcony doors, and a full bag of Dr. Lodi's chelation cocktail hung on the IV stand beside my bed. I nearly cursed in surprise. But before I could, Doro stepped forward.

"I want to apologize, Meg," Doro said. "You were right. I did lie to you. And it was wrong of me."

I shifted my weight and tugged my T-shirt down over my thighs.

"My family didn't inherit Ambletern," she went on, her voice sounding choked. "My father bought it when I was a girl. He is . . . well, he's not dead. Not in the true sense, just dead to me." She swallowed. "I was ashamed to tell you that we'd fallen out. Why we'd fallen out. He's not right, Meg. He was . . . disturbed. Maybe even mentally ill. He did things—interfered in my life, ran off people I loved. He made it so I couldn't have a life. So, for the well-being of me and the people I cared about, I made a break—"

"Doro," I interrupted.

She blinked. "There's more. He—"

"I get it." Our eyes locked. "I know what it's like to live with a parent like that."

"I'm sorry. Really sorry."

"Yeah, okay." I sighed.

Her eyes shone in the darkness. I wondered if it was with tears; I wondered if she still ached when she remembered how Pete Darnell had deserted her. If she missed her mother and father. I wasn't a monster. There was no need to hurt Doro any further. I didn't require a grand mea culpa from her.

But the fact remained: I wouldn't confide in her anymore. She couldn't be trusted.

"I asked Koa to give you your treatment. I'll finish up and then come back and check on you."

I nodded. "Fine."

After she slipped out, I climbed into bed and Koa caught my arm. His hand was warm, rough. I covered it with mine.

"Was my mother poisoned?" I asked.

His eyebrows shot up. "What? What the hell are you talking about?"

"She thinks Doro put something in her soup."

He shook his head. "No. No chance. I helped Doro with lunch. I was with her the whole time. It was a bug or something. I promise you, Meg."

I pointed at the IV stand. "I'm going to need to look at the bag."

He furrowed his brow.

"The bag," I repeated. "Give it to me."

He unhooked the bag from the IV stand and handed it to me. I turned it over, examining the seams intently.

"You can think whatever you want of me. But I swear, I would never let anyone hurt one of my patients." He was so close, I could smell his breath. It smelled like something spicy.

I handed the bag over.

"Just a little stick," he murmured. I lay back on the pillows and turned up my arm again. Watched him hold up the needle, then lower it to a vein. He pressed it against the skin, then looked up, catching my eye. My stomach fluttered.

Then, like a shard of ice, the needle pierced my skin and slid into the vein. Air whooshed out of my lungs, releasing the pressure that had been building over the past few hours. My body melted onto the mattress.

"Good?" he asked.

I nodded.

"Be right back." He slipped out just as Doro came back in.

"Knock, knock," she said, and I motioned her over. She positioned herself at the foot of my bed. I felt her hand drop lightly onto my leg.

"You're going to feel better soon," she said.

I didn't answer.

"I'm sorry, Meg. I truly am. You know, I used to lie when I was younger. About my age, mainly. I said I was seven, all the way up until I was ten or eleven. I don't know why I did it."

"Seven must've been a good year for you."

"It was a terrible year, actually. It was the year my mother died."

"Oh. Doro. I'm sorry." I struggled up. She was wiping her nose. Dabbing at her eyes. "You were so young. You must've been devastated."

"She was an exceptional person. So compassionate. Always wanting to lift others up. The ones who couldn't help themselves. That's how she wound up getting involved with the Indian Movement. Anyway," she said briskly. "I don't remember if I cried. It was such a long time ago." She smoothed the covers between us. "You should lie down. Try to sleep."

I obeyed but didn't close my eyes. "I'm afraid when my mother dies, I'll be secretly glad. I'm afraid everybody will think I'm a monster because I don't cry."

She laid her hand on my leg again. This time it felt warm, reassuring, and I was glad it was there.

"I wouldn't worry about it, if I was you. Crying is overrated. Your connection to your mother is much deeper than a few tears."

I wondered how she'd come to know better than all the accepted research on the psychology of grief, but sleep smothered me before I could arrange the thoughts into a question.

KITTEN

—from Chapter 18

Fay nibbled tentatively at the edge of the cookie. When the powdered sugar hit her tongue, her resolve crumbled, and she crammed the entire thing into her mouth, then the other two.

While she was still chewing, Fay felt a thin stream of chilled air hit her, and the skin on her arms goosepimpled. She looked up. The house's great front door was open—cracked just enough to let the air-conditioning escape. Fay dropped the foil and raced across the porch, into the cool house, banging the door closed behind her.

It took her eyes a while to adjust to the gloom.

A voice greeted her, floating through the cool of the foyer. It didn't sound human.

"You've come back," it purred.

She turned, convulsed in horror, then screamed.

Ashley, Frances. *Kitten*. New York: Drake, Richards and Weems, 1976. Print.

Chapter Thirty-Eight

I woke sometime later in the night to see Koa standing beside my bed. I bolted up. Gasped. My pulse racing, images of Billy Kitchens and that horrible Confederate flag on Captain Mike's truck flashing in my head.

He held up both hands. "Meg. Breathe. It's me."

I clutched at my T-shirt.

"I didn't mean to wake you," he said. "Doro went to bed. I came up to finish your IV."

I lay back down, my heart still knocking away. "Good Lord, you people should carry defibrillators with you."

"I'm sorry." He pointed at the stand beside my bed. "Mind if I have a look?"

"Sure."

He edged his way to the bed and fiddled with the bag. "Looks good. I think you're all done here."

"What time is it?" I looked around for my phone. I must've never pulled it out of my purse when I got back to my room.

"A little past two a.m." In a few seconds, he had removed the catheter and wrapped the line around the used bag.

"Sorry for keeping you up so late," I said, but he just shrugged. "You can throw that away in the bathroom."

When he reappeared, his hair looked wet, like he'd smoothed it down. He stood awkwardly in the center of the room, waiting, I guessed, to say good night. I contemplated telling him about William Kitchens and Farrow. The spiked tea and our struggle and the stolen truck. I wondered how much it would freak him out. I wondered if he would offer to stay with me. If he did, I could see myself telling him everything.

I could see myself falling asleep in his arms.

I shook my head, clearing the cobwebs. Koa's reason for being here was still a mystery. And even though my gut told me I could trust him, I wasn't sure. It was possible that feeling was just plain, old-fashioned sexual chemistry. Unburdening myself should wait.

But there were other things we could do in the meantime. Things that didn't include talking. Koa might have said we should keep our distance, but here he was, standing in my room. Looking tense and gorgeous and like he might be persuaded to stay.

I propped myself up on one elbow. "You want a drink? I have some whiskey."

"No, thanks."

He didn't move. The smell of gasoline or oil, from whatever piece of lawn equipment he'd been working on that day, wafted over me. My eyes dropped to his arms, brown and muscled. They looked like they could snap a tree trunk. Possibly the best arms I'd ever seen. Top five, easy.

"I Googled you," he said abruptly, and I couldn't help but break into laughter.

"Great opener," I said. "Very smooth."

He shrugged. "I figured you were used to people doing that. But I wanted to tell you up front. So, sorry, I guess. It's really weird, now that I'm saying it." He smiled.

I sighed. "No, I'm glad you told me. That was very considerate, actually. And it's okay you did it. I don't mind."

He was quiet.

"So. I'm guessing you want to know if the gossip's true?"

"None of my business."

"No. But I'll still tell you."

He hesitated. "You dated Graeme Barnish? The guy who wrote the Aggregate series?"

Heat crept up my neck. "Yes."

"I read those. They're good."

I made a face.

"He's kind of a big shot," he said.

"Yeah. A married big shot. Which is one reason why he's an ex."

Koa didn't respond.

"It's a pretty nasty story," I said. "Worse than anybody knew."

"I'm sorry that happened to you," he said. "But we don't have to talk about it."

I nodded.

"Or any of your old boyfriends, really."

"I just thought you might be wondering." Now my face was legitimately burning, and my mouth had gone dry. This conversation was beginning to feel like it had taken a wrong turn.

"I wonder about you a lot," he said.

He was studying me. Not smiling. Just looking and my stomach fluttered in response, just like when he'd put the cath in my arm. I felt a small stab of regret about the heinous, ratty T-shirt and pajama pants I'd thrown on.

"What I mean is," he said quietly, "I think about you."

I swung my legs over the side of the bed, walked to him, and put my hands on his chest. The heat from his skin warmed my fingers. Slowly, I let my hands drift down and dip under his shirt, touching his bare skin. I moved them up, palms flat against his chest, and closed my eyes. He'd broken into gooseflesh under my touch.

"You've never told me your last name," I said.

"Pierson."

I withdrew my hands, but he caught my wrists before I could move away.

"Why did you do that?" he said.

"I don't know. I wanted to?"

He kissed me then. A thorough, urgent, crushing kiss, like he'd been holding back for a very long time. I threw my arms around his shoulders and pressed myself against him in response. After a few moments, he pulled away, but kept his face pressed close to mine. I could feel his breath in my ear.

"I guess being Meg Ashley," he said, "you're used to getting whatever you want."

I closed my eyes and breathed in the traces of cut grass and gasoline. He couldn't know how wrong he was. Being who I was meant hardly ever getting what I wanted.

After a moment, I spoke.

"Sometimes I think about what it would be like if my mother wasn't my mother. If I could've grown up someplace like Bonny Island. If I could wake up to that sunrise and the ocean and the marsh every morning. Just breathe without worrying about all the bullshit."

I opened my eyes. He was looking down at me.

"Ridiculous, I know," I said.

"No."

Our eyes were locked.

"You can talk to me," I said.

He was quiet.

"You can tell me about Neal Baker. What you're really doing here."

He inhaled deeply, and I felt my body move toward him in response, pulled in with his breath. He shook his head. "I can't. I'm sorry."

I couldn't believe it. A man of honor. A man who kept his promises. Other than Edgar, I hadn't encountered many of them. Unexpected tears filmed my eyes, followed by the hot sting of embarrassment. I looked away.

"But you don't have to know everything about a person to kiss them," he said.

I didn't move.

"You know enough. The main thing, anyway."

I raised my eyebrows.

"That I want you."

He dipped his head, found my mouth, and kissed me again. And my God, it was perfect, and he was right, I didn't have to know his secrets. Not tonight. I could let him kiss me for the sole reason that we both wanted it. So I did, and he kissed me—again and again and again—the force of every kiss pushing me away, so that he had to keep grabbing my arms or my shirt or the elastic waistband of my pajamas and reeling me back to him.

We'd worked our way over to the balcony doors, where I finally managed to grab two fistfuls of his T-shirt as well, just to anchor myself. The doors were open just enough for the breeze to billow the curtains like flags. Koa looked past me, over my shoulder, out into the darkness, breathing hard.

"What," I panted.

He was quiet for a minute and I couldn't read his face. "It's nothing," he finally said.

But he reached around and slammed both doors shut behind me, bolted them, then yanked the curtains closed. I started to ask him what he'd seen, but he pushed me up against the door, just firmly enough to make my stomach flip.

I wrapped my arms around his shoulders and laced my fingers through his hair. He lifted me up to him, his arms like steel around my torso. I let out a barely audible moan, and that was it. The next thing I knew, we were on the bed, the regrettable T-shirt and pajama pants gone, his shirt too and then anything else that could possibly keep us from doing what we wanted.

KITTEN

—FROM CHAPTER 19

The thing that had spoken was hidden in the shadows halfway up the wide staircase, shivering and gripping the banister with two red-slicked fists.

Outside, the clouds must have pushed east, because a thick shaft of light from one of the upper windows fell across the thing, and Fay could see the side of its head. Its scalp hung in ribbons over its ear. Round eyes blinked out from the red, glistening mask.

With a shock, Fay recognized the shape of Carl Cormley's close-set eyes and covered her mouth with her hand. He lifted his face toward her, beseeching.

"I stayed behind," he rasped. "I hid. I wanted to make her confess." Blood burbled somewhere in the depths of his throat.

Fay couldn't move forward. She took several steps back. She felt dizzy, light-headed.

Her back hit the massive front door, and she felt for the doorknob. When at last her fingers found it, she gripped it, twisted, and pulled. The knob turned but the door wouldn't budge. She pulled again with no luck. The door was locked. Her hands flew up to the bolt for the key that always hung there. It was gone. Someone had taken it. Taken it and locked the door from the outside.

And then she smelled the smoke.

Ashley, Frances. *Kitten*. New York: Drake, Richards and Weems, 1976. Print.

Chapter Thirty-Nine

I woke, dry-mouthed and disoriented. Strange light slanted in from between the curtains—afternoon light, I realized, when I squinted at the time on my phone. Past one.

And then I remembered.

Koa's kisses. The way they had propelled me across the room. His skin on mine in the sheets, his mouth. His body.

He was gone. He must've left sometime in the early morning. I remembered the pressure of him against me during the night. His breath caressing the skin of my shoulder. That had been nice too. Better than nice.

But what if last night had just been a diversion? A strategy to throw me off balance? Koa hadn't exactly been forthcoming about his background or why he'd come to Ambletern. Maybe he thought I'd be too starry-eyed after last night to ask any more questions. *He may be right,* I thought. The details from last night were filtering back to me, giving me shivers. As nervous as the whole thing made me, I wanted more.

I clicked on my voice mail and listened to a message from Aurora. She was boarding her parents' private plane for a Mother's Day getaway, screaming over the engine roar. She yelled that she'd gotten my email, that she supported me no matter what, and that if I found myself homeless in the near future, I'd always have a room at her place. She signed off with noisy kisses.

There was no message from Asa. No missed calls. I dialed his number, and his voice mail chirped.

"Asa," I sighed. "I'm still waiting for pages, and I . . . there's something I need to talk to you about. Call me, okay?"

I threw the phone on the bed, then collapsed back on the twisted bedclothes.

Fuck. Where was he? And why wasn't he returning my calls?

I was dying for coffee but didn't relish venturing out and running into Frances. Then memories of last night—the part at Billy's—sliced through me. I looked down at my arm. A large, angry green-and-purple bruise bloomed around my bicep where Billy had grabbed me. I touched it.

Doro said she'd lied about her father being dead because he was mentally unstable, even dangerous, which I could confirm from my encounter with him. The guy was a five-star paranoiac for sure, obsessing over his grown daughter and my safety. And maybe had even gone so far as to hide a murder weapon so his hotel could benefit financially. Regardless, at this point, if I kept my distance, he was a nonissue.

Right now I needed to focus on Susan Doucette's theories. If she was right—if Billy had hidden the murder weapon on the island or handed it over to Frances—that changed everything. And if I could actually find it? My tell-all would rocket into the stratosphere.

So my next task was to find the rock—or whatever had killed Kimmy Baker. Although I'd been to her cabin, I hadn't exactly searched the place. And I hadn't had a chance to investigate the ruins or the middens, either.

And I had to consider it might not be a rock that I should be searching for. The Cultists—Susan included—were convinced that was the murder weapon, or maybe it was an ashtray, like the one described in the book. But what color was it? And how big? Besides that, if Frances had killed Kimmy, would she really have been reckless enough to describe the actual murder weapon in her book? The reality was, the thing I was looking for could be something no one had thought of.

I knew it was probably a million-to-one chance, but maybe if I was able to find the rock or ashtray or hammer—whatever the thing was—there might be a way to match Kimmy's injuries to the shape of the weapon. And possibly some of the victim's DNA. But not the killer's—that was probably too much of a stretch. I didn't know how, exactly, but maybe the police could use it to peg the real killer. Either Vera Baker, Billy Kitchens, or Frances.

Or Doro. I guess I had to keep her in the running.

On the other hand, I got most of my ideas of how these things worked from reruns of *Law & Order*, so I was probably living in a dreamworld. But, even though all of this seemed like a reach, I had to believe having the murder weapon would be better than not having it.

Then, of course, there was Susan's other theory: that Billy had given the rock to Frances in exchange for money. Now that I really considered it, the idea seemed extraordinarily far-fetched. Frances had never liked getting her hands dirty—not for any reason. I couldn't see her willingly incriminating herself by stashing a murder weapon. She was too god-damn committed to preserving her own precious hide. If she'd killed Kimmy and gotten a hold of the rock again, she definitely would've gotten rid of it.

My head throbbed. The sheer number of possible scenarios and what-ifs was becoming ridiculous. I was going to need one of those murder walls, like TV detectives have, with hundreds of photos and clippings and notes all connected by red string. Which reminded me of Pete Darnell, Amberlern regular and Doro's friend. I'd forgotten I needed to do a little research on him.

I retrieved my laptop from the desk, typed in his name along with *"Dalton, Georgia,"* and watched the search results load. There were dozens of entries—more than the usual social media or ads for "search a classmate." Most of them had to do with Pete Darnell's parents—a wealthy family from north Georgia who'd made their money (and were still making it, from the looks of it) in carpet manufacturing. They featured prominently in the local news of Dalton and Atlanta, throwing charity galas and auctions, donating money to the Martin Luther King, Jr. Center and dedicating various parks and art complexes.

I scanned the articles. One in particular caught my eye:

> Peter, adopted by his aunt and uncle at the age
> of two after the death of his own parents in a
> car wreck, has been accepted to an overseas
> exchange program in Cairo. He will be studying
> archeology and ancient Mesopotamian history.
> Following that, he plans to attend Columbia
> University as a recipient of a Robert C. Byrd
> Honors Scholarship.

Young Darnell had published a handful of professional articles about ancient Mesopotamia, as well as a couple of pieces in *National Geographic*. He continued his parents' legacy of philanthropy and married well—Laura Thomaston, a striking lawyer from London. She was tall, thin, and blonde. Almost a doppelgänger of Doro, I noted. The Darnells spent part of the year in London and the other at their horse farm in east Georgia, where he commuted to his teaching job at the university.

I sat back and thought about Pete and Doro, and the evolution of their relationship. I wondered if he'd been angry about the joke she'd played on him when they were teens. Or if they'd just drifted apart because his family wanted someone more sophisticated for their brilliant son.

I pushed aside the computer. Pulled on my ragged jeans, a T-shirt, and a long-sleeve denim shirt from the pile on the chaise. A hint of sweat and bug spray wafted up. God, I really needed to get my laundry done. Or do it myself, which was probably how things happened around here. But it would have to wait. I had things to do. Long-lost murder weapons to find. Vague clues to uncover.

Whatever those clues might be, I needed to find them soon. Before my mother—or Billy Kitchens or anybody else—figured out a way to shut me down.

ᴄᴐ

I emerged on the ridge of sandy bluffs, the middens snaking out before me in both directions. I pushed my sunglasses on top of my head and looked down over the blinding white wall of shells that rose from the sand.

The curving wall stretched a good quarter of a mile. It was high, but even at its highest point, ten feet maybe, I could still see the sparkling sea beyond it. The water was calm today, deep blue in the sun, and the waves hardly seemed to have the energy to crest as they lapped the sand on either end of the wall. The breeze slipped over me. I closed my eyes, letting the warmth soak in and settle my nerves.

This place—I didn't know why, but it felt like I belonged to it. And also, simultaneously, it made me feel ill at ease. The same way I felt about Frances, come to think of it. Maybe I just had to accept it—for me, the idea of home would always carry with it a shadowing of discomfort.

I eased down the bluff, past pocked holes where kingfishers nested, and across the narrow strip of hard-packed sand to the wall. I pressed my hands against its uneven, scabrous surface. It was hard to believe these were just shells, put here by the Native Americans hundreds of years ago, cemented together into something impermeable by the wind and rain and heat. I thought about how, after Kim Baker's death, they'd found her mother here, sawing into her flesh with a shell. I wrapped my arms around my torso and headed east.

The thing was enormous, probably hundreds of square feet in total, front and back. If Billy Kitchens had dug out a hole and mortared the rock into the wall, it would blend in so well that in all likelihood I'd never find it. I might as well try. I'd start at one end and work my way down to the other.

Nothing jumped out at me in the first section, so I continued on to the next, running my fingers over the bumpy shells, covering as much of the surface as I could. I forged on, sweating and squinting into the sun, until, two-thirds of the way down, I stopped.

About a foot off the ground, the shells were a different color, like they'd been dyed a dingy brown. It looked like someone had flung a paint can across the bottom of the wall. I ran my fingers over the splotches, and a bit of it flaked off under my nails. I studied it, then wiped it on my jeans.

Just then, a deafening boom split the air. I shot up, and my fingers and toes tingled in response. Another boom sounded, and I shaded my eyes, searching the line of trees along the bluff. I decided to try to run around the end of the wall, where I could take cover. As I ran and the booming continued, I realized I was stinging all over. But it wasn't the neuropathy. Something real and very sharp was raining down over me. I stopped and scooped up a small, dark pellet beside my feet. What the hell . . .

Another boom rang out. A shotgun blast, I knew now. And another shower of pellets. I covered my head with my arm.

"Hey!" I yelled toward the tree line. "Hey, stop!" I crouched and scuttled along the wall, back in the direction I'd just come. Rounding a bend, I found myself suddenly in the midst of the herd.

The horses were agitated—milling about, snorting, stomping their hooves. I scooted between them, threading my way back to the wall, hoping I didn't get kicked in the head or crushed in a stampede. At last, my outstretched hand hit the wall and I managed to feel my way in the direction of the nearest end. Another crack of gunfire rang out and the horses seemed to converge and roil, undecided on which way to go. I broke into a run, just as they coalesced and turned to run with me.

In seconds, they'd overtaken me, their hooves thundering as they split and then crashed past. I crouched and threw my arms over my head. Sand sprayed me from all directions. It felt like shards of glass, shooting into my eyes and nose and mouth, and even though I knew I should keep my mouth shut, I screamed—a long, drawn-out shriek as they rumbled past.

After they were gone, I spit long strings of sandy mucus onto the ground. My hands and feet were numb, and I was trembling from equal parts relief and terror. I wiped my gritty eyes and strained to see who was on the bluff.

"Come on out, you asshole!" I screamed.

I could still hear the herd thundering their way west along the wall. The waves crashed against the other side of the middens.

"Coward!" I yelled hoarsely. I turned to see a horse, one horse, who'd left the rest of the herd. It stood alone by the middens wall. The foal.

"Hey, girl," I said and reached out a hand to touch her. "Look at you."

She nosed close to me, searching me for some kind of treat. She'd grown since Koa and I had released her a little over two weeks ago. Her spindly legs seemed so much stronger, her coat smooth and glossy. I ran my hand down her neck. "You've gotten so big."

"Seems like she knows you."

I turned to see Doro and Koa at the top of the bluff. She wore a green bikini top and jean shorts, the skin of her chest and belly and legs freckled and creased from the sun. Still, I couldn't help noticing she looked decades younger than her fifty years. It was uncanny. Beside her,

Koa held a shotgun. It was double barreled, but shorter than it should've been. Sawn off, I guessed, like in the movies. It wasn't exactly how I'd imagined our next encounter.

I started toward them, across the sand, as they made their way down to me. I charged up to Koa and shoved him, hard. He staggered back with the gun.

"Meg," Doro said.

"Are you insane?" I yelled at Koa. "You could've killed me."

"I wasn't—" Koa said.

Doro leapt forward, put her hand on my arm. But I jerked away from her, slipping in the sand. The foal nosed up to me, but I brushed her off and started marching away.

"Megs, c'mon," Doro called out. "Wait a second."

I glared back at her. "He was shooting at me. I'm going to call the police," I said.

"We were shooting in the air to get the horses moving," Doro said. She nodded at the foal, who was nosing the crotch of my jeans. "She thinks you have something for her."

Koa averted his eyes, embarrassed.

"I don't have anything," I said and stepped away.

"We didn't see you, I swear," Doro said. "But it was just birdshot, anyway. It wouldn't hurt you, falling from the air like that. We were trying to get the horses to move away from the middens. Sometimes they get confused and stuck there."

"Okay." I looked uncertainly from her to Koa. "Whatever."

"Koa," Doro said, and I saw them exchange a look. "I'll get Meg back to the house. Will you finish up here?"

"Sure," he said. Glanced at the foal. The shotgun hung by his leg.

"Hold on," I said.

Doro put a hand on my arm.

"Wait a second," I said. "What's he finishing up? What are you going to do?" I didn't know who exactly I was addressing, her or Koa, but I had a feeling it didn't matter. Something had passed between the two of them. They were in this together.

"What are you going to do?" I yelled at Koa and started toward him again.

Doro snagged my shirt. "Megan. Stop." Her blue eyes were locked on mine. "Come back to the house with me."

I looked at Koa. "Don't do it. Don't hurt her." I went to the filly and ran my hands over her withers. Draped my arm over her neck, like I'd done in the mission ruins that night when we caught her. I faced Doro. "We saved her, Koa and I did, from a snakebite. She almost died. I didn't know that you let them . . . that you let them die that way. I just couldn't let it happen. You can't . . . you can't kill her."

Doro smiled at me. She spoke in a low voice, the kind of voice people typically use for a cranky toddler or psychotic person.

"No one's going to kill the horse," she said. "We don't do that on Bonny. We protect the animals here. Yes? Okay?"

I shook my head. "That's what you guys were talking about in the library, right? You were telling Koa you knew about the foal, about what we had done. And that he had to shoot her?"

They exchanged glances.

"Meg," Doro said. "No. You misunderstood. We were just talking through all the options."

"And one of them is to kill her. Right? That's one of the options?"

Doro sucked in a breath. "We did discuss it, yes. But that's not what's going to happen."

I felt myself trembling now. "I'm not leaving until I know she's safe."

"She's safe. You have my word."

I wiped my nose.

"Meg?"

"Okay," I said.

"Koa's just going to make sure the foal catches up with the rest of the herd, so she doesn't get separated from them. She's still young. She still needs her mother." Her eyes were gentle. "Do you hear me, Meg? Do you believe me?"

I looked at Koa. He was gazing past the wall, past the far end, where the horses had slowed and were cropping at the grass along the tree line. The foal butted me with her bony head. I scratched between her ears.

"You have to know, Meg," Doro said. "It would never be my first choice to hurt a living creature, least of all the horses."

"You said you manage the herd," I said.

"I meant we don't take heroic measures." She glanced at Koa. "Typically. On very rare occasions, we have to make hard decisions. But that's not what's happening here. Okay?"

I stepped away from the foal and raked my fingers through my hair. It felt like the sun was scouring out my skull. A bead of sweat traveled down my back, between my shoulder blades. "It's not my business anyway. I just . . . I'm tired, I guess. Sorry," I said dully.

Koa finally looked at me, his eyes dark, the wind whipping his hair around his shoulders. There was a crease between his brows. He glanced off into the distance again, and it made my heart ache in a way I hadn't felt in a long time.

Doro broke the silence. "I'll run you up to the house, Megs."

"It's not his fault," I said. "It's mine."

She smiled at me. "Don't worry, I'm not going to fire him. Let me take you back and get you something to eat. Koa, we'll talk later?"

He turned, the gun shouldered. "Yes, ma'am."

She looked past him, at the foal, who had moved down the wall a piece and was nipping at the sparse clumps of sea oats. "She's a sight, isn't she? Quite the survivor. Reminds me of you, Megs."

KITTEN

—from Chapter 19

Fay's nose and mouth and throat burned with a metallic tang. The smoke had risen and thickened in the foyer such that she could barely make out Carl Cormley's gruesome visage now. Somebody—Kitten, undoubtedly—must've done something with the gas in the kitchen, switched on the oven and then lit a match.

"You're hiding her, aren't you?" Cormley said, baring his teeth and clawing one hand in her direction. "The little demon."

"No."

"I'll throttle you, too, I swear it, if you're hiding her. Come closer. Tell me where you've put her."

Ashley, Frances. *Kitten*. New York: Drake, Richards and Weems, 1976. Print.

Chapter Forty

Doro got us iced tea, and we sat in the salon. I eyed my glass, sweating on the table between us, but didn't drink. I'd had enough of tea to last me a lifetime.

She sat beside me. "You want to talk about anything?"

"Do you?"

She sighed. "You still don't believe me about the foal. Because I lied to you about Billy."

I looked down.

"Seems a bit hypocritical, since you lied to me too."

I shrugged. "I guess."

"Look, I'm sorry for misrepresenting certain . . . things about my life and the way I run the island. And I know you're sorry for not telling me about the foal. So I've got an idea. How about, from this point on, you and I start dealing in the truth?"

"Okay."

I didn't trust Doro, but I still needed her in order to finish the book. I wanted to keep things cordial between us. She had come clean about most everything. I had to give her credit for that. And I had to admit, I wanted to believe her. Her friendship had become something I couldn't imagine not having.

She went back in the office to make some calls, and I closed my eyes and let myself drift. If I could just climb in a bed and sleep until all the lead was out of my system, I'd be golden. I hadn't realized how run down I had gotten used to feeling in the past year. And how it made living my life seem like an insurmountable task.

Just then I heard something in the next room. Footfalls on the stairs. A tentative voice calling down. "Doro?"

It was Frances.

"Doro?"

I sat up. Crept to the arch and peeked around. When she saw me, she froze.

"We need to talk," I said.

She turned and scurried back up the stairs.

"Well, that's just swell . . ." I muttered, then charged after her, all the way up the stairs, down multiple halls, and back to her room. I pounded on the door.

"Frances! Open up! You're going to talk to me, do you hear?"

There was no answer. I pushed into the room and looked around. Her suitcase lay open on the bed, neat stacks of clothing already packed inside. Piles of jewelry and lingerie surrounded the bag. Two other bags already waited by the door.

"You're leaving?" My voice was a screech.

She bustled in from the bathroom, arms full of zippered bags. "I have work to do back at home. And I miss my husband." She swept her eyes over me and crinkled her nose. "Good Lord, Megan, you really ought to think about a shower once in a while."

She dumped the bags, then flitted to the wardrobe, where she flung open the doors. She swept an armload of dresses from the rod and brought them to the bed.

"I went up to the middens," I said. "To look for the murder weapon."

"A fool's errand, if there ever was one."

"I don't think so."

She smoothed a stack of clothing in her suitcase. "Megan, think about what you're saying. Even if you did find the murder weapon, the chances of finding any DNA on it are minuscule. This isn't *CSI: Bonny Island*."

"Well, maybe not, but I did find blood there, on the wall—dried blood, I think from where Doro has shot horses. I caught her, I think, about to shoot another one."

Frances went on with her folding. "You *think*. And even if that's what she was doing, it's part of her job, to manage the herd on the island. Doesn't mean she'd kill a human being."

"It means she's capable of violence. Right? It can't be easy to shoot an animal. A horse. That would have to take a seriously cold-blooded person."

"Or someone who grew up understanding the balance of nature."

"Mom."

Frances stopped and gave me a look, the one that meant she'd had enough and was about to slam shut the door on this conversation.

"I'm going to let you in on a little secret, Megan," she said. "I made the whole thing up. Everything about Kitten, the poisoned guests and the murder. All of it. I made up the whole goddamn story, just like a million writers do every day."

She straightened. Her hair had come loose from the pins that held it back. Her mouth was a grim line. She looked old. Tired.

Goose bumps broke out on my arms. "That's not what you said before."

"It's what I'm saying now."

"Were you lying then? Or are you lying now?"

She just glared at me. And then the realization hit me.

"You know where it is," I said. "The murder weapon. The rock. You know where he hid it, and you don't want me looking for it."

I thought I caught a flash of alarm in her eyes.

"Where's the murder weapon, Frances?" I asked. "The house, the ruins, or the middens?"

Her face hardened; her mouth clamped shut.

"Susan Doucette really did her homework, didn't she? She actually figured it out, so you had to shut her down. Where is it, Frances? Where's the rock? The house, the ruins, or the middens?"

And then, all at once, I didn't need an answer because I saw my mother's face. After all these years, trying to get close to her, studying her for a sign of love or approval or . . . life, I knew my mother's every expression. I knew why her face had suddenly turned a sickening shade of gray.

"Oh my God," I breathed. "I can't believe it."

I took a step toward her, and I could've sworn she flinched.

"You have it," I said. "You actually have it."

She didn't move. Not a twitch or a breath. She stared at me, her eyes huge and watery, and I let out a crow of triumph.

"You stashed it somewhere in the apartment."

She shook her head. "No."

"I don't believe you. It's hidden in the apartment. You kept it close."

I started mentally cataloguing the place. "Where'd you hide it? Where?"

Her phone trilled on the bed between us.

"Who is that?"

"Nobody."

The phone jangled again.

"You put it in your safe, didn't you? The one in your closet?"

I could see her hesitate, frantically tear through the files in her brain for an excuse. The phone was distracting her, and it was almost comical to see her struggle to come up with a lie.

"I don't have it," she said lamely. She was flushed now, staring down at her phone.

"Or in a safe-deposit box."

"Stop thinking you can bully me into confessing something that's not true!"

I fought an urge to laugh. "But it's true, isn't it? Susan was right. Billy gave it to you."

"He absolutely did not."

"There's a chance it could still have Kim Baker's DNA on it. What do you think of that? Frances? What do you say to the fact that you could be obstructing a murder investigation right now?"

The phone finally, blessedly, quit ringing.

"I'm going to call the police," I said.

"Don't you dare—"

"Don't *you* dare misdirect me anymore. I'm not asking the right questions! I don't know what I'm doing! I'm just another stupid Kitty Cultist, those poor pitiful losers imagining things that never happened because their lives are so sad and gray. Your lies are so obvious, Frances. You shut Susan Doucette down eight years ago because she figured out that you and Billy worked out some kind of deal and hid the truth. She got your fucking number and scared you to death, so you threatened her and her parents."

She was listening to me now. I finally had her attention.

"You've always known what happened that summer. But it wasn't Doro who killed Kimmy, was it? It was someone else. Was it Billy? Or you?"

I moved to the suitcase, the big one she'd just closed. I pushed it over and tore at the zipper. Once I had the lid up, I started pawing through the contents. She tried to pull me away.

"Stop it! Stop it, Megan!"

I shook her off and pushed through the slippery garments. "I know it's here. I know you brought it." I jumped up to face her. "You wouldn't have come down here without your insurance. Tell me, have you already threatened Doro with it? If she cooperated with me?"

"What could I threaten her with?"

"That you'd turn in her father? That you'd kill her yourself if she talked?"

"Megan, I would never!"

"You have no right, Frances. No right to play with the truth like that! A little girl was murdered."

"You don't know what you're dealing with here, Megan. You don't know what you're talking about."

I turned back to the wrecked suitcase. "Where is it? Where the hell did you put it?"

The phone rang again, but before Frances could reach for it, I dove across the bed.

"No!" she screamed.

I jabbed at it without bothering to check the screen. "Hello? Who is this?" She leapt to grab it from me, but I dodged her. "Hello?"

"Meg?"

A voice from what sounded like the other side of the planet, and my brain seemed to buzz and scramble.

Asa.

KITTEN

—from Chapter 19

Cormley, rigid against the banister, groaned every couple of minutes. It was a low, feral sound that erased everything else but the tight bud of terror blooming in Fay's stomach.

She flung open one of the windows near the check-in desk and kicked at the storm panel. Kicked and kicked, over and over again, but it held fast. She ran into the salon and tried another window, and another, but the plywood wouldn't budge.

Then she remembered: the panel in Kitten's bedroom, the one Kitten—or Cappie—had repeatedly pushed out, was only loosely secured. That window was her only chance. Her only way out.

She paused at the foot of the staircase and looked up at Cormley. Intermittent bursts of air and bloody spittle blew from his lips, and he still stared at her. Hungrily, like he couldn't wait to get his hands on her and devour her. She would have to make it past him to get to Kitten's room. Revulsion rolled through her, but she sucked in a smoky lungful of air and charged up the steps.

Ashley, Frances. *Kitten*. New York: Drake, Richards and Weems, 1976. Print.

Chapter Forty-One

Fury washed over me. I felt like I could crush Frances's phone in my bare hand.

"How are you?" Asa said on the other end.

"How am I?" I screamed. "HOW AM I? Why don't you tell me how YOU are? And how it is you're calling my MOTHER?"

I looked at Frances, but she'd turned away. I realized, with a flush of guilt, how much I was sounding like her. Well, so be it. I had learned from the best. I knew how to fight to the death.

"Are you all right?" Asa said. "Is everything all right there?"

"Oh, yes, Asa. Everything's all right. Just kindly answer the question."

"The question?"

"Why you've been avoiding my calls. Why you're calling Frances."

"Look, Megan—"

"Tell me what business you have with my mother."

"I couldn't figure out how I was going to tell you. I really respect everything you're trying to do."

I was quiet. My stomach had twisted into a series of knots.

"Are you there?" he asked.

I bit my lip to prevent another outburst. "Tell me what's going on. Now."

Asa cleared his throat. "I think Frances should be the one to tell you."

"Okay, fine." I hit the speakerphone button and held the phone out to Frances. "You're on."

She smoothed her blouse and leaned toward the phone. "Asa?"

"I'm here."

"All right. So, Megan, Asa has come to the decision that he is ready to make a move."

"A move," I said.

"Let me back up. Edgar's passing was very difficult for me," Frances said.

I snorted.

Frances continued. "The truth is, he was everything to me, personally and professionally, and his passing left a void. A very large and unmanageable void that only a singularly skilled person could fill."

She hesitated a beat, and it dawned. I cackled in disbelief.

"Asa?" I said. "You're telling me that Asa's your new agent?"

"He is."

"He's a newbie, Frances."

Frances pursed her lips. "He got you a book deal, didn't he? A fat advance based on nothing else but my name and his charm."

I closed my mouth.

"It was time I moved on from Rankin Lewis," she went on. "I'd gone as far as I could go with them. I considered my options and decided to ask Asa if he would represent me." Here, she smiled, an oily, self-satisfied smile. "Amazingly, he accepted. So while my lawyers work on getting me out of my contract, Asa and I are working on a couple of new projects."

I couldn't catch my breath. I felt sick to my stomach.

"Megan?" It was Asa again, from the phone. "Are you there?"

"Where else would I be?" I snapped.

"Look. I'm really sorry, Megan. It just felt like the right thing to do."

"For you."

Silence.

"At least, I hope it was," I said. "I hope she made it worth your while, Asa."

"It was the right move for Asa as well," Frances said. "I just signed a contract with Pelham Sound, a nice deal for my next book."

"What book?" I asked.

"It's going to be an autobiography," Asa chimed in. "A kind of chatty behind-the-scenes, writing-craft sort of thing—"

Frances took the phone from me. "Asa, let me handle this." She looked at me. "In exchange for my book, and a few more after that, they've agreed to drop yours."

"What?"

"Your book is dead, Megan."

I shut my mouth.

"And though it may be too much to hope for, one day, I hope you'll understand. I did it for you."

She stood there, holding the phone between us like an offering. My mind felt like a computer that had been wiped blank.

She had been right earlier. I didn't care about the book. Not really. I was just tired of the lies. Weary from trying to find my life beneath all of them. I was just trying to find a way to be free by fighting her.

Asa's voice came, tinny and pathetic, from the phone. "I'm so sorry things worked out this way, Meg. If it's any consolation, it wasn't an easy decision for me."

I brushed past Frances and tripped against the wall of luggage, sending everything toppling. As the stinging tears rose, I barreled through the door.

"She'll be okay," I heard my mother say to Asa as I fled.

I kept going, the neat click of her door echoing back to me. At the head of the stairs, I stopped. I still had questions that needed answering—but I could talk to Doro. She would tell me what was really going on. I wiped my eyes and inhaled.

"Doro!" I called into the still house. I clattered down a flight of stairs, then ran down the hallway. Another flight, and I pulled up short in the foyer. It was deserted as well.

"Doro!"

I felt my phone buzz, tucked in the back pocket of my jeans. I whipped it out.

"Megan?"

"Yes?"

"Hi, it's Dr. Lodi."

"Oh, hi . . ."

"I've called you several times. Is everything okay?"

"Oh sure, yes, I've just been a little . . . preoccupied."

I darted into the salon—it was empty—then threw open the double doors to the dining room. Empty too.

"I'm fine," I said. "Totally fine." I crossed the foyer and checked in the office. No Doro. I trotted down the narrow corridor to her living quarters.

"I'll try to make this quick," she said. "It's actually good news. I think I finally know why your lead levels are so high. I found something really interesting on your X-rays, on your ankle, where your birthmark is. It's actually not a birthmark."

I balanced the phone between my cheek and shoulder and pushed open her bedroom door. Then checked the adjacent sitting room and the bathroom. Everything was in order, but Doro wasn't there.

"What?"

I caught a glimpse of something—a leather-bound ledger on a high bookshelf—and reached for it. The 1990 guest registry. *Oh my God.*

"I wasn't sure at first," Dr. Lodi continued. "But I think when you broke your ankle, it dislodged something that had been in the tissue in that area for a long time."

Half listening to the doctor, I tore to the month of May and found what I was looking for—a signature: *Pete & Laura Darnell.* Pete Darnell, that bastard, had married and brought his new wife to Ambletern. To throw it in Doro's face. Or maybe to force a meeting with his first love—one last fling for old times' sake. But Doro had felt it necessary to hide the evidence. Why?

Something in the window caught my eye. I pushed aside the heavy brocade curtain. The driveway was empty, except for the Jeep Doro and I had driven back from the beach. No one in sight, just the sway of the palmettos and the distant curtains of dripping moss. I tried to get a view of the front of the house, but the angle was impossible.

"Hello?" I heard my mother trill out in the foyer.

Dr. Lodi was still talking, but I was barely registering her words. ". . . pellets, two of them. I've never seen anything quite like it," she said. "But it has to be where the lead—"

"Dr. Lodi, I'm sorry. Can you hold that thought?"

"Ah, sure. Of course."

Frances was standing at the front door, laden down like a pack mule with her luggage.

"Where is she?" she snapped at me.

I tucked my phone in my pocket. "I don't know. If you can just wait, Koa can—"

"I can't wait. The man with the boat is at the dock now—"

"You called Captain Mike?"

"He's waiting on me. I have to go." She looked around the room and spotted a set of keys on a table by the door. She swept them up.

"You're not going anywhere. You need to stay here and deal with this avalanche of shit you've created. I need to know what you said to

Doro, if you threatened to blackmail her or hurt her. You're not leaving. You're going to stay and deal with all this."

I lunged for the keys but she snatched them away from me. I slipped in between her and the door, planting my feet, folding my arms.

"Meg, for God's sake. Move." She tried to push past me, but I blocked her again. She sighed. "Your book is over. This whole ordeal is over."

I just stared at her.

"Get your things. You're coming with me."

"No."

Her eyes were hard glittering holes, her skin like marble. But her voice was raw, pleading. I couldn't make it all mesh. I didn't know what to believe.

"Megan. I know you're angry after all that's happened. But if you could just look past it all for a moment. If you could just trust me, for one minute—"

"I'm never coming home," I said. "I'm never . . ." The rest of the sentence died in my mouth. This was my mother. She was never going to be what I wanted. She was never going to love me. It was time to accept it.

"I never want to see you again," I finished.

I stepped aside, and she brushed past me. She flung the door open and dragged herself, strapped down with all those ridiculous bags, across the porch, down the steps. I could hear her struggling to heave the suit-cases into the Jeep, but she must've done it, because after a moment or two, I heard the engine rev and roar down the driveway.

I sank down on a bench under the staircase and waited for the tears to come. But they didn't. I couldn't cry over my mother. I didn't feel anything but glad that she was finally gone. I thought of Dr. Lodi, what she'd been saying on the phone. Something about my X-ray. I reached back for my phone.

"Megan."

Billy Kitchens stood in the bright foyer, in the exact center of the dusty Persian rug. He lifted the hem of his shirt, another faded plaid shirt like the one he'd been wearing yesterday, revealing the oily black handle of his gun. He moved to me, and I jerked in surprise, my phone pinwheeling away from me, across the polished wood floor.

I reached for it, but he grabbed my wrist and yanked me up, hard.

"Why didn't you listen to me?" His sour breath warmed my face. "I told you, you're not safe here." He yanked me into the crook of his iron arm. "You've got to come with me."

KITTEN
—from Chapter 19

Cormley clawed at her legs, managing to close one hand around her ankle. Then yanked once, hard. She bumped down the steps, two, three, four. She would've screamed, but her mouth filled with smoke. The next instant he was on top of her—pulling at her shirt and hair, breathing his hot, bloody breath all over her.

"Where is she?" he rasped. "Bring her to me, and I'll kill you both."

She flailed, kicking him off, and he banged down the steps.

Ashley, Frances. *Kitten*. New York: Drake, Richards and Weems, 1976. Print.

Chapter Forty-Two

Billy's forearm pressed against my windpipe until I saw a spray of stars. I flailed my arms wildly, trying to find something, a piece of furniture in the foyer, a random vase or lamp I could grab and swing at him.

"Don't fight me!" he snarled into my ear. "If you'll settle down, I can help you."

I relaxed, and the next instant, he released his pressure. He grabbed me by the back of the shirt and swung me toward the door. I felt his face against my ear again. His breath was sour in my nostrils.

"We don't have much time. We have to run to the dock. I hid us a boat there."

"No—"

"I've been watching. Keeping tabs. I know the signs when Doro's about to do something bad. I already warned the other one, the Native man who works for her. I told him he better get out. Now I'm here to help you. Now open that door, you hear?"

He was unhinged, Doro had said it. But she hadn't said he was dangerous. And he'd paid Koa a visit. Whatever that meant. If I could just stall him, settle him down somehow, maybe I'd be able to talk my way out of this.

I gritted my teeth. "Billy. I'll go anywhere you suggest, if you'll just let go of me."

My head banged against the door, and I gasped in pain.

"I'm sorry to do that, but you've got to mind me. Now open that door."

I obeyed, and he pushed me out onto the porch. He guided me down the steps, then the front walk.

"Now run," he ordered.

"I don't understand," I said.

"Run."

My legs felt weak, but I knew it was just the fear. I was strong enough to run. I started up a jog. Billy still clutched my shirt and jogged with me. We made it all the way down to the end of the drive, between the two tabby pillars that guarded the entrance, and then turned on the rutted road toward the dock. He pushed me forward.

"Faster," he panted.

I stumbled, and he collided with me, and we both fell. I leapt back, poised to spring away from him, but he was pointing the gun at me. At my head.

I held my breath and closed my eyes, suspended in time, waiting for the blast.

But nothing happened. No gunshot. No explosion of pain and blackness. He spoke instead.

"It was Pete Darnell. You know after he got married, he brought his brand-new wife to the island? Flaunted her in Doro's face. His wife had no idea, but it broke something inside of my girl. One day when the new wife was off at the beach, Pete and Doro, they . . . ah . . . slept together." He flung out a hand. "That piece of filth seduced my daughter in her very own house."

I thought of the missing 1990 ledger. Of course Doro had hidden it. She was ashamed.

"So you sued Frances?" I said.

"It was all her fault, I figured, in the end. She was the one who set the whole thing in motion." He rubbed his eyes, and I saw my chance. I sprang off the road and fell into the dense palmetto thicket.

"Hey!" I heard Billy call, but I scrambled up again and pushed forward. Thorns tore at me as I thrashed through the brush, but I kept running until I'd made it deep into the woods. I stopped for a second, trying to still my breath, to listen for crashing footfalls.

Nothing.

I picked a different direction and dashed through another formidable-looking wall of brush, weaving through the tangled trees. I was heading to the dock, just like Billy wanted, only not the long way on the road. I would get there first and take his boat while he was looking for me in the woods. Maybe I'd catch up with Mom. At least I could get myself to St. Marys and call Koa.

Koa. Fresh panic sluiced through me. Billy had said he'd been to see him earlier. What the hell had he done?

I kept up my pace, sprinting through the woods, branches of palmetto and blackberry slicing at me until I spotted the sound. I burst out onto the shoreline, then slowed. I'd overshot it; the dock was a couple of hundred yards to my left. Frances had already gone, apparently, with Captain Mike. I trotted along the tangled shore, looking for the boat Billy said he'd hidden. There was nothing. Just the Jeep Frances had parked nearby.

Had the story about the boat been a lie? Was Billy planning to get me out here and shoot me so he could dump my body in the sound?

I retreated back into the woods. At least there I'd be safe. I walked for a while, wondering what my next move should be. Finding Koa seemed like my best bet. He had a gun and could help me find Billy's boat, if the thing actually existed. I angled toward his cabin, picking up my pace.

Then stopped. I'd come upon the edge of a huge saw-palmetto thicket, a sea of the hostile-looking bushes stretching out at least a hundred yards in a vast semicircle. Their serrated fronds formed a formidable barrier. If I ventured in there, I'd encounter skunks and snakes and who knew what other animals, not to mention the spiny thorns of the plants themselves. I'd be sliced to ribbons.

Leaves crunched in the distance.

Billy.

I looked around wildly for some kind of ditch to duck into. A boulder to hide behind. But there were only trees—among them a huge live oak, dripping with moss and a couple of low spreading branches. The crunching became crashing. Billy was closing in on me. I had to move. Now.

I jumped and swung up over the lowest branch, the rough bark burning my hands. Billy was old, I told myself, my triceps and lats screaming in protest. He probably couldn't see worth a flip. If I camouflaged myself in the tree branches, he'd have a hell of a time shooting me. And he'd never be able to come after me. I might be a princess, but he was an old fucking man. I'd stay up here all night, if that's what it took—beat him on sheer stamina alone. I finally made my way up onto the branch, then stood and edged my way closer to the trunk where the branches were thicker and closer together. I pulled myself up, farther and farther into the tree, until I was out of sight.

I shrank behind the curtain of silvery moss. Pressed my back against the tree. Willed my breath to slow. I could hear Billy's heavy work boots stumping through the underbrush. He was getting closer. The rustling got louder and louder until, at last, it stopped.

A squirrel chirped. Birds cawed over the treetops on the water. I could hear a boat engine in the distance, puttering away. I held my breath.

"Megan!" he yelled right beneath me, then, "Goddammit."

I opened my eyes and looked around at the curtain of leaves and moss. And then I saw something that nearly stopped my heart: a snake—a rattler—was coiled in the crook of another branch, just to the right of me at eye level, so close I could see its diamond-shaped head resting on the layers of brown-and-black coils.

"Fuck," I mouthed. "Fuck, fuck, fuck."

I reached around to my left, groping. My fingers closed around a branch the size of a switch. I bent it toward me, slowly, slowly, and, after a long time, I finally felt it crack. The snake hissed, jerking its head up. I froze.

"Megan! Come on out!" Billy was pointing his gun into a stand of pine trees. "I told you, I don't want to hurt you. But if I've got to use this gun to slow you down, I will. I'll do it for your own good, if I have to."

He squeezed off a round, and a boom cracked the air. The snake's body quivered, and a section looped below the branch. I looked down. Billy had backed up all the way to the tree, my tree, and was directly under the snake.

I pictured myself reaching over, flicking the snake down with my stick. In my mind I saw it fly down past the branches, its body flailing in the air. Saw it land on Billy. I imagined him screaming. Contorting his body to rid himself of the beast. Screaming again when it sank its fangs into his neck. Yes.

I reached forward, moving the stick toward the snake. Carefully slid it through the narrow U-shaped loop. *That's it. Thread the needle. Don't move. Don't breathe.*

In one fast motion, I whipped the stick downward toward Billy, then released it. The snake sailed down toward the ground, hitting a few branches and ricocheting. The next instant, Billy screamed and began dancing over the leaves, swinging his arms wildly. I peered through the branches and moss, straining to see.

Billy whirled around it like some kind of possessed dancer, brushing frantically at his shoulders and groping blindly for his gun. He danced back, pointed the gun at the ground, and fired twice. Dirt and leaves sprayed out from the craters.

Shit.

The creature must have glanced off him on its way down. I missed. Billy shoved the gun back into his waistband and peered up into the tree.

"Megan," he called out.

I didn't answer.

"I gave you that cassina back when you came to see me just to slow you down a little," he said. "So I could talk to you. It's a natural drug. It doesn't give you anything but a bad bellyache."

He was peering up at me, shifting his balance from foot to foot, waiting for me to answer. When I didn't, he bent down then and yanked at one of his bootlaces that had come undone. And I saw a movement around his feet, just to his right—a flash of brown and black that darted out and hit him.

"God fucking dammit!" he yelped, jumping back and grabbing his arm. I jumped too, banging my head against the tree.

Billy struggled to his feet, still holding his arm, and backpedaled until he was a couple of yards away. He was puffing and frantically searching the area around his feet. Then, gradually, his movements slowed. Then he wasn't moving at all. Just swaying, the slightest bit, and his head drooped. He drew in a breath and fell back against the trunk. I heard a *shush-shush* sound: his breathing.

Was the venom already taking hold? Did it really happen that quickly?

The woods were silent, except for the *chee*-ing birds and squirrels. I didn't move for what felt like an eternity, just sat crouched in the heart of the oak tree, holding my breath and waiting for Billy to leave.

He never did.

At last, I stretched out my cramped legs and dropped down, branch by branch, to the ground. I tiptoed to Billy. He had sunk to the ground and was staring up at the sky, blinking. When I drew close, he turned his head toward me. He was pale, slick with sweat. I saw his hand. It was red and purple, already swelling in strange, bubbly formations.

"I tried," he said.

"Where's Koa?" My voice shook. "What did you do to him?"

He didn't answer. Just looked at his hand.

I leaned closer to him. Gathered a handful of his shirt and pulled him close. I could smell his breath. Tobacco and tea.

"Tell me what you've done to Koa, Billy," I said.

His eyes met mine. "I would never hurt you," he said. Saliva webbed his lips. His face looked waxy and bloodless. "You were the sweetest little thing, Meg. So small. So innocent. I tried to keep you close. I tried to protect you from her. But I couldn't . . . I couldn't, and she hurt you."

Fear prickled across my skin.

One tear slid down his cheek. "She'll kill you, Meg. If you don't go now, Kitten'll finish what she started."

I couldn't breathe. Couldn't move or think straight. Was he telling the truth? Lying? Or completely out of his mind? I couldn't tell.

"Run," he said.

I did.

KITTEN

—from Chapter 20

Fay ran.

To the top of the stairs, down the halls, all the way to the back of the house, she ran, her breath coming in great gulps. She threw open the door to Kitten's bedroom.

The room was dark, and the air smelled of Kitten's peppermint shampoo. The bed was made, toys neatly lined up on the window-seat cushion. Fay flew to the nightstand and opened the drawer. Under the periwinkle book of poems, she saw a glint of red-brown stone. The ashtray. Kitten's make-believe mico's bowl.

And a small foil packet with a double row of tiny blue pills.

She grabbed the ashtray, ran to the window, and pushed it open. She sat on the sill carved with Cappie Strongbow's name, and closed her eyes. Holding the bowl with both hands, she jumped.

Ashley, Frances. *Kitten*. New York: Drake, Richards and Weems, 1976. Print.

Chapter Forty-Three

At the dock, I found the keys sitting in the driver's seat of the Jeep. Minutes later, I was skidding into Koa's yard. I leapt out of the Jeep, tore through his cabin, banging open every door and calling his name.

The place was deserted.

I drove into the woods, north, toward the middens. A silent mantra repeated in my head: *let him be there, let him be there.* Fifteen minutes later, I emerged from the woods and killed the engine. I ran to the edge of the bluff, the serpentine line of the shell wall a beacon shining white in the sunlight. I shaded my eyes against the glare.

Then—a whinny, deep and guttural, like a groaning through the pounding of the surf. The foal. I scanned the wall until I spotted her, the smallest blob, near the western end. Panic rising in my throat, I slid down the bluff and across the flat stretch of beach. As I neared the wall, I could see she was lying down, and the wall above her was stained with blood.

No.

Had she been shot? I couldn't see the wound, but there was blood pooling around her, and she wasn't moving. I'd been right after all. This was the killing place. It had been done here before.

The Weight of Lies

I reached her and touched her head and she twisted around to me. Then scrambled up. I exclaimed and nearly flipped myself backward in shock. She pranced around and stuck her nose into my lap, searching for a treat.

She was unhurt. Completely unhurt.

I touched the blood spattered on the wall. "Whose . . ."

And then I knew.

I pushed the foal out of my way and made for the end of the wall. The tide had come almost all the way in, and it and the wind roared together. There was only a narrow strip of sand, now, between the water and the wall. I ran down the wall, scanning the water desperately, not even sure what I was looking for. Then, as I neared the far end, I spotted something dark, half on the sand, half in the water. It appeared to be a body, bobbing in the shallow surf.

I broke into a run, splashing through the rising tide.

When I reached him, I grabbed his soaked shirt and tried to roll him over. After the third attempt, I finally succeeded, frantically pushed the wet hair away from his mouth and nose.

"Koa!" I screamed.

I felt for a pulse, the waves tossing his body against mine relentlessly. It was impossible to hear or feel anything. I had to get him out of there. He appeared to be bleeding from the head—the water that swirled around my shins was tinged pink—but I couldn't tell how serious the wound was. The tide was coming in fast, though. By now we were both more than half-submerged.

I looped my arms under his shoulders and lugged him up to the small strip of sand between the water and the wall. He gasped twice, then heaved up a fountain of bloody sea water. He groaned.

"Koa, it's Meg. I'm going to look at your head." I examined his bleeding head, but I couldn't find the source. I tried to wipe the blood from his eyes, nose, and mouth, but he screamed and jerked away.

A raw strip of skin, the size of a child's hand, dangled against the side of his head. It had somehow been partially peeled back, and now it was open, exposing layers of red and white beneath.

I was looking at his skull. I felt faint, a rush of dizziness, and lurched away from him. I gulped air into my lungs. I couldn't pass out. I had to help him. I approached him again.

"Koa, the tide is coming in. I've got to get you to the other side of the wall. Can you stand? If I hold you, do you think you can walk?"

He lifted his arm. I took it, hooked it over my shoulder, and hauled him up. God, he was heavy, heavier than I'd expected. His clothes were soaked with seawater and blood, and I had to steady myself against the rush of each wave.

"Try to walk," I said and I felt him draw himself up the slightest bit.

We staggered along the wall, stopping every time a particularly large wave hit us, until we finally made it around the edge of the middens. The foal trotted over to greet us, but I shooed her back and let Koa sink down against the wall. I crouched beside him.

"The tide's coming in, so I've got to get you to higher ground. The Jeep's just up on the bluff. Do you think you can make it?"

His head was bowed, exposing the open, glistening gash on his skull. I swallowed the bile rising in my throat and rested my hand on his chest.

"Koa, can you hear me?"

A voice rang out above me. "Meg!"

I looked up—at a black figure standing on the top of the wall, blocking the sun. Aiming a shotgun on me. I jumped back, my heart jackhammering my ribs.

"Don't shoot. It's Meg."

I stood and shaded my eyes. The features of the figure sharpened. It was Doro, staring down the barrel at Koa and me.

"Are you okay?" she called out. "What are you doing?"

"Koa's hurt. His head is bleeding. I think Billy attacked him."

"Oh, shit." She lowered the gun. "Oh, no."

"I was with Billy before. He held a gun on me and was taking me to the dock. A snake bit him, and I got away."

Doro sat on the wall, then dropped to the sand. "Oh my God. I knew it. I knew—" She knelt beside Koa. Touched his face. "This is my fault. He doesn't want anyone to have this island but him. He's crazy." She sounded like she was about to cry.

Something about what she was saying—it was starting to make sense. My brain was finally starting to make connections. And things were finally adding up.

Crazy Billy.

Dr. Lodi, earlier, on the phone.

Saying she'd found something on my X-rays, something in my leg. *Pellets.*

Doro reached across Koa and grabbed my shoulder. "Meg. What is it? What's wrong?"

I shook my head. "It doesn't matter right now. We have to get Koa help."

"He said something, didn't he? Billy said something to you about me."

She gripped my arm, so tightly I gasped.

Doro was a proven liar. Billy had poisoned me and pointed a gun at my head. I didn't know who to believe and I didn't know how I'd gotten here—stuck in the middle of this insane father-daughter blood feud. All I knew was I wanted out.

But Koa needed me.

"Meg, talk to me," she said. "Don't you understand? We need each other right now. The only way we can get through this is if we trust each other."

KITTEN

—from Chapter 20

Fay gulped the air, then attempted to stand. She gasped in pain. Her leg—
or rather her knee. She'd wrenched it so badly she couldn't stand. She scanned
the grass around her. The mico's bowl—the ashtray—was lying a dozen feet
away. She dragged herself toward it and, when she reached it, panted over
it—a mother hen protecting her egg. She let the sharp, cold edge press into
her cheek. Then a voice above her:

"Now it's got your fingerprints on it."

Fay rotated her face into the sun and squinted. Kitten was looking
down at her. The child was wearing a green gingham dress edged with ruffles.
It was stained with blood. Her head was wrapped in some kind of red silk
turban—*Beverly Cormley's scarf.* Henrick's prized white ostrich feather drooped
from the back of it. Miss Bolan's silver necklace, the one that had gone missing
before everyone got sick, hung around her neck.

Ashley, Frances. *Kitten*. New York: Drake, Richards and Weems, 1976. Print.

Chapter Forty-Four

I stared at Doro, kneeling in the water on the other side of Koa. Her top half—tan, freckled skin and green bikini—was crosshatched with red. Koa's blood. I noticed, hooked to her belt on her soaked jean shorts, a knife in a leather sheath.

She was staring at me, wisps of her hair blowing around her head, the wild electric blue of her eyes. Eyes that pleaded.

We need each other . . .

She was right. I couldn't help Koa alone. We needed each other.

"I always thought it was a birthmark," I said. "But I still have the pellets, lead shotgun pellets, inside me." I looked at her. "Somebody shot me when I was little. That's what's been causing the neuropathy. The tingling and the numbness."

"No," she whispered hoarsely.

"That can't be true, right?" I said. "Because that would mean I was here on Bonny Island when I was just a baby."

Her lips parted.

"Which isn't true," I said. "Is it?"

She shook her head but still said nothing. Her eyes had grown large and red.

"Why would I have been here when I was a baby? Unless . . ."

She raised one hand to cover her mouth, her eyes shiny with horror and shame.

". . . unless I'm yours," I finished.

She dropped to her knees in the sand, the gun splashing into the water beside her. She brought both hands to her face, like she had to hold it in place.

I touched her. "Doro." She didn't look at me. "Doro, we have to help Koa."

"I can't. I can't," she gasped. "This wasn't how I wanted . . ."

"Okay, just . . . just, take a breath. Just take a breath."

A deep, guttural groan tore from her throat—a keening sound unlike anything I'd ever heard. My scalp prickled. She wailed, long and low. A wave of chills rolled through me. I wanted to run. To plug my ears with my fingers and run until I couldn't see sand or moss or water any longer.

I checked Koa again. He wasn't moving.

I pried her hands from her face and wrapped my arms around her narrow shoulders. Without one second of hesitation, without even a thought, it seemed, her body molded to mine. I held her as she shuddered with sobs. Then, before my brain could register what was happening, she held me back, her hands in my hair, up and down my back, like she couldn't embrace me tight enough.

She was crying, and suddenly, I was too. Our tears fell and mingled on both our faces.

She cupped my face. "When I got pregnant with you, Billy was so angry. Pete was a married man. He wasn't going to help out. And Billy said I was too unstable . . . not cut out to be a mother." Her voice cracked, lips trembled. "One night, he took you. He brought you here, to the middens, where he used to bring the old horses and shoot them." She inhaled. "I followed him. I saw him put you there, against the wall."

I held my breath.

"He pulled the trigger, but I pushed him and he missed. I grabbed you. I ran through the woods, drove his skiff to St. Marys, and called Frances. She was the only person I knew who could help. She had money and connections. Everything I didn't have."

I couldn't fathom it. It was too big. Too impossible.

That I could be the daughter of Dorothy Kitchens and Pete Darnell?

That I wasn't Meg Ashley? That Frances had agreed to keep this secret from me all these years? I didn't understand.

My breath hitched in my throat. I brushed away the sand and tears and blood from her face. Her eyes—filled with shame and fear—pleaded for belief, for acceptance. Absolution. I could feel her love for me—it was a palpable force in the air around us.

"Koa," was all I said to her.

And "Yes," her simple reply.

The two of us hoisted him together, and when our eyes met, I had only one thought.

I've found you.

KITTEN

—from Chapter 20

Fay thought back to the curio cabinet in the salon. The etching of Osceola, the great Seminole chief. She knew how Kitten liked to play dress-up. She felt cold with fear.

"Silly," Kitten said. "You should've left the bowl in there, to burn with the house."

Fay's head was spinning from smoke and the fall. She felt separated from her body—like she'd left Bonny Island and flown someplace else.

Kitten crouched beside her. "Did you see Dr. Cormley?" She was talking in that bright, childish voice. "Did you see what I did to him?" She produced a knife, a strange curved knife Fay remembered from the curio cabinet as well. "I killed Cappie with the mico's bowl. But I did better with Dr. Cormley. I killed him the Guale way."

Ashley, Frances. *Kitten*. New York: Drake, Richards and Weems, 1976. Print.

Chapter Forty-Five

Back at the hotel, I stayed outside with Koa in the Jeep while Doro ran inside to retrieve my phone. I held my wadded shirt to Koa's head. It was soaked through with blood, but he was still breathing, his chest rising and falling in short bursts.

A few minutes later she reappeared and tossed me the phone. "No cell service. And the landline's down too. It does that sometimes, with the weather . . ." She trailed off, looking dazed. I hadn't noticed any clouds when we'd been at the beach, but the air did have that crackly pre-storm feeling.

"Where does the line come in the house?" I asked her. "I'll check it."

She looked confused.

"Doro!" I barked. "We have to call an ambulance for Koa."

It was getting late, and I could feel the panic rising in me. Billy was out there, in the woods, snakebit. Dead, maybe. Koa was dying too. We needed to call the paramedics, somehow. And the police.

"Maybe we should go to the dock and see if my phone works down there," I ventured. "We should try to find Billy too."

"No," Doro said. She wiped her mouth with the back of her hand. "Let him stay out there, in the woods. That's where he belongs."

"Okay, well. But we have to help Koa. He'll die without it."

"It's the honorable way," she said quietly. "The Guale said the Maker of Breath sits on a hill and sends everything down to us—Sister Sun and Brother Moon, the rain, the wind, even storms. All those are gifts to us from the Creator. In special cases, the Maker sends Sint Holo, the horned serpent, as a gift to the wise ones."

I chewed at a ragged nail, feeling the tingles gearing up. Her ramblings were starting to unnerve me. She was losing her shit.

"That snake, the one you saw that bit the foal, it was meant for Koa." Her gaze drifted down to Koa. He was pale, but breathing steadily. "It was because he lied. Because Neal Baker hired him to come down here and pin Kimmy's death on me."

I blinked in surprise.

"I don't know who did it—Billy or Frances or Kimmy's mother—but I know I didn't. I didn't kill her!" Her face was red now, her eyes glistening.

"Doro, I know." I rubbed my hands together, more out of habit than anything. "Nobody's saying you did anything. Just calm down. What we need to do is head to the dock, okay? It's getting dark."

Suddenly, from somewhere inside the house came a loud crash like shattering glass. Doro whirled. I stiffened. She turned wide eyes on me.

"It came from the back of the house," I said. "From the kitchen."

I started up the porch steps, intending to head around to the back of the house, but she grabbed my arm.

"It's Billy. He's come back to shoot me," she whispered.

It couldn't be. He could barely walk when I saw him.

"Get the gun," I said anyway.

She pulled the shotgun out of the Jeep. Propped the barrel over her arm. I glanced at Koa's slumped form, then up at the house.

"Stay close," I mouthed and motioned her to follow.

Around the back of the house, the row of kitchen windows was dark. The window at the very end was ringed with jagged shards of glass. We peered inside. The pantry door was ajar, and a sliver of light shone from it. The counter and sink were littered with broken glass.

I did a quick assessment. If Billy had managed to revive himself and come back to the house, he'd be desperate. Probably shoot to kill. We'd need to be nimble.

"We should get Koa out of here," I said. "The dock."

"The mission," Doro said. "It's the highest point on the island. We'll be able to get a signal and call the police. And hide."

Doro started back toward the front of the house, and I moved to follow her, then glanced back one last time through the broken window. Just inside the pantry, in the small wedge of light, I could see rows of empty shelves. A couple of cans lay on the floor, like someone had knocked everything off with a sweep of their arm.

∞

We drove the two miles to the mission ruins as slowly and carefully as we could, right up into the chessboard of broken rock walls. We decided to leave Koa in the Jeep. While I arranged some extra towels I'd gotten at the house around his head, Doro found an extra lantern in the back, then started over the network of low walls.

"Meg!" she shout-whispered. "Come try your phone over here."

She held up the lantern. Shadows on the jagged walls behind her as they blanched to a spooky gray. "It's the highest point on the whole island."

Reluctantly leaving Koa, I joined her in front of the open arch and held up my phone. No reception. Not even the hint of a network.

"Maybe we should wait here for a while," Doro said. "See if some of the cloud cover will blow over so we can pick up a signal."

I looked back toward the Jeep.

"Meg. I didn't mean what I said before. I don't like what he did, but I don't want him to die. We're going to get him help. He's going to be all right. Okay?"

"Okay."

She made me sit on a couple of logs that ringed the blackened fire site, then pointed up to a spot at the top of the main building. "The Jesuits built this place so the sun would shine as it set through the arched windows and down onto the altar, which was covered in gold. It would catch the sun and glow like it was on fire. Probably scared the living shit out of the Guale." She rolled her eyes. "Exactly the way the Jesuits wanted them. Scared."

"I know how they must've felt," I said.

She lifted her face to the star-strewn sky. "I've never been scared on Bonny. My father always said I was fearless, like my mother."

She shifted on the log. Gazed off, past the grid of rocks, into the moss-draped woods.

"My father said my mother was the last of the Guale. It wasn't true—she was as WASPy as they come, but she did have an affinity for Native Americans. And she felt like she was one of them. They both believed that we all get to decide who we are—inside. When I was seven, my mother heard about the American Indian Movement. And something that happened up in Custer, South Dakota. A white guy stabbed a Lakota man to death. They slapped the white guy on the wrist, let him out on a five-thousand-dollar bond. It was a joke. The guys from AIM and the Pine Ridge Reservation were going to go meet with the prosecutor and demand justice. Demand to finally be heard. My mother convinced my father that we should go and join the fight."

She toed a chunk of charred wood.

"Even though all the AIM guys wanted to do was talk, the Custer police acted like it was a revolution. They wouldn't let but a few of them into the courthouse. They set up roadblocks, stood guard in riot gear. Eventually, the talks broke down and the police got what they wanted . . . a riot. They set fire to the courthouse, the chamber of commerce. Couple of police cars."

She laced her fingers. Studied them.

"My mother wasn't doing anything wrong. But she got mouthy with a cop, and he didn't appreciate it. She got shot. Three times. Two in the neck, one in the gut."

My mouth opened, but no words came. Susan Doucette had said Vicky Kitchens was accidentally killed in the fire in Custer. Not gunned down in cold blood by a cop. But there was no reason to believe Susan knew more than Doro. No reason at all.

"I'm sorry, Doro," I finally managed. "I'm so sorry."

She folded her arms around her knees. "You know, when I was a child, my father told me that story many times, but it took me until I was a teenager to really understand the lesson in it."

"What do you mean?"

"Our enemies are all around us, ready to take what is ours. But you can't let them. Once you've lost what belongs to you—your belief, your faith, your land—you've lost everything."

The night had gone from a turgid gray to a velvety black. The jagged stone walls rose like teeth in a giant's maw. Crows' silhouettes dotted the trees. Doro's eyes had locked onto me, like a missile radar beam.

"You never leave your land, Meg. Do you hear me? You never, ever leave."

All of a sudden, behind Doro, between the darkening stone arches and walls, I saw the slightest hint of movement.

KITTEN

—from Chapter 20

The Guale way?

Fay couldn't think what Kitten meant by that. The very next moment, her vision filled with strange spots—like bright, white-hot stars, sparking and popping all around her—as she felt an intense sensation of burning along her scalp.

Then she understood.

Ashley, Frances. *Kitten*. New York: Drake, Richards and Weems, 1976. Print.

Chapter Forty-Six

A soughing sound drifted out from the warren of crumbled mission half rooms, and we both jumped up. Doro held up the lantern to the arched opening. My entire body was trembling.

The mare clopped out of the dark. Long nose, arched neck, burtangled mane. Her ears twitched forward and back, and she whinnied. Doro laughed, then I joined in, a giddy harmony of relief that rose up and softened the night.

When our laughter finally drifted away, the only sound was the mare cropping at a patch of grass. Neither of us sat, though, and I noticed Doro put the lantern on a low wall along the edge of the courtyard. Its glow illuminated the line of trees flanking us, a spotlight trained on an empty stage.

Waiting for Billy to lurch in from the woods.

I strained to see the Jeep and Koa. I could just make him out in the blackness. He was still in the same position. He looked like he was sleeping.

"She still hasn't accepted the foal." Doro was running a hand down the mare's sinewy neck.

"Will she ever?" I said.

Doro glanced at me. Her fingers traveled along the mare's broad back. "Animals are funny about attachments. They're not like us. They don't mourn their losses."

I glanced at the Jeep. At Koa. I was starting to think it had been a terrible idea to come out here. A spectacularly bad idea.

Her voice was low, musical, as she stroked the horse. "Meg?"

"What?" Every nerve ending in my body was firing.

"You trust me, don't you? Isn't that what you said, back at the middens?"

I opened my mouth, but couldn't say anything. She was my mother, my real mother. But something inside me was still holding back. Hesitating around the fringes.

She went on rubbing the horse. "I trust you. You're my daughter. Anything I've ever done was for you and Bonny Island. The things you've done have not been from such a pure place, have they? Sneaking around behind my back. Contacting Susan. Going to see Billy. Keeping secrets for Koa. Writing those lies about me in your book."

I stared at her.

"But I understand, Meg, you didn't know any better." She smoothed the mare's mane. "Mothers always understand."

A beat of silence settled over us.

"Holding forth on motherhood, Kitten?" came a voice from the shadows.

The next instant, Frances stepped into the nimbus of watery lantern light. Her skin was glistening with sweat, the collar of her silk shirt torn loose. Her smudged eyes flicked over me for a brief moment, then went right back to Doro.

"It's in such poor taste, don't you think?" Frances said.

"Frances," I said.

"You left," Doro said.

Frances turned to me. "I never called Captain Mike. I drove to the dock, then walked back and hid near the house. Doro might think she's the almighty ruler of Bonny Island and everybody on it, but she isn't. She doesn't understand that as long as there is breath in my body, I will do whatever it takes to protect you."

My breath caught in my throat. Waves of pinpricks zoomed up and down my body, and my hands fisted by my sides.

Doro sauntered toward my mother. "How curious. How strange. You couldn't care less about Meg for her whole life and then, the minute she comes down to Bonny Island, the minute she returns to me—presto!—you appear! A howling, growling mother bear."

"You're a liar, Doro," Frances said in a low voice. "A liar and a murderer."

"It's too late, Frances," Doro snapped. "She knows what really happened. She figured it all out on her own."

Frances's eyes slid to me.

"She knows you and Billy stole her from me," Doro said.

Frances let out an incredulous laugh. "Stole her? *Stole* her? The only reason you didn't go to prison was because Billy couldn't bring himself to turn in his precious, darling Kitten for attempting to murder her own infant daughter." She shook her head. "All he ever wanted was to protect you and Megan. He moved to that godforsaken town just so he could keep an eye on you. And this—"

She thrust something out to Doro, and the thing flashed in the moonlight: a silver julep cup, identical to the ones I'd seen on the bar at Ambletern. Doro stiffened. Moved back.

"Billy gave it to me the same day he gave me Megan," Frances said. "He said keeping it safe meant keeping her safe."

Frances walked past Doro and slammed the silver cup on the wall. When she stepped away, I saw the dent, a caved-in spot around the engraved letter *A*.

"I don't understand," I said.

Frances shook her head. "I was scared they would take you away from me. I thought if I didn't hide the cup—keep the whole house of cards standing—everything would unravel. The truth would come out about you, and I'd lose you forever. To protect you, I had to protect her. But I was wrong, Megan. I should've gone to the police that day and told them everything."

I couldn't feel any tingling anymore; I'd gone completely numb.

"I don't understand," I said. "There's got to be more."

I felt Frances and Doro exchange a glance. A current, almost electric in nature, passed between them.

"What!" I practically screamed. "What is it?"

"Don't, Frances," Doro said in a low voice. "It won't solve anything."

"You have your cup back, Doro. Take it. Just let me and my daughter go home."

Doro snickered. "I don't tell Meg where to go, Frances. She doesn't belong to me. She belongs to herself."

Frances took a step toward me. "I know I haven't been what you wanted. I know I failed you. Just, please . . . please come home with me."

I pointed at the silver cup. "That's the murder weapon? That's what killed Kim Baker?"

Frances's stricken face told me the truth.

"Billy asked you to hide it?" I asked.

"Yes," she said.

"To protect who, exactly? Him? Doro? Who killed Kimmy?"

Her face creased in anguish. "I wanted you to be happy, Megan. And you couldn't be happy if you knew about your real mother. What she had done to . . . other people. What she did to you."

"You BITCH!" Doro burst out. "Don't listen to her. She took that cup from Ambletern this week, and now she's making up some crazy story to turn you against me."

"No, Doro," I said. "She may be lying about everything else, but she's telling the truth about that. That cup's been sitting on a shelf in her office ever since I can remember."

"Then she took it when she was here years ago," Doro said. "It's not the murder weapon. I didn't do it. I was a child—an eight-year-old beanpole. You think I was capable of smashing somebody's skull with a little silver cup?"

Some half-formed thought, something I couldn't quite capture and distill, flitted through my brain, then evaporated.

"That leaves her." Doro pointed at Frances. "She was desperate for attention. The only problem was she didn't have a story. She didn't have anything that would make the world notice her. So she killed Kimmy and wrote a book that blamed me."

"I thought you said Billy did it," I said.

"I was mistaken." Doro picked up the cup and threw it at Frances. She ducked and it bounced off the rocks behind her with a clang. "You already got your pound of flesh, Frances," Doro snapped. "Why did you come back? Are you still not satisfied, after all you took from me?"

"No, Doro, I'm not." Frances's jaw worked in the light of the lantern. "I'm not satisfied. I want my daughter back."

Doro roared. "How dare you make this about yourself? I was the one who lost everything, not you!"

"You tried to *kill* your baby," Frances said and my heart sputtered, like it might cease to beat. "Your daughter is the one who almost lost everything!"

"It was Billy!" Doro screamed. She turned a pleading face to me. "Meg, you have to believe me. She's twisting everything. It was Billy who wanted you dead, not me." She flew to me, grabbed my arms. "I named you Aiyana. It's Cherokee. It means 'eternal blossom.'"

Laughter bubbled up from Frances. "God, no! No, it doesn't. It's just some made-up name she found in a novel or something. You're not Native American, Doro, no matter how hard you pretend. You're not Guale or Cherokee or Creek or anything. And neither is Meg."

Doro ignored her and reached a hand out to me. "I named you Aiyana, because I wanted you to know your heritage. Your true heritage. This island is yours and you deserve to rule over this place with me."

I shook my head.

"I saw the pictures. I always thought you and Frances were so happy together. But when your agent wrote me and told me how badly she had treated you all your life—your *adoptive* mother—I knew it was a gift from the Creator. He had brought you back to me, so you could know your true home. Your real mother."

I backed away from them both. Pressed my fingers to my throbbing temples. Oh, God. What was she saying? What did this mean? Had Doro tried to kill me? Or Billy? Who was I supposed to be afraid of here? Who was I supposed to believe?

"Megan," Frances said.

"Aiyana," Doro said at the same time.

No, no, no . . .

The word worked its way from brain to mouth, taking on a force I couldn't suppress.

"No!" I screamed. "Just stop. Stop. I don't believe anything you say. You scare the shit out of me, okay? You fucking terrify me. And I don't trust either of you." I took a few uncertain steps away from them. "I need you both to just . . . to just . . . go. Or I need to go, I don't know . . ."

Doro moved toward me. "You don't love her, Meg. You've always known something was wrong. And you were right. She wasn't your real mother."

I looked into her eyes. Felt tears slipping down my cheeks. Dripping past my chin and rolling over my neck. But I couldn't speak.

"This is why you came back," Doro said, softly now. "To find me. To be where you belong." Her electric-blue gaze burned into me. "I love you. And you love me. Tell her. Tell her the truth. Now that you've found your mother, your real mother, you don't need her anymore."

I ripped away from her and stumbled back.

Doro said, "Aiyana."

Frances reached out to me. "Megan . . ."

"No," I said again. "Don't either of you touch me. I can't deal with this now." I looked back, trying to find Koa in the Jeep, but it was so dark, I couldn't see a thing.

"Megan, will you just listen to what I have to say?" Frances said.

I shook my head. "I don't have to listen to you anymore. You're not my mother. You've never been my mother."

In the light of the moon, Frances's face was a Picasso painting, the wrinkles deepening and casting strange shadows over the folds of her face. She didn't reach for me again. Her arms hung limply at her sides. "Please," was all she said.

I looked away.

The next instant, I felt her arms encircle me, the familiar spicy-floral scent of her French perfume mingling with my own sharp smell. She pressed her face against mine, and I bit my lip to keep from crying. I didn't want to cry anymore. Not over this woman. This liar.

"I have always loved you," she said. "Not the way I wanted to. Not well. For that I'm sorry."

I pushed her away. Her eyes searched mine for a moment, then went wide—and blank. Her hands fluttered up and her mouth gaped, worked for a second or two silently.

"Frances?" I said.

She pitched forward, the weight of her body sending me staggering backward. I caught her and saw Doro, panting and clenching her knife.

KITTEN

—from Chapter 20

"Don't go anywhere, you hear me?" Kitten said. "I have to hide the bowl."

Fay didn't see her leave. Her eyes felt gluey and wouldn't open. The pain had dulled, thankfully, and she had gone to a gray place, gentle and warm. It was just as well she couldn't move. She needed to conserve her energy until someone came—the deputy, maybe—and took her back to town.

When she got there, she'd try for a job. Not in a diner; a shop near the marina, maybe. Then she would take an apartment or carriage house behind one of those lovely Victorian mansions. A cozy home with some history. She'd decorate with wicker and Indian blankets and ferns. At night she'd cook and watch TV shows.

Her own home.

She was ready to go there.

Ashley, Frances. *Kitten*. New York: Drake, Richards and Weems, 1976. Print.

Chapter Forty-Seven

Doro bared her teeth and nodded when she saw me holding Frances.

"Good girl, Megs. Aiyana. Good girl."

Frances slipped from my grasp and thudded to the ground. I crouched beside her and looked up at Doro. She wiped her mouth with the back of the hand that held the knife. The blade flashed.

"We did it," Doro said. "The island is finally ours again. Just you and I and the Maker of Breath." She smiled.

Terror swelled in my gut. Frances was shuddering on the ground beside me. Her eyes gone glazed and unfocused. And the sounds she was making—strangled, dry gasps that made the hair on my arms stand on end.

"Mom." I touched her face. Spoke softly. I had to stay calm for her. She had to know I was here. I would save her. "Just lie still, okay? Lie still."

Doro spoke behind me, in a singsong voice. "'You tell me a story, you weave me a tale.'" She laughed harshly. "Frances thinks she owns all the stories, but I have stories too."

The words flooded me with fear. I looked at her.

"I'm going to tell you one now."

She picked up the silver cup, turning it around in her hands. "One of the friars, Father Miguel, tried to install his own choice of chieftain—mico—over the Guale here. The men of the tribe were angry. They came here one night, dragged him to the central chapel, and clubbed him to death at the altar. They cut him to pieces, here, in his very own mission."

I couldn't pull in a breath. It felt like my lungs had telescoped.

"This is the secret, Meg. The beautiful truth . . ."

I felt the blood pound in my ears.

"Bonny Island has always belonged to me. From the moment I set foot here. The Maker of Breath gave it to me as a reward for my mother's sacrifice."

I was locked in her gaze. Paralyzed by it. "So you did kill Kim."

Doro jutted her chin. "She used to taunt me—say she was Guale, and she was to be the next mico of the island. She didn't understand that I was the only true mico."

"There's no tribe here anymore, Doro," I said. "No tribe and no mico."

"You're wrong about that. My father's only mistake was thinking he could bring in other people to share it with us."

And then I knew. She'd hurt Koa. She'd tried to kill him. Like Kitten had killed Carl Cormley and Fay in the book. My brain shifted into overdrive, buzzing and connecting every unanswered question. Making sudden, horrible sense of it all.

Laila. Esther. Where were they? What had Doro done with them?

I almost leapt at her, but something stopped me. The half-formed, flitting thought from earlier. The realization that crashed over me was so powerful, my knees buckled. "There's no way you could have killed Kim alone. Someone helped you," I said.

Her eyebrows lifted the slightest bit.

"Who was it?" I said.

But I knew who it must've been. Doro's only true friend. The one who returned to Ambletern year after year, and then even after he was married to another woman. Pete Darnell.

Doro knelt on the other side of Frances's still form and pressed the cup into my hands. It felt like a stone in my hands, heavier than I expected it to be. But then, it was an antique, an Ambletern cup, made of the purest, heaviest silver. With Doro so close, I could smell her scent—that familiar woody, smoky smell. Another memory pricked at me. That same earthy smell, drifting in my room at Ambletern.

Doro picked up Frances's limp hand and pressed it to her cheek.

"Look," she said. "See the way her nail beds curve slightly? Billy taught me it was the sign of a predator. The way you spot an enemy is look at their nails. Kimmy had nails like that. Koa does too." She dropped Frances's hand, her gaze fastened on me. "She's not gone yet. If you hit directly on the temple, you won't have to do it but a few times." She leaned forward. "Do it, Meg. Hit her."

Doro and Pete. Creeping through the marsh. A silver cup in hand. Just two children, off to play. *To kill.*

"End it," she ordered.

I shook my head. "I can't . . ."

"You can."

"No, I can't. She's my . . ." I was going to say *mother*, but I found myself thinking something else instead.

. . . *my everything.*

"No," Doro hissed, her eyes blazing. "I'm your mother. Do it or I will."

I was shaking uncontrollably. She reached across Frances and snatched the cup out of my hand. In one swift move, she raised the cup and cracked it down on Frances's head. I gasped. The cup flashed back up again, poised over my mother's head.

"No!" I shrieked.

Frances was moaning, reaching into the air with one hand.

Doro smashed the cup down on Frances's head again, and I launched my body at hers, knocking her onto the grass. She rolled, then popped back up and came at me. On instinct, I shoved the heel of my hand upward, driving it into her jaw. To my utter surprise, she dropped. I tripped over her, snatching the cup.

I turned. Doro, her face twisted in an ugly sneer, was charging at me. I swung the cup, and it clanked, connecting with her skull. She staggered sideways, a spray of blood arcing from her face. I pounced again, aiming for her nose, and connected. She howled and skittered back.

I turned to check Frances. The mare had clopped up to her, stopped right beside her still form and dipped her head. But my mother wasn't moving. In front of me, Doro was staggering to her knees.

"It has all our blood on it now," she said, panting. "Kimmy's blood and Frances's. Mine." She grinned. "Yours." She nodded at my hand. I'd cut myself and was bleeding now too.

I pictured myself smashing the cup on her head. Cracking her skull with it. I could grab the shotgun and blow a hole through this crazy woman. My mother.

A shadow moved behind the jagged mission wall. I remained motionless, then it moved again, and a man stepped into the weak light. Rivulets of blood from the stray shotgun pellets ran like tiny, gory, dark-red ribbons down his face and neck.

I froze.

The shadow lifted his clasped hands, tilted his head slightly, and squeezed the trigger of a black-and-silver pistol.

The bullet ricocheted off the stones to my right. He fired again, and this time I heard a strange thudding sound, and Doro collapsed. I stood, paralyzed, waiting for something else to happen. For her to jump up and whirl and attack again. She looked so normal, lying there just beyond the fire ring—with her green bikini top and frayed jean shorts. But then I saw the pool of blood under her head.

The cup clanged on a log we'd been sitting on and rolled to a stop in the sandy grass. Billy stepped over the rubble of stones and looked down at Doro. Then me.

"You were a difficult baby," he said in a monotone. "You wouldn't breastfeed. You wouldn't sleep. Cried all the time." He knelt beside Doro, and his voice gentled. "It was what we did to the foals rejected by their mothers, to put them out of their misery. I shouldn't have been surprised it was what she thought to do to you."

I felt the heat, the tears, the horror rise up in me. I covered my mouth with my hands to keep myself from vomiting.

"I followed her down to the middens and saw what she meant to do. But I pushed her and she missed . . ." He cleared his throat. "Mostly. You were bleeding, though, from a couple of the pellets, and I knew the situation was bad. I took you, got the cup, and ran. Crossed the sound. I couldn't think what to do. I couldn't take you to the hospital. If anyone saw your little leg torn up the way it was, they'd get the law involved. You know what they do to a person who takes a shotgun to a baby?" He shook his head, swallowed heavily. "So I called Frances. She had the means to take you. And I trusted her. I knew, for her own reasons, she would keep the whole situation quiet."

"You told Frances you would drop the lawsuit if she took me," I whispered.

He nodded. "We came to an agreement." His jaw was working now, shuddering with the pain, and his chest heaved.

"She told me she thought Doro killed Kim Baker, right when she got here." Even as I said it, I could hardly believe it. "She was telling the truth. She knew it all along. Both of you did."

And then it all made sense. Why Frances couldn't tell me who I was. She would have had to admit her appalling litany of sins—that she had always suspected Doro, but instead of reporting her suspicions to the police, she wrote a book about it. Then, when she realized her reputation—and millions—were at risk, she took me to keep the story quiet.

I backed away—from the cup, from Billy and Doro, then remembered Frances was behind me. I ran and knelt over my mother. Lowered my ear to her mouth.

"She's breathing," I said to Billy. "We need to call for help."

But he'd already lain down beside his daughter. His head was turned toward her, and his eyes had gone unfocused and glassy with shock.

KITTEN

—from Chapter 20

Kitten slipped between crumbled arches and crawled under a tunnel-like pile of rocks until she reached a small, shadowy room in the center of the mission ruin.

Herb and Delia, slumped together against the rock wall, head to head, appeared to be posing for a family picture. They were not. Their mouths and chins and clothing were stained purple from where they'd been sick, deathly sick from the berries Kitten mashed into their jam.

Kitten put the ashtray in Herb's lap and arranged his hands around it. She sat back. Imagined his voice:

"When you were born the moon and the sun met in the sky, and the four directions each blew their winds, all at once."

Her voice answered. "This island is mine, Father? Really?"

"Of course, my little Indian princess, every square mile. Created for you by the Maker of Breath. But we've forgotten our poem. Why don't you start us off?"

A child's voice carried through the mission, high and clear and full of promise.

> *You tell me a story,*
> *You weave me a tale.*
> *But I travel alone*
> *Down the dark, twisted trail.*

Ashley, Frances. *Kitten*. New York: Drake, Richards and Weems, 1976. Print.

Chapter Forty-Eight

"Ready?"

"Yes . . . No. I don't know."

"We can leave. Right now. There's a cab behind you."

"No. I'm ready. Let's go."

As I walked into Bemelmans Bar at the Carlyle Hotel, Edgar's old haunt, silence fell, and the sea of people parted. Eyes focused like lasers, and a murmur, low but insistent, rose around the wood-paneled edges of the room.

The launch party for the fortieth anniversary of *Kitten* had been underway for at least an hour, but my entrance managed to record-scratch everyone into stunned silence.

Koa stood beside me. He was wearing a dark suit—tailored in all the right places—which made him look like a movie star. A gorgeous, nearly bald movie star. The doctors had shaved off all his hair in the process of reattaching his scalp, and a scar, shaped like a crescent moon, glowed red against the pale skin and brown fuzz.

But it was me the people were staring at. I didn't feel a single pin-prick—I hadn't had an episode in weeks, thanks to the surgery that removed the two pellets of birdshot in my ankle and the continued chelation. But I still felt a knot of dread in the pit of my stomach. I briefly considered running out of the place and never looking back.

I inhaled shakily and let Koa guide me across the room to my mother. I air-kissed Benoît, then hugged Mom, trying to avoid the wound still healing on her back. She pressed her face against mine, hard, her lips to my ear.

"You're here." Her voice was fervent with gratitude.

Yes. I was there, with my mother. Because in the end, I was Megan Ashley, daughter of Frances Ashley. I was making peace with it. We both were. Even while the real world raged around us.

And, my God, how it raged.

The news that Dorothy Kitchens was a delusional psychopath who had, for years, imagined herself the chief of a defunct-since-the-seventeenth-century Native American tribe had whipped up quite the media storm. The revelation that I was Dorothy's birth child, and reports of Doro's attempt to murder Mom? That news had caused the Kitty Cultists to lose their collective mind.

Unfortunately, that wasn't the end of it. After I was finally able to reach the police and they'd taken care of everything else, they'd discovered Esther's and Laila's lifeless bodies—torn from shotgun blasts and pushed behind a hot-water heater in a closet in Ambletern's kitchen. Doro had shot them both. Sometime in the days that followed, I'd been able to talk to Esther's son on the phone. He'd been quiet, respectful. Then asked me not to come to the funeral.

Billy Kitchens died of cardiac arrest brought on by a snakebite, in the center of the mission ruins. He was lying beside his daughter, the precious daughter he'd raised to think she could do and be anything she wanted. The child he coddled and pampered and protected who grew into an adult—and monster. In a way, he paid for his sins and hers.

The mare was found a couple of feet away from Billy and Doro. The foal was with her. Incredibly, someone had managed to snap a picture of them. When I saw it in the *New York Post*, I cried uncontrollably.

The fortieth-anniversary edition of *Kitten* had instantly presold hundreds of thousands of copies. Mom's people were in a frenzy, talking movie sequels, a cable series, a theme park down in Georgia. "Mom's people" meaning Asa Bloch. I'd decided to let that one go. I was finding it nearly impossible to hate anyone; I just didn't have the energy. And also he'd gotten a five-figure book deal for Susan Doucette. So maybe he was okay.

Everyone—from shopgirls to waiters to cabbies to friends—keeps asking how I'm handling it all. I find it hard to express my feelings in any coherent way, so I'll just say this: any day I don't come across an in-depth think piece about "The White Savior Syndrome as Represented in Western Pop Culture," featuring my mother and Doro Kitchens, is a good day.

And there are good days. A lot of that has to do with Koa. He was able to fulfill the promise he'd made to his old friend Neal Baker and tell him that Doro was the one who'd killed his daughter, Kim. I think it made him feel like he'd closed an important chapter in his own life. The night he flew back from Texas to New York, I met him at the airport, and I could see the peace in his face. It was the same night he told me that he loved me.

A couple of minutes after my grand entrance at Bemelmans, the clink of glasses and roar of voices returned to its previous volume. Koa and I pressed our way through the crowd to the bar, where we ran into Aurora. After I hugged my friend and we each fawned over the other's dress, she nudged my shoulder.

"Your six o'clock," she murmured.

I turned. In the amber light of the bar, a tall man with carefully coiffed black hair, a long, bent nose, and a face composed of a series of sharp planes lounged against a far wall. He was dressed in a tight, expensively tailored suit and was staring intently at our little group. When I caught his eye, he hunched and rotated away. I faced the bar again.

I would need at least two more drinks to deal with that situation.

Sometime near the end of the evening, the Bemelmans's pianist plunged into the theme from one of the *Kitten* movies, a haunting but beautiful piece. I hadn't meant to, but, spurred on by the music, I found myself searching the room for the tall stranger. I finally located him, standing alone against the whimsically muraled wall. He was watching me, the way he had been earlier. I gave Koa a swift kiss on the cheek and made my way over to him.

"Peter Darnell," I said.

"That's right."

I gazed at him in fascination. His face was dark like mine. *My father.*

"How did you get in?" I asked.

"I know people." He gave me a tense smile.

"You know who I am, right?"

"Of course I do. You're why I came. Megan." His voice had a hint of a Southern twang to it. We shook hands, and I waited for my fingers to bloom with prickles. They didn't.

"Megan. Or Aiyana," I said.

I thought I detected a flush along his neck, just above the blinding-white collar of his shirt. He pulled at his navy tie. He was handsome, but not dazzling. Like an actor you'd cast if you didn't want to upstage the female lead.

"And the last name," I went on. "I have my choice of three. Ashley, Kitchens, or Darnell. Depending on which version of the story I believe."

He smiled again, this time broadly, baring a row of beautiful white teeth. One incisor jutted out, making me think of a feral dog. A wolf.

"Well, we all choose who we are, ultimately. Don't you agree?"

I upended my whiskey, then set the empty tumbler on the table beside us. A waiter promptly swept it up.

"No. We are who we are, and we either choose to face it or live in denial." I studied him. "Speaking of which—"

"I'm Egyptian. Half. Adopted by the Darnells."

I nodded. Half-Egyptian in an otherwise all-white family. We were more alike than I thought.

"Forgive my awkwardness, Megan. I came here expecting . . . hoping to see you. My daughter. But now that you're here, I find that I'm unprepared. And probably not saying anything the way I practiced it."

I returned his smile. But I doubted this man, my father, had ever rehearsed a speech. He was a murderer, if Doro had told the truth. He'd been close to her, then turned, toying with her and using her. It sounded crazy, but he might be more of a psychopath than Doro. And yet, I was still standing here.

"You're lovely," he said. "And certainly accomplished, I imagine. What I was hoping . . . maybe it's not possible. But I'd like to think you're open . . . perhaps . . . to a relationship. Between us."

"Maybe. I don't know. It's hard to say right now."

Silence fell, and he glanced at Frances, surrounded by a knot of well-wishers.

"Have you met her yet?" I asked.

"No. But I think I'll wait until another time to introduce myself. I really just want to talk to you."

I folded my arms. "About what? Kim Baker's murder?"

His eyes danced over the crowd. "I don't need to hear the lies Doro told about me. Doro was a troubled woman. A deeply disturbed girl."

"So that's your official position? It's all lies? You didn't help her kill Kim Baker?"

He sent me a sharp look. A probing one.

"Because you know they haven't closed the case just yet," I said. "I understand there are a few more details they're investigating."

He fidgeted with the knot in his tie. Smoothed the end of it. "I just want to talk to my daughter right now."

I looked over at Koa and Aurora, standing at the bar. They were both watching Peter Darnell and me, straight-backed and hawkeyed.

Ready to fly to my aid if I gave the signal. My heart surged with love. I turned back to him.

"I'm living here in New York with my mother until she fully recovers. In a month or so, I'll be moving in with my boyfriend and starting a new job."

"Congratulations. Where?"

"A nonprofit in town."

He nodded in an easy way. Doing the father routine.

"I'm also working on a book," I said. "Something you might be interested in. A novel."

"Following in your mother's footsteps. Brava. What's it about?"

I cocked my head and let a smile curl my lips. "It's about a damaged woman, the daughter of a world-famous bestselling novelist, who finds herself at the center of a decades-old unsolved mystery."

His lips parted, revealing the wolf's tooth again.

"I'm calling it *The Silver Cup*," I said.

He wasn't looking so relaxed anymore, his face flushed a deep crimson. He cleared his throat.

"It was nice meeting you," I said. "Mr. Peter Darnell. Dad. Maybe we'll cross paths again one day."

Maybe in court, when you're being tried for murder, I thought.

"We should—" he began, then stopped. A spot just above his eye twitched.

"Introduce yourself to Frances on your way out," I said and smiled. "I'm sure she'd love to meet you."

He started to puff his chest, but I turned my back and walked to my friends at the bar.

ACKNOWLEDGMENTS

To everyone who bought my first book, *Burying the Honeysuckle Girls*, or checked it out of the library; to those who read it, wrote reviews, wrote to me; who told their friends to read it or chose it for their book club . . . I thank you. Your passion for the book warms my heart every day, and this book wouldn't exist if it weren't for you all.

Thanks to my crackerjack agent, Amy Cloughley, at Kimberley Cameron & Associates and to my enthusiastic and tireless editor, Kelli Martin, and the whole team at Lake Union. I am so grateful that I get to work with such a talented and supportive team.

Thanks to editors Heather Lazare (in the early days) and Shannon O'Neill (in the latter days) for wrangling the manuscript into something polished and pretty. Y'all are magic—that is all.

To Erratica: Chris Negron, M. J. Pullen, and Becky Albertalli—your early reads were invaluable. Thank you. George Weinstein, you're up for the next one. Thank you also to Katy Shelton for an eleventh-hour read. As always, thanks to Michael Brown and Valerie Connors of the Atlanta Writers Club for their continued support of me and all of us local writers.

Dr. Gladstone Sellers kindly provided everything I needed to know about lead poisoning and its treatment—so any mistakes regarding those sorts of details are mine. I'm grateful also for Rebecca Roanhorse's generous thoughts and advice concerning Native American characters in the book. Ken Madren, it's not exactly about a pirate . . . but thanks for the island inspiration all the same.

Finally, Rick, Noah, Alex, and Everett—I can't thank you enough for your stalwart encouragement and steady stream of sass. I love you.

ABOUT THE AUTHOR

Photo © 2015 Christina DeVictor

Emily Carpenter, a former actor, producer, screenwriter, and behind-the-scenes soap opera assistant, was born and raised in Alabama. After graduating from Auburn University, she moved to New York City and now lives in Georgia with her family. She is the author of Amazon bestseller *Burying the Honeysuckle Girls*. Visit Emily at www.emilycarpenterauthor.com and on Facebook and Twitter.